Night Bells

A Primoris System Novel • A Tale from Niflheim: Book One

L.M. Sherwin

Enjoy!

L.M. Sherwin
2013

This is a work of fiction derived from the author's imagination. Any resemblance to real places, persons, or events is either coincidental or used fictitiously.

NIGHT BELLS

This book is dedicated to Zachary Sherwin for being an unending source of love and support, to my parents for saving all my old stories, and to Leigh Anne Conduff for making us do our third grade writing project—that's where the seed was planted.

Prologue

The following letter was discovered in the ruins of New Kristiansand many centuries after the events surrounding the sons and daughters of the Maslyn family line had faded into memory...

Dearest Louisa,

The boy has been traumatized, to be sure, and I feel that destiny will not free him from this tale of treachery and woe. A great tragedy has occurred here, but I know in my old bones that fate will see him through to the end, though there may be storms along the way. It does my soul good to know that you have missed the fell deeds that passed over us in the night. Your good friends, Lord Maslyn and his dear wife, Lizbet, were both brutally killed—possibly at the hands of their own child, Fenris. The culprit, along with Olan, has disappeared and Soryn, poor Soryn, is left utterly alone and lies locked away for his own protection.

I do hope that I will be of some use and help to him, even in my old age. This place is one of cruel and terrible destiny. A blessing it might have been that you passed on when you did. I miss you more than I can sometimes bear, but this cold, harsh place is often only a den of suffering. I take comfort in one of the psalms. "The Hope of the Faithful," it is called. The hope of the faithful...yes, that is what I have, sweetest Louisa. Hope that one day, this boy will rise to meet his new beginning—whatever it may be. Hope that I will see you again after my light here on Niflheim burns out. Hope that all will be bright and good again for this broken family.

I must blow out my candle now, beloved, and welcome the sounds of the snowy night. My eyes grow tired earlier these days. My joints ache with the frigid winds. My mind wanders across the paths in the wood behind the church. My body longs for sleep. I still place the dried wreathe of lavender on your pillow at night—the one we were able to weave that summer long ago—a symbol that you are ever in my heart, though your body has been gone these sixteen years. I kiss your memory each time the moons pass over me and sleep comes.

Say a prayer for the boy, dearest Louisa, and for me that I might be of help to him. Tell our Lord that I desire only to serve Him. Watch over me in the night.

All my love and devotion,

Kimbli

Chapter One

In which the young master discovers a secret...

Late in the month of Jol, 903 PAE (Post Ancient Earth)

A red glow lazed about the room like an unwelcome guest, reluctant to leave. Odors from the distant kitchens meandered across the floor stones and ascended to his nostrils. He snorted. The scent of burnt flesh—even stag— had always sickened him. Bringing a gloved, bejeweled hand to his face, he covered his eyes. The red lights from the room's two lanterns dulled his senses and lulled him into a hazy half-consciousness. Footsteps resounded on the stairs leading to his room. A scowl escaped his freshly licked lips.

It was Jori, his manservant.

"My Lord Maslyn," Jori politely chimed when he arrived at the top of the staircase.

The manservant was met with silence. Lord Maslyn continued to cover his face and feigned sleep.

"Lord Maslyn," Jori nudged the young noble's shoulder.

"What?" the boy asked, disinterested.

"It's almost Night Bells, sir," Jori informed him.

Lord Maslyn sighed and stretched. He hated Jori's roundabout way of ushering him to bed almost as much as he hated the infernal Night Bells that the village church rang each night. Jori walked behind him, like a dog, over to the four-poster bed. Lord Maslyn rolled his eyes when the manservant promptly started to undress him. Jori deposited Lord Maslyn's linen nightgown over his master's head and put his day clothes into the wicker basket adjacent to the door. The servant girl would pick it up in the morning.

Once the noble was properly tucked beneath the covers, he dismissed Jori and pretended, once again, to fall compliantly asleep

7

as his manservant walked down the staircase. It was almost impossible for Lord Maslyn to hear the great door slam, for it lay far and away at the end of the long corridor that ran from his tower to the main castle. He didn't bother to strain his hearing in order to make sure that Jori was truly gone. Lord Maslyn listened carefully for any telltale sounds of life around his room—his nightly custom. There used to be birds nesting in the rafters of his ceiling, but they were gone now. Even though it was the month of Jol—the dead of winter on Niflheim—it was colder than usual outside. No summer birds would survive the frigid cold of his lofty domain this time of year. They would have long since gone underground to their nesting caverns.

Lord Maslyn's window was tightly bolted and he never attempted to open it, not once in six long years. Still, sometimes, he pulled back the drapes and looked at the outside world to which he was denied access. In summer, he saw birds and other animals that lived in the forest behind his tower frolicking in the snow. The bars and bolts over the glass made the whole world look as though great black stripes ran through it. Often, at night, he would pretend that he knew of a sort of power that could move objects from far away. If he ever mastered that imaginary skill, he envisioned that he could open the latch on the outside and open the windows, even if only for a frigid breeze. He knew that he would never survive a climb or a fall from the height of his window; it just would have been nice to feel fresh wind on his face.

Instead of wishing for magical powers, tonight he was content to lie in bed, awake. He opened one eye. Only silence and the red aura of the lanterns piqued his senses. Again, he detected the horrid smell of cooking meat. The kitchens were probably preparing venison for drying the next day. Or the servants could have been eating dinner together. He didn't really know. He always ate by himself, or with Father Kimbli. It was not permitted for him to associate with the rest of the castle. The same people came every day, week, month, year. The same three people: Jori, Jordis the servant girl, and Father

8

Kimbli. His entire social sphere consisted of those who were either assisting him with every aspect of his life or offering him counsel about it.

Thoughts of such things irritated him. The covers were scratchy against his legs, and bile rose in his throat. He truly hated everything about his life in the tower. He hated the red lanterns, the putrid smells seeping from the air shafts, the stone steps, and, most of all, he hated the silence that permeated every single crack in his broken existence. Never, in six long years, had he left that room. Being a twelve year old boy, he was sure his social development was being stunted from such isolation.

The tower was like a stone cell. But, of course, he guessed that was exactly what it was meant to be. They threw him in the tower ages ago, though he couldn't remember the exact night. He remembered his life before the tower, the fire that killed his family, and his life after, but he didn't remember why those men had locked him in the tower room. Before, he had a father, mother, and two older brothers. After, he had only his loneliness. Why did they want to isolate him? He still remembered waking up after the fire with the disgusting scent of blood and burnt flesh in his nose and the memories of people he would never see again. The stone prison was grating on his nerves. The empty noble's title he bore did him no good. It was all meaningless.

After a while, his mind wandered and his thoughts settled on his weekly visit from Father Kimbli that happened the afternoon before. He didn't mind the priest's visits, if only because they dispersed some of the monotony of his increasingly dull waking moments. The priest had come up the stairs, like smoke, meandering about as shadows would before settling over one area. Kimbli was kind, but somewhat of a mother hen type. He always asked after Lord Maslyn's health and seemed immensely interested in any little detail of the boy's life and daily pursuits. He never asked Lord Maslyn about his past or about his family. The noble thought this a little odd, since he remembered the priest from the time before the tower, but he never brought it up.

Yesterday, as usual, Father Kimbli descended onto the cushioned chair at the table and stared at the boy like a great, moth-eaten vulture. For all his kindness, the man looked to be nearing the further side of ninety. Not for the first time, Lord Maslyn wondered what had happened to the priest that caused his face to permanently freeze in a contented smile. Again, as usual, Father Kimbli opened with, "So, what have you been doing this week, Lord Maslyn?"

A sigh.

"Lord Maslyn, you must remember that you are free to tell me anything you wish about your life and your thoughts. I have watched over you since you were very young. Please, tell me about your week. It would please me to hear."

Rolling eyes.

"I have infinite patience, my lord, and I assure you," Kimbli said with a chuckle, "That I will continue to come every week, regardless if you feel like talking or not. I should think it would break up the monotony for you."

This was always how their visit went. Father Kimbli said everything and Lord Maslyn said nothing. In the early years, the boy had attempted to ask the priest about the tower and why he was there. He also tried asking about the incident, but Father Kimbli always changed the subject, a cloud descending on his wrinkled face. Years later, Lord Maslyn was at a loss as to what he was supposed to talk about—given that he did the same thing every week and nothing ever changed. He was never allowed to go anywhere or do anything that would entice sinning, excitement, or mischief. So, every meeting was an exhausting hour of sighs, nods, eye rolling, and staring off into blank space. Eventually, Father Kimbli exhaled heavily and, with great ceremony, stood. Ending as he always did, the priest said, "Until next week, my Lord Maslyn. I will pray for you. I hope you can find something to spark your interest in the coming days."

The memories of these events always troubled him. Though the priest's visits were ultimately harmless, they still annoyed the young lord. What bothered him so much was the fact that the priest knew exactly what the boy wanted: something to interest him. He desired more than anything to leave the tower, to discover, to explore. The red lamps had finally dimmed to the ember-like shade of a dying fire. Lord Maslyn raised himself up. Even with the bolted window, heavy drapes, and coverlets, he shivered. It was utterly barbaric that he was not allowed to keep logs in his room. They never let him have anything that could be considered "dangerous", though he did not know why. Perhaps it was because he was a boy and, traditionally (at least in the books he read), boys were rambunctious and unruly. He supposed that fire most certainly fell under those categories.

Chilled, he still left the warmth of his bed, sliding into his slippers to walk towards the impotent fireplace situated in the center of his stone prison. Wind licked at the shaft of the chimney and he could feel a frozen draft pooling around the base of the hearth. A shudder racked his small frame. He tightly held his arms about him as if they could provide any warmth. He continued to sit in front of the windy alcove and felt utterly consumed by sadness. A cold facade remained on his face in front of the servants and Father Kimbli, but in his room, in the dark with the Night Bells ringing, he let himself become the scared young boy that he was.

The cold air tugged at his nightshirt and his limbs grew stiff. As his mind started shutting down for sleep, he sensed another draft near the fireplace. From the bottom left corner, he felt a warmer sort of air spilling out of a crack. Now, he was intensely interested. Never in six years had anything interested him about this room. For the first time in eons, he felt the urge to do something. Smiling to himself, he thought he may indeed have found something to talk about with Father Kimbli. Lord Maslyn knelt down and pressed his small face to the crack, tried to smell and feel the air. It smelled fragrant—like flowers. It was a familiar scent...like someone he once knew, though he could not say whom. The air definitely came from below instead of from the chimney lip twenty feet up. Lord Maslyn craned his neck to look up the tunnel. He saw the snow swirl around outside the mouth of the chimney and he pressed his body closer to the warmer air that came up from the crack.

As he scooted his body closer to the corner of the fireplace, he felt his spine come into contact with a sharp object. At first, he thought he had hit a rock or a piece of jagged brick in the hearth. When he turned and felt it with his fingers, he discerned a handle. Lord Maslyn went very still. "Just what is hidden in this fireplace?" he thought to himself. Hesitant, he lifted his frozen hand and felt of the metal latch. It was warm. He pulled on the handle. There was a small *click* and a hidden door swung inward, open. Lord Maslyn realized that some of the bricks in the fireplace were an illusion, merely plaster, fastened to a wooden door that posed as the left panel of the hearth.

The air blew full-force out of the opening, and the boy reveled in the warmth of it. He looked behind him, over the table that blocked his view of the staircase. Listening, he only heard silence and he could see the dying flames in the red lanterns. Lord Maslyn smiled to himself. That night, for the first time in six years, something different would happen to him. Mustering any courage he had, he peered down through the small doorway. It was just big enough for his small body to crawl through. He felt sure that a grown adult would have had difficulty fitting through such a tiny opening. There was something comforting about that, as though the doorway were there just for him.

After his head and shoulders squeezed inside, he let his eyes adjust to complete darkness. With the fingers of his right hand, he cautiously reached forward and felt the stone floor. Astonishingly, it was smooth and seemed as if it had been hewn by an artisan. Letting his fingers travel further along the floor, he felt a lump in his stomach when the floor suddenly stopped and only empty air remained. This was discouraging, but then a thought occurred to him...*stairs*. He backtracked to where the floor seemed to end and he did, indeed, find an edge that ran downwards until it hit another horizontal floor. *Stairs*.

A delicious thrill curled in his chest and he slowly eased himself out of the opening, carefully shutting the false door. He made sure that he could use the hidden latch to reopen it at will. As much as he wanted to explore the entirety of the secret passage at once, he knew that it would be more prudent to wait and do so the following night, after he had had time to plan and secure some light for the tunnel. He made sure that nothing looked amiss in the fireplace or the hearth around it, and shuffled back to bed. Excitement kept him from sleep right away, so instead, he pulled back the curtains and stared out at the snow falling over the castle grounds. He could see the church, far away on the hill and footmen who cared for carriages down in the yard, nodding off at their posts. He closed the curtains and buried himself under the mountainous covers. The next night, he would explore the tunnel and perhaps find something wonderful nestled beneath his dark prison.

* * *

He felt a gentle shaking bring him out of his dream. Jori. Groaning, Lord Maslyn rolled over and was disgruntled to feel his whole face dragged through the drool that had escaped to his pillow during the night.

"Ugh!" he grimaced.

"Sir, shall I have your sheets laundered?" Jori asked, not the least bit concerned.

The boy raised himself and ran a hand through his tousled hair before wiping the slime from his cheeks.

"Uh…yes. That would be fine, Jori."

Lord Maslyn could tell that there was a slight smile at the edge of his manservant's face and felt embarrassed by the whole thing. He had always slept with his mouth open. Casting insecurity aside, he

13

rose and stretched while Jori took his nightclothes and put them in the basket near the door for Jordis. The manservant also left a basin of warm water on the table with a cloth for Lord Maslyn to bathe. Then, Jori left without further comment and descended to see that his master's breakfast was ready.

Lord Maslyn craned his neck to see around the doorframe and discerned the tall, skinny figure of Jori walking down the corridor leading to the main castle. The boy stole a glance at his everyday bathing amenities to see if they could be of any use to him in his exploration of the tunnel that night. Soap and a basin of clear water rested on the tray. Beside these things were a comb and his clothes for the day. "Humph," he thought to himself. "It will take some imagination to find anything useful in this room."

He washed, inspecting his surroundings as he did so. There were four walls in the tower. On the south wall stood his bed and window. On the east wall was the fireplace. The west had the doorway and the north wall—the *north wall*…Lord Maslyn took his wet washcloth with him and smiled when he realized that the north wall contained his answer! There was a shelf there chocked full of books. He now knew how he could inconspicuously get candles for the tunnel. When Jordis came, he would ask her for a candle, because he was trying to work up the discipline to read each night. It was a long shot, and all the servants supposedly knew he was not allowed to have fire, but he felt certain that Jordis would understand. She was nearly his age after all, perhaps only a year younger. Surely she would be sympathetic if he told her that it could be a secret. She would not suspect anything amiss if it was for something as common as *reading*, especially when he was the most boring creature alive, as far as his servants were concerned. Lord Maslyn made sure never to be a bit of trouble.

Jori returned to find his master freshly washed and ready for dressing. Lord Maslyn always hated that part. He found it rather stupid that he had to allow someone else to dress him. A previous attempt to dress himself had resulted in a tongue lashing from the

14

servant. "Wretched man," Lord Maslyn thought, though he truly didn't mean it. Jori was acceptable. A slight smile threatened to form on his face, but he was careful to squash the urge. If anyone suspected his altered behavior, who knew what the servants might say? In the future, with the façade in place that he was reading every night, he was sure that he could get away with seeming more excited or alert. He would simply say that he had read the most interesting book the previous night.

His manservant did not seem to notice the boy's excited mood and left soon after the dressing was over. Lord Maslyn knew that Jordis would soon come with breakfast and retrieve his laundry. The young noble thought it would be the perfect time to ask for a reading candle, since she would have all day to try and get it without being detected. He hoped he wouldn't get her into any sort of trouble. She *was* sort of pretty—and very nice. In fact, he wondered if speaking to her would change something between them. They never really spoke to one another and he felt a little sorry that he never thanked her for all the things she did for him each day.

Strolling over to his window, the boy stared out at the snow that shrouded all things in mystery. Snow was a beautiful thing— and yet so cold. Hopefully Jordis would not be icy and unforgiving like that. Shouts from the guard drew his attention to the right. Plastering his face to the window, he strained to see out to the far edge of the castle. The scene was happening far away, but he was able to discern a stray horse that was causing chaos for the stablemen. It was none of his concern, so he left the window to pace the floor until Jordis arrived ten minutes later.

Chapter Two

In which the young master obtains a piece of advice…

She entered the room silently, as always, carrying a loaded laundry basket under her arm. Its contents included new sheets for the bed and freshly laundered clothes Lord Maslyn had worn earlier in the week. The boy moved to the back of the room to let her attend to her duties. A flurry of activity began around his bed as she turned back the coverlet and stripped the linens. All her hair was hidden underneath a starched white cap that tied under her slender chin. Her dress was very clean, neat, and every stitch was orderly. It was clear that she took great pride in maintaining her appearance.

Jordis turned around and Lord Maslyn could see that she was, indeed, very pretty. Her lips sported a healthy pink glow and her eyes were the strangest grey. Lord Maslyn's own eyes were a flat, muted brown just like his father's had been. His older brothers had had the red-brown eyes of their mother. Jordis' eyes looked wise and old—like an oracle's. She stole a glance at him while she smoothed the comforter on his bed. Heat flushed Lord Maslyn's young face and he turned away, hastily. A stifled intake of breath rang out in the room. The boy had startled her.

"Uh—J-Jordis!" he said, unintentionally loud.

Again, she looked up and then swiftly lowered her gaze as she curtseyed.

"Yes, Lord Maslyn?" her response was schooled to be calm and friendly, though her white hands were clenched at her sides.

Fluttery sensations invaded his stomach when she looked at him from beneath her blonde lashes, inquisitive. "What is wrong with me?" he thought to himself. Swallowing hard, he looked at her square in the face. She blushed, her skin turning the most beautiful

17

scarlet color he had ever seen. Her face then reminded him of the red lanterns and the Night Bells. It made him nervous.

"Um, Jordis, Can I ask a favor?" he managed.

She looked genuinely surprised. Her shoulders relaxed.

"If it pleases you, milord."

The boy's eyes darted around. His mind scrambled for what to say next. He skirted to his bookshelf. He hadn't thought through the plan that far, so he grabbed a book in a hurry. The spine looked like it was freshly bound and never opened once. *Fabulous.* An eager smile plastered itself onto his face when he turned around. She looked a little confused at his behavior. He held out the book to her and announced proudly,

"I need some candles to read with at nighttime. The red lanterns are far too dim and the suns set so early, I haven't been able to read at nighttime like I want. It helps lull me to sleep, you see."

The most skeptical expression darkened her pretty face,

"I can see why you picked it. *The Common Ailments and Treatments of Horses* would put anyone to sleep."

Lord Maslyn thought, "Oh no! What book did I pull off of the shelf!?"

He bustled in his mind for something to say so he wouldn't rouse her suspicions. Suddenly, as if by a miracle, it came to him.

"Well, it seems the guards are having trouble with one of their horses. I noticed outside the window and I was just wondering what might be wrong with it. There isn't much to occupy my time up here."

He even believed it himself. It was a brilliant excuse to have such a ridiculous book in his hand. Curiously enough, he found that he *did* want to know what was wrong with that horse.

"Oh. Well, I suppose that makes sense. The horse's name is Sable and he's a vicious nightmare." She flushed again as she realized she had criticized one of her master's horses. "I'm sorry, sir! I did not mean to speak ill of your property, milord."

"Jordis, I haven't been outside this room in six years. I have no idea what my 'property' consists of. You criticize as much as you like," he reassured her.

A real smile lit up her face this time. Lord Maslyn thought she seemed just as glad of the conversation as he was. He hoped they would talk again like this.

"Well...*candles*," she began. "I believe I can secure a few for you and a candle stand. You may want to hide them, though, when you're not using them. I don't know how Jori would feel about you having access to fire, no matter how small the flame is."

"I suppose you're right," Lord Maslyn admitted. He was thankful she agreed to grant his request.

"I can bring them later this evening after my chores are done. What will I tell Jori if he should see me?" she asked.

Another flaw in his plan. It was becoming increasingly clear that he would have to think well on his future schemes. He thought about several options.

"What if you told him that you forgot your laundry basket?"

"No, that would be something I'd never forget."

"Well," he tried again, "What if you said that you forgot the sheets from the bed? You just put fresh linens on, so it might make sense for you to walk out without the old ones."

"Hmm. Unless I come up with something better, that's what I'll say."

She went to the laundry basket at the foot of the four-poster and grabbed the old sheets, placing them on the floor in a pile. Her skirts swished in circular motions when she came around to the front. The young master leaned against the table and smiled at her.

"I'll do this for you on one condition," she announced.

"What condition is that?" he replied.

"In the future, don't call me, 'Jordis'."

"Why not?" he asked, surprised.

"I hate it. It was my grandmother's name and she was the meanest woman I have ever met. I much prefer to be called 'Arna', which was my great-grandmother's name. It's my middle name."

He laughed, "Arna it is, then."

She turned to leave him and he touched her arm, gently. Again, those peculiar butterflies raced around inside his stomach. Again, she turned and blushed.

"Before you go, I have another favor."

"Yes, milord?" she muttered, polite and reserved once more.

"Please don't call me that. I have a name I like best, too. I also haven't heard it in a while. Please don't call me by my title."

There was something desperate within him as he asked this. It looked as though Jordis—Arna—could be a potential friend in his bleak life. For some reason, it was vitally important that they be on familiar terms. There was intense hesitation in her eyes, but he could see that she was considering the idea. He hoped she would agree. He wanted to hear his own name.

"What *is* your name?" her expression turned sheepish.

"It's Soryn. Soryn Jens Bialas Maslyn." Hearing it aloud made him feel strangely brave for the night ahead.

"That's quite a name. One to be proud of I should think. Fine; I won't call you by your title when we're alone like this. I'll bring you candles tonight so you can get on with *The Common Ailments and Treatments of Horses*. It sounds simply riveting…"

She went to the top of the staircase and peeked over her shoulder to wink at him. In that moment, he felt keenly aware of all the time he had wasted in not talking with her all these years. Ever since the first morning he awoke in the tower, he remembered her being there. Never had they said anything more than, "good morning", or other such empty pleasantries. It truly was a shame; she was a nice girl.

* * *

20

Throughout the day, he listened closely for chapel bells to the south in order to gauge the hour. It was painfully boring to trudge about the frostbitten tower, accomplishing the useless tasks that Jori brought for him. Apparently, his title still carried a miniscule amount of weight in the castle and each afternoon, his manservant brought him a small mountain of papers to be sealed and signed. Soryn never read them. He had a distinct hatred of paperwork and resented Jori for bringing it each day. He never wanted to be a lord anyway. A boy his age should have been able to be something else. Fenris, his eldest brother should have inherited the horrid task of signing papers all day. The thought of his elder brother had been fleeting, but he felt keenly alone once it had passed through his mind. Though Soryn had been young when Fenris and Olan were taken from him, he missed them.

After wading through the pile of papers and sending them away with Jori, he sat and fidgeted for about twenty minutes before he finally persuaded himself to move. Since Arna had not yet returned and he knew Jori wouldn't be around until dinnertime, Soryn walked over to the north wall, which housed his bookshelf. Thankfully, he had remembered to place the horse book on his nightstand, to maintain his façade of interest. He could see the blank space between the books on the second shelf and it reminded him of the secret door in the fireplace.

All of a sudden, he was unbearably filled with excitement. "Oh, please hurry up, Arna," he whispered. Much to his chagrin, she did not bound up the stairs at that moment. He looked at the spines of the books on his shelf. He saw many that were about matters related to running a town—the upkeep of a large castle, land treaties of years past, the history of his country, Oban, the ancient history of his planet, Niflheim. All of these books, he usually avoided. His eyes were drawn to the bottom shelf.

This shelf had successfully evaded his attention for six years. Never had he taken the time to pay attention to its contents. Since he still needed to wait for Arna, he folded his legs underneath himself and sat level with the lowest shelf. It would make sense that the most insignificant titles would be placed here. Many people reserved a bottom—or top shelf—for items that were forgotten. However, after only a moment of browsing, he began to see that most of the books were very interesting, indeed.

This shelf only contained thirteen titles when all of the other shelves had a full load. These books were grouped according to common theme and importance. All of them were oriented around the containment, use, and history of the Seidh on the planet Niflheim. From what he understood from conversations with Jori and odd tidbits he heard from guards through the window, the Seidh was what common people called *magic*. His heart fluttered in delight and he scanned the spines of each of them.

The books were incredibly dusty and old—in fact, he felt certain that, if he hadn't sat down and looked closely, he would most likely never have given them a glance at all. "What unusual books to have in this room," he thought. Magic had never really been discussed much around him. He never talked about it with Father Kimbli. He felt it was acutely unusual to have such things in his tower room.

A strange excitement bubbled up his spine, and in the pit of his stomach he could feel a feathery sensation building. What if *he* could learn magic? As irrational as it was, the books were making him feel as though the Seidh were some real power. "Silly of me," he thought to himself as he raised himself from the floor and walked to his window. "Belief in magic is only for superstitious old people and fools." Still, he found that he rather liked the sound of the Seidh; perhaps if it *were* real, he could someday come to learn how to use it.

Six tolls came from the church bells. Annoyed, he thought, "Won't Arna ever come back?" Impatience started to settle into his bones. A thought occurred to him that had never crossed his naïve mind before. He left the window and crept cautiously toward the doorway that led to the extensive corridor attached to the main castle. An invasion of behavior that was out of character for Lord

Maslyn had filled the day, it seemed. He had never explored the corridor; it had simply never occurred to him to try. The door would be locked at the end, but why not explore a bit? Jori would not arrive with his dinner until six-thirty in the evening, and Soryn would have plenty of time to reach the end of the cloister and back.

The hard-soled shoes provided for him each year were far too loud for such an expedition. He was sure it was best to move as silently as possible, so Soryn removed them and tested the first stone step. No sound. The next step…no sound. Good. Fearing the servants would hear even at the faraway end of the corridor, he moved as stealthily as possible and stayed close to the stone walls. It felt oddly thrilling to be sneaking about in an area that was wholly different from the tower. Even though it was still part of his prison, it seemed different, closer to the rest of civilization.

Voices of far-off servants resounded off of the stones. Soryn caught snippets of small talk being tossed about. The air was warmer the closer he moved towards the door. He still hadn't caught sight of the door itself. The tunnel was almost pitch black because of the fact that the windows were all boarded up. Apparently, his captors did not want him looking outside too close to the main castle. A streak of light manifested itself and Soryn could tell that he was nearing the great door that barred his life from the rest of the world. The noises of the house were far louder there. He was careful to stay out of the path of light that extended from the crack underneath the door.

Footsteps came dangerously close and he froze. His heart beat faster than it had in six years and sweat broke out on his forehead. Soryn instinctively closed his eyes, as a key was inserted on the other side of the door. Metallic clicks and clangs rang out as the door latch opened. Soryn plastered himself as close to the shadows as he could. The door opened. Arna walked in, carrying his dinner tray and a small parcel underneath. She hadn't seen him.

Forgetting himself, he breathed a sigh of relief. She turned quickly, only to gasp at the sight of him. They both gave a stifled shout and clamped their hands over their mouths, but it was clear that no one else was near the tower corridor entrance. After she realized there was no danger, Arna closed the door, locked it back, and made sure nothing was amiss with his dinner tray or the parcel. Next, she turned on him with what he could imagine as the most severe look she possessed.

"What do you think you're doing?" she hissed.

"I was just exploring. I got bored," he mumbled.

She scowled and stomped off in the direction of the tower room. Soryn followed along like a chastised dog and glumly ascended the steps. She did not say a word the entire time they walked back. His feet started to go numb on the cold floor. He quickly put his shoes back on as she plunked a tray on the table without the usual amount of grace she showed in her work.

"I can't believe you could be so careless! What if Jori had seen you? You aren't supposed to leave this room!" Heavy breathing accompanied her outburst.

"If they didn't want me to leave this room, why didn't they put a door *before* the stairs?" he countered.

She realized that he had a point, but she just clenched her jaw and tossed the parcel on the table before turning to leave.

"W-Wait! Arna, don't be angry with me! I was just impatient. I wanted you to come back." Soryn watched a blush rise to her cheeks. "Uh…I mean…I was really excited about my reading for tonight, you know…"

She raised her chin up a little higher than it had been and marched over to his seat. She smelled of jasmine and lavender. He could not help smiling. Leaning down, she said,

"If Jori or Father Kimbli finds out you are going 'exploring' too often, you can be sure they *will* install that door you mentioned." Her voice was serious. "If I were you, I would know what was good for me and stick to reading my little books and doing as I am told."

With that, she elegantly tossed her head and marched down the steps into the darkness. He sat dazed at the table. There was no time to recover before she stomped back into the room and grabbed the pile of laundry that she left earlier in the morning. At least she had a good memory.

"Have fun reading about sick horses, *Lord Maslyn*."

And she was gone.

He uncovered his tray and found an extra piece of fish, an apple, and a raspberry tart. He reached for the parcel and gingerly untied the sack, dumping its contents next to him on the table. She brought eight candles, stand, flint, and tinder. There was also a small book entitled, *The Behavior of Horses in All Seasons*. Lord Maslyn smiled to himself. Arna was thoughtful, despite her snappy tone. Again, he was sorry for how long he had waited to talk with her. Perhaps they could still be friends if he tried to speak with her more often. In the back of his mind, however, her advice pulsated like another heartbeat. Her opinionated outburst was most likely correct. Angering Jori or Father Kimbli was something he never wanted to do. Even though they put strict parameters on his life, they had always been kind to him. He put the candles back in the bag along with the rest of the stash and ate his dinner. All the while, he thought about the tunnel in the fireplace

Chapter Three

In which the young master stretches his legs…

The ringing of the Night Bells filled his bedroom with small vibrations and chimes from other objects that were stirred by the sound. Lord Maslyn lifted his eyelids and stared at the canopy hanging over his four-poster bed. Sitting up, he stretched and turned to pull back the curtains attached to the frame. Soft, red light seeped into his coverlet and bathed the room in rich color. He strained his ears, listening for any movement from the corridor. Jori left long before, but the young master was still cautious. If he were caught, it could get Arna into trouble as well, because she had given him the candles.

He reached underneath his bed and felt the parcel he had stashed between the frames. The candles were long and thin. He removed them carefully so they wouldn't break. The stand was a circular dish with a raised well in the middle. He placed one candle in the dish and rested it on his nightstand. The bed squeaked a bit as he stood and walked to his dresser. Earlier, he had been able to locate several pieces of black clothing in his drawers. Swiftly, he dressed.

Thanks to his dark hair and being garbed head to toe in black, it would be easier to hide himself if he had to. A feeling of adventure settled over him and he could not help the boyish smile that came to his lips every time he thought about the secret passage in the fireplace. He went back to the bed and sacked up the rest of the candles", attaching them to the belt he had found in his wardrobe. His appearance most likely looked thievish, but he was too excited to care. Going to the table, he pulled the flint and tinder from his pocket. He had never lit a candle before, but he had seen Jori and Arna do it plenty of times.

Soryn took the tinder—a wad of cotton—from the table and positioned it on the stone hearth at the fireplace. The candle dish clanked against the stone when he set that down. Next, he retrieved the steel piece that Arna had included with the flint and held it in his left hand. The flint was awkward to hold, but he was able to get a good grip on it. He positioned his hands near the tinder on the stones before he made his first attempt at striking a spark. A pitiful little clash came out, but no fire. Not to be discouraged, he struck the flint a little harder this time, making sure to angle it towards the cotton.

Sure enough, a spark singed the outer edge of the tinder. "Perhaps this time," he thought. The third time, a little fire sprang up from the cotton fibers. He quickly lit the candle before blowing out the flame on the tinder. That way, he would be able to use it again in the future. The wax exteriors of the candles were marked for hours, so he would know how long it would take for him to explore the passage. With the light, he was able to see the hidden door latch clearly. If he had not known it would be there and what it was, he was sure he would not have noticed it. Tugging on the latch, the false stone wall swung open, silently, as before.

Somehow, he knew that door and that tunnel would change him. Lord Maslyn already felt more excitement than he had in six years, and his frozen body was beginning to thaw with the warmth coming from the open tunnel. He smelled that familiar fragrance again and felt the warmer air circulating through the space. The light showed that the stairs were even, smooth, and steep. The return trip up to the tower would be taxing—especially since he was accustomed to so little exercise. Still, nothing deterred him from stepping firmly onto the first descending step.

He went down a few and turned around, keeping his balance, and pushed the door so that a small crack was open for him to return, but so that it would look like a normal fireplace from the other side. The bed curtains were closed so it would appear that he was still in bed if Jori returned. Turning back around, he started down the staircase. The walls of the tunnel were a strange sort of material—

28

not stone precisely, but almost dirt-like in its makeup. It reminded him of the strange bumpy earth that he played in as a child, when he and his brothers would dig deeply enough through the snow in summertime. The soil of Niflheim was a purple sort of color and the composition was more foam than particulate. It was seldom that any soil could be reached, since snow covered the world year-round and only partially thawed in the summer. Nevertheless, the tunnel walls surrounding him looked just like the dirt he remembered. It must have taken quite an effort to obtain so much of it.

There was no chance that he was underground—not with the tower being so high—so he wondered if the person who had created the tunnel had brought the earth here to insulate the walls. He attempted to keep count of the steps he went down and was already up to thirty when he realized the staircase was going to continue for quite some time. It was not a spiral, or a straight staircase, but one that wound on and meandered without a discernible pattern. Just when he thought he had it figured out, the tunnel would start off in a new direction, only to change again just as quickly.

He made it to step fifty-seven before he stopped to rest a bit. A skin for water would have been appreciated, but he had not planned on there being so many steps. His candle had not even passed the half-hour stripe. Given his frail and weak constitution, he supposed he was making good time. Perhaps the trips down from the tower and back could provide him with much needed exertion. Though he had no one to compare himself to, he figured he was stunting his growth by living his sedentary existence. He imagined most other twelve year old boys would have been more athletic. Air was flowing easier now, and he no longer had to gasp for breath. He steadied himself and continued to descend.

"Fifty-eight...fifty-nine...sixty..." On and on he counted this way. The candle lost an hour. The wax began to disappear past another half hour mark when he began to see level ground below. Almost in disbelief, he patted the floor with his foot to be sure he had reached the bottom of the tunnel. There were a total of one hundred and twelve steps. It was a long way down. On the way, he had discovered two things. The steps were created by someone with exceptional masonry skills. They were incredibly even despite their steepness and they had carvings Soryn could barely make out with the candlelight. Also, he was extremely lacking in physical strength and muscular fortitude.

He gently laid the candle stand on the last step and slumped to the carved stone floor, resting his back against the earthen wall. Empty silence permeated every inch of the tunnel. Soryn turned his head to his left where the tunnel remained flat and seemed to curve towards a room or alcove. If he was not mistaken, there was a faint glow coming from the direction of the flattened path. A knot of fear tied itself intricately into his chest. What if he got caught? Still, wouldn't it be better to explore and risk discovery than to live forever in that tower room without experiencing anything different?

Taking all the courage that remained in his exhausted body, he raised the candle to his lips, took a deep breath, and blew it out. All was dark for several minutes, but he could eventually make out the muted orange light coming from farther down the tunnel. He left the candle on the floor and stood up, careful to make as little noise as possible. He removed his shoes. Walking in his sock feet, he tiptoed through the tunnel in silence. If there were people ahead, he hoped he would have more success in stealth than he had with Arna in the corridor earlier.

Using as much agility as he could muster, he managed to silently step his way over to where the corridor opened a little wider and curved to the right. That familiar scent he noticed the first time the door opened was very strong there and his brain suddenly began to flood his mind with snippets of disjointed memories. Unfortunately, he could not make any of them out. He was only able to glimpse brief snatches of color, white hair, a blurry face. Uneasiness tightened the knot of fear growing in his chest. "What is this place? Who built it? Does anyone else know about it?" Soryn's thoughts raced through his mind.

The glow became a light when he turned the corner. He almost despaired when he saw more stairs until he counted them: only five. The light came from the top and he discerned a bumpy, purple-brown room. Shadows crawled across the rough ceiling and pooled in its corners. Deep breaths filled his lungs as he gathered his bravery. He climbed the five steps quickly and stood at the top of the short staircase. Lord Maslyn marveled at the sight before him.

* * *

The room was small, perhaps half the size of his tower room (which was not spacious by any stretch of the imagination). Light flickered across the surface of thousands of objects that cluttered the floor, desks, counters, shelves, and walls throughout the space. Soryn could see the source of light hailed from something altogether foreign to him. Candles, lanterns, fireplaces, torches…those were the forms of brilliance he was used to in the tower. *This* room contained a light he had never seen before, even in his memories of the years before the tower. It was spherical and hovered above a small spire resting in a circular base. It sat on a desk in one corner of the room. The sphere seemed to be made of a swirling liquid, rotating in regular turns. It reminded him of one of the three suns that could be seen in the sky on a clear day. This little "sun" was a fierce, fiery orange like one of the larger suns of Niflheim called "Adden".

He stepped closer, fascinated by the object. All time and priority was forgotten while he walked closer to the sphere. Soryn felt radiating heat, welcome and warm, bathe his body. A smile threatened to break out on his lips. This place had, indeed, already shown him new and exciting things. The miniature Adden continued to rotate over its spire and he reached a hand towards it. The closer he came to its surface, the hotter the heat beaming from it became. He felt sure he would have been burned had he not been startled out of his skin and turned around.

I wouldn't touch that if I were you.

31

Despite the heat, ice settled in Soryn's spine at the comment. What frightened him even more was the fact that the sound hadn't occurred audibly. It had resounded in his mind. Jerking around, he scanned the room. He could see the entryway to the tunnel, the cluttered shelves and surfaces, but he did not see any living creature in the room with him. Moving away from the sphere, he skirted around, carefully avoiding the messy piles and articles. His heartbeat slowed when he was sure he was not about to be killed by a hidden assassin.

In fact, the room appeared to be abandoned, even though the shining orb remained. A thin layer of dust covered every inch of the place and cobwebs threaded themselves between shelves, prominent objects, and the walls. Few spiders on Niflheim were poisonous, but nevertheless, Soryn made sure to avoid their webs. The voice did not return even after he waited several minutes. "Mostly likely my imagination," he thought. Soryn brushed it off as nerves from his first expedition. Perhaps his mind had gotten a bit overexcited.

All around the room were things utterly new and intriguing to him. It was puzzling that he had no conceivable idea of how such a room came into existence. There was only one way in and out that he could see. Whoever had used this room must not have visited in the last six years. Unless…A perilous thought fluttered into his mind. "What if someone is visiting this room when I'm asleep at night?" The thought terrified him. Still, the dust made it seem unlikely. As far as he could tell, the only footprints amid the dust in the room were his own.

Another unusual object caught his eye while he was sorting through his thoughts. Unlike the sphere, it emanated no light and instead seemed suffused in shadow. It rested high on a shelf sitting in the only corner of the room that wasn't covered in the light from the "sun". Lord Maslyn walked closer to it, peering up, trying to see the features of the item. The shelf was rather high and the object looked to be a small statue. Because it was black, it absorbed all the light around it, and Soryn had a hard time seeing what it was. Confused, Soryn was willing to dismiss the thing.

The rest of the room's contents proved equally interesting and he found that it would most likely take years to sort through the bits of flotsam and jetsam that drifted on top of every available surface. Though the room looked like a rat's nest, he could tell that there was some semblance of organization to the piles. On the table were various loose pages and scribbles. The counter that ran in an L-shape across two walls was filled with mysterious instruments and baubles. The shelf, of course, housed books. When he looked at the shelf again, he was drawn to the top where the black object perched. He squinted to see if he could make it out any better, but to no avail.

Want me to come down?

The velvety voice invaded his faculties again. That knot in Soryn's chest coiled with more loops with every scare he experienced. The voice most certainly qualified as frightening. Because of the nature of the comment, he could only assume the voice was coming from the statue. Soryn swallowed hard and said weakly,

"Yes?"

He felt rather stupid talking to a statue, despite the seriousness of the situation.

Done.

Instead of a statue above him on the shelf, Soryn realized it was a black animal about the size of a plump cat, though he was positive it was *not* a cat. Its body was pudgy and bulbous even though it was petite. Short legs ended in cleft hooves. Perky ears framed in a face with a snout and beady black eyes. Soryn searched his mental repertoire for any image he could to associate with this animal. He had seen it somewhere before. The black creature moved from its perch and hopped from the shelf to tall piles of matter on the counter. The boy was surprised the animal did not knock everything down in the process. In fact, the thing gracefully descended to the floor as if it had performed the same feat hundreds of times.

Is this better?

The creature turned around slowly, as if it was allowing Soryn to get a better look. Lord Maslyn took the opportunity seriously, still trying to figure out what sort of animal it was. When he saw the curled tail, the word leapt to his mind. *A pig.* He had seen them in the barns when he was a little boy, outside the castle walls with his mother. Admittedly, he had never seen a black pig before, or one that appeared to be mature despite the miniature size. The pigs he had seen in the barn were huge in comparison. He was sure this fellow would be able to fit into a serving bowl.

Is my size a problem? the pig asked, clearly offended.

"No! I was…just surprised by it, is all," Soryn muttered.

The pig trotted around the floor, neatly dodging every bit of clutter. Lord Maslyn felt his mouth hanging open in astonishment that an animal had lived down here for so long without any identifiable source of nourishment—let alone the fact that it talked and gave advice!

"What are you doing down here?" Soryn asked.

The pig swiveled its head around and gave what Soryn imagined to be a bored expression. Without answering the question, it hopped from the floor to a chair that the boy had not noticed before. Then, it jumped to the counter near the "sun".

I live here. Are you here to force me out?

"Not at all. I was just startled to see you."

The pig ignored him and turned towards the orange sphere.

You could have lost your hand, you know; had you touched this.

Soryn walked over towards the counter and watched the pig reach with its jaws towards a metal rod lying next to its small body. He—at least Soryn *thought* it was a "he"—clenched the metal tightly in his mouth and directed it so that it made contact with the "sun". Instantly, the metal turned red and dripped its melting liquid onto the sphere, disintegrating. Soryn agreed with the pig's assessment. Before the entire rod could turn red, the pig tossed it from his mouth onto the stone floor where it slowly grew grey and cold once more.

The affectionate name you've given it is quite accurate. This is a sun, just a very small one. It was patterned after Adden, in fact, as you guessed.

Annoyance at the pig's self-important attitude washed over Lord Maslyn. Also, how did the pig know what he called the sphere?

I have a name, you know.

There it went again! Soryn thought, exasperated, "Just what kind of a pig is he!?"

I'm a sentient pig and I don't appreciate you thinking such insipid thoughts about me.

"Ugggghh! How are you *doing* that!? How can you know what I'm thinking!?"

I'm...talented.

"That's rather obvious. It would take talent for a human, let alone a pig!" Soryn spat.

I grow rather tired of you calling me "pig," instead of by my name. Do you think you could humor me?

"I suppose," the boy replied.

I prefer to be called "Ulla".

"Oo-lluh?" Soryn tried out the strange name on his tongue.

That's it. Now why don't you tell me the reason you have invaded my study? I have worked quite hard to keep it a secret.

Lord Maslyn didn't know how to answer Ulla. There were many reasons he decided to go explore the tunnel. Was it curiosity alone? The pig didn't seem to mind that Soryn was taking his time. He decided that it was simple. "I wanted to get out," he thought to himself.

"I wanted to leave the tower," Soryn said aloud.

Oh?

"I wanted to...get away for a while."

Hmmm.

Ulla sounded truly interested, if not a little amused. The boy felt uncomfortable in the pig's presence, but he tried his best not to let on. The fact that an animal had talked to him was not so strange. All

35

animals could communicate effectively with humans, even if they did not speak the same language. Some animals chose *not* to talk to people. What made Lord Maslyn nervous was the fact that Ulla seemed to know what he was thinking. He was certain that something like *that* wasn't normal.

Oh, you'd be surprised, Ulla interrupted.

Chills crawled up Soryn's arms and he quickly became both frustrated and fearful.

"Would you *please* stop doing that?"

Doing what?

"Reading my thoughts! It's annoying!" Soryn snapped.

Would you stop breathing if I asked you to?

That pulled the boy up short. He couldn't tell if the pig was trying to make a joke or if he was serious.

Oh, I am very serious. Just as it would be absurd for me to ask you to pause your breathing, it would be quite unreasonable for you to ask me to stop reading your thoughts. It's something I do as subconsciously as you breathe.

The young noble scowled and tossed his hands in the air, giving up.

The pig hopped from the counter with the "sun" to the chair again and promptly clambered onto the table with the papers. If Soryn didn't know about the pig's exceptionalities, he would have taken him for a stray barn animal, despite its being confined to the room at the foot of the stairs. He appeared to be just like any other pig, only a little cleaner than Soryn remembered other pigs being. Lord Maslyn looked down to find Ulla staring at him. It was rather unnerving. Soryn turned around and drifted over to the shelf stuffed with ancient books.

Would you like to read them?

The young master was surprised at the question. He had scarcely looked at them before the pig called out. The titles *were* interesting. Soryn was surprised when he saw that every single book on the entire shelf was related to the Seidh. These books were also different from the thirteen in his tower room. Thinking back, he felt sure that those thirteen books were from the same collection as the ones on this shelf. The boy thought, "How did those books get into my room?" He turned around.

Don't think you'll get answers from me, Ulla said. *I don't know how they got into your room.*

"You're a pig, Ulla. Why should I suspect you?"

Still, Soryn felt sure that Ulla could have had something to do with all the mysterious things surrounding this room. Lord Maslyn expected Ulla to speak up about his thoughts, as usual, but the pig stayed silent and merely stared at him. The pig snorted and shook his head in the direction of the shelf.

Why don't you take a look at one of those?

A strange sensation filled the boy as he walked closer to the shelf. It was almost as if Ulla *wanted* him to take one. He glanced in the pig's direction, but found that Ulla had jumped down again and was trotting over to the corner. The boy ran his fingers gingerly across the old, fragile spines. Some had titles so worn, they couldn't be read—perhaps they had come over on the colonization ship *Elena,* almost a thousand years ago. Again, he noticed an uneasy feeling building within. He waited for the pig's snide remarks at his discomfort, but none came.

He pulled a book from amongst the others entitled, *A Rudimentary Commentary on the Seidh.* The cover's color was a pale grey, most likely from age. Soryn blew the dust off of the spine and cautiously opened it, the odd feeling in his body growing. It was difficult to put his finger on the precise emotion he was experiencing, but the longer he stayed in the room, the more uncomfortable and paradoxically excited he became. The first paragraph on the first page read,

"One must observe the strictest vigilance when entering the practice of the Seidh. The proper rituals must be observed if any knowledge is to be gained; remember your own human frailty…"

37

Soryn closed the book. Admittedly, he was intrigued with the idea of the Seidh and its potential uses for him, but…something about the whole room gave him the worst sort of disquiet. Perhaps it was—

Were you going to think "the pig"?

There Ulla went again. He apparently liked to meddle in the young master's thoughts. Soryn decided to change the subject.

"What does the book mean by human frailty?"

Ulla gazed up at him with his round, black eyes and tilted his head.

Why do you want to know?

"You're the one who told me to get a book and read from it!"

I merely suggested. I didn't tell you to do anything.

"What does it mean?"

If you must know, it refers to the fact that the Seidh takes a great deal of mental and physical effort to practice. Not many can discipline their minds and body enough to become practitioners.

"You're a pig. How do you know so much about magic?"

Are you determined to look common by calling it "magic"?

"I just want to know how you know so much about it. How do you read minds? How did you know the orb over there was a miniature sun?"

I'm entitled to keep my secrets to myself. I think that you, however, are running out of time for tonight and won't get any more secrets out of me during this trip.

A small sliver of panic knifed the boy in the back. He had lost track of time. Since he had blown the candle out, he had no way of knowing how many minutes had passed. He stood still, thinking.

I expect you'll be back tomorrow night?

"Yes, I'll come back."

Soryn fled the room and hastily grabbed his candle stand before beginning his struggle up the stairs. It took far longer than he remembered it taking to descend. He was utterly exhausted when he reached the top and slumped down inside the fireplace once the trap door was shut. His breathing eventually slowed and, as he closed his eyes, images of what had transpired rolled around in his head like marbles on the stone floor. "What in the world have I discovered?"

Though it seemed, at first, to be a harmless study, it was no coincidence that the books on his shelf matched the ones in the room downstairs. As well, mind reading pigs—smug ones at that—didn't just show up out of nowhere. He knew that the room and its oddities were very significant. Yet, for tonight, he would have to let his thoughts return to his immediate surroundings. The red lanterns had gone out completely, and the window drapes remained dark.

Hauling himself up, he carefully removed his adventurer's garb and hid it under the bed with his sack of candles and supplies. Soryn mentally walked through everything in his mind, making sure he missed no details about his evening. He even opened *The Common Ailments and Treatments of Horses* and thumbed through some pages before marking the next chapter, as if he had read them in detail.

When he climbed into bed, he found he could not sleep and was overwhelmingly confused about the whole time he had spent in the study. He was relieved to know that, despite his stress and confusion at his situation, his excitement remained. The Seidh was, indeed, a seductive subject. Lord Maslyn wanted to believe that it could help him somehow and that Ulla could teach him things about it. "I wonder if it can help me get out of here, or at least help me remember how I got here in the first place?" Outside the window, he heard a bird calling out to its mate. He fell asleep listening to the sound and wondering if it talked with humans telepathically, as Ulla did.

* * *

Down in the study, Ulla sat gazing at the "sun". He pondered the boy that had disturbed his rest. Closing his eyes, he saw the boy asleep in his bed and the room around him. Opening them, he allowed the light from the orb to fill his brain, this time thinking about how he would entice the boy to learn about the Seidh. Finding it an uninteresting topic for the middle of the night, he hopped over to the counter and climbed back onto the shelf where he preferred to rest. Within minutes, he was just as still and silent as the time the boy first laid eyes on him.

Chapter Four

In which the young master begins a beautiful friendship…

"Ahem, Lord Maslyn, sir…" Jori attempted to rouse the young master.

Soryn remained asleep despite the fact that the slight cough was the manservant's third try at waking him. Jori sighed and went to the window, throwing the drapes aside. He had already opened the noble's bed curtains. It was strange that the boy was not up with the dawn, but Jori thought little about it. As soon as he walked around the bed again to go for a fourth attempt, the young lord opened his eyes and yawned, stretching.

"Good morning, Lord Maslyn," Jori greeted, bowing.

"Goo-hhhh (yawn) murnin…" Soryn replied.

"Late night, sir?"

Lord Maslyn felt dread sprinkle itself all over his skin. He sought in his mind for an excuse for the dark circles that no doubt rested beneath his eyes. Then, he remembered,

"I've been reading about horses and I was particularly interested in the chapter I read last night."

"I wouldn't imagine the red lanterns would give you much light," Jori quipped.

"It seems I have relatively good eyesight." Lord Maslyn hoped his excuse would be enough to get Jori to stop prying.

The manservant seemed content with that and continued about his business. He laid out the boy's bathing amenities and then disappeared down the corridor, assumedly to see that Arna was getting Lord Maslyn's breakfast ready. Once Jori left, Soryn exhaled heavily. "That was close," he thought. He trudged sleepily over to the table.

Washing, eating, Jori helping him dress…all of it passed without the boy having to focus much on what he was doing. Throughout the day, the young lord paid little attention to *anything* except the shelf at the other end of the room. He stared at it in between visits from Jori and Arna. Those thirteen books on the bottom teased him and made him want to steal away to the study again. Already, Soryn's curiosity about the Seidh and Ulla was beginning to get the better of him. Despite his urges, however, he avoided the shelf the entire day. Instead, he spent time on devising intricate excuses for the purple lids and sleepiness that would no doubt accompany him for many mornings to come.

That way, he reasoned, he would be confident when spouting his excuses. Perhaps he would get used to the late hours. By nightfall and the ringing of the Night Bells, Soryn was wide awake. Jori had left only moments before, but Soryn jumped out of bed and walked towards the shelf. "I only mean to look at the titles," he told himself. He wondered about the reason for their presence in his tower room. Shouldn't they be down in the study? His thoughts troubled him. Crouching, he gazed at the titles again. Many of them were more specific than the ones down the staircase. These were all about something called "yreth".

Feeling sure that Jori and Arna were truly gone for the night, he pulled one of the books from the bookcase. The title read, *Yreth: the Blessing and the Curse*. He turned to the first page.

"By now, you are interested in the Seidh, its potential uses, and the mechanics of practicing magic. As I am sure you are aware, magic takes a toll on those who have been practicing for years, and even more so on an untrained mind. The reason behind this is not the Seidh itself, but the talent necessary to practice this art. Yreth is the term used to describe one's latent ability to use magic. Scientists on Niflheim are unable to pinpoint the exact source of, or reasons behind yreth in the body, but it is a hormone within certain individuals that allows the practitioner to use the Seidh. Those who

42

do not produce yreth within their own bodies cannot learn to use Seidh magic—all recorded attempts have proved fruitless. An overproduction of yreth within the body, however, can cause hyper-function of the body's endocrine glands which results in the potentially fatal, but reversible disease called Yresses. Yreth overproduction is the result of a practitioner using more magic than their body can handle.

The only cure for Yresses is to temporarily cease the use of magic to allow the body's production of the yreth hormone to normalize. Though curable, this disease is very painful, with symptoms including a high fever, hallucinations, and severe joint pain."

Lord Maslyn put down the book. He thought that people who used magic were merely talented and gifted. It now seemed that in order to use it, he would have to find out whether or not he possessed this yreth hormone. His tutoring had taught him about human biology, but he had never heard of such a thing. "How will I know if I am someone who can even use the Seidh?" Soryn grumbled to himself. He carefully placed the book back exactly where he had found it on the shelf and changed into his dark clothing and shoes. Soryn did not want to waste the candles and felt sure that he would be able to feel his way down the stairs in the darkness. The light of the small sun would surely fill the tunnel once he reached a certain point.

Coming to see me? Ulla's voice rang out in the boy's mind.

Soryn paused in his walk to the hearth. The fact that Ulla's words could reach him so far away was disconcerting.

Oh, don't let it trouble you. I'm awake, if you wanted to know.

Irritation swelled Soryn's nerves and he ignored the pig. He chose, instead, to open the false door and step gingerly into the pitch black passageway. Soryn felt that it took him less time to make it down the staircase, despite the fact that he couldn't see his own hand before him. He was right about the light from the sun. When he was halfway down, the dim orange glow illuminated the stairs.

Yes, you're very smart.

"I know you can hear me and you might as well know that I am not the least bit interested in these internal dialogues of yours," Soryn barked.

That's too bad. I was fully prepared to discuss that hormone with you, but if you'd rather I didn't, then I can just as easily go back to sleep on my shelf.

"Ulla, don't do that! I just don't want you in my head all the time. I have questions for you and I want you to answer them, but I don't want you reading my private thoughts!"

Very well. I'll try not to intrude upon your...intriguing thoughts.

"Good."

Soryn hit the bottom of the staircase and made his way into the study. He found Ulla sitting on his haunches near the warmth of the small sun. He looked less statue-like today, though the sun made the pig's eyes appear more red than black due to the glittering reflections. In fact, everything about the way Ulla looked was a little upsetting.

Am I that intimidating? Ulla chuckled.

"You said you'd stay out of my head," Soryn reminded him.

I lied. Your mind is far too amusing. I suppose you'll have to deal with it if you want to know my secrets...

"Fine. I'll just continue to ignore you."

I imagine you'll find that almost impossible to do, but I'll leave you to your little resolutions.

Soryn ignored him and walked to the bookshelf in the corner. As he browsed the titles, looking for that same beginner's book he picked up the night before, Soryn asked, "Ulla, what is yreth really? I never heard of it before reading about it upstairs."

Ahhhh. Curiosity is forcing you to speak to me, eh?

"I am curious. The book in my room talks about it like it is almost a mystery to our scientists."

44

It is a hormone that didn't exist on Ancient Earth. They say one is blessed if they possess the natural ability to produce it. Why? Are you interested in using magic?

"I just want to know what all of this is, that's all. I'm not saying I'm interested in anything."

Soryn tried his best to keep his mind blank. It was most likely impossible to keep anything from Ulla, but he did not want the strange creature to know that he was deeply interested in the subject. Lord Maslyn kept his mind as clear as possible and pulled the book he had looked at previously off of the shelf again, intending to pick up where he left off.

You won't find what you're wondering about yreth in there. They didn't want to scare away any new apprentices when they wrote that one. It's an old book. There's probably not even that much information in that book upstairs. I suppose I'm your only hope for the real knowledge. It sounded as though Ulla sighed with his words.

"Scare them away? Just how dangerous is this stuff? If your own body produces it, how can it be that bad, even if you get that disease they were talking about? Why do you have to produce yreth to use the Seidh?" Lord Maslyn was frustrated.

The Seidh, magic, power, whatever anyone calls it, is very dangerous and humans on Ancient Earth only dreamed about using it. It takes a tremendous amount of mental energy to even focus enough to begin to harness it. Yreth, in some people a naturally occurring hormone, helps in that process. It successfully allows your mind to focus itself in an amplified manner on one thing—to the point of altering reality. No one can do that without its help. Some may try, but they will not succeed for very long before their own mind wears out. Yreth allows you do to it every time without that happening.

"But upstairs it said that it could make you ill if you use too much magic."

Oh, it is dangerous. It is very easy to cause your body to overproduce yreth, and there are side effects.

"What kind of side effects? The hallucinations and joint pain?"

Probably not ones you want to talk about just yet. As you thought earlier, you don't even know if your body makes it naturally. Why don't you give that beginner's book another shot and I might tell you more.

Soryn was suspicious of the pig's knowledge and chose to remain quiet for a few moments.

If you are about to say how uncanny all this is, save your breath. I already know you don't trust me and you are reluctant to delve too deeply into Seidh matters. However, I will say one thing...have you ever thought that it just might not be a coincidence that you discovered this place? That those thirteen books are nestled in your bookcase upstairs? Hmmm?

If Soryn was honest with himself, he had not thought too deeply about the reasons behind finding the staircase. He assumed that it was just chance, a bit of fortune from the universe.

Don't go thinking you're anything special because you found this place. What I am saying is this: how do you know that someone isn't pulling the strings that allowed you to find this place? Perhaps for their own reasons?

"Someone like you?" Soryn quipped.

I'm a pig. There is no way I could haul thirteen books up the stairs. I don't know why you're here. I spend a good deal of my time asleep. Perhaps you should spend more time finding out about those closest to you rather than that hormone at present. In the meantime, you could accomplish quite a bit of reading.

Soryn considered Ulla's words. Although he did not trust the pig, the reasoning made sense. Still, the entire matter was overwhelming. While Soryn was thinking, Ulla stared at him again with his unnerving eyes. Soryn grew frustrated with the direction his thoughts were taking him and decided to leave for the night.

Probably a good idea. You look tired. Maybe you should rest.

46

"Be quiet, Ulla."

Soryn stalked out of the study and made his way back to his bedroom, sore and stiff from his earlier climb the night before. He was reluctant to think about anything specific, knowing Ulla would be able to hear his thoughts and comment on them whenever he liked. This both annoyed and worried him. It felt as though all his privacy had been stripped away.

Oh, it's not like that. Most of the time, you won't even know that I'm listening, Ulla commented.

Gooseflesh covered Soryn's arms and sweat broke out on his face as he entered his icy room, closing the fireplace door behind him. All at once, he regretted discovering the study. A sense of foreboding settled over him. Quickly, he undressed and ran to his bed, forcing himself to sleep at once. That way, he wouldn't have to think anymore about the pig or the Seidh for tonight.

* * *

Down in the study, Ulla smiled to himself. The pig was well aware of how bizarre and frightening his powers must be to the boy, but he was happy to know both that Soryn was visiting him and that he did not care if Ulla scared him. What mattered was that Soryn would keep returning and that he was becoming interested in the Seidh. For the sake of the boy's present sanity, Ulla decided to ignore Soryn's thoughts for the night and, instead, focused his attention on the small hole in the wall underneath the counter on which the miniature sun sat. He had seen the familiar, yellow eyes sitting there throughout his conversation with Soryn. He smirked.

What are you *two doing here?* Ulla asked.

At his question, two lithe, grey tabby cats slithered through the small hole and into his study. They quizzically cocked their heads at him in unison. Answering together, they said, *There isss ssssomething you should know about thisss boy.*

And what is that? Ulla asked.

47

He issss being helped by a girl-child.

Yes. Jordis. I know of this. Do you have anything useful to report? Ulla rolled his eyes.

We don't like thisss girl. She isss sssusssspiciousss to usss. The cats hissed.

Is that all you have to tell me tonight? Ulla's tone took on a bored, desperate quality.

Yesss. We mussst be going, they said.

The two felines turned together and squeezed through the small hole like water flowing between rocks. Ulla rolled his eyes again. Geri and Freki had never been particularly helpful to him, but for some reason, he liked having them around to tell him useless bits of information that he already knew. Sometimes it helped Ulla work through his thoughts. Tonight, he used all of his mental energy to avoid the *boy's* thoughts. He had none to spare for the cats' opinion of the girl or Soryn.

Ulla knew that upstairs, Soryn had already slipped into a dream of fire and screaming. The pig let his concentration slip just enough to pay closer attention to the boy's nightmare. Soryn tossed and turned, tangling his sheets around his legs. Visions of monsters and blood haunted him and he soaked his mattress with sweat.

Hmmm…now isn't that interesting, Ulla thought.

* * *

The next morning passed very slowly for Soryn. He awoke abruptly before dawn from his nightmare. He had dreamed of the fire before, but the fact that this dream occurred after his encounter with Ulla made him wary. Lord Maslyn ran a shaky hand through his sweat-soaked hair and trembled, both from the cold and his nervousness. He wanted to compose himself before Jori came.

He rose from his bed and walked across the freezing stones to the table. Snippets and phrases of the last several days flashed through his mind. In a very short time, his world had become increasingly complicated, perhaps more than he was ready for. Every second, Soryn was poised to hear some snide remark from Ulla in his mind. Every second that Ulla did not speak made Lord Maslyn even more anxious.

Jori came and went. Soryn was dressed at the table and eating breakfast when Ulla finally greeted him.

Good morning. I trust you slept well.

"I'm sure you know exactly how I slept."

No need to be belligerent. I'm here to help you, after all.

"Are you, Ulla? Because sometimes I think you are just trying to get me to do something that *you* want me to do. I'm not sure it's something good, either."

What gave you that idea? Haven't I been helpful? Haven't I tried to tell you to take things slowly and not overload yourself all at once?

Soryn considered the pig's statement. Ulla had tried to tell him not to read into things too quickly and to investigate the people around him first before delving deeper into the Seidh.

"I suppose you're right. I'm sorry. My life has just changed pretty dramatically in a very short period of time," Soryn apologized.

That is something I can relate to, my young friend. Now, why don't you ask that pretty servant of yours about life in the castle? After all, you have been shut off from quite a bit these last six years.

"How do you know about that? How do you know how long I've been in the tower?"

I know a lot about what goes on in this castle.

"How? I've never seen you come through the fireplace to leave the study. Is there another way out?"

Maybe. Maybe not. I have sources for the information I need.

"Why don't you tell me, then, about what goes on in this castle?"

Why would I want to take away your opportunity to speak with a pretty girl? Besides, she may be of use to you later on. I think it is far more important for you to get to know her better. I also think it is far more entertaining for me to listen in.

Soryn bristled at Ulla's comment. Arna was not someone he wanted to "use". He wanted to get to know her. Besides, he needed someone else to talk to other than Ulla alone. The pig made him nervous more often than not.

That hurts me. I'm just trying to be helpful.

"Sorry. Give me some time to get used to your mind reading, Ulla. Also, I've never really talked to girls."

Ah, well...you're twelve. You've got your whole life ahead of you for experiencing new things. Think of the last two days as the beginning of a much larger journey.

"I suppose."

She's coming. Bye-bye now. Don't forget to tell me all about it.

Soryn could sense the sarcasm dripping from Ulla's encouragement; as if the pig would not hear everything going on in the tower room.

As Ulla foretold, Arna's footsteps rang out in the corridor and she appeared in the doorway carrying her laundry basket under one arm.

"Good morning," she said.

"Good morning, Arna." Soryn tried to sound as friendly as possible.

She immediately changed the sheets and picked up other laundry about the floor. She reached for his black clothing that had fallen from the under-frame of the bed in the night. Soryn sprang from his chair to stop her. Their fingers met on the top of his shirt. Again, they both blushed as their eyes met.

"Alright, this is just silly," Arna giggled, clearly embarrassed. "We both act as if we have never interacted with the opposite gender before. Let's just clear the air before we continue with our work, shall we?"

"What?" Soryn stuttered.

"If we're going to be friends, Bialas, we have to be honest and open with one another."

"Bialas? Why are you calling me that and what are you— friends?" he coughed.

"Yes. Friends. Don't you want to be my friend, Bialas?" she asked, still touching his hand.

"I would like that very much," he admitted.

"Good. Now, first things first. Do you think I'm pretty?"

"Huh!? I-I…well, I mean…"

"Yes…?" Arna prompted.

"Yes. I think you're very pretty," Soryn confessed.

"That's grand. I think you're very handsome as well. Now that we've gotten that out of the way, I say we interact with one another very adult-like and dispense with all of this blushing nonsense. It clouds my head and I've got lots of work to do. Agreed?"

"I suppose that sounds agreeable," Soryn managed.

Now that was entertaining.

"Now is not the time, Ulla," Soryn said aloud without thinking.

Realizing what he had done, horror lodged in Soryn's throat and he desperately looked up at Arna, snatching his hand away.

"Who's Ulla?" Arna asked, a smile on her face.

Soryn tried to think up a proper excuse when he heard the pig again, *Why not tell her the truth? She wants you to be honest and open, remember?*

Arna continued to stare at Soryn and it unnerved him in a way that was entirely different from Ulla's stares.

"Arna, can we talk sometime? Sometime when you don't have to work?"

She seemed surprised by this question. Instead of answering right away, she merely reached again for the black clothing on the floor. Soryn blushed again, cursing himself that he could not control his emotions around her.

"I think that would be nice, Bialas," she told him.

"Really!?"

"Yes. How does tonight sound? After Jori has gone to bed?"

"So soon," Soryn muttered in disbelief. He suspected she would try to suspend such a meeting.

"Well, truth be told, I have been bored to death lately and it would be wonderful to have a little conversation in my life." Arna smiled.

Soryn merely grinned and said, "That would be nice. I look forward to it."

Without saying anything more, Arna took her laundry basket and waltzed out of the room. Soryn felt the huge pit of snakes in his stomach suddenly uncoil and he sighed a great breath of relief.

I think it went rather well, don't you? Ulla chimed.

"I suppose."

I told you she might be more agreeable if you tempted her with serious talk.

"You were right, I guess."

Ulla was quiet for the rest of the day. Though this made Lord Maslyn uncomfortable, he brushed it off and went about his daily routine with increased vigor. The thought of Arna's clandestine visit to his room made him feel warm inside. Since he was six years old when they placed him in the tower, Soryn never really remembered friendship. He had been alone for half his life. He appreciated the thought of a friend more than Arna could ever know.

Soryn half expected Ulla to pipe up with some terse quip about his thought, but nothing came. If Ulla had anything to say about the matter, he stayed quiet. While Soryn waited for the suns to set, he studied his room some more. Since he had discovered something so extraordinary in his fireplace, he thought it a worthwhile task to seriously inspect the rest of his room. He started with his bed.

The candles and flint still rested beneath the frame, but Soryn found nothing of further interest under the bed itself. He tried to lift the mattress, but found it too far set in the frame to move it much. Abandoning this pursuit, Soryn stared at the wooden finials and posts that held up the curtains. They were ornately carved, but harbored no secret compartments. After examining the bed, he checked the stones on the same wall. Using his fingers, he gingerly traced the grout between the rocks. To his disappointment, he did not find anything suspect. He continued to the center of the next wall, examining the section on the right side of the fireplace. All he found was a mouse hole. He made a mental note to ask Jori to fill it up later.

On the left of the fireplace was a desk that Soryn never used. He had always preferred to work at the large table running down the center of the room. Soryn admitted to himself that it was a shame he had never used the desk. It was a lovely old thing, carved in a similar fashion to the steps that ran down to Ulla's study. He wondered, again, who had created all the wondrous things in his tower and if someone important might have lived there. His parents and his brothers certainly never came to the tower from what he remembered. Lord Maslyn found the tower itself to be a mystery that needed solving.

The desk had a small shelf section connected to the top, with tiny compartments filled with all sorts of scholarly artifacts. There was a dried up ink well, styluses, and old parchment paper. No books or notes were stacked on top of the desk. He searched the ubiquitous drawers running along the bottom of the desktop. Each was narrow and deep.

He found nothing of great interest in the drawers—merely stores of parchment, ink wells, twine for joining notes, etc. Shutting the drawers in disappointment, Soryn crossed the room to his window. It was dusk. The suns were beginning to set. Purple and pink clouds yielded to grey, heavy ones. It would snow again tonight. Soryn hoped it would not keep Arna away. He had no idea if she lived within the castle walls or elsewhere. He hoped she would be safe and that they would have their meeting. Jori would soon arrive with his dinner. The boy went to the table and sat. While he waited, he continued to meditate on all of the changes that were taking place and the new adventures to come.

Chapter Five

In which the young master brings an accomplice into the works…

Finally, Soryn was alone after his meal and nightly routine with Jori. A tingling sensation in his stomach caused him some considerable discomfort. He felt sure that having a girl as a friend would come with some rather undignified side effects. The Night Bells rang faintly outside his window from the village church. Lord Maslyn could almost see the ancient Father Kimbli padding his way down to the altar to make his prayers to the empty crucifix hanging on the wall. Though Soryn had not been to the church since he was a young boy, he still remembered it well. As he listened to the plaintive chimes, he wished—not for the first time—that he, too, could go to the church altar and pray. Soryn had never been overly religious, but with all of the changes in his life, some direction and guidance would not go amiss.

When Soryn was young, his father, the Maslyn, would take him and his brothers each week to the church services. Sometimes Father Kimbli would speak, and Soryn remembered how wise and kind the old man sounded. He was glad that the priest still visited him each week, even if Soryn did get bored every time. There was something extraordinary about the kindly old man, something vibrant beneath those aged eyes.

The Night Bells ended their homage to the dying day and Soryn went to the table to wait for Arna. He had no real idea of when she would be coming. Jori had only left about twenty minutes previous, so he knew a long wait might be in store. At first, Lord Maslyn drummed his fingers on the table. Then, he shifted in his chair for a while. After it had been almost an hour, he tired of sitting and went again to the desk. Though he had searched it thoroughly during the afternoon, he was still drawn to it like he was to Ulla and the books in his room and the study. Soryn bent down to look underneath the desktop drawers. Perhaps he would find something he had missed.

Though it was hard to see with only the red light from his lanterns, Soryn used his fingers and was able to discern markings on the wood above him. The carvings were fluid—almost like a water pattern. They were very difficult to make out, but he traced them and thought he made out a swirled image.

"Want some help?"

Soryn was so startled by Arna's voice that he sprang up, instantly smacking his head on the underside of the desk drawers.

"Aggh!" Soryn yelped.

"Sorry! I didn't mean to startle you!" Arna exclaimed.

Soryn nodded while he plastered his left hand over a scratch just above his hairline. Arna extended her hand and helped him up from the floor. When Soryn brought his hand away, he saw a dark swath of blood.

"Ouch."

"Here, sit down and let me take a look. Let's make sure it isn't deep." Arna shuffled him to a chair and began to examine his head.

Soryn had not even heard her come into the room. He wondered what sort of training serving girls underwent to be so graceful…and stealthy.

I told you she might be useful. If she can move that quietly, she may be able to help you get out of the tower, Ulla suggested.

Soryn was surprised that Ulla had spoken after nearly a day of silence.

I was busy today, Ulla said in response to the boy's thought.

Lord Maslyn refused to comment on Ulla's words. Instead, he spoke to Arna, "I didn't even hear you come up."

"Ah, sorry about that. I have always been quiet," she replied.

"Really?"

"I guess I take after my mother. Before she married my father, she was a maid for Governor Frey and they had the best training in

56

treading lightly through a household. I suppose I just picked it up from watching her."

He felt her small fingers pick through his hair and rub his scalp. When she came across the spot Soryn had wacked on the desk, he winced.

"Be still. I think you're alright. You might want to have Jori bring up some ointment tomorrow. I'd get some for you, but serving girls aren't allowed in the medicine cabinet." She removed her hands from his head and sat down at the table.

Soryn realized once she sat down that he had not honestly looked at her until this moment. He hardly recognized her. Instead of her uniform, she had on a simple wool skirt and a tunic tied with a burgundy belt around the waist. Instead of her cap, he saw her hair for the first time. In the dim light, he guessed the color to be ashy blonde. It was cut short about her face and was somewhat boyish, but he thought it suited her. He blushed again.

"I hope you don't mind my casual dress. I just get so bored wearing the same old thing every day. I do apologize about not wearing my cap. I hate it and refuse to wear it after I have finished work for the day. It makes my head itch."

"Oh, no, it's fine. I mean, uh, I think you look very natural this way," he stammered.

"Well, thank you."

They sat in silence for a few moments. Arna did not seem uncomfortable in any way. She smiled and looked about the room. Soryn noticed her prettiness and the relaxed way in which she carried herself. This satisfied him for some reason. Since he hoped they would be friends, it was important that she felt comfortable around him.

"So, what were you looking for under the desk?" Arna asked pointedly.

Soryn did not know what to say or how to start the conversation about his adventures.

"Go on," she prompted.

"I thought I saw some markings under there. Something like a swirl pattern."

"A swirl pattern? That's not so unusual. Lots of furniture in the house has swirl patterns. It's a popular motif for carvings in our country."

"Really? I just don't remember much about the rest of the furniture in the castle, I suppose."

His response triggered some emotion that registered on Arna's face.

"What is it?"

"I just wish you didn't have to be up here," she sighed.

"Do you know why they keep me here?" Soryn asked, instantly forgetting what he had intended to talk about with her.

Arna looked away, seemingly pained by his question.

"Please, Arna, if you know, tell me. I can't remember much about the night of the fire."

"You really don't remember what happened?" She was shocked by his admission.

"I remember fire, screams, and my mother sheltering me. And then…nothing. Everything went black and I woke up here with Father Kimbli staring over me with the saddest eyes."

Arna seemed uncomfortable and looked around as if someone was watching. Soryn grew pensive and images from that terrible night flooded his mind.

Unpleasant memories won't help you with escaping from here. Forget those things and talk with her about more important matters. In time, I'm sure you'll find out more about that night, Ulla scolded him.

For once, Soryn was relieved to hear Ulla's intrusive dialogue.

"Anyway, that's not really what I asked you here for," Soryn brought up.

Arna exhaled, apparently relieved at the subject change.

"Arna, I don't really know how to say all of this, but I suppose I'll just get to it. I found a secret door in my fireplace over there.

That's why I asked you for the candles and flint box. That's why you saw the black clothing on the floor when you came for the laundry earlier. I've explored where the door leads and I want to show you what I found."

He looked into her grey-blue eyes for some reaction. What he saw filled him with hope.

"You found a secret passage, didn't you? What did you see!? Did you find a way out of your tower?"

Soryn laughed a little at her obvious interest.

I thought you might find her a valuable friend in all of this. See how interested she is? Ulla couldn't help but appreciate Arna's zeal. He was growing deeply interested in her.

"Well, there's a staircase in the fireplace that goes down quite a ways. That's why I was interested in the carvings on the desk—they seem to be the same as the sorts I found on the stairs in the passage. Although, I think you'll be far more interested with what's actually down there."

"What's down there?" she asked, intrigued.

"In all honesty, it would be far easier to show you than to tell you about it. Do you want to see?"

"Of course!"

She hopped up and elegantly pushed her chair in before heading to the hearth. While Soryn retrieved his flint box and candle stand, Arna peered around the inside of the fireplace at all of the bricks and iron fixings. When Soryn reached the hearth with his candle accoutrements, she had the glowing aura of adventure about her.

"Bialas, this is an amazing find. I had always suspected there were secrets in this castle, but everyone laughed me off like a silly child. I knew they were wrong. Thank you for including me."

"You're welcome," he said, feeling that he was truly the thankful one.

He believed, somehow, that he and Arna would be spending a lot of time together from now on. He could tell from her exuberant interest in the passageway. He just hoped she would be as interested after she met Ulla. The pig was unusual to say the least.

Lord Maslyn bent down and lit his candle—quickly this time— and activated the secret door handle, swinging it open. He stepped in first so he could offer his hand if she needed it. Arna accepted his help down to the steps. Reaching past her, he closed the door. The candle created a warm, comforting bubble of light around them and her pretty face gleamed with excitement. She looked all around at the purplish walls and at the stone steps below their feet.

"What a wondrous place," she commented.

Oh I like her, Ulla said to Soryn.

The boy could not tell if the pig was joking. Soryn merely smiled and guided her down the stairs. When he saw the glow from the miniature sun, he stopped and blew out his candle. Arna gasped, alarmed. Soryn pointed down towards the bottom of the staircase and she saw the amber light spilling into the passage.

"Feel that?" Soryn asked her.

Arna stood very still.

"It's warm here," she observed, astonished.

"Yes."

At this juncture, Arna seemed a little uneasy, so Soryn took a huge gamble and reached for her hand. His stomach fluttered when she squeezed his in return. They continued towards the light and turned into the small alcove that led up to Ulla's study. Soryn looked at her to make sure she still wanted to go. Arna nodded. Their hands remained clasped as they walked up the few steps into the room. Arna gasped when she saw the cluttered room and the mysterious, floating orb on the table. She let go of Soryn's hand and explored the space. Her fingers gently brushed some of the piles of papers and instruments on the center table.

"What *is* this place?" she asked.

"I don't really know," Soryn admitted. "I suppose it's a study of some sort, or it used to be."

What an informed guess, Soryn. I'm impressed.

Soryn could practically see Ulla's rolling eyes accompanying that statement.

"It certainly seems as though no one's been here in a long time." Arna's remark seemed to drift from her lips halfheartedly.

Soryn saw her staring, fascinated by the miniature sun in the corner of the room. He watched her carefully, knowing that she might try to touch it as he had the first time he visited the study. Slowly, she edged towards it.

Keep an eye on her, little Maslyn. We don't want her to lose all of those pretty fingers.

He knew Ulla's words were the truth and when Arna raised her right hand, Soryn warned, "You probably want to follow the 'look but don't touch' rule in the case of that thing. Trust me."

As if in a trance, Arna moved her hand away and looked at the floor. It seemed to Lord Maslyn that she was deep in thought.

"Is everything alright, Arna?"

"Yes, I'm alright. It's just such a fascinating little thing." She continued to gaze at it with bemused eyes.

Better go ahead and prepare her for meeting me. I can't exactly let her leave without seeing me. It would be a terrible injustice to her. I am quite dashing, after all.

This time, Soryn rolled his eyes and went to Arna. He gently nudged her and jerked his head in the direction of Ulla's perch on the top shelf. She glanced up.

"See anything interesting up there?" Soryn asked.

Arna could see a spot on the top shelf that did not seem to fit. It was very dark there and she saw a statue of a pig, but the area around the pig was most interesting.

"Why would someone have a statue of a pig down here?" She was puzzled.

I'm not a statue, my dear.

Soryn saw her eyes go wide and she backed away from the direction of the shelf. Arna looked at Lord Maslyn in apparent horror.

61

"D-Did you hear that, Bialas!?" she sputtered.

"Yes. Just stay calm. He's what I wanted you to see down here. Well, him and the sun."

Soryn is rather besotted with that old thing over there. I think I'm far more interesting, personally.

It was clear that Arna had heard Ulla speak again. Soryn could tell from the terrified look on her face.

"Who are you?" she whispered in Ulla's direction.

My name is Ulla and I have lived in this study for a long time. Who are you?

She gasped, her eyes almost as round as saucers.

"Don't let him fool you, Arna, he knows very well who you are and he can read your mind, too."

"What!?" she shouted.

Oh, don't be so put out. As I explained it to Soryn, it would be as unnatural for me to avoid reading minds as it would be unnatural for you to dispense with breathing and sleeping and so on. I have very little to do down here and a gift like this certainly makes life a little less monotonous.

She stared at Ulla. At this point, he had not yet melted from his rigid stance on the top shelf. Soryn wished that he would just hop down so she could see that he was alive and harmless.

"Ulla, come on down. You're scaring her to death," Soryn demanded.

Oh, you're no fun, little Maslyn.

The pig's body unfroze from its statuesque state and Arna watched in amazement as Ulla hopped down from the shelf to the table, then neatly to the floor. She had never seen such a small pig before, much less one colored jet black. She knew most animals talked of course, but she had never met the kind that could read minds or had such apparent interest in humans. Most animals kept to themselves, preferring not to converse with humankind.

Yes, it is true most animals keep to themselves, but you can see that I am quite different from most of the livestock around here. An altogether different animal.

"How can you read our minds, Ulla?" Arna asked, boldly standing free from Soryn.

Ulla liked how the girl challenged him and how she stood so defiantly strong—obviously an empty posture. She was frightened of him.

As I said, it comes naturally to me. When you have a thought, I know it.

"Then can you hear everyone in the castle? If you could, wouldn't that get rather frustrating?" she countered.

You misunderstand. I cannot read everyone's minds. I can only read those minds that are within a certain radius; those who are in close proximity to me. In Soryn's case, I can hear him and anyone else who walks into that tower, because they are within my telepathic radius.

That seemed to satisfy Arna, though she still looked incredulous. "How big is your radius?" she wanted to know.

Oh, I am not sure. Obviously not farther than Soryn's tower. As you can imagine, the extent of my acquaintance with Soryn's mind is only because no one has spent much time with him up there. When you started talking with him, it made for something very interesting to listen to down here.

"So you've been spying on us, haven't you?" Arna quipped.

Now, now, Arna, I am hurt that you think me a spy. Who would a pig like me be reporting to if I'm a spy? I assure you that my attentions are innocuous. I am merely a curious creature at heart.

This conversation agitated Soryn a bit, so he decided to inform Arna about the link between the books in his room and the contents of Ulla's study.

"Arna, other than the pig, my room upstairs and this study share an interesting link."

"What sort of link?" Arna turned away from Ulla, much to the pig's chagrin.

"The books on the bottom shelf of my room and the books in here are all about the Seidh. Have you heard much about anyone in the castle who might practice magic?"

"Books about magic? Here? In this castle?" Arna's doubt was clear in her response.

"Well, yes. Don't the servants talk about magic or the Seidh or whatever one should call it?" Soryn was surprised by her reactions.

"Bialas…you really don't remember much about what happened that night, do you?" She looked at him with a sad, melancholy expression.

"I told you what I remembered and I'm sure Ulla knows by proxy."

Indeed I do know what you remember. I also know what happened in actuality.

"You do?" Arna and Soryn asked together.

Mmm. I was there, you see. It was quite a spectacle.

"You call the death of my whole family a spectacle?" Soryn whispered.

No, not that. Death is tragic, of course, and worth getting upset over. I just meant that there was a most extraordinary use of magic that occurred that night.

Soryn was not sure that Ulla found death tragic at all. Anger building, Soryn shouted, "Tell me, Ulla!"

Soryn, my boy, you have far more pressing matters at hand. I know you want to discover the truth about what happened the night your family died, but you will not be able to wrap that hotheaded brain of yours around the facts unless you know more about the Seidh. As much as you think they might help you in learning about magic, these books are mostly useless to you.

"What do you suggest, then, if you're so smart?" Arna tilted her head and raised an eyebrow at the black-eyed creature.

Soryn nodded in agreement.

Well, it's obvious that you must escape the tower.

"He'd never make it out by sneaking through the castle. Someone would most certainly see him," Arna scowled.

Did I say anything about methods, yet? Give me time, give me time.

Arna rolled her eyes and looked over at the sun on the desk. It seemed to momentarily calm her nerves.

"Go on, Ulla." Soryn grew impatient.

Thank you. As I was saying, these books will not truly help you. They are for those who already know the depth of the Seidh and are looking for some development in their craft. Aside from that beginner's book, you need someone able to show you the power of the Seidh, if you are to learn anything.

"What if I can't learn?" Soryn huffed. "What good would it do me anyway?"

Soryn, how many times have I heard your impotent thoughts upstairs drifting towards desires to alter the world around you? I've heard your thoughts as you peer over those books up there. I know you would like to know more—

"Why do you want to help me?" Soryn interjected.

Arna thought this a very good question. She did not trust Ulla.

Arna, Soryn, I guarantee you that I am trustworthy. The fact that I know you do not trust me makes me want to prove even more that you can. I want to help you. Soryn, I have seen you suffering in that tower. I know your loneliness. I share in this loneliness myself. Not many people make it down to my study, you see. In fact, Soryn was the first in eons. I want to help, because I have a vested interest in your future, Soryn. I want to see what you will do when you are out of that stone prison.

"Why? How is my future interesting to you?"

Oh, that is unimportant. What is important is that you need to get out of this tower in a secret fashion that would allow you to return each day unnoticed. Then, no one will suspect you are leaving.

"Why not let him escape once and for all? Why should he come back once he's gone?" Arna asked, miffed at the pig's suggestion.

Because. This will take time and Soryn needs a stable, structured environment to return to in order to keep his wits about him. As well, has Jori or Father Kimbli ever treated you with anything but kindness? How would the manservant and the priest feel if you left them like that? They have been your only family after the incident. It would be rather cold to leave them all at once, don't you think?

Soryn had to admit that Ulla's words made sense. "You mentioned that we would need someone to show us things about the Seidh. Do you know someone who could help us, assuming, I could in fact get out of the tower?"

I hear of an old snow woman out in the forest behind the castle. Fanndis is her name. My friends tell me that she is one of the most respected practitioners of magic in these parts. She won't let just anyone into her inner circle. You may need to bargain with her.

"What could I have that she wants?"

Not important right now. You can cross that bridge when you come to it. What you do need to worry about at the moment, is escaping.

"Well, if he can't sneak through the castle and he can't climb out the window, what do you suggest, Oh Wisest Swine?"

I do not appreciate your rudeness, little girl.

"And I don't appreciate your tactics. Come clean and tell us how to get out, since you obviously know." Arna's distaste for the pig grew with every minute.

Soryn, have you ever thought if one side of the fireplace has a secret door that the other side might as well?

It was as though a white light struck Soryn's mind and he felt exceedingly foolish. All that time he spent checking his room he should have spent inspecting that fireplace from top to bottom. He wanted to get up there immediately.

Without so much as a "goodbye" to the black pig, Soryn grabbed Arna's hand and said, "Let's go!"

Up the stairs they went. Soryn took them two at a time in the dark. Arna was too preoccupied with the thought that they would to die a horrible death from falling down the stone steps to protest Soryn's abrupt exit. After they had lost sight of the sun's glow, Soryn slowed down and stretched out his left hand (his right was holding Arna's) and felt for the door. It was still some time before he came to it.

He opened the latch and let Arna go through first.

Lord Maslyn's room was quiet. Everything looked the same as when they left earlier. Arna quickly skirted to the other side of the fireplace so Soryn would have room to come out of the passage. When he did, he silently closed the false door and knelt in front of the right-side fireplace panel. Arna made sure he had enough room to access the area by moving onto the hearth. The red lanterns made it difficult for them to see what was right in front of them, but Soryn kept feeling around with his hands looking for a hidden latch.

"I don't feel anything yet," he muttered, disappointed.

"It's strange that it isn't symmetrical with the other side. I wonder if maybe it's a hidden brick or something this time around," Arna offered.

"Maybe."

Soryn felt into cracks between bricks to see if he could feel any that were loose. No areas of interest surfaced. Arna realized they had left their candle stand below and mentioned that she could go back for it, but Soryn shook his head. He wanted her close, in case he found it in the next few moments.

Arna felt jittery waiting for Soryn and decided to examine the center panel of the fireplace while he focused on the right. She heard his frustrated scowls while her deft fingers roamed over the back panel behind the log stands. There was a smudged spot that did not quite match the others. She reached towards it and as soon as she touched the smudge, the brick slid further into the wall. They both gasped in astonishment when the right panel of the fireplace swung open to reveal another staircase. Excitement splayed on both of their faces when they looked at one another. But Soryn's expression grew worried when a thought occurred to him,

"What time is it, Arna?"

"Perhaps six hours or so from Morning Bells."

"If we did discover a way out, we would want to check into it. We wouldn't get much sleep. I wouldn't want you to appear too sleepy tomorrow. I don't want you to get into trouble." As much as Soryn wanted to go immediately, he stifled a yawn and knew he was too sleepy.

"Why don't we go tomorrow night? We can go get some sleep and then meet again. Same time?" Arna was tired as well.

"Sounds good. Be careful going to your room." Lord Maslyn had no idea where she lived in the castle.

"I'll be alright. This was a very interesting night, Bialas. Thank you, again, for bringing me along." She leaned down and patted his shoulder, then put the hand to her mouth to cover a yawn.

Watching her leave made Soryn melancholy. He had enjoyed her company far more than he had anticipated. It was intoxicating. Already, he was dying to see her again the next night. His curiosity about the second passage was somewhat dulled by his extraordinary sleepiness. Crawling to the four-poster, he threw all of his clothes at the foot of the bed and kicked them underneath the frame before donning his nightshirt.

Once the covers were securely over his head, he thought about Arna and her pretty hair and eyes and skin and clothes. With the chill in the air it was easy for him to tell he was blushing.

Don't get distracted now, Soryn. You have an important iron in the fire already. Besides, you're far too young to think of entangling yourself with some female.

"She's just a friend, Ulla," the noble whispered dreamily.

Within seconds Soryn was asleep and Ulla chuckled to himself before propping up against the wall at the top shelf. Satisfaction curled behind his pig lips and he closed his eyes. The next steps in his plan formed in his mind. His attention was broken when his two feline underlings caught his mind's eye. They were within his telepathic radius, but still outside the castle walls. Ulla focused on their thoughts. Geri was thinking about a fish she was hoping to catch for breakfast later. Freki was imagining a long nap by the fire in the woodshed. Ulla smirked at their petty preoccupations. Though he was not sleepy, he was far too tired to be bothered with his informants at present. If they wanted to talk, he had already chosen not to listen and would pretend to be asleep instead. With that decision made, he became very still, like a stone, and all the while kept his mind engaged in thought.

* * *

A frigid wind seemed to have destroyed every bit of the roof over Soryn's head. Though it seemed solid enough upon waking, he felt sure there was a draft blowing in from above. It was barbarically cold in his room and all he wanted to do was stay in bed. He knew Jori would arrive with his breakfast soon, but he didn't care. All he thought about was burying further beneath his ample blankets.

"Blast it all," he spat. "If only I could have a fire in here, perhaps I could sleep without getting frostbite every night."

A thought nudged his consciousness. He was a noble, was he not? Nobles should be allowed to have a few demands every now and then. Soryn decided to tell Jori that he refused to work on *anything* whatsoever until they provided him with a fire. He could throw a small tantrum if he wanted. In fact, he would refuse to get dressed if Jori would not allow him some means of warmth in this icy cage. While he had his brain going, Soryn devised a plan for retaining Arna as his personal servant. It was certain he could use one with all the work they brought in for him each day. More than that, he was almost a young man and he was tired of being alone all the time.

By the time Jori ascended the steps later in the morning, Soryn had cocooned himself under the covers. When he sat up, it all looked like a great mountain of bed sheets.

Slightly confused, Jori mumbled, "Morning, sir."

Soryn gave no reply and continued to sit in as resolved a manner as he could.

"Breakfast, sir," Jori said without much enthusiasm, starting for the bed.

When Jori turned down the covers, he was a little shocked to see Lord Maslyn wide awake and staring at him. "Good heavens, Lord Maslyn. I thought you might've been asleep still. What do you mean by staring at me like that?"

"I want a fire, Jori. I am frozen from head to toe. I have no idea why you all won't let me have a fire, but I want one and I want it within the next half hour."

"I'm sure that could be arranged, but, you see…well…we don't want you to be..."

"Alone with it. Yes, I know. That is why I request you to assign Arna to me as a personal assistant each day. She could perform all her usual duties in here as well as make sure the fire is going, along with helping me with the paperwork you send each day. I don't want to be alone for upwards of sixteen hours a day and I no longer want to freeze to death while I go about my business."

Jori was quite taken aback by his master's comments. The man had never heard Lord Maslyn make such a request in the six years he had served the boy. He did not mind his job and, in fact, rather liked the quiet and simple demands. Still, Jori was impressed by the outburst. Lord Maslyn was usually rather boring. It was almost nice to have a spirited order of this sort.

"Your terms are acceptable. I don't know any 'Arna', though. You shall retain Jordis as your personal assistant from this moment forward."

The boy forgot Arna went by "Jordis" in front of everyone else. It was nice that they called each other special names. Soryn was a

70

little disappointed that it had been so easy to have his demands met. Jori was far too easygoing.

"Won't anyone be upset about me having fire?" he protested.

"It will be alright, I should think. The steward didn't want you to have a fire when you were young, because he felt you might be tempted to play with it or some other such nonsense. I always said it was a silly presumption. The reason Asmund does not think of it for you now, is he supposed it would upset you; give you bad memories," Jori said, while he stripped the sheets and rushed the young master out of bed.

"It snows ninety-five percent of the year! It never occurred to anyone that a twelve year old boy might freeze to death in a drafty old tower? So what if it gives me bad memories!" Soryn had been bothered by the cold before, but today he had had enough.

"My apologies, Lord Maslyn. Now, since you have requested Jordis as your assistant from this point on, I will have her come retrieve your midday and evening meal. Is that sufficient? She'll have her meal in the kitchen, of course, while you have your meal in the tower."

"That's ridiculous! How can we have friendly conversation if she is somewhere else? No, I'm afraid that will not do, Jori. She must dine with me. I'll not be an elitist noble who acts better than those who work with him."

"As you wish, sir. I'll send her up as soon as I explain her change in station."

"Change in station? What do you mean?" Soryn asked, perplexed.

"As your personal assistant, she will need a new uniform, as well as certain keys and other such items. It might take an hour or so to arrange everything."

"Ah, very good." Soryn had not remembered all of the things servants had to do each day or that the clothes they wore were actually uniforms.

He sat quietly and thought about this as Jori helped him dress. Jori left without another word, while Lord Maslyn ate his breakfast. Down the corridor, Jori smiled to himself—again delighted that Lord Maslyn had finally spoken up about something he wanted. The manservant always remembered Soryn as the Maslyn's most subservient and introverted child. It was a good change of pace to hear him act like a Maslyn for once; demanding and somewhat pretentious. Jori still knew the master was a kind and intelligent child, and that he really just wanted some company.

"I don't blame the lad," Jori thought to himself, "I would have gone crazy long ago if I were shut up in that tower."

* * *

Within the hour, Arna reported to Lord Maslyn's quarters, her laundry basket in hand. However, instead of her usual servant's attire, she now wore a very nice dress that had fur trim around the neckline and sleeves. It was a becoming green that somehow made her grey eyes change color. Her face flushed and he noticed that she kept swirling her skirt, just slightly as she walked. She dropped her basket to the floor by the bed.

"Good morning, Arna," Soryn smiled.

"Good morning, Bialas. I hear that I'm to be your personal assistant from now on."

"Is that alright with you?" All at once, the boy realized he had not considered her feelings on the matter or even asked her about his idea before demanding that it be carried out.

"Are you joking?! I'm *ecstatic*! This will give us time to go exploring in that tunnel! I want to see what other secrets this old castle hides," she neatly remade the bed while she spoke. Then, she went about her other daily duties.

Soryn supposed that habits were too hard to break and stayed quiet while she worked. He was dressed for the day, ready to go exploring, and had Arna with him, but was still glum. They had one

72

or two problems to solve before they were free to go gallivanting in the tunnel and perhaps to freedom.

"Arna," he cleared his throat. "We have a couple of things to consider before we start planning trips down that tunnel."

"You're referring, I assume, to Jori's visits and Father Kimbli's weekly chat?"

"Yes, actually," Soryn affirmed.

"Here is what I think: during the daylight hours today, we observe Jori's comings and goings. I know that we are both already familiar with them, but since you have retained me as your assistant, things may change a little for Jori's rounds. I will be taking care of our lunchtime and dinnertime meals. I'll go get them, bring them back, we'll eat, and then I'll take the dishes back. There are so many dishes in the kitchen, Inga won't notice when I bring them. If I like, I can take them all down at the end of the day when I *supposedly* return to my room for the night. Jori will still bring your papers around lunchtime, so we should make sure we are always in the tower during the half hour before and after noon. He also returns just before Night Bells, correct?"

"Correct." Soryn enjoyed hearing her scheming at work.

"You'll need to be in your room a half hour before Night Bells, then. Does Jori come at any other times during the day?"

"Never. Not unless I summon him, which I haven't in a long time. I think the last time was when I was ill about three years ago. He's always very precise with his time and activities."

"Alright then. We'll still watch him today to see if anything changes. Now, Father Kimbli visits you on Freya's Day, right? What time?" Arna looked very serious and involved.

"After lunch, usually, and he stays about an hour or so." Soryn was amused by her business-like manner.

"So…he'll be coming the day after tomorrow. You'll need to make sure that you are there for that. I think we've taken care of the main issues, then."

"I believe that about covers it. Now, as enthusiastic and excited as I am about the potential of getting out of here, I *was* promised a fire in my room. I have nearly frozen to death for the last six years of my life. Do you think you could oblige me and let us have a fire while we experimentally watch the day go by?" The prospect of being warm tantalized him.

She seemed a little put out by this suggestion. Soryn felt a bit guilty. He knew it would make things much messier in the hearth than the night before.

"I suppose. It will be a great big sooty mess, but the cold is quite intense in here isn't it? I'll go get firewood right away. While I'm gone, why don't you talk to that scrawny pig of yours and see what he thinks of our plan.

I am sure you are aware that I can hear everything you're saying. Ulla snorted at the idea that he was "scrawny".

"Yes, I know, Oh Wisest Swine." Arna stuck her chin up and swirled her skirts regally around herself. She trotted down the steps humming.

Though Soryn was extremely fond of the girl, he was bewildered by how much she had come to life in the last few days. Again, he was reminded of his sorrow over not becoming friends years ago.

You certainly wasted a lot of valuable time feeling sorry for yourself. You would have done better being a little more bold and outspoken. Well, no matter. It seems you two will make up for lost time. I like this plan you have concocted with that hellcat.

"Don't call her that. She's nice, Ulla." Soryn frowned.

I think you are beginning to develop a small obsession with her...

"That's ludicrous and you know it. I'm just happy to have some human interaction, that's all."

Well, it is of no consequence to me. I'm just a part-time-advice-giver and bystander anyway. I think I'll go to sleep.

"You do that."

Arna returned after a few minutes with a brass firewood rack hung over one arm and a sack in the other hand. Soryn rushed to help her with the brass rack and was astonished when he felt how heavy it was. Arna was certainly much stronger than him. He hoped that he could gain some muscle with their endeavors in the tunnels. He sat the rack down on the hearth and watched Arna place kindling underneath the stacked logs. He offered assistance, but she just smiled and waved him off.

"I like my job. Don't worry about trying to help too much. I feel useful when I'm being productive."

Within a minute, she had a small flame going on the hearth. She had wisely moved the metal log stands out of the fireplace, so that once it burned down by the end of the day, they would safely be able to step around the ashy remains to access the secret doors. Soryn was fascinated by the fire. He had not seen it in years, except for the oil lights in the red lanterns and the candles. Immediately, the radiating heat coming off the flaming tendrils warmed his face and hands. Relishing every minute, Soryn planted himself on the floor near the hearth and bade Arna to sit as well.

"So, what would you like to do today?" he asked her.

"Shouldn't I be asking what you would like for *me* to do today?"

"Nonsense. You are my assistant, not my slave. I'd much rather have you for a friend than an assistant. We'll just let Jori think you're merely my servant. We'll know better, won't we?" Soryn smiled while his back grew deliciously toasted. It seemed as though he had not been warm in years.

"Hmmm…what would *I* like to do today? Well, other than observing Jori's comings and goings, I would like to…." She narrowed her eyes and put on a mischievous face. "Talk."

"Talk?" Soryn lifted his brows.

"Yes. As you can probably imagine, a servant's life isn't exactly filled with chatter. I never really get to sit and talk with anyone. I'm one of the youngest servants, so there aren't many people my age

75

around that I can talk to. I was thrilled when you started up a conversation with me the other day."

"Well, let's talk," Soryn chimed.

"Alright." Arna grinned.

"Um…what do you want to talk about?"

"Tell me about what you do all day up here? Don't you get bored to death?" Her eyebrows went down and she listened intensely.

Soryn thought about his answer and, before long, realized that he was a very dull creature. "Well…" He made circles with his thumbs. "I wander about, look out the window, sign all those dreadful papers, and…"

"Yes?" she prompted kindly.

"I sit and think. Sometimes I read. Sometimes I write in a journal that I keep in my nightstand."

"That's it? Oh dear, that tunnel must have truly upended your world, huh?"

"You could say that. I've had more activity in the last few days than I've had the rest of my life." He smiled, despite the pitiful nature of his daily pursuits. She was easy to talk to. "Well, enough about me. As you can see, I'm rather boring. What do *you* do all day—at least when you aren't doing chores in here?"

She leaned back against the hearth, well away from the fire. Soryn watched as she crossed one leg over the other knee and bobbed her foot lightly in the air.

"I'm afraid I'm not boring at all. I stay busy all day long. I rise with the suns, don my uniform, and head to the kitchens to report to Inga. She gives me a list of items to procure down at the village market and I go get them. When I return, I drop them off and then come up here to fetch your linens. I take them to the laundress, Salme, and then I eat my breakfast in my quarters. After that, I help Darby, the assistant chef, with his chopping and dicing. I take any vegetables he gives me to Inga for the evening's supper. By then, it's time for lunch and I eat again in my quarters. If I have time, I read

76

from one of the books in the library—Steward Asmund lets the servants borrow one at a time. During the evening, I polish the silverware in the dining cabinets, wash the kitchen floors, help Inga clean, and give Salme a hand with folding. After evening prayers, I'll read some more. Then…I go to sleep."

Her life sounded extremely productive. It made Soryn feel even more useless and commonplace. Arna looked over at him and could tell he was feeling a bit low.

"Cheer up. I think your life has taken a turn for the busier." She winked. "I don't know what I'll do with myself now that my routine has changed so much." Her smile widened.

Over the next few hours, they talked and laughed together. Once, Soryn took Arna to the window and showed her the things he looked at each day. He pointed out the horses in the barn and his view of the village chapel. Later, she showed him how to play a game he had never heard of called, "Expikaer". It had Ulla so interested he often gave suggestions to fortify each side's strategy.

Arna retrieved lunch and they ate together, still talking. Jori came shortly after to drop off Lord Maslyn's paperwork for the day. Soryn and Arna sat, wading through the dreaded flotsam and jetsam for the better part of an hour and a half. After, they played another game of Expikaer and explored some of the Seidh books on the lower shelf. An hour before Night Bells, she stacked the dishes together and told Soryn that she would return about an hour after Jori left him for the night. After she had gone, Lord Maslyn went to his window and gazed at the falling snow. Though their planet was covered with the white blanket all year, he never tired of watching it fall. It made him feel peaceful in the same sort of way that Arna did.

It is nice to have friends, isn't it, little Maslyn?

"Yes, Ulla. It is a wonderful and mysterious thing."

Soryn continued to watch the falling flakes. Shortly before Night Bells, Jori arrived to help Lord Maslyn dress for the night. Soryn was all smiles when Jori entered and when he left. The manservant was pleased that Jordis' assistantship had brought the boy so much happiness. It was good to see Lord Maslyn interact with someone his own age.

Once he was alone, Soryn sat by the dying embers of the day's fire and closed his eyes. A strange feeling of contentment settled over him. He was still in his tower, but he had made a friend and he was about to explore the other passage in the fireplace. He wanted her to come back. While he waited, he talked to Ulla.

Oh you will talk to me now that she's gone?

"Don't be silly, Ulla. You're important, too. You helped us find the other passage."

So you will tolerate me because I'm useful to you?

"You're a cynic, Ulla. You need to have more faith in me."

And you need to have more trust in me.

"Fair enough. What do you know about the second passage?"

I know that it can lead you outside the tower.

"Is that all you know about it? Do you know where outside the tower it leads?"

From what my friends tell me, it takes you to a door that faces the forest.

"Who are these friends of yours? You've mentioned them before." Soryn was very curious about the sort of company the pig kept.

I befriended two felines several years ago. Geri and Freki are their names. They are flighty little creatures, but they're loyal and have all sorts of gossip about the castle and its inhabitants.

"Ah, two busybodies: just what you need. You already spend your waking hours eavesdropping on my life. Now you have those two to help you nose your way into everyone else's business."

You wound me, Maslyn. And here I was thinking that we were comrades. I thought we were...friends.

In truth, Soryn did consider Ulla to be somewhat of a friend. However, despite his appreciation for the animal, the pig was somewhat creepy.

I get it. I'm helpful, charming, kind…but I make you uncomfortable.

"Well, to be frank, Ulla, yes you do. This whole mind reading thing of yours is strange. I've never even heard of such a thing. Telepathy is one thing. Mind reading is entirely different."

Ah, I understand. I suppose you just need time to get to know me. I do have many idiosyncrasies. I think your friend is coming up the stairs. She's thinking about the tunnel and the day she spent with you. I think this relationship is developing nicely.

Ulla faded out of Soryn's mind and the boy sat up. Arna came up the stairs and walked into the room. She wore the same attire as the night before. He, thankfully, had the good sense to change back into normal clothing after Jori left. It would have been painfully embarrassing for her to see him in his nightclothes. He smiled and thought she looked pretty in the dim red light of the lanterns.

"You came early! I'm glad. I was getting antsy with only Ulla for company," Soryn said as he stood up.

"Better watch out. Ulla heard you, I'm sure."

Humph, was all the black pig muttered.

"Well, shall we?" Soryn extended his hand towards the right panel of the fireplace.

Pinpricks of excitement inched their way up Soryn's spine. He stepped onto the hearth and made sure there was room for Arna. He was careful not to touch any of the remnants of the fire or the ash around it. She reached past him to push the secret brick in the center panel of the fireplace. As expected, the right side panel swung open, revealing a dark descending corridor. They looked at one another and Arna nodded to Lord Maslyn. Taking the lead, Soryn stepped into the blackness below. Just as he set foot on stone, he remembered they did not have a candle. The stand was still down in Ulla's study.

I think you should be alright without it. Go on. Have an adventure in the dark, Ulla told them.

Arna shrugged and Soryn nodded for her to come into the tunnel. She followed behind, checking to make sure that the reverse

79

side of the panel had a latch as well. She tested it before closing it behind them. Total blackness swallowed them up. Soryn reached back until he found her hand. She clasped it firmly while he felt along the walls with his free hand. They were rough against his skin. Slowly, they made their descent into greater darkness.

There were many steps. Arna kept a count of them in her mind. When she made it to one hundred and sixty, she began to wonder if they would descend underground. Eventually, Soryn discovered his feet were on a level plane. He stopped and whispered to Arna that he thought they were at the bottom. Arna stopped and waited for him to check out the area. He let go of her hand and felt around ahead for other walls or openings.

The floor remained level for a few paces. Soryn decided it might be better to try and guess the dimensions of the width of the passage before moving too far forward. For all he knew, they could be in a huge room or hallway. He stood still and oriented himself. Since he had only tried walking forward, he turned slightly to his left and walked slowly, arms outstretched, towards what he hoped would be a wall. After about seven paces, he felt it. He traced his steps backwards toward the stairs and easily found them. Instead of going out towards the center again, he followed the width of the bottom stair and followed the wall to his right. He kept a hand on it this time and called for Arna to follow him.

Together, they made their way across the level floor. It took several minutes, but finally, Lord Maslyn felt the wall curve slightly towards the left and his right hand brushed against wood—very cold wood.

"What is it?" Arna asked, noticing they had stopped.

"I think I may have found the door."

She exhaled, and reached until she felt the wood as well. Soryn let go of her hand again and felt the door's surface for a latch. When his hand brushed against metal, he grew very still and quiet.

"Are you alright, Bialas?" Arna whispered.

"All this time…the exit was right here. All those years up there…"

She took hold of his hand and squeezed it. "Open it. Let's see what's out there."

He nodded. Soryn grasped the door latch and turned it. It took both of them to wrench the door open. It scraped inward across the floor. Loud screeches and metallic clanks announced the door's reluctance to open. After considerable effort, the pair finally had it opened as wide as it would go. What they saw when they opened the door made them both gasp with shock.

A great white-blue wall stood before them. It glowed as though it were lit from within. Soryn touched it…ice. Arna could not help herself and touched it as well.

"I suppose the door is buried under a snow drift," she frowned.

Soryn's excitement dwindled with the realization that they had no tools with which to dig a tunnel up and out.

"Well, Ulla, you didn't mention that this door would be buried under who knows how many feet of snow," Soryn grumbled.

How was I supposed to know something like that?

"Didn't your friends, Geri and Freki, mention anything about the door being hidden beneath the drift?" Arna retorted.

I seem to recall they found it during a summer some years ago. The drift would have mostly been melted, then.

"Yes. I suppose it would have," Soryn turned to Arna, "Do you know where we could get some snow shovels?"

"Of course. I'll get some tomorrow morning before I come up. Now that we know Jori hasn't altered his schedule, we'll be able to work on it during the morning and the afternoon."

"You might want to find us some boots, too. If the snow we dig out melts and refreezes in that small passage, we'll need shoes with good traction, right?"

"Right." She winked at him and Soryn liked how her face appeared blue in the light from the snow wall.

"I remember my mother giving us boots to walk across the creek when we would take walks in the forest. She loved the forest," Soryn told her.

Arna smiled and closed the door over the ice wall. It went back into place easier than they expected and they turned to hike back up the staircase. They did not speak to one another. In all honesty, they were both disappointed that they were delayed in getting out of the tower. Arna started to say something comforting, but imagined it would be better to stay silent.

When they returned to the tower room and left the fireplace, Arna turned around and knelt to make another fire.

"You don't have to do that, Arna," Soryn mumbled.

"Yes I do. I'm still your assistant, after all. Can't have you frozen in the morning with all the work we have ahead of us." Arna saw a small grin settle on his lips.

"That would render me almost entirely useless, wouldn't it?"

She did not reply and finished building a neat, warm fire for him. Before she left for the night, she put a firm hand on his shoulder.

"Don't let this get you down, Bialas. You *will* get out of here, you know, possibly as early as tomorrow." Arna squeezed his shoulder before taking her hand away.

She left and Soryn watched her go, his heart sinking. He changed back into his nightclothes and sat by the fire, warming himself. For a few minutes, he let the waves of heat crash over his back and allowed himself to ponder Arna's words. He should not let it get him down. In the last few days, he had discovered that there was far more to life than he had guessed. He had a friend, a warm fire behind him, and the prospect of leaving the tower whenever he wanted. He had a good life, even if it was still spent in the tower. There were many blessings to be thankful for. That thought sparked another memory of his mother. He could see her soft, red-brown eyes over him as she tucked him in. He heard her bell-like voice saying, "Remember to thank God for all your blessings before you go to sleep. Whenever you're sad, look up at the pretty stars and count a blessing for each one. Soon…you'll be too full of happiness to be sad." She told him that many times when he was a young child. Thankfulness for Arna flooded his heart. She helped him to remember things long forgotten. That was a blessing.

Lord Maslyn left the fire and crawled into bed, moving to the edge so he could pull back the drapes over the barred window. It was a clear night and a great sparkling net of stars spread wide over the castle. Making sure he could still see them, he buried himself under the sheets and covers. Taking his mother's advice to heart, he counted a blessing for every star he saw. He found within minutes that his disappointment had washed away and a smile formed behind his lips. The dimmed red lanterns cast a warm glow over his head while the orange light from the fire flickered over his feet. If anyone had looked over him in those moments, they would have thought he was illuminated from the inside. As he fell asleep, he realized that Night Bells had come and gone. He had not even noticed.

Chapter Six

In which the young master develops a fondness for birdsong...

After Jori left the next morning, Soryn stood by his window looking at two of Niflheim's suns in the sky. The third was obscured by a large cumulonimbus cloud. He gazed up towards the village chapel and then to the stables. He saw that horse, Sable, giving the stable hands trouble again. The thought passed his mind that he might ride that horse someday. He smiled as he crossed the room toward his long table to eat the breakfast Jori had brought. While he ate, he stared at the dying embers of the night's fire. Fire was a new addition to his life and he relished everything about it. It was beautiful in every stage: the framing of the wood, the orange flames, the crumbling logs, and the grey ash—like snow that had wilted and died. The night before, he had counted Arna's fires as blessings with the stars.

You sound very cheerful this morning.

"Hello, Ulla," Soryn said, sipping his milk.

Hello, indeed. I trust you slept well?

"Yes, Ulla. I slept very well. How did you sleep?" Soryn made empty conversation. His mind was preoccupied.

What are you thinking about?

"As if you don't know?" Soryn smiled.

I'm learning it is polite to ask, even if I already know the answer.

"I'm wondering what I will be like once I'm able to leave the tower whenever I like."

An interesting question, to be sure.

"I've lived in this tower for half my life. I'm not sure I'll enjoy freedom as much as I imagine. Perhaps I've grown suited to confinement."

As one who has spent an enormous amount of time being confined, myself, I think you will enjoy freedom very much.

"What do you mean?" Intrigued, Soryn sat down on the hearth, listening.

I haven't left this tower in a very long time, either.

"Really? I suppose I didn't really think about how you got down there or why."

Yes, well, I'd rather not talk about the how or why. Let's just say we're much in the same position. I want to leave as much as you.

"Why don't you come up here to my room and then go down the other passage with us?"

Getting out of the tower is not exactly my top priority. Let's talk about that another time. Your lady-friend is arriving.

Sure enough, Arna came up the stairs just as Ulla had said and carried with her two snow shovels and a bag slung over her shoulder.

"Good morning, Arna," Soryn's face brightened.

"Good morning, yourself. Shall we get started?" She dropped the shovels carefully, so they would not clank too much, and took the bag from her shoulder. Soryn watched as she untied the mouth of the bag and began to dump its contents on the long table. Out poured two pairs of rough workman's gloves, two strips of felt cloth, a pair of boots, a change of clothes for each of them, and a bar of soap.

"How did you sneak past with all that?" he laughed.

"Ah… I have my ways," she smirked. "I made a list when I returned to my room last night and I found all the items this morning."

"Did anyone see you?" Soryn suddenly grew afraid of the consequences of their pursuits.

"No, and no one will miss these things. I made sure of that. We should be able to keep them for quite some time."

He walked over to the table. Soryn found his pair of clothes and took them down the hallway that led to the main castle, thinking Arna might like to change in his room rather than in the dark, cold corridor.

86

She smiled at his gesture and proceeded to change into the work clothes she had brought for herself. Arna slipped on her wool trousers and secured the boots over them. After she had changed, she went to the window and looked out toward the left. She tried to imagine where the door below would take them. The tower was circular like any other tower, but Soryn's room was rectangular, like all the rooms in the castle. Perhaps the secret passages used the extra space in the tower that was not taken up by Soryn's oddly shaped room. Ulla's study was also rectangular—which meant that it was built within the inner space of the tower and not around the perimeter. It was clear from their journey last night, that the second passage went around the perimeter of the tower until it ended with the door.

Soryn returned in his work clothes and went to the table.

"You'll need these." She lifted the boots and tossed them to Soryn.

The boy slid on his boots. Then, they both slipped their work gloves over their hands.

Soryn asked, "How will we know how much time we have down there?"

Don't worry. I'll let you know when you should start making your return. You mustn't be late in retrieving your midday meal or they might become suspicious. Leave it to me.

"Thank you, Ulla. You're being awfully helpful today." Arna remained skeptical of the pig's real intentions, but was thankful for his promise of help.

It would have been impossible for her to get a watch without someone missing it. Watches were hard to come by in New Kristiansand, despite it being the capital of Oban.

I'm pleased you are finally seeing how helpful I am.

Arna ignored him and picked up the shovels. She handed Soryn one of them and went to the fireplace. Sidestepping the remains of the fire she had made the night before, Arna pressed the hidden brick in the center panel. The right side swung open and she slipped inside, starting her descent down the tunnel. Soryn followed, awed by her enthusiasm at the prospect of so much work. Since they still had not returned to Ulla's study for their candle stand and Arna did not see any point in wasting energy getting another one, they went down the stairs in darkness once more.

Carrying shovels in their left hands and keeping their right hands on the wall, their descent went much quicker than the previous night's. It seemed they were at the door in mere minutes, though both of them knew it took longer to get there. Excitement made the time pass more quickly. When they reached the bottom, they propped their shovels against the wall by the door before opening it together. Again, they both gasped at the beauty and wonder of the ice wall that stood in the doorway. Despite its beauty, it was the only thing keeping Soryn within his tower. Therefore, it had to be destroyed.

A fleeting thought passed Arna's mind—maybe she could sneak him out of the castle without anyone seeing. Perhaps they could do it at night, but then she remembered the guards and night servants and banished the thought. She knew this was a better way—and much more adventurous, as well. With the daylight, the ice was lit up with blue and white lights. It was a pity to destroy such a beautiful thing, and a pity that there was no way to capture its glory before they removed it. Ancient Earth's photographic technology must have been a grand luxury. Niflheim had very few cameras and the ones that did make it through the colonization voyage were antiques and didn't work very well.

They nodded to one another and picked up their shovels. Soryn laughed at his lack of strength and gave the hardest thrust he could into the wall. Laughing again, he opened his eyes and realized he had only pushed the shovel's tip about two inches into the ice. He shrugged to Arna and jerked the shovel out.

Hmmm. This may take you two quite some time to sort out.

They chose not to reply to Ulla's remark and, instead, Arna lifted her shovel over her head with the shovel blade pointed concave side out and made downward hacking motions. Sheets of ice fell away, to Soryn's amazement. He realized that she was working on shaving the ice instead of trying to dig through it. Her ingenuity and intelligence was commendable. They cleared a small vertical layer of the ice within minutes, even though there was still no sunlight peeking through at the top of the door frame.

They worked until Ulla gave them a half hour warning to return to the tower room. By that time, they had made quite an impressive dent in the wall, but they realized they would need to prioritize the top half nearest the door frame in order to make quicker progress. Once they could no longer reach that top section, they would focus on the bottom. This way, they surmised, would allow them to dig a tunnel while they searched for the top of the snow drift.

They left a small puddle in the door's passage when they returned to Soryn's room. They were sweaty and out of breath, but made it with plenty of time for Arna to change back into her work uniform. Soryn rested while she went to retrieve their lunch. He was glad of the physical exercise, but again reminded of his poor strength. If it took a while for them to dig their way out of the door, he may even develop muscles.

When she returned, they ate, talking intermittently. After the meal was concluded, she pushed the dishes down to the end of the long table, as she had done the day before, and rested while Soryn went down the castle-side passage to change into his normal clothes. Jori came soon after lunch and the two children used the time to rest and to get the documents signed for the day. Arna pushed the completed papers towards the center of the table for Jori when he returned that evening.

After they had both changed back into their work clothes, they went back down the passage. The puddle they had left earlier had refrozen in the time they had taken to eat and sign papers. They were careful not to slip as they went back to work on the ice wall. Within a few minutes, the ice directly around their feet had melted again.

Slowly, they created the beginnings of a tunnel. After they were able to walk about three paces in, Soryn had an idea.

"What if I stand in the tunnel and thrust my shovel up through the roof of the snow? Perhaps we are closer than we think. Maybe I can do it!"

"I think that's a great idea, Bialas. Just prepare to get very wet and very cold." Arna raised an eyebrow.

"We can always build a fire later, right?" Soryn smiled and then set to work chipping away at the ceiling.

Do you realize just how wet and cold you are about to be, little Maslyn?

"Oh hush, Ulla. I'm trying to work," Soryn snapped, chipping away, while ice shavings fell on his clothes and began to melt into the fabric.

Within a few minutes, Arna's excited voice rang out loudly, "You've done it, Bialas! I can see light!"

Soryn had been working so hard that he had not noticed the small bits of sun' light coming through the hole he made. He stopped and peered up. Tears unexpectedly sprang to his eyes. She was right. He had broken through the top of the snow drift. Arna squeezed into the small tunnel and looked up with him.

"You could get out of here tonight, Soryn. You're as close to freedom as we are to breaking through that snow drift."

By all means, don't stop.

For once, they both smiled in response to Ulla's sarcasm. Their motivation spiked and neither Soryn nor Arna held back. They attacked the roof of their small tunnel and, soon, light spilled over them both. Soryn saw sky—sky without bars. Birds flew over the clouds. The tears fell quietly from his eyes. Arna leaned her head on his shoulder and his heart gave a delighted leap.

"Let's see if we can get you out of here, Bialas."

Well once you do, just don't forgot what I told you about that Fanndis woman. You need to see her if you want to learn more about the Seidh.

"Yes, Ulla. How much time do we have?" Soryn was not going to get so sidetracked by their discovery that he would get caught or get Arna into trouble.

You have about another two hours or so. Plenty of time to at least explore a bit, I should think.

The children said no more and went back to their furious attack on the tunnel roof. When they cleared the width of it in the center, the ice closest to the door frame suddenly collapsed, leaving bits of ice and snow all over both of them. They laughed at this and continued to hack away at the ice in order to make a way for them to climb out. The height of the snow drift was about five and a half feet. Soryn chose not to look up too much, for fear he would get distracted and be unable to actually get out of the hole they had made. Time was still a precious commodity.

Finally, the two of them made an incline that would allow them to climb out. Arna thrust her shovel several feet up and Soryn thrust his shovel several feet above hers.

Arna smiled at Lord Maslyn, extended her hand, and said, "After you."

Nodding, excitement surging through him, Soryn Jens Bialas Maslyn climbed his way out of the tower and stood in the snow, breathing in the free air. Arna watched him lift his face to the open sky and laugh. Joy filled her heart as she looked on his display of total happiness. She climbed out of the tunnel and slipped her hand in his.

"You're free, Bialas. You can leave anytime you like."

He leaned his head against hers and sighed. They looked out at the forest. The deciduous trees looked like great dark skeletons against the horizon. Towering firs and pines painted the vista green and white with their needles. The wind coaxed the branches to sway slightly.

If I can reach you, I'll try to let you know when you should return.

91

"Thank you, Ulla. That would be nice," Soryn said, keeping a hold of Arna's hand.

Giving his friend no warning, Soryn fled the base of the tower for the forest. He could not explain the utter elation that he felt. It was like being awakened from a long sleep, as though his years in the tower had been one long nightmare from which he was only now able to awaken. Arna looked around the castle turrets and parapets for guards. Thankfully, they were facing other directions. It was as though some unseen force was on their side. Together, they ran for the tree line.

When they made it, the suns had inched lower in the sky and the castle stood bathed in a pale pink glow. Soryn looked back at his tower and marveled at its beautiful exterior. Exhaling heavily, he turned towards the forest and darted in. Arna shook her head, amused at his vigor, and followed along. All around them were tangled and gnarled snow-covered roots. Snow drifts were deep and more than once, they were thankful for their knee-high boots. They went in a straight path through the forest and never looked back.

Soryn had no idea which direction the old snow woman's cottage would be, but he didn't care. All he had on his mind were the sensations of freedom—the frigid wind on his face, the tingling numbness that threatened to claim his toes, the feel of Arna's strong hand in his. He felt more alive than he had ever felt in his life, even before his days in the tower. He felt as though nothing could puncture his happiness. Arna's soft crunching footfalls reminded Soryn that he should carry on. He moved forward without talking, so he could listen to the sounds of the forest. Off in the distance, he caught the sound of crows squawking.

Once, Lord Maslyn slipped, but Arna caught him. His legs dangled off a steep bank, hovering over a frozen creek bed. A ribbon of fear tightened around his heart, but he realized Arna was too strong to drop him. She pulled him up and they giggled nervously as they continued on. The suns were almost entirely set by that time and each one knew they should return before they could no longer find their path. Suddenly, a wolf howled—not too near, but not too far away either. They froze in their tracks, petrified. They heard movement and rustling around them. Jerking their heads and looking, they grew even more anxious. Arna closed her eyes and Soryn stared straight ahead.

A harsh, orange light broke through the coming darkness about thirty yards ahead of the pair. Snow fell in fits from the sky, but Soryn thought he made out the shape of a person holding a lantern standing there looking at them. He could not tell if it was a man or woman, but a strange nostalgic sensation washed over him. Too soon, the person's image, along with the lantern's light, was swallowed up in a gust of snowy wind. Soryn wrapped his arm around Arna and tried to shield her from the icy blast as they turned around in their path. The pair trudged back towards the field behind the castle.

"Who do you think that was?" Arna asked, shivering.

"I don't know. Let's get back inside and talk there."

They hurried. Snow fell so heavily that it started to fill in their footprints. After only several minutes, they broke through the trees and saw the tower door in sight. Both worried that the hole they had dug around the door would be filled in with the coming blizzard. Thankfully, they found it mostly intact and carefully climbed down. They removed their shovels from the remaining ice wall and moved inside out of the cold. The door slammed shut and the two children breathed a sigh of relief at having come in out of the storm.

"I think we may have to dig out our hole again tomorrow," Arna laughed, panting from their hurried return.

"Ah, that's alright. We know it isn't far."

You two are back early.

"It started to snow," Soryn coughed. He leaned his shovel against the wall and sat on the stairs to catch his breath.

Find anything interesting in the woods? Ulla asked.

"We saw someone holding a lantern, but they were too far away to make out and the snow was falling too heavily to stay and find out." Arna said, sliding down next to Soryn. "I suppose we should start heading upstairs. We'll need to wash off and change into normal clothing. I'll make a fire."

"That's alright, Arna. I'll make the fire this time." Soryn wanted to try his hand at a fire for once.

"That's fine with me," she grinned.

* * *

A fire roared in the hearth. They both knew it would be futile to attempt to leave the castle during the night, particularly with the inclement weather. The fierce storm outside could be seen through Lord Maslyn's window. Since they knew they would not be seeing each other again until the morning, they agreed to plan their next day during dinner. Arna rested at the table and Soryn leaned back in his chair with his arms behind his head. Neither was hungry just yet. Arna had not even gone to get their meals. They were content just sitting for a few moments.

"I think it's obvious that we should wait and see what the weather does in the morning, but if it is nice enough to go out, we should explore as much of that forest as we can without getting lost," Soryn said.

He was so eager to get out into the world that the thought of being confined for an entire day was unbearable. Once he had felt such freedom, he could not imagine waiting to taste it again for more than a few hours.

"If we're ever going to find Fanndis, I think you're right. I wonder if she's the one we saw in the woods last night." Arna had been frightened by the strange person they had seen. If it *was* Fanndis, she hoped her fear would dissipate when she actually met her.

"What sorts of things will we need?" Soryn asked.

It had taken both of them almost thirty minutes to thaw out from their exploits in the forest and each one knew a heavier coat would be a necessity from now on.

"Do you have a heavy coat, Bialas? If you've never been out, I don't suppose you would…" Arna thought about a place she might find an old coat that had been thrown out.

"Well, I have never looked for a coat in here, but that doesn't mean I don't have one." Lord Maslyn got up and headed for his dresser.

While he searched each drawer, Arna made mental notes of the places she could look for gloves, scarves, extra socks, warm hats, and other articles that would help them in their long escapades outside the tower. Soryn startled her when he exclaimed, "Aha!" She looked up and he held a thick, wool overcoat that had been shoved in the very bottom dresser drawer. It looked a size too big for him, but she knew that several layers underneath it would help him stay warm in the frigid Niflheim air.

"That looks fine. Start looking for knitted sweaters and things. We'll have to layer up if we're going to be out there very long— which I imagine we will." She went back to her thinking and he went back to work on the dresser.

Umm…little miss…shouldn't you be going to get dinner right about now?

"Goodness! Ulla! Thank you! I had nearly forgotten!"

Without saying anything to Soryn, she dashed down the steps to the castle passage, thankful that she had changed back into her uniform already.

"Goodbye?" Soryn said, obviously having missed Ulla's interior dialogue with the girl.

Sorry to leave you out of that. Takes a little bit more energy to communicate to two people at once and I'm rather tired today.

"What have you been doing that's so strenuous? I thought you stayed indoors all day."

Those two pesky cats came to visit me and their incessant whining has worn me out. They are always complaining about some animal or another who has spurned them or won't talk to them et cetera, et cetera.

"Ah huh…" Soryn continued pulling out sweaters, wool trousers, and all the socks he could find from his dresser.

No sympathy? Ah, I see. You are too busy for me now. You haven't been down to my study.

"We've got a fire going at the moment, Ulla." Soryn had not really thought about the fact that they had not returned to the study in quite some time. The boy felt a bit guilty. Ulla sounded lonely.

Well, since there is a blizzard going on outside and you've no need to work in the other passage tonight, why don't you come down to my study? Once the fire has burned out, of course. We can talk.

"I'll see what I can do. I'm not sure how long it will take for it to burn down all the way."

Arna returned about that time with their dinner on two trays. Panting, she set the meals down quickly.

"Things went well?" Soryn left his work at the dresser and sat at his place at the table.

"Yes…things…went…well…" Arna tried to catch her breath.

"You didn't get into trouble, did you?"

"No. Inga had the trays on her kitchen island. She was out of the room. I grabbed them and left without anyone really noticing me. I don't think I was late or anything."

"That's good news. When you dashed out like that, I wasn't sure what had happened. Ulla didn't include me in his brief conversation with you," Soryn smiled.

The two of them attacked their food as if it would disappear if they did not ingest it as quickly as possible. After all their hard work, it was little wonder their appetites had increased. Ulla let them eat in silence. Though he wanted to talk to them, he just sulked about the study. He had grown indignant that they had left him alone for so long. He thought, *Aren't I the one who has helped them with all their*

96

little intrigues? Scowling, he hopped down from his top shelf and planted his squat, petite body near the miniature Adden. The small sun's warmth never ceased to comfort him. Just as he had grown contented and relaxed, he heard the familiar hissing of his feline lackeys. Ulla groaned and pretended to be asleep.

Sssir, are you asssleep? The cats' synchronized way of speaking irritated the pig.

No. What do you two want, now?

We jussst wanted to ssssee how you were handling the boy'ssss defection in hissss loyaltiesss.

He has NOT defected in his loyalties. The girl is no threat. She is just trying to help him. That's the honest truth of it, Ulla protested.

We'll ssssee.

Any news? Ulla hoped they would get right to the point.

Dependsss.

On what? The pig grunted. Those cats truly knew how to try his patience.

Dependsss on how much you want to know our sssspecial newsss…

What if I said I didn't care?

Then we wouldn't tell you. We want to know our ssservicesss are appreciated.

The two tabbies' tails waved like twin snakes as they turned their heads and closed their eyes—attempting to look coy.

I assure you, your services are most appreciated. I can't collect the information myself, can I? I am at your mercy, Ulla soothed—knowing full well he had already discerned their "special news" with his mind reading.

Well then, we can tell you that the one you sssseek isss not far from the village. He'sss in the north, near the foressst. We heard thisss from our coussssin in the next village.

Really? That's a stroke of luck.

Yessss. We thought sssso asss well.

Ulla smiled the only way a pig could, which turned out to be more of a grimace. Geri and Freki turned together and slithered out the same hole they came from.

The pig sat back on his haunches and soaked in the warmth from the sun. *So you're this close, are you?* Ulla felt a deep satisfaction that he could read the minds of the children but they could not read his. If they could, they would not associate with him at all. They would probably think he was using them. How little humans knew, always looking at the forest and never at the trees themselves. He listened in on Lord Maslyn's conversation with Arna above.

Soryn stretched after eating too quickly. Arna stared at the fire. They were silent for some time. While eating, they had been far too busy to talk. At the moment, their hunger mollified, they were merely happy to catch flickers of heat from the fireplace and rest.

Well, you two are not very interesting at the moment.

"We're tired. Don't you have something important you can be doing?" Arna quipped as she folded her hands and put her head on top of them.

Fresh out of important things to do, I'm afraid. I'll just have to bother the two of you.

"You're not a bother, Ulla. Like she said, we're just tired. We worked very hard on that tunnel."

Seems like you made quick work of it. What was it like for you in the outside world, little Maslyn?

Soryn thought hard about the question before answering. He could not really explain to *himself* what it had been like, let alone another person. To know that, at any time, he could leave…it gave him a bold feeling of independence.

You don't need to voice it. I heard you loud and clear. I'm happy that you were able to get out and about.

"Thanks," Soryn muttered through a yawn. He looked over at Arna who was almost asleep. "Arna," he said, nudging her arm gently. "Wake up. Go on down to bed. I'll see you in the morning."

"Mmmm," was all she said. She carefully picked up the dishes and waved as she descended the few steps to the castle passage.

Ulla decided to leave Soryn alone for a while. If the boy chose to come to the study, he would. The pig hopped up to his shelf and went to sleep. Meanwhile, in the tower room above, Lord Maslyn sat in his chair, taking in every ounce of warmth from the fire that he could. He closed his eyes and took in the sounds of the wind and snow pummeling the window and stones of the tower. He had no idea what they could expect tomorrow when they opened the door below. Still, he knew that even if they had to dig all over again, it would be worth every bead of sweat.

It had been surreal, being out in the forest, almost as if it could not have happened. But it did. It happened, and he was truly free to leave whenever he wished. He knew he would have to make sure that no one took his freedom away. The door would have to remain secret to everyone but Arna and Ulla. If ever again he was locked away without any hope of escape …he had no idea what it would do to him. The first time around, he had nearly expired of boredom. If it happened again, who knew what would become of him? It was still quite some time before Night Bells. He knew he needed to put away the clothes he had gotten out of the dresser before Jori saw them and asked questions.

It was difficult to make his body move when he was so tired, but he went to the dresser, anyway. He decided the best thing would be to organize the shelves so that one would be for their outside explorations and the rest could be for things he wore inside the tower. Organizing the dresser and the clothing he had pulled out did not take nearly as long as he had imagined. Without much desire to read, he found himself at a loss for what to do. When Arna was gone, it was lonely. He went to the fire, still amazed by the overpowering heat it brought into the room.

Jori found him asleep on the hearth when he arrived to take the day's paperwork and help Lord Maslyn prepare for bed. When the manservant found he could not wake the boy, he picked him up and carried him to the bed. After the covers were secured, Jori dimmed the red lanterns and left the little noble alone. Jori smiled, marveling at the effect that Jordis and the fire were having on the boy. It was as though he was finally peaceful after all these years. Humming, Jori strode down the castle passage and went to drop the papers under Steward Asmund's door. After that, he went to his room, dressed for bed, and went to sleep.

* * *

"I'm sorry Ulla!" Soryn shouted when he awoke abruptly the next morning.

Ulla laughed when he heard the boy's exclamation.

Soryn jerked his head left and right, trying to reorient his mind after waking so suddenly. He had a horrifying dream, but he didn't remember it.

It's alright, little Maslyn. I knew you wouldn't come to see me. Really, I understand.

"You're sure?" Soryn was still half asleep.

Yes. Don't worry about me. Besides, you need to get out there and enjoy the day. I hear it is sunny. Your manservant came already. He left the breakfast there for you and your clothes. His thoughts indicated a desire to let you have your rest. He did not seem suspicious, so no need to get anxious.

"Mm," Soryn murmured as he swung his feet over the side of the bed and clamped his hands to his head—he had a frightful headache. Wobbling initially, the noble was finally able to right himself and walked to the table. Without even bothering to change, he ate his breakfast. His appetite from the day before had failed to wane in the night. After he scraped the plate clean, he changed his clothes and scribbled a note to Arna on a spare piece of parchment from the desk. It read:

"Gone to visit Ulla. Come on down when you're ready. I think he's getting lonely."

-Soryn

Ooh, goody. I get a visit. To what do I owe this honor?

"Ulla, be sensible. We've been very busy the last few days," Soryn scowled as he activated the secret passage to Ulla's study and climbed down.

Alright, alright. I know you've been busy. I just like to give you a hard time.

"I guessed that."

The passage to Ulla's study was so much warmer than the passage on the other side of the fireplace. Soryn relished the warmth, especially since the evening's fire had died out sometime in the night. Soon, he bounded up the few short steps to the study and leaned against the threshold. Ulla sat, his head cocked to the side in a strange fashion, next to the miniature sun spire.

"I'm here. What do you want to talk about?" Soryn folded his arms.

Whatever you would like. Don't you have burning questions for me?

Several questions came into his mind at once, but only one question interested Soryn at the moment: "Is it likely that the person we saw in the woods was Fanndis?"

Could be. But how should I know?

"You always seem to know a lot about what goes on in the castle and elsewhere."

True, but I don't know specific details about anyone, really. What I know about this place and what goes on here was pieced together over several years of information from Geri and Freki. It also comes from my own experience. I know little about people that live in the forest.

"You said you knew Fanndis was there," Soryn countered.

I only know that because my feline companions apparently caught wind of the information through a friend of theirs.

"Oh." Soryn frowned.

Your little friend just arrived upstairs. Better go and fetch her.

"I left a note for her. She'll come down when she's ready."

She still doesn't like me, you know.

"She's entitled to her own opinion of people. It's none of my business what she thinks of you. I like you. You are a bit odd and usually spend your time making us uncomfortable in some way or another, but I like you."

I appreciate your sentiments.

While they both waited for Arna to arrive, Soryn looked around at the arbitrary objects that inhabited every square scrap of counter space about the room. He saw many notes that had been hastily scrawled—most seemed unintelligible. Arna bounded in and Soryn turned around, smiling.

"Good morning, all," Arna said, brimming with energy.

"Good morning."

Good morning, my dear.

"What are you two up to?" She smiled at Soryn and glared at Ulla.

We were discussing the woman you saw in the woods. Soryn had asked if I thought it might be Fanndis.

"Well, was it?" Arna rested her hands on her hips.

I have no idea. How could I know? From what you two have told me, you did not get a great look at the person holding the lantern, correct?

"Yes, I suppose." Arna pursed her lips and mentally prepared for the forest exploration ahead.

"Is there anything else you want to talk about Ulla? I think we both would like to head to the woods now."

Nothing comes to mind. You two go and have fun. Be careful and remember that you will be too far away for me to prompt you to come back. You're on your own. Also, Father Kimbli comes today.

Soryn nodded.

He slipped his hand around Arna's and they bounded up the stairs. When they arrived in Lord Maslyn's room several minutes later, Arna promptly grabbed her spare clothing and sauntered down the castle passage. Soryn took that as a cue to prepare for the day's business. She returned, after giving him plenty of time to change, and firmly planted her hand on the table. Her gesture somewhat startled the boy.

"We have a problem," Arna announced, looking very serious.

"We do?" Soryn words squeaked a bit.

"It's sunny today and the guards can see everything for miles. The only advantage we have is that the castle's main building is far from the tower. However, they could still walk the parapet that runs along the top of the passage from the main castle to the tower."

"Do you have any ideas for avoiding them?" A bead of sweat formed on Soryn's brow and a fit of anxiety brewed in his chest. It would be torturous to spend the day inside when it was so beautiful out.

"Let's get down there and check on the hole outside the door." Soryn agreed.

The two of them hobbled down the other fireplace passage. Soryn silently scolded himself for having forgotten their candle stand when he had visited Ulla just minutes before. When they reached the bottom and opened the door, they were relieved to see that their hole had not filled in too much from the night's snow storm. It took about ten minutes to dig their way out again.

"Let me think," Arna said, pacing.

Soryn peeked through the gaping hole above him and glimpsed a flock of birds flying overhead. He was fascinated by their wings and flight patterns. The songs they sang were spirited and beautiful.

"Okay. I think if I scout out the guards' movements, we should be alright. It may take a few minutes. Don't worry. I'll be back soon." Arna nimbly climbed out of the tunnel and skirted the tower's exterior until Soryn could no longer see her.

He smiled. She was awfully brave. While he waited for her to return, Soryn stood very still and closed his eyes. He wanted to listen to the sounds of the birds chirruping in the forest trees. Most of the birds on Niflheim were very big, and their heavy feather coats kept them warm in the frigid temperatures of the planet. The smaller ones lived in great caverns the majority of the year. Soryn opened his eyes and marveled at their grace as they flew overhead. Their iridescent, ebony wings spread the height of a grown man with each flap. They seemed to dance across the sky. Arna might know what they were called, and he intended to ask her when she came back.

She returned suddenly, looking flushed. Soryn worried that she had been spotted, and raised his eyebrows in question.

"They didn't see me. I think we have only one shot at this."

"Alright," Soryn said.

"He's just turned to head back the other direction and he's facing the village, *not* the forest. We have to go *now*." Arna turned and crawled back up onto the highest level of snow and ran towards the forest.

Soryn climbed out and sped after her. It took them only a minute or two to reach the trees. Arna signaled for Soryn to squat behind the trunk of a large pine and she peered out, checking for movement or alarming activity from the guards. When she exhaled heavily, Soryn knew they were safe. She nodded at him and they turned towards the rest of the woods.

"Do you think we'll find her?" Soryn whispered.

"I don't know. Let's go and find out," Arna whispered back, slipping her gloved hand into Soryn's.

The woods were flooded with tangling rays of sunshine. The snowy evergreens reflected the light and cast a green hue over the blanketed forest. The bare deciduous trees looked like wispy fronds amid the powerful firs and pines. It was a glorious day, and the two children forgot the cold as they navigated their way through the wintry flora. Any tracks they had left the previous night were gone, so they were content to make new ones and worried only about finding the snow woman's dwelling place.

"What are the giant birds called, Arna? The ones that make such pretty sounds?" Soryn asked, still curious.

"Oh, them? They're called fifa birds. They sure sing prettily, but they make a giant mess if they nest in the thatch of your roof. People have to set traps and things to keep them away—especially during summer. It's their breeding season."

"Fifa birds...I like their name. It sort of sounds like the calls they make." Soryn hoped they would see more of them.

Arna laughed and picked up her pace, hoping they could explore more of the forest before they had to return for lunch.

After they had been walking for close to a half hour, Arna heard the unmistakable sound of an axe splitting a block of wood. Soryn was alarmed, never having heard that sound before, and she had to assure him that it was most likely safe.

"Perhaps there's a cottage up ahead," Arna suggested.

Though Soryn felt a bit timid about it, they pushed ahead. The sounds of the axe grew louder as they continued walking. Within minutes, they caught sight of a stone house with a heavily thatched roof. Smoke gushed out of the three chimneys. The sound of the chopping came from behind the cottage. Soryn's heart beat loudly in his chest and he felt he would explode from his fright and excitement.

"I'll go first," Soryn said, trying to assert his own bravery.

"You don't have to," Arna told him.

"It's alright."

Soryn tried to move quietly through the bushes, with marginal success, and pushed through knotted branches. He stepped into the small clearing surrounding the cottage. A sigh escaped his lips and he relaxed a bit after realizing he had not been discovered yet. Just as he stepped further into the snowy yard, the door of the stone cottage swung open to reveal an older woman standing in the doorway. A fur hood covered most of her face. A fluffy grey and white cat wound itself around her legs.

"What do you want, Lord Maslyn?" the woman's severe voice demanded.

Soryn was taken aback at her words. Arna was stunned and stayed firmly hidden in the thicket.

"And you! Girl! I know you're in the woods, so come on out and let's talk like civilized people," the woman barked.

She turned around and, to the children's amazement, beckoned them into her house. Meanwhile, the sound of wood chopping continued in the back. The children knew this meant she was not alone. Soryn grew apprehensive. They might have found the person they had been looking for, but he had no idea if they would actually learn anything from her.

"Do hurry up, you two. I don't have all day, you know. I am *quite* busy."

Holding hands, Soryn and Arna bravely entered the woman's cottage. There was still no proof that this was the "Fanndis" that Ulla had mentioned, but they hoped it was. As they ducked under the short door frame, they saw the old woman shedding her coat and moving to stoke the large fire that blazed in the hearth. The room was smallish and had two dark corridors leading off of it—one on either side. The woman was short, thin, and her grey hair lay braided down her back loosely, allowing stray hairs to escape at their leisure.

"You can hang your coats on the pegs by the hearth. We keep it quite comfortable in here," she commented, busy with the fire.

Arna and Soryn did as she said and stood awkwardly, waiting for her to talk. She was quiet until she finished with the hearth. The old woman looked up and stared directly into Soryn's eyes. Her own were ice blue and cold, like the sky at dawn.

"You never answered my question, Lord Maslyn. What do you want with me?" Her eyes never looked away from his for a second.

Soryn felt like his whole personhood was unearthed by her glare. Her manner was far more direct and blunt than Ulla's. This fact comforted Soryn, even as it intimidated him.

"We... um, that is to say...are you Fanndis, the old snow woman?" he blurted out.

Merest hints of a smile graced the aging face and she chuckled, "The *old snow* woman?"

"Yes?" Soryn said, unsure of himself under her piercing eyes.

"Yes. I am *Fanndis*. Though, I should tell you, I'm not quite that old yet. Why were you looking for me?"

The boy looked to Arna and seemed at a loss for words. How could they explain Ulla and his ideas? Soryn was afraid he would muddle it up and squeezed Arna's hand.

"Well, we wanted to know if you could do something for us— not for free of course. We just wanted to know if you could tell us about the Seidh."

Fanndis pursed her lips and crossed her arms over her grey apron. The children were growing afraid she would not answer them when a back door somewhere in the cottage opened loudly and heavy footsteps entered the house. The children tensed, but Fanndis seemed unaffected. They turned their heads when a tall, broad-shouldered man entered the room. Arna blushed when she looked at him. He had a strong face with tanned skin, blue-grey eyes, and sandy blond hair that seemed to stick up on top as if he had not combed it in years. On his face was a scraggly, closely shorn beard that seemed etched into his skin.

"Stigg, meet the young Lord Maslyn and his friend." Fanndis gestured to Soryn and Arna.

Soryn was again struck with confusion that she knew who he was. He had never seen her before in his life. The man called "Stigg" nodded to Soryn and bowed slightly to Arna. In his arms was an enormous stack of firewood. He was so tall that he had to bend over slightly as he moved about the room. Still, he was remarkably graceful and navigated the room's sparse furnishings and people

107

quite well as he made his way to the hearth. Each piece of wood was then placed in a brass basin. Stigg never said a word, not even when he left the room—through the other side of the cottage—and disappeared.

"Don't mind my son. He is not a man of many words." Fanndis smiled after him.

Soryn could not stand it any longer. He felt almost like he did when Ulla was toying with his mind. "How do you know who I am!?" he demanded.

"Soryn, I know who you are because I was the one who brought you into this world twelve years ago. I also brought your brothers before you. Your mother and I were old friends before she passed away. I was also your brother Olan's teacher."

Arna was surprised the woman was so forthcoming with her information. Something within told the girl that Fanndis spoke the truth. No façade or pretense. Despite her sauciness and blunt nature, Arna found she rather liked the "old snow" woman. She glanced up at Soryn who stared at Fanndis with a look of hopefulness.

"You knew my mother?" the boy asked.

"Yes, I knew your mother. Lizbet was a remarkable woman. It's a shame what happened. It's a grand shame. Not a day goes by that I don't miss her."

"Can you tell me about her?"

"I certainly can, but not today. I want to know why you two came here asking about the Seidh. That's a dangerous topic for everyday conversation." Fanndis crossed her hands in her lap.

"Well...I don't know where to start," Soryn admitted.

"Typically, one starts at the beginning—which in your case means the night of the fire, I suppose." Fanndis leaned back as far as she could in the straight-backed chair and propped one leg over the other in a masculine fashion.

"I don't remember much about the night of the fire. You seem to know more than me," Soryn began.

108

"Yes. I know, as well, of some strange circumstances surrounding the event."

"Well, all I really remember is the fire itself and that I woke up the next morning in the tower room and I never left it for six years. No one really talked to me about the whole thing, not even Father Kimbli."

"Is that ancient man still around? My goodness, I haven't seen him in ages..." Fanndis smiled at the mention of her old friend's name.

"He comes to visit me and he asks about how I'm feeling each week. He doesn't mention much about what happened that night, though."

"I should think not. Priests don't typically dabble in matters involving the Seidh."

"Anyway, things carried on like that for six years. About a week ago, I discovered a secret passage leading from my fireplace down to a study in the bottom of the tower. In this study, I met a rather unusual creature. His name is 'Ulla' and he's a black pig." Soryn felt a little sheepish telling this wise woman about Ulla when he knew she wouldn't believe the pig's mind reading.

"A pig, you say?" her expression changed to one of immediate and eager interest.

"Yes. He talks to me and he thought it might be a good idea to learn about the Seidh, so I could better understand what happened the night my parents died."

"How does he know so much about that night?" Fanndis retorted, narrowing her eyes.

"Well, I don't really know, but he said that he does and that he knows I'm interested in learning magic."

"Are you?" Fanndis asked.

Soryn did not answer right away. He thought for a moment about what he should say. He could tell from her tone and questions that she was as distrustful of Ulla as Arna was. Still, he wanted to know about the Seidh, if only to unravel the mystery of the night that put him in the tower.

"Yes, but I'm not interested just because Ulla suggested it. I've always been interested in magic," Soryn confessed. He felt the truth would go further with her than falsehoods.

"The Seidh is not just about altering perceptions. It's also about depth of character, discipline, commitment. As well, one must have a biological aptitude for it." She raised an eyebrow.

"Yreth, right? The hormone that lets you use magic?" Soryn hoped she would tell him more.

"Yes, as a matter of fact. Does your little friend want to learn magic as well? She's been overly quiet."

Arna was startled when Fanndis brought the topic of the conversation to rest on her. She looked pleadingly at Soryn before saying, "I…uh…well…I just wanted to come along and help Lord Maslyn." Arna looked downward in the trained servants' way.

"Oh, come now, child. We're all friends here. I do not intend either of you harm. In fact, I am quite intrigued by your visit. You would do well to tell me what you're up to. I may be able to help." Fanndis smiled, then, and Arna felt her heart melting at the sight.

The girl felt some strange kinship with this woman, though she knew they were not related and that they had never met. She knew she should tell Fanndis the truth.

"I want to learn the Seidh. I have always dreamt about learning it, just as Lord Maslyn has."

Again, the old woman smiled at Arna's words. It had been quite a long time since children were in the cottage. Stigg had been a grown man for many years now. Fanndis decided that, for the time being, they should take a break from their conversation. Fanndis offered everyone hot tea from the kettle that hung over the fire in the hearth.

"Yes, please," they both said, graciously.

She poured the steaming liquid with poise that belied her years. Arna felt the older woman had some youthful spirit that enabled her to be so vivacious and blunt in her advancing age. Fanndis caught the girl staring at her and smiled kindly in return. She knew the girl was fascinated with her. The interest flattered the woman, but it also amused her. She had, apparently, been made up to be quite a powerful woman in their eyes. Fanndis wondered more and more about "Ulla" and how he knew about her.

Everyone sipped their tea in silence. Soryn was enchanted by the sounds of the forest outside the cottage and with the company inside it. He wondered where Stigg had gone until he heard the sound of wood chopping again a few minutes later. He wondered why Fanndis did not offer her son tea as well. There was a comfortable sense of ease in this woman's house. Soryn was far more tranquil here than in his tower room or Ulla's study. It felt almost like home—as though it would be a shame to leave. This thought made him remember that they did not know how long it had been since they left.

"Fanndis, do you happen to know the time?" Soryn asked.

Her eyes gazed above Soryn's head. He followed her gaze and saw a small clock hanging next to one of the windows. It was 10:45 in the morning. The children knew they would have to leave soon. Arna looked crestfallen and Soryn was glum as well.

"Whatever's the matter with you two? Is the time that saddening? You may stay as long as you like," she said.

"It's just that…" Soryn did not really know how to tell her that no one knew he had escaped from the tower. More than that, he realized she had not even asked him how he had gotten out. He chose, again, to tell the truth. If she had known his mother, he felt he could trust her. He *had* to.

"I escaped the tower using another secret passage leading down from the fireplace in my room. No one but Arna and Ulla know about me being able to leave my room when I like. The thing is, we have to make sure we get our meals at regular times and my manservant, Jori, brings the paperwork I need to sign after we've had our noon meal. Also, Father Kimbli will come to see me this afternoon."

"I see," Fanndis replied.

Arna was sad that it was time to leave and stayed quiet.

"You can come back and visit me anytime, you know," the snow woman said, attempting to encourage the two of them. "I won't give away your secret."

"Could we, really?" Soryn beamed with excitement. "May we come back this evening?"

She thought for a moment. The lad had mentioned the name, "Jori". Fanndis wondered if it was the same Jori who had served the Maslyn before the incident. If it was, he was a good man—very trustworthy—one who would most likely keep the boy's secret. However, she could always arrange for more time with the children than just spare moments in the morning and evening. It was impressive that Soryn had escaped when he was only twelve. She had anticipated it would have taken longer for him to find the secret passages she had made so many years before. Perhaps she had not hidden them as well as she had supposed. Still, she was wary of this Ulla character. Fanndis wanted to know who he was. He certainly had no business in her old study.

"You may return this evening, but I have some matters that I will need to attend to, so plan on staying in your room until I can send a message to you." Fanndis stood to see them off.

They left, promising to return after they heard from her. She walked with them to the edge of the woods and watched them enter the bottom door of the tower without the guards seeing. A plan formed in her mind. If it didn't work, she would have to provide them with better protection from the watching eyes of the castle guards. Fanndis found it hard to quell her excitement. She had hoped for many years that there would be another chance to help the Maslyn family. The first time around, disaster had ensued and she was exiled to the forest by Steward Asmund. Perhaps her "meddling", as Asmund had called it, could now help set things right.

Her steps crunched through the snow back to her cottage and, instead of entering the front door, went around to the back where her son was working. Stigg had his overcoat off, and sweat soaked through his shirt despite the fact that the temperature remained below freezing. Fanndis admired how hard he worked at every task. She did not wish to disturb him, but it was necessary this time.

"Stigg!" She raised her voice just enough that she could get his attention without startling him.

He turned and rested the axe on the stump he used to station the wood blocks. "Mmm?" he asked, wiping the sweat from his forehead with a cloth that hung from his back pocket.

"Lord Maslyn has found our passages in the tower. He left through the outer door passage and has even been to my study. But some sort of creature now lives there who has been talking to the boy about the Seidh."

"What sort of creature?" Stigg was as surprised as his mother that something was living in the study they had once used for their work.

"A pig, apparently. One named 'Ulla'. Have you heard that name before?" Fanndis queried, frowning.

Stigg thought long and hard about it. Eira, the cat, wound herself round his legs while he pondered it. He shook his head. "I haven't heard a name like that. What about you, Eira?"

He leaned down to scratch the feline's tufted back. She meowed and shook her head. Though Eira understood human speech perfectly well, she preferred not to converse with people. At her negative reply, Stigg smirked. He was distrustful of this "Ulla" creature, especially since it had taken up residence in their *very* secret passageways.

"I think it is time to peacefully end our exile. Saddle my horse, if you please. I think I'll be going to pay Father Kimbli a visit before the children come back," Fanndis told him.

113

She went indoors to change into warmer clothes. By the time she came through the back door of the cottage, her son had saddled her longhaired horse, Liv. Stigg helped her up and secured her stirrups.

"Be careful. People in the village may not be happy to see you." Stigg warned.

"Well, I suppose I'll find out one way or another, though I'll try to be secretive. I'll return as soon as I can." Fanndis clicked her heels on Liv's sides and the horse trotted obediently into the woods.

Fanndis was an expert at navigating the snow-covered brambles, soil, and roots of the woods. It took her only a few minutes to make it through the tree line and into the field behind the castle walls. She gave the great stone edifice a wide berth and entered the village streets without attracting the guards' attention.

She stared at a village she had not visited for six years and wondered how all their lives would change once she accomplished her goal. Shaking off any apprehension (for, in her opinion, she was too old for such nonsense), she nudged Liv forward towards the village church. Most of the townsfolk failed to notice her as she rode through the streets. Others simply stared at the gorgeous horse she rode—blonde horses were rare in their country. When she reached the churchyard, she dismounted and stared at the great red doors before her. Exhaling heavily, she led Liv to the hitching post by the gate and prayed that her trip would not be fruitless.

Chapter Seven

In which Fanndis arranges a meeting...

She was careful not to let her cloak drag the stones in the church. Seeing a few faithful parishioners kneeling in prayer, she made sure her footsteps were soundless. To her left, a young priest walked quietly with a village merchant that Fanndis had once traded with. Fanndis kept her hood over her head and walked over. She didn't want to disturb them, but she needed to find out where Father Kimbli was.

"Excuse me, Father," she whispered.

The young priest turned in surprise at her beckoning.

"Yes, my lady? Is there anything I can help you with?"

"I was wondering if I could speak with Father Kimbli about a private matter," she quietly asked.

"He's counseling someone at this moment, my lady. He should be finished soon. Have a seat over there, if you like. If you need anything else, please let me know."

Though she was a Seidh woman, Fanndis had always felt welcomed by the village priests. She sat where the young man had instructed her and could hear the soft murmurs of Father Kimbli's voice guiding the parishioner through their conversation. The church hadn't changed. Stained glass windows depicted the colonization of Niflheim and scenes of the first settlers arriving in New Kristiansand. Vaulted ceilings towered above her and the smoke from the incense and candles mingled with dying light. She observed women and men praying. Being among the people of the village brought a smile to her lips. Stigg was wonderful company, but it grew rather dull being confined to the forest for six years. Still, she reminded herself that she had not been locked in a tower as the young Maslyn had.

115

Fanndis broke off her thoughts when she heard the office door opening and watched a middle-aged man leave. After a minute or two, Father Kimbli came to the doorway and waved at the man he had been counseling. Turning his head, he caught sight of her. The old man jumped a bit. His mouth hung open and his eyes widened in surprise.

"Hello, Kimbli," Fanndis greeted.

She could not help smiling with her words. Kimbli drew a sharp intake of breath and grinned.

"Fanndis, is it really you? It has been so long…I thought I'd never hear your voice again. How are you?" Kimbli stammered.

"I'm well. I'm getting tired of the lonely woods, though. I think it is high time I caused a stir, don't you?" She hoped he would understand the implications of her comment.

"Let's talk in my office," he said, ushering her inside. "What's happened, Fanndis?" Kimbli knew she'd never leave the woods without something extraordinary to tell him.

"He's out of the tower. Soryn found my secret passages. Everything we had hoped for is coming to pass—just a little earlier than we figured, old friend."

"I knew he would discover them, eventually. Jori certainly doesn't know about the passages, but after all those days I spent with you in that study, I knew the boy would find them sooner or later. I'm glad of it. It was painful for me to see him suffering all alone." Kimbli bowed his head and prayed a prayer of thanks.

"Many things have happened in the boy's last week. He's made a friend. I believe she is a serving girl. Her name is 'Arna'. Soryn is quite taken with her, I think, and she with him."

"Oh, really? I've only heard of a serving girl named 'Jordis'. Perhaps she prefers 'Arna', for some reason. I'm happy that he has some company. I've never been able to help him open up or share his thoughts. I'm just a kind, senile old man to him," Kimbli chuckled.

"I'm sure you've been tremendously good company for the boy. You were always a good friend to me." Fanndis smiled.

A comfortable silence fell over them. It seemed as though six years had been only six days.

"What is it that you came to talk to me about, Fanndis?" Kimbli inquired.

"I want to know if you can help me arrange a small coup in the castle. It is time everyone knew that boy's potential and that he was openly accepted as the new Maslyn. The village seems to be doing fine without a village leader, but if only for Soryn's sake, they need to know he is ready to take command and make decisions for their welfare. He needs to meet with Governor Frey and transition into his mayoral role. A transition of that sort will obviously require him to undergo intense training, but I think time will run out if he isn't allowed to start now. That fool Asmund, has kept him locked away longer than was necessary. The monster that ran away the night of the fire hasn't been seen or heard from in years. The boy is no longer in danger. Will you help me convince everyone of this?"

"Of course, Fanndis. The village has been peaceful for several years now. I agree that the threat is gone. I will speak with Asmund about this, if you like."

"That would be grand. I'll have Stigg pay a visit to Jori. I think that Lord Maslyn should make his debut in the village no later than next Freya's Day. He has been hidden away for far too long and will be nervous. However, if he is to be anything like his father was, we've got to help him find his courage to step into the light as a leader."

"How can I contact you?" Kimbli asked.

"Don't you have that ratty old crow of yours? Have him send me a message." Fanndis had hoped to see Kimbli's pet bird, Aquinas, again. They had been quite fond of each other, back in the old days.

"Yes, he's still around here somewhere. I think I sent him off a few hours ago to forage. He eats all the time, as I'm sure you remember. I'll send him when we need to talk," Kimbli replied.

"I know you're supposed to visit with Lord Maslyn today, but do you think you could postpone your meeting until I can get this sorted?" Fanndis asked.

"Certainly."

Fanndis stood up and prepared to leave. Kimbli rose as well, saddened that their meeting had been so short. They both had much work to do if they were going to help Soryn gain his rightful place in the village. He watched the old woman put her hood back up and extended his hand.

"Come here, you old fool," Fanndis said, reaching to hug Kimbli. "It's good to be among friends again."

He smiled in return and nodded. Fanndis left the room, closing the door carefully so that she wouldn't startle the parishioners. Outside, she unhitched Liv from the post. Once she had mounted her horse, Fanndis clicked her tongue and they moved forward. There was one more visit she needed to make. The back roads south of the church meandered and zigzagged through cottages until she broke through and faced the frozen River Ingrid. Liv nimbly trotted across the ice and up the bank. Another cluster of cottages lay on that shore. They rode on snowy cobbled roads between thatched houses, which became increasingly elaborate and sturdy. Within minutes, she stared at the town's second, smaller castle, the home of Governor Frey. Guards met her at the castle gates and she politely announced that she had an appointment with the governor.

The guards bade her to wait and one went to confirm the appointment. Fanndis scheduled no such meeting, but she was sure that the governor would see her from his meeting room. The large glass window above the great front doors framed his body as he talked with several men. Fanndis watched from below and saw the guard interrupt the meeting and mention her arrival. Governor Frey peered out the window and Fanndis nodded when he saw her.

Returning to his post, the guard helped her dismount and then led Liv off to the stables. The second guard retrieved a housemaid to show Fanndis inside. She was a middle-aged woman sporting a sour expression. They said nothing to one another. Downtrodden and hunched, the servant opened the Governor's private office door for Fanndis and left her without comment. Fanndis raised her eyebrows at the woman's back as she walked away. "What a happy woman," she remarked to herself.

When Fanndis walked into the office, Governor Frey sat in his straight-backed chair with a furrowed brow, accompanied by pursed lips.

"What are you doing here, Fanndis?" he asked, massaging his temples. "Shouldn't you be out in your forest thatching the roof or something?"

"Well, it's lovely to see you, too, Frey. And here I was, thinking you wouldn't be excited to see me. I'm glad I was wrong. To what do I owe this cheerfulness?" Fanndis loved to push the politician's buttons.

"Humph. You're here, might as well tell me what is important enough to interrupt my exports meeting," he scowled and stared at his bookshelf.

Fanndis cackled, "I'm here because I'm tired of staying out of the village and because it's high time you ordered that coward Asmund to let Lord Maslyn out of his tower. Things have gone on long enough."

Frey just stared at her.

Fanndis waited a couple of minutes and then prompted him, "Well? What have you to say about it?"

"You mean Asmund hasn't let him out after all this time?" Frey asked.

Fanndis realized the governor's surprise was entirely genuine and was dumbfounded.

"You didn't know?!" she gaped.

"No, I did not. I don't make a habit of personally checking in on every noble in the country. His papers were signed with the Maslyn's seal and I've received them regularly. I know that Asmund would never be allowed to touch the seal, let alone use it falsely, so I assumed that the boy was protected until the threat had passed and was then let out. Was that not the agreement?" Frey knew he would soon have a word with the Maslyn's steward.

"It *was* the agreement. Those of us who were closest to the family, however, knew that the immensity of the threat merited keeping him in the tower for several years. Several years, however, turned into a permanent arrangement, from what my trusted sources tell me. Apparently, Asmund had an easier time dealing with the boy when he did not have to talk to him face to face. I think the stingy miser has been having his fun pretending to be the Maslyn, himself. I know that Asmund's not a wicked man, but he is certainly both naïve and ambitious." Fanndis frowned. The fact that Governor Frey knew nothing about Soryn's extended "protection" did not encourage her.

"Step out there and tell my servant, Mika, to saddle my horse at once. This ends tonight. That boy is the Maslyn of the village, such as it is. He cannot be permanently locked away like some criminal. Nothing that happened that night was *his* fault. I can't believe this! Asmund shall be dealt with immediately," Frey shouted. He stood up and wrenched his cloak from the back of his chair.

Fanndis assumed that Mika was the woman who had shown her the way to the office. She glimpsed outside the door and sure enough, the dour, plump lady stood there, shoulders slouched forward. Fanndis wished she would smile or at least do something to improve her unfortunate appearance.

"Excuse me, madam, but the Governor needs his horse saddled immediately." Fanndis grinned in an encouraging fashion, but Mika just grunted and left.

Fanndis shrugged and turned to see Frey walking up towards the door. She moved out of the way for him in deference, though she vividly remembered their days as children, when they refused to step aside for each other in any event. They usually ended up stuck in a doorframe, somewhere, after trying to fight the other to get through first.

Frey stomped down the hallway, clearly angry. Fanndis was thankful that his anger was not directed at her. She followed, laughing inwardly. Things were working out much easier than she had anticipated. Apparently, they would have the boy freed within a few hours. This would allow him to make decisions as the head of the castle and the village. She knew he was not ready for such a responsibility. Asmund was not fit to act as a mentor. It would have to be someone else; Kimbli, perhaps. He was the only one who knew enough about the family and about running the village to help the boy. She hoped that the church elders would release him to do so. Fanndis knew she was leaping ahead again. For now, she needed to calm down and see where Frey's tirade would lead.

He threw open the front doors. Guards and servants scrambled around him to get out of his way. They knew what he was like in his black moods. One of the grooms from the stables held the reins to Frey's grey longhair, tremors of nervousness causing his hand to shake. The beast was a magnificent animal—several hands taller than Fanndis' Liv. Frey mounted and waited for Fanndis' horse to be brought out. When she was settled, they both set off together at a gallop towards the Maslyn's castle. They rode in an awkward silence. Talking with people other than Stigg had brought on a sort of giddiness. Frey's fuming silence was disappointing. She had hoped for more conversation from her childhood friend.

Frey's grey hair whipped in the wind, distracting Fanndis. Her aging heart still ached at the thought that, many years ago, they might have been married. She had been too stubborn and willful to answer his proposal favorably. For years, she regretted the decision. Some of his harsh behavior might be due, in part, to her refusal of him years ago. Despite her pleas, Frey never took her back. In the end, she managed to find love. Stigg's father had been one of the fishermen in the village. He had been a kind man. He died at sea, poor soul. Fanndis realized she was brooding and shook off her thoughts, trying to pay attention to the matters at hand.

A dreary malaise overtook the two of them as they rode towards the Maslyn's castle. The sight of it was somewhat overwhelming. It was far larger than Governor Frey's own castle. Built several hundred years after the colonization ship landed on Niflheim, it was one of the oldest buildings in Oban. It had been designed as a communal shelter and fortress for the people of New Kristiansand. Years later, it became the home of the Maslyns—the village's leading family. Eventually the mayoral title itself became known as "the Maslyn". The Governor of Oban began living and working in New Kristiansand about fifty years ago. A separate house was set aside for the first governor so that the existing Maslyn line did not have to uproot and move out of their majestic ancestral home. Frey much preferred his own home to the Maslyn castle. In the twenty years he had reigned as Governor of Oban, he had made many improvements to it.

Fanndis thrust her chin high in the air as they neared the castle. The two of them entered through the gates and dismounted. Guards swarmed around the governor to attend to his horse and person.

Frey tersely declared, "I need to see Steward Asmund, if you please."

Fanndis said nothing. She kept her hood over her face and followed Frey when the guards opened the doors for them. Familiar scents and aromas filled her nostrils as she stepped into the castle. It had been six years since she had lived there. Everything was just as it had been and she did not need to look up to know where Asmund's office was located. She knew without being told that the steward would have taken over the previous Lord Maslyn's private office in order to conduct village affairs. She smirked. It had been hard for her to accept Asmund as steward in the past, but the previous Lord and Lady Maslyn had been very fond of him—only God knew why.

A servant announced the governor's presence and Frey stormed into the study. Asmund, a thin waif of a man, sat behind the great pine desk with eyes as large as saucers.

"Why, G-Governor F-F-Frey, sir, how n-n-nice of you to drop in. What can I do for you?" Asmund sputtered, obviously startled by Frey's unscheduled visit.

Frey, a man of strong stature, loomed over the desktop and drummed his fingers on the pine surface. One fist was stationed firmly on his left hip. Any fool would have been able to tell that he was furious.

"Do you mean to tell me that Lord Maslyn has been imprisoned in that infernal tower for six years? *Six years*!? This is an outrage, Asmund! You ought to be thrown in prison for this! The agreement was made years ago so that the boy would be freed when Fenris' threat had passed. Was that not the agreement?!" Frey's voice resounded loud enough that that entire wing of the castle had certainly heard.

"Y-yes, your honor..." Asmund sunk lower in the great chair upon which he sat.

"Why was he not freed? That beast hasn't been seen or heard from in at least three years! This is preposterous! Lord Maslyn should have been free to roam about after the first year had passed!" Frey took his right hand off the desk and paced as he spoke. "I am infuriated, Steward. You are no longer fit to be caretaker of this village's wellbeing. I am formally removing you from this post. You may seek employment elsewhere. We will find a *suitable* replacement immediately."

Asmund's face grew ghostly white and he was struck dumb in shame and shock. He had never intended harm to Lord Maslyn. He had just conveniently chosen to ignore the boy's existence, save for needing his signatures and seal on legal documents. Being the sniveling coward that he was, Asmund stood up, mustering what little dignity he could, and bowed to Governor Frey. On his way out, he paused and peered at Fanndis' cloaked figure. Peeking underneath the hood, he gasped.

"You!" he spat in disbelief. "What are *you* doing here?"

"I grew tired of living in those woods. Thanks to the governor, here, it looks like your edict is null and void. I truly wish you the best, Asmund. I don't think this job has agreed with your health. You seem pale..." Fanndis smiled mischievously.

Frey sighed and walked to the other side of the desk, collapsing in the chair with dramatic flair. He had been too harsh on Asmund— the coward was not a dangerous man, after all, just dimwitted and ambitious (a potent combination). Still, Lord Maslyn's rightful place was behind the desk where Frey now sat, not up in that drafty, frostbitten tower. He rubbed his forehead with his right hand.

"Fantastic...who will we get to replace him? I can't think of anyone who would know the family history well enough to be an adequate replacement for that idiot. What do you suggest Fanndis?" Frey looked up desperately.

"You're asking me? You actually care what I think on the matter?" She sounded more caustic than she intended.

"Yes. You are a very wise woman. Just think if you had gone against your wise judgment all those years ago, we would've gotten married. Imagine what a disaster *that* would have proved to be. Your judgment is sound and I trust you. Who would you appoint as a suitable replacement?" Frey asked, seriously.

Fanndis had prepared her answer long before. "Father Kimbli. He has been the closest friend to this family for several generations. It would be unthinkable to appoint anyone else. He already counsels the boy each week, and Soryn trusts him. There can be no one else, Frey."

The governor considered Fanndis' words carefully. It would not be too difficult to convince the church elders that Kimbli should be the advisor for the boy. It would be hard to convince *Kimbli* of it, however. Frey grimaced and rubbed his forehead with his fingers.

"Will you talk to Kimbli? I'll smooth things over with the church elders if it becomes an issue. Once I explain the situation to them, they should not be difficult to convince. Are you certain Kimbli has kept the boy's imprisonment a secret from the other priests?"

"I'm not sure if he has or not. I think that, before we do anything else, we should find Jori and let that boy out of the tower. I was going to send my son to talk to the manservant, but things have progressed more quickly than I imagined. I should have known I could count on you to act with haste. Forgive my disbelief. Thank you, Frey." Fanndis turned to leave in search of the manservant.

"Fanndis..." Frey began.

She paused. "Yes?"

"I'm sorry you've lived out there alone all these years. I should have protested when they banished you. I shouldn't have let them do it. It was all so chaotic after the fire. I didn't know who to trust. I'm sorry," he said.

Frey's eyes were honest and he gazed at her with an expression that held too much emotion to be merely apologetic.

"It's alright, Frey, truly. You're helping now, and that is what's important. Besides, I've not been alone. Stigg has been with me the entire time, bless him. I expect he's been the lonely one with only his persnickety old mother for company," Fanndis jovially replied.

Governor Frey stood up and followed her out the door. Since he had set foot into this quagmire, he might as well see it through to the end. Fanndis appeared to know where she was going and he tagged along like a faithful dog. He was reminded of what had almost become their engagement and how they would have spent their entire lives quarreling if they had married. He knew that they were better off as comrades in arms. This way, they were entitled to be at each others' throats while remaining firm friends. Still, they were getting along quite well today.

They came to a large oak door. He had not paid attention enough to the passageways they had taken to know where in the castle they were. Fanndis tried the handle to no avail.

"I knew it would be locked. I just thought I'd try it, just in case," she admitted.

Fanndis calmed her nerves and commanded her mind to empty. Small pinpricks of sensation began to work their way up through her core and into her right arm. It had been a while since she had used the Seidh for breaking and entering, but she figured the situation called for that sort of thing. Placing her tingling hand on the handle, she formed the mental command in her mind. Through her body, the yreth in her blood danced and the shout in her mind ordered, "Open!"

This time, when she pushed down on the handle, the door opened. Frey had seen Fanndis work spells and such before, but having been away from such displays for so long, he was taken aback when the door swung inward. Icy air bombarded them as they entered the passage to Soryn's tower room. They did not hear any talking or sounds of any kind as they walked over the stones, their footsteps loudly ringing in their ears. They climbed up the few stairs leading into the bedroom, and then stood in the doorway. The two children stopped eating their lunch and stared at them in surprise and confusion.

"Well, I see we've come too late for the noon meal. Shall we go for a stroll in the fresh air instead?" Fanndis offered cheerily.

Chapter Eight

In which arrangements are made…

When Arna and Soryn returned from Fanndis' cabin, they spent a while in Ulla's study to let him know they had found the old snow woman. He asked how the meeting had gone and they replied that they would be returning during the afternoon. After spending nearly an hour or so with the pig, they returned to the tower room above. During their lunch, they discussed their surprise at Fanndis' mention of Soryn's mother. They also talked about their interest in the cottage and how comfortable they felt there.

"I wonder if she'll really teach us the Seidh," Arna mused, during their meal.

"I don't know. Maybe she'll tell us more about the night of the fire," Soryn whispered.

Arna shivered in the drafty room. They had not had time to make a fire when they arrived. Sitting quietly for a little while, they were startled when Ulla's voice seeped into their minds.

I think you may want to stop eating. You have two visitors coming down the hallway…

Ulla said no more and Soryn's and Arna's bodies tensed. They listened intently to the footsteps moving over the stones of the passageway. Silence and utter stillness overcame the children when they saw Fanndis come into the room with an old man dressed in fine clothing. The woman smiled kindly at them as she had in the cottage and said, "Well, I see we've come too late for the noon meal. Shall we go for a stroll in the fresh air instead?"

The man behind her said nothing. Instead, he pulled his cloak more tightly about himself.

"Fanndis…what are you doing here? How were you able to come?" Lord Maslyn was bewildered by her strange entrance into the tower.

"I was as tired of exile as you were of being stuck in the tower. Why not gain freedom for us both at once?" She sat down in one of the chairs at the long table.

"Who gave you the key to the tower?" the boy asked.

"No one— I let myself in," the old woman replied.

"You let yourself in?" Soryn repeated.

"With the Seidh. It's not difficult to command a door to open."

Arna stared at the old man. She knew it was Governor Frey and could not fathom what he was doing with Fanndis. Arna saw him looking at Lord Maslyn with what she perceived to be both kindness and pity.

"You've been living in *here* all these years, Lord Maslyn?" Frey asked as he looked about the stony prison. He shivered even in his heavy clothing. "It's abominable…and *freezing*!" the old man added.

"Yes. It's been…interesting," Soryn laughed, trying to keep the mood light despite his confusion.

"I am truly sorry that you have had to endure this situation. It was only brought to my attention this morning by your benefactress here. I was under the impression that you had been released many years ago. I received your papers—signed with your seal—and I assumed…Please forgive me." Governor Frey bowed his head to Soryn and continued, "Let me assure you that from this day forward, you are free to move about the castle and the village at will. You need not remain in this tower any longer. Your father had exquisite quarters in the main castle that you can be moved into immediately, if you wish."

Soryn's mind had trouble processing the stranger's words. He still had no idea who the old man was, but Soryn was sure he had some estimable power. Suddenly it struck him—*Governor Frey*!

Soryn promptly responded, "Thank you very much, Governor."

The boy thought he should make some gesture, so he stood up from his chair and bowed before the man. Soryn saw Fanndis smile when he righted himself.

Governor Frey sat at the table next to Fanndis and looked at Arna. "I do not believe we have been introduced, my dear. What is your name?"

Arna blushed and stood up to curtsey as she gave her name. "It's Jordis, sir, but I prefer to be called 'Arna,', if you please."

"Well, Arna, it is a pleasure to meet you. May I ask what your connection is to Lord Maslyn?" He smiled and hoped his words did not sound overly suspicious.

"I am his personal assistant. I fetch his noon day meal and his dinner, take care of his laundry and cleaning, and help with paperwork." She kept her eyes downcast as she replied, out of respect.

"I see. Well, from now on, I expect you won't have to act alone in your duties. Once he is out of the tower, he'll have the entire household at his service," Governor Frey said.

He liked the girl's countenance. She seemed to enjoy her post. He suspected that Arna and Soryn's relationship was one of friendship, rather than merely master and servant.

Isn't it a shame that they came to your rescue after you've already found a way out yourself?

Ulla's voice gave Soryn pause.

I don't know much about the governor. Fanndis is the one you want to help you. Ensure that you remain on her good side. As far as the governor is concerned, do as you wish, but I recommend remembering the importance of powerful allies.

Soryn, acknowledging the wisdom of Ulla's words, chose his next words carefully, "Governor Frey, Fanndis, I have been locked in this tower for six years. If I were to go down to the castle and take up my post as the Maslyn, I don't imagine that the house would take me seriously, let alone the village. I need to learn how to be the town's Maslyn before I take up the position. I would not want to let everyone down."

In truth, Soryn was troubled by his new freedom. He had wanted to continue, in the secrets of the passageways, learning about the Seidh. It did not seem terribly attractive to be out in the open and responsible for an entire town—especially without any training. He fought hard to hold back tears. For some reason, he had trouble controlling the emotions welling up within. The older woman saw the change in expression on the young noble's face and suspected the boy's conflicting emotions.

"My lord, we don't expect you to begin your full duties immediately. In fact, we believe that you should have ample time to train for your position as the Maslyn. No one would expect you to start right away. You're only a boy. I do not speak for the governor, but I would propose something like the following: perhaps you should be given tutoring in the mornings and, in the afternoons you should be allowed some choice in your activities. You have been cooped up in this tower so long you need a chance for social interaction and the pursuit of leisurely activities that befit your station in the city. How would you feel about that arrangement?" Fanndis' words seemed sincere and encouraging.

Soryn was reminded of how much he liked her. The young master cleared his throat and looked at Arna. She appeared to be as overwhelmed as he was by the sudden change of events. Soryn was at a loss for words. Fanndis' suggestion seemed ideal. Since he had been locked in the tower, he had no idea what was expected of him as a noble and the Maslyn of New Kristiansand. Even though he held no real affection for his title, he owed it to his family to be the best leader he could. He also longed for interaction with other people. Deep down, he knew he desired to learn the Seidh and discover its role in the events of the night his family died. Fanndis' arrangement would allow him to do all the things he wanted to do. In his heart, he silently thanked the old snow woman.

He mustered what courage he could and tried to sound dignified as he said, "I think those terms are agreeable."

Arna smiled at him. Though she knew they would still use the secret passageways, it would be nice to know that Soryn could walk freely. Governor Frey's fidgeting caught her attention. He seemed overly nervous. She remembered her servant's training and asked, "Governor Frey, is there anything that I can do for you? Would you like anything to eat or drink?"

He looked up in surprise, "Why, no thank you, young lady. I'm afraid I must attend to some business concerning the stewardship position of this castle. Because Lord Maslyn is still unable to fully inherit his duties at present, we will need a suitable replacement for Asmund."

Soryn remembered that the steward had worked with his father when he was young. Lord Maslyn suspected that Asmund was the reason he had been in the tower for so long. If that was the case, he was glad that Asmund was going to be replaced. Governor Frey stood, and everyone in the small tower room rose out of respect. He promised Lord Maslyn that they would speak again soon and left without further comment. Fanndis turned to the two children and smiled.

Once Governor Frey was gone, Lord Maslyn blurted out, "What in the world did you do, Fanndis?"

She shrugged and said, "I thought you would have a better position if I took action immediately. I'm sure it would have been enjoyable for you to go traipsing around in secret, but this will allow you far more freedom and less heartache."

The boy admitted that she was probably right. Asmund might have kept him in the tower indefinitely. A comfortable silence settled over the three of them and it was only after several minutes that Lord Maslyn began to wonder why Ulla was so unusually quiet. After that thought, he waited for the pig to reply with some cynical comment, but none came. He found this very odd, indeed.

Soryn offered, impulsively, "Fanndis, would you like to visit the study or see the other passage?"

The old woman was not surprised by his offer. She was keenly aware of how hard the animal below was trying to communicate with the children; something that she was not about to let him do in her presence. It took quite a bit of her mental willpower to block his messages to Lord Maslyn and Arna. The Seidh was a powerful tool, but she knew she would later feel drained by the amount of effort she was expending. It was obvious that the creature was highly intelligent and crafty. She wanted to meet him in person.

"That would be splendid, Soryn. Still, you don't want to leave and explore the castle a bit first? Father Kimbli won't be coming today, since you're officially free of the tower. He'll visit soon." Fanndis smiled.

"No, I think I'd like you to meet Ulla before we go anywhere else. He's been feeling left out the last few days and I want him to know how thankful to him I am for his help." Soryn stood up and Arna followed his lead.

The old woman laughed inwardly when the children were showing her the secret latches to the passageways. She had designed and created them so long ago that it seemed like returning home after many years away. She assured the children that she would be fine following them down. When Soryn and Arna had already disappeared down the stair to the study, she eyed the ornate desk on the wall to the left of the fireplace. It had been Stigg's desk when they lived in the tower. Smiling and remembering Stigg's younger years, Fanndis bent down and entered the passage. The staircase felt so familiar to her, though it had been ages since she had been down to her study. She wondered what sort of mess the animal down below had created.

The darkness did not bother Fanndis. She rather liked the close feelings the walls gave her as they continued deeper down the tower steps. The familiar orange glow from her sun spire flooded her heart with nostalgia and longing, even though her cottage suited her tastes far more than the frigid stone. She caught up to the young ones easily and they soon were at the bottom of the tunnel. The three of them walked up the few steps into the study together.

The black pig rested on the table in the center of the room. The air about him was strange…as though all the color had been absorbed and only darkness remained, shrouding him. Fanndis' wariness of the animal grew exponentially. He threateningly peered at her with eyes as black as jet. Soryn and Arna were both taken aback by his malicious appearance. They still heard nothing from him in their minds. Suddenly, Arna had the idea that Fanndis might have blocked his attempts to talk to them.

She asked, "Fanndis? Is he trying to speak to us right now?" Arna was impressed by the old woman's power if her suspicious were true.

The old snow woman's eyes never left those of the animal's when she replied, "Yes. He's quite put out that I'm not allowing it."

Ulla let out an unnatural growl—one that Soryn could not imagine coming from a real pig. Arna shivered. Fanndis simply held her resolve and steeled her hold on the pig's mind.

"I want you to know who the master is here, Ulla. I'll not have you talking to the children until I know for certain you mean them no harm," Fanndis declared. Meanwhile, Ulla was desperately pleading with her.

Why would you think I mean them harm? Ulla spat.

You knew about me. You want him to learn the Seidh…I've never seen you before. Clearly you are not what you seem and I don't trust you, Fanndis replied mentally.

Ulla responded, *I have only ever wanted to help the boy—I referred him to you, didn't I? As you are aware, animals know much about the connections between humans in the villages. I heard about you through two friends of mine—cats, if you must know. The boy wanted to learn the Seidh and escape. I thought I'd help him do both.*

133

How can I be certain that what you say is true? The woman raised an eyebrow.

Because, in return for your trust, I will tell you my darkest secret.

Oh? Fanndis thought she knew his secret already, but she wanted to hear him admit it.

Arna and Soryn kept quiet, as they could tell that the others were engaged in some sort of mental battle, which could be perceived by only the occasional, tiny changes in expression by the combatants. Fanndis stood perfectly still and Ulla menacingly poised on his four legs, making vicious grunts at irregular intervals. Soryn wished he could hear what they were talking about.

Are you still listening, old woman?

What's your secret, Ulla? Fanndis demanded.

I'm not an animal at all. I am human.

Fanndis had been suspicious before about the pig. His abilities to converse with humans were far more advanced than an ordinary beast. He could read minds—but not hers. She kept hers well guarded. His interest in the Maslyn's life was very unsettling. She smirked in response to his admission.

I see, she said.

You see? *That's all you have to say?* Ulla was already furious with the woman. He had hoped Fanndis would turn him human again or at least teach Soryn to, but now he knew this woman would not help him willingly. He had to make her trust him.

How did you come to be in my study, Ulla?

That is my business. I think you should release your barrier so that we may all speak freely. The pig desperately wanted the topic to move away from him.

Very well. You and I will chat again later.

With that final remark to the pig, she lifted her mental barrier from the children's minds and relaxed. It was as though a coil had been released from around her head. The tingling sensation receded and she felt wholly herself again, albeit tired.

Soryn and Arna could tell something had changed. Ulla immediately spoke to them.

This woman is a master practitioner of the Seidh. You would be privileged to be under her tutelage, Ulla said, truthfully. Though he did not like Fanndis, he knew she was an expert with magic.

The children were relieved that they were able to converse with the pig again. Ulla and the woman were clearly not on good terms with one another. Soryn did not know what to say to the pig now that he was free to leave whenever he wished.

"Ulla, I wanted to come down and thank you for all your help in freeing me from the tower. We were able to find Fanndis because of you. Thanks to her, I'm now free to leave the castle as I please. I am going to train for my position as the Maslyn of New Kristiansand. Thanks to you, my life is about to begin." Soryn said, hoping it would be enough.

The pig jerked his head to look away from the three humans in the room and smirked. *It was a pleasure. I'm glad I was useful.*

Arna grew antsy—the day's events were overwhelming. She put a hand to her forehead and leaned against the table. Soryn, keenly aware of her movements, impulsively put an arm around her shoulder.

"Are you alright?" he asked, blushing at the contact.

"Yes, it's just been a full day. I think I'd like to get some fresh air. What do you think, Fanndis? Would you like to come along? Ulla?" she replied, sounding tired.

"That would be lovely, dear. Shall we retire to my cottage in the woods?" Fanndis offered.

"That sounds wonderful. What do you think, Soryn?" Arna asked.

"A walk would be nice. I'd like to talk to Stigg, if he's at the cottage. Ulla, would you like to get out of this study and enjoy the outdoors with us?" Soryn hoped the pig would say yes.

No, thank you. I'll stay down here and sulk, if you don't mind.

"Ulla…" Soryn groaned.

Enjoy your day. I'll be here, should anyone ever want to talk to me again.

With that, Ulla hopped from the table to the counter running along the back wall and then onto the top shelf, where he slept. Within seconds, he was as still as stone. Soryn sighed. He wondered just what had passed between the older woman and the animal.

The two young ones turned to head back up the stairs, but Fanndis was feeling along the wall to the right of the sun spire. Her movements caught Lord Maslyn's attention and he asked her, "Fanndis, what are you doing?"

"I'm sure there was a shortcut here, I seem to remember...yes! That's the one!" Her indiscriminate ramblings led to her pushing on a stone towards the corner of the wall, causing a loud scraping noise. Before their eyes, part of the wall began to push itself back. Fanndis used all her strength to move it aside to reveal a doorway.

The children were dumbfounded to see the wooden door that led to the field behind the castle. Whoever had created the passages had connected those two staircases. Not for the first time, Soryn admired the creator of all the hidden secrets in the tower. Then a thought struck him. He felt foolish for not recognizing it before.

"Fanndis," Soryn asked, "Do you know who created these secret stairways in the tower?"

Arna, wanting to know as well, gazed up at the Seidh woman. Fanndis was quiet until they had opened the great door and began to climb out of the hole. She smiled and chuckled before she said, "Stigg and I did, long ago." She looked up at the birds overhead, grinning at their flight.

Soryn asked, "How?"

"It took hard work, the Seidh, and time—from when Stigg was ten years old to his fifteenth year. The study was completed soon after the first passage and we were able to use that for our work when we needed a break from construction. The secret study and exit were actually your father's idea. He thought it would be an excellent hiding place for the family, should they ever be threatened by an enemy." Fanndis grew pensive as she continued, "I suppose that, in the end, I was unable to help them. Secret stairways are of no use when the enemy already knows the castle."

The three of them were quiet as they walked towards the forest. Snow shone brightly in the suns' light. Each one shielded their eyes. The field they walked through was like a great mirror reflecting the sky's brilliance. It took Soryn's mind off of Fanndis' words. He turned back to look at the castle and was startled to see a line of guards on the parapet that led from the tower to the castle. They were holding their swords aloft to the sky in what he imagined to be a salute. He squinted at the tree line and saw nothing that would illicit such behavior. When he turned back to his companions, he was struck with an indescribable emotion.

Fanndis and Arna were glancing at him with teary smiles on their faces. He cocked his head to the side in confusion and then looked back at the guards. Then it hit him. Fanndis confirmed his thoughts,

"They're saluting you, Lord Maslyn."

He stood up a little straighter. He did not know much about being the Maslyn of New Kristiansand, but now, for the first time in his life, he felt like it. He bowed to the guards and, when he straightened up, saw that they were all bowing in return. Small tears formed at the corner of the boy's eyes. He had never felt respected before. The sensation, wholly new and strange, was almost more than he could bear.

He turned and led the way to the forest, attempting to hide his tears. It wouldn't do to appear weak, especially now. Arna's hand gently slipped inside his and he looked at her before he could hide his face. She was smiling at him and a small tear rolled down her own cheek.

"It's alright, Bialas. We have all been waiting for the day you would walk out in freedom. It's alright," she promised.

Soryn did not reply, but squeezed her hand instead. They navigated through the snow-covered forest in silence. When they were closer to the cottage, they heard sounds of Stigg's work in the clearing, shoveling the snow away from the cottage's foundations. He looked up, saying nothing when they came nearer.

"Stigg," Fanndis chided him, "Come on inside and take a break before you work yourself to death."

Without a reply, he set down his shovel, took a cloth out of his trouser pocket, and wiped the sweat from his forehead. He followed the children into the house. Once inside, Fanndis and the children sat around the fire. Stigg disappeared into one of the rooms branching off the center. Fanndis laughed under her breath.

"Don't mind him. He's not a talker, if you'll remember." She stoked the fire as she had that morning when the children visited.

Arna and Soryn were deeply intrigued by Fanndis' silent son. They wondered what he was like, why he was so quiet, and why he had never gone off into the world. He looked like he was in his twenties at least. Stigg returned to the room, dressed in a simple tunic and trousers. His face was washed, his hair combed, and he wore different shoes—clean ones. He sat on the hearth near the fire and leaned back against the stones, hands behind his head in a relaxed posture.

"Good morning," Arna muttered, her heart pounding in her chest.

He nodded with a small, "Mmfph."

"*Stigg*…you can do better than that, for heaven's sake." Fanndis frowned.

He glared at his mother, sat up, and cleared his throat before he mumbled, "Good morning…"

"There, that wasn't so hard now, was it? It won't kill you to speak once in a while." Fanndis patted him on the knee in a way that Stigg felt was keenly patronizing. Still, he knew his mother meant no harm and he tried his best to appear pleasant. He was not fond of speaking, and preferred to keep his mouth shut and listen. It was rare that he had anything he wanted to say.

The old woman stood up and asked Arna to follow her into the other room for a moment. Soryn was surprised that Fanndis would leave him alone with Stigg when the man hardly said or did anything social. He managed a smile at the man, but Stigg was gazing out the window behind Fanndis' chair. Fanndis and Arna walked into the kitchen. It was a bright room with two windows, on opposite walls, and an open door leading to the clearing behind the cottage. Arna shivered when she looked at the open door. She went to shut it, but Fanndis stopped her.

"Keep it open for Eira, dear. The cold is a test of will for a practitioner of the Seidh, you know. You must learn to dress warmly and steel your mind against the rest. That is something you will learn."

"Something *I* will learn?" Arna felt excitement welling up inside.

"Yes. I want your training to start immediately, but we'll need Lord Maslyn's formal permission for you to be dismissed from your castle duties. I sensed it the minute I saw you last night in the dark. You will be an exemplary practitioner. Your training must start today."

Arna gasped when she understood that it was Fanndis they had seen with the lantern the night before. Everything that she and Soryn had hoped for had more or less happened within a twenty-four hour period. It was all a bit overwhelming.

"What about Lord Maslyn? Won't he learn the Seidh as well?" Arna questioned.

"If what I can sense about him is true, he will not have the yreth necessary in his body to support magic. I can't be sure until he is given the test, but I'm not frequently wrong about such things. One practitioner can recognize another, even if they are untrained and unskilled. That is how I know *you* will become a great one," Fanndis explained.

Arna felt an ambitious fire spring up within her. She hoped with all her heart that Fanndis' words were true and that she would be a tremendously powerful Seidh woman. Arna remembered well from many years ago how Great-Granny Arna would walk off into the night when the full moons would appear together in the night sky. Sometimes, Arna followed her and would watch her sitting before a fire, entranced by some invisible visage. She often heard her repeating prayers in the same breaths as she would beseech the natural world for answers to her questions. Arna wanted to experience that world. Fanndis could show her.

"Will I ever get to see Lord Maslyn again?" Arna whispered, without thinking.

The old snow woman smiled and laid an aging hand on the girl's shoulders. "Just because I can't teach him the Seidh does not mean there is nothing he can learn from our way of life in the woods. Since the boy has been locked up there for so long, it's obvious that he is sorely in need of physical exertion. I'm sure Stigg would help teach him the way of the forest—things he should know, not only as a Maslyn, but also as a person. You'll see him, perhaps daily. I do not imagine he'll want to stay away from you for very long, anyway."

Arna blushed. The girl had always liked the young noble ever since she had begun serving him alongside Jori. She hoped they would be able to remain friends now that Bialas' time would be filled with more responsibilities and commitments. A gust of cold wind blew in through the open door and Arna was reminded of the drafty tower her friend had been forced to live in for so long. She wondered if he would maintain that room as his residence or if he would move down to his late parents' quarters. Fanndis looked at her with an odd expression and Arna shook her head.

"Sorry. I got distracted and was thinking of many different things," she apologized.

"Quite alright...*this* time." Fanndis smiled before adding, in a more serious tone, "You will also have to learn to still your mind and to call things into focus instead of allowing your mind to run rampant. It's a difficult ability to learn, but one that will improve your magical skills."

The girl nodded, knowing that the woman had criticized her for good reason. Arna *wanted* to learn how to do those things. She wanted to become like Fanndis.

"Now then," Fanndis began again. "We need to perform the test and we must do it outside. It shouldn't take more than a minute or so."

The spry old woman bounded out the door without telling Arna anything further. The younger girl shrugged and walked out into the snow after her. Fanndis was fidgeting around with some small trinkets on top of an overturned barrel. Her hands were unwinding some twine and she turned towards Arna, holding a small piece with the thumb and forefinger of each hand. She held it horizontally aloft in front of her chest.

"This is the most ancient test used for knowing the yreth capabilities within someone's body. Yreth, as you know, allows you to perform the Seidh—to perform magic. You must still your mind, like I told you before. You must focus all your thoughts on one thing...*fire*. The easiest bit of magic to create in the entire world is fire. The twine is necessary the first time to help you concentrate your efforts in a single location. In the olden times, they did not use the twine. Because they had nothing to concentrate their power on, some extraordinary peoples' fire would engulf everyone around them. The twine gives us parameters that enable us to focus our energy in one location. Once you are focused enough, the yreth will begin to course through you. Watch as I perform this task. Learn what you can." Fanndis spoke solemnly and Arna felt chills rise on her arms—chills that had nothing to do with the frigid temperature.

Fanndis closed her eyes and stood exceptionally still. Arna kept her eyes on the twine the entire time. It took two or three seconds for the old woman to ignite the whole length of string. It continued to burn for several minutes while Arna watched in fascination. The girl noted that Fanndis had controlled the fire to the point that it burned around the flesh of her fingers, never touching them.

"Does the heat bother your hands?" Arna inquired.

"One learns to control the body's reaction to different elements. Fire can be friendly: generating heat, but not hot enough to damage skin. This fire is warm…go ahead and run your fingers through it."

A fluttery sensation bathed the girl's fingers as she ran her hands slowly through the fire. She had absolute trust in Fanndis' words and did not hesitate when the old woman asked her to touch the flames. It was, as she had promised, warm, but not hot. Red and orange hues danced within and Arna was astonished that the fire did not even singe the twine at all.

"Could this fire burn through the twine if you asked it to?" Arna queried, curiosity racing through her.

"Of course," Fanndis replied.

Before their eyes, the twine suddenly disintegrated and Fanndis quickly whipped her hands through the air to ward off any lingering sparks. All was silent for a few moments. Arna wanted, more than anything, to perform the task herself. She eyed the old woman with a hopeful expression.

"Take a piece of twine from the barrel. If you have the gift that I think you do, it should not take you more than a minute to perform this feat."

Arna held the twine aloft in front of her chest, stretched out between her fingers, as Fanndis had. Many fleeting thoughts flitted through her mind, but she pushed them all back to some unused corner of her brain. She breathed rhythmically to help calm her nerves and still her thoughts. When her mind cleared, she called forth the image of fire. Though her eyes were closed, she imagined the stretched twine; saw it engulfed in "friendly" fire. She commanded the fire not to burn her hands or the twine she held.

Strange tingling sensations began to creep from her spine down into her arms. It was an odd sort of feeling. Arna imagined that it was similar to the sensation of a limb that had been asleep regaining its feeling. When would she know if it had worked?

"Open your eyes, Arna," Fanndis whispered.

Arna peered down at the twine stretched between her two hands. It was blazing brightly with fire twice as large as Fanndis' had been and was warm, but not scorching. In her excitement, she lost part of her focus and the fire singed her fingers. She gasped, but Fanndis reminded her, "Focus. Ask it to become harmless and it will." Arna did as she was told and the fire once more became tame.

"This is…" Arna could not finish her words. She was utterly enchanted by her own abilities. It was incredible and impossible, yet the fire burned strong and lit her eyes with wonder. The fire burned down through the twine when she asked it to, but it avoided her fingers. The ashes fell and melted tiny black holes into the white snow below.

"Well done, apprentice." Fanndis bowed towards the young girl.

Arna bowed in return and replied, "Thank you, master."

Fanndis chuckled and linked her arm with Arna's. "We're going to have great fun, you and I."

With that, they walked back into the cottage kitchen and headed to the sitting room to bring Soryn, what they imagined to be, greatly desired conversation.

Stigg sat in precisely the same position as when they had left the room minutes before. Soryn looked stressed. Arna thought it might have been because Fanndis was already teaching her the Seidh. She sat down, feeling a bit self-conscious. Soryn looked at her with a thankful expression, but before he could ask her what the older woman had wanted, Fanndis announced, "Lord Maslyn, I need to see you for a moment. Follow me, if you please."

The older woman turned back towards the kitchen. Arna squeezed Soryn's hand as he walked towards the hallway. She hoped that Fanndis was wrong about him and that she and Lord Maslyn would be able to learn the Seidh together, but something in her heart told her that would not be the case. Soryn winked at his friend and followed Fanndis out of the room. In the kitchen, he saw that Fanndis had already gone out the open back door. Outside, Fanndis held a piece of twine in her hands.

"Lord Maslyn, I am about to do something that *you* will need to be able to do in order for me to teach you magic. If you are unable to perform this task, it means that your body does not possess the necessary yreth to support the use of the Seidh. Are you ready to accept the outcome of this test?"

Soryn pawed at the ground with his foot, kicking the snow away in little semi-circles. Soryn knew he would be disappointed if he could not perform magic. Instead of dwelling on it, however, he just shrugged.

"I'm ready," he said, simply.

Before his eyes, Fanndis lit a length of twine on fire using magic. He smelled the smoke and could see that it was real. A small bead of sweat ran down his face—not because he was warm, but because he was afraid he wouldn't be able to do it. She slowly told him the steps to perform the test and then handed him a fresh piece of twine.

"Hold it between your hands and close your eyes. Imagine the fire burning, but not harming you. Concentrate as hard as you can…call it forth," she told him.

He held the twine between his two hands as she had. Concentrating with all of his might, he imagined the burning fire in his mind and envisioned it blazing over the string he held. After about two minutes, Fanndis broke his concentration.

"Soryn, open your eyes."

He knew, without looking, that he did not have what it took to become a Seidh man. It was useless for him to try. He knew, too, that Arna had passed. Though Fanndis did not mention it, he was sure of it. Soryn was surprised that he was not as disappointed as he had expected to be. Still, he was sad that he would not get to spend as much time with his new friends.

"Lord Maslyn, there is no shame in being unable to use the Seidh," Fanndis assured him.

"I know," Soryn said.

"There is something I would like for you to do, however. Now that you have some free-time in the afternoons, I was wondering if you would like to come and help Stigg out with things that need to be done around the cottage and in the woods. Since I will be spending my time training Arna, there will be lots of chores to do around here."

Fanndis hoped that Soryn would not perceive her offer as a patronizing attempt to make him feel better. She truly thought the boy would benefit from working with her son.

"Could I? I haven't really gotten the chance to do much of anything physical. That would be great!" Soryn was overjoyed that he would still get to see Arna, Fanndis, and Stigg each day.

"It certainly will. We'll expect you here each afternoon—you are welcome to have lunch here with us, if it is alright with the steward and with Jori," Fanndis stated.

"Who will the new steward be?" Soryn asked.

"I expect you'll find out soon enough," Fanndis assured him.

Soryn thought they might go back inside the cottage to talk with Arna and Stigg, but instead, Fanndis continued to speak, "Lord Maslyn, there is one other matter we need to discuss before we go inside."

"Yes?"

"If Arna is to train with me, she'll need to live here. That means that you would need to formally discharge her from your service in the castle. There will be paperwork to sign—ensuring that she was not dismissed on negative terms and such. Jori will be able to explain things to you. She'll need to return to the castle tonight to get her things, but after tonight, you'll need to have another servant assigned to you. Arna needs to be able to focus all of her time on the Seidh," Fanndis explained.

"I understand," Soryn responded. "I'm glad that I'll get to see her. I would have missed her a lot."

"I think these arrangements will work out nicely." Fanndis winked at him.

With their discussion ended, the two of them returned to the cottage and sat down with the others to talk for a while about the events of the day and about the future. Stigg even contributed arbitrary, noncommittal noises every now and again to assure them that he *was* in fact listening and approved of various things. They sat and talked well into the evening and Soryn's growling stomach alerted them to the lateness of the hour.

"Well," Arna said to Soryn as they walked back to the castle, "I suppose everything is about to change, isn't it?"

"I suppose," Soryn whispered so Stigg, who was ahead with the lantern, would not hear.

"I think things will work out marvelously from here on. After all, if anyone deserves a 'happy ever after', it's you," Arna beamed, laughing softly.

"A 'happy ever after'? I've heard that phrase before," Soryn said, thinking.

"I imagine that your mother or father read you fairytales as a child and all *good* fairy tales end with, 'and they lived happily ever after'. Isn't that wonderful to think about? I suspect that, in the end, you'll have a 'happy ever after' for others to tell stories about." Arna smiled as they broke through the tree line. The suns were setting and both children were reminded of how hungry they were.

"Everything is going to change," Soryn repeated. "I just hope that you're right about how it will all turn out."

Arna slipped her hand into Soryn's. He smiled and squeezed hers. Stigg remained at the edge of the forest when the children broke through the trees. They continued to the door in the bottom of the tower. Each tried to imagine what their lives would be like and how they would interact with one another after Arna was no longer a servant in the castle. Later, when they were both in their beds, each secretly prayed that, whatever the ending, they would be together when it came.

Chapter Nine

In which a great deal of work is carried out…

Soryn awoke to the sound of the birds singing outside his tower window. He had chosen to remain in the tower instead of relocating to his father's quarters. The blazing fire he made the night before had died down to embers, but the room was still warm. Yawning, he turned over and pulled the covers tighter around him. He knew that Jori would not be far off in bringing breakfast, but he wished he could sleep for hours. The previous day had been intense and he was not sure what he thought about the differences between his old life and the one that was about to begin.

He had almost drifted to sleep again, when he heard a muffled, throat clearing sound. Turning over, he saw the face of his manservant. Jori smiled, eyes twinkling. Soryn wondered if the manservant had suddenly gone mad.

"Jori?" the young noble inquired, "Are you quite alright?"

"Good morning, Lord Maslyn. You must dress quickly. Breakfast is waiting for you in the great hall," Jori announced.

Lord Maslyn was astounded. "The great hall?"

"Of course; you are master of this castle not only in name, but in truth now. You must come and eat among your people. The steward is waiting for you," Jori said as he helped Lord Maslyn out of bed to dress.

Soryn followed the manservant down the hallway in a daze. He was really going to see the rest of the castle. That knowledge made him both nervous and excited. As Jori turned the latch, and held the door open for his master to walk through, Soryn felt the surreal knowledge that he would be able to walk freely through the door at the end of it. Lord Maslyn took a deep breath as he gazed through the open door, seeing a curving hallway of stone lit by lanterns set in sconces. Warm air moved through the passage and he wondered if it warmed the entire castle. He was embarrassed that he did not remember the castle's layout as best as he should, and he honestly had no idea where the great hall was. Heart beating madly, he took his first free steps into the castle in six years.

Jori went ahead of the boy after he had closed the door (without locking it this time) and led his master through the castle hallways. Soryn tried to keep count of all the rooms they passed, but he could not keep track. He was too intrigued by the paintings hanging on the walls. He saw many he did not recognize before they came to more familiar portraits. In one, his mother rested on a chair with her hair plaited down over her shoulder. She wore a pale lilac dress he remembered well. Her silvery white hair shone brightly in the light from an open window. A stabbing sadness welled in his heart while he gazed at her beauty and remembered her tender voice. Her red-brown eyes held mirth and joy as she looked emptily out from the canvas.

His father was the next painting. He stood stoically, also illumined by the window. Dark brown hair, very much like Soryn's own in shape and texture, framed his handsome face. The artist had captured the kind but serious air that his father was remembered for. The boy hoped that he would be like him when he grew up. He hoped he would be a Maslyn that both his parents would be proud of.

Jori gave the Maslyn plenty of time to look at the images of his parents. Though the manservant passed those portraits every day, he knew that his master had not seen them in six years. He knew it must have been painful for Lord Maslyn. When Soryn finally peeled his eyes away from the images, Jori was ready and continued on. Just as they were nearing the end of the passage, the last portrait caught Soryn's attention.

An image of three boys in formal attire haunted him. He had been five when the painting was completed, his brothers eleven. The memory was not hard to recall. Fenris had heckled the artist the entire time and Olan had tried to keep his brother from distracting the man. Soryn had said nothing—he never said anything much in front of his brothers. They were vastly different from him and, though he missed them, he had never really known them at all. He looked away from the picture and they moved on.

The castle was long, making up for in length what it lacked in width. Soryn noticed that the great hall branched off of the straight, central corridor. The boy looked up to see vaulted ceilings with bright lanterns hanging from beams at regular intervals. Enormous, clear-glass windows on each side of the hall let in rays of suns' light and the young master found that he had left his mouth open in his awe. There was a long, rectangular table in the center of the room that had only one occupant. Soryn was surprised to see Father Kimbli sitting next to the empty throne-like chair at the end of the table.

Jori seated him next to the priest.

"Good morning, Lord Maslyn," Father Kimbli said, smiling.

"Good morning, Father," Soryn replied, surprised to see the old man.

"Sir, meet the new steward," Jori announced.

Soryn was dumbfounded. He had no idea that Father Kimbli would have been allowed to hold such a title. The decision pleased him. Though he was often bored by the priest's visits, Kimbli was a kind man and Soryn respected him.

"I'm very pleased with these arrangements, Father. Thank you, Jori," Soryn said.

Jori bowed politely and walked away. After he left, Soryn could not even speak because two serving women came from a door towards the back of the room, near the enormous floor-to-ceiling windows, holding great pewter trays of food. The boy's eyes widened with delight and he was ecstatic to have such a grand breakfast with his ancient friend beside him. Father Kimbli said a humble blessing over the meal and the two of them eagerly ate.

"I had no idea it would be you, Father Kimbli. I'm glad you're the new steward."

"I'm very glad of that, my boy. I, myself, am petrified of the idea, but I suspected it would bring you happiness and help ease you into the life of the town's Maslyn better than throwing you in with some stranger. I thought all of this freedom would be enough for you to handle, even without having to get used to some other person to work with."

"It's hard for me to believe that I'm free to go wherever I wish, mostly *whenever* I wish." Soryn set his fork down as the enormity of that thought settled in his mind.

"Indeed. I am thrilled that I have lived to see this day." Kimbli sighed, "I'm sorry that your confinement lasted so long. We wanted to keep you safe, but then Asmund decided to extend your stay in the tower. I'm very sorry we did not challenge his decision. Can you ever forgive us?"

"Of course, I forgive you. Although, I still don't understand— what was it you were trying to protect me from?" Soryn wished all the adults in his life would come clean about the events of the fire.

"We will most definitely have that discussion, Lord Maslyn, but today is not the day. Today, we need to talk about your tutoring."

"Oh yes," Soryn muttered, "tutoring. If I'm to run a town, I suppose I should know how to be a Maslyn."

"Even though Governor Frey resides in this city, he does not readily involve himself in the town's affairs—that is your duty. You report to him just like all the other mayors in Oban," Kimbli informed the boy.

"That makes sense," he allowed.

Soryn felt the weight of his title as he contemplated all of the things he needed to learn in order to become the leader he needed to be. Suddenly, Soryn missed Arna and wished she could be with him while he was studying. He asked, "Who will my teachers be for tutoring?"

"Apparently, I will be your teacher. I will be responsible for several things while I work here," Kimbli chuckled.

"You?" Soryn retorted, surprised.

152

"I studied politics and government before I went to seminary to become a priest," Kimbli told him. "I suppose they thought I would remember enough from sixty years ago to be useful." He hoped that Governor Frey and Fanndis had been right.

Soryn's curiosity having been assuaged momentarily, they sat for a while, chewing their food. When they finished their meal, the two serving girls who had waited patiently for the dishes emerged from the perimeter of the hall and retrieved the plates and utensils. Soryn and Kimbli thanked them and left. It became apparent to Soryn that their lessons would take place in the previous Maslyn's office. He was excited to be in a place where his father had spent much time.

It was a beautiful room full of ceiling-high shelves covered with books. There was a pine desk in the center, closest to the draped window that overlooked the castle gates and the village. Soryn saw that a smaller desk had been stationed near the great one, imagining that was where he would sit during lessons. He was surprised when Father Kimbli directed him to the larger desk, taking the smaller one for himself. Soryn saw that there were several books stacked there: *Leading with Humility*, *New Kristiansand Politics and Economy: a Commentary*, and *Interpersonal Relationships in Business*.

Soryn felt intimidated and grew uncomfortable. He had never had an interest in any of those subjects, but he knew that, if he was going to succeed, he would need to summon some quickly. Father Kimbli said that they should dive right in. Soryn picked up one of the books and began his first lesson on being a village leader. To say the least…he was a little overwhelmed. Father Kimbli assured the boy that he had what it took to be the new Maslyn. Soryn was glad of his friend's confidence. He read the passages the priest outlined for him and took copious notes. By the time the morning was over, he was dying to see Arna. Father Kimbli laughed and waved him off. Soryn grabbed his coat and fled the castle for the woods.

* * *

Arna awoke, feeling as if she were frozen from the neck down. Sleeping by the hearth in Fanndis' cottage had not provided the warmth she'd hoped. The fire had died out long ago and the windows were not well shielded against drafts. She shivered and tried her best to cover every inch of her body in order to slink back into sleep. No sunshine peeped through the shutters and no sounds crept through the house. Morning had not yet come. For all the girl knew, it was closer to midnight than the dawn. She wished she had decided to stay in the castle for the night instead of coming right back after she had gathered her things the day before.

When she could not fall asleep after several minutes of trying, she rolled over and looked at the grey ashes of the dead fire. She did not know if Fanndis would object to her building a new one. Arna was certain that she would be frostbitten in the morning if she did not find some way to warm herself. A sudden spark danced across her mind. She wanted to try lighting the fire with the Seidh. Ever since she had made fire in Fanndis' test, she was dying to try it again. "This is my chance", she said to herself.

Arna sat up, tugging her covers tightly about her, and looked at the blackened hearth. She closed her eyes and concentrated, regulating her breathing and focusing her mind on one thought only: fire. She imagined a fire that would burn brightly and hot through the night without need of wood or kindling. She focused for several minutes until she felt sweat running down her temples. When she opened her eyes, she was overjoyed to see a silent, beautiful fire burning before her. She extended her hands to warm them and relished the glorious heat that thawed her frigid frame.

Fanndis watched from the entrance to her bedroom. She had wondered when the girl would try to make fire again. The results were impressive. There was great potential in her apprentice. The old woman had been startled when Arna returned to the cottage after dark and was excited by the girl's eagerness to begin learning immediately. Fanndis had shuffled the girl off to bed by the hearth so that she would be rested and ready for the day when morning came. Fanndis was satisfied with the fire the girl had created— thankful, too, for it would heat the cottage through the night. Fanndis returned to bed.

Arna stared at the fire and found she was no longer sleepy. She thought of many things while she hugged her knees close to her chest and watched the enchanted flames. Would she ever command other elements? Perhaps she could try summoning water or wind with magic. A yawn escaped her lips and Arna decided she was too tired. After her mind drifted from thoughts of the Seidh, her thoughts settled on Lord Maslyn. She blushed at the image of his happy face. She had been fond of him for many years, and truly hoped that she would get to see him the next afternoon after his lessons were done for the day. A chill came over her and she scooted closer to the fire, letting the heat course over and through her.

An hour passed and countless thoughts bounded through her brain. Arna felt her eyelids drift closed. She scooted her sleeping pallet closer to the hearth so the fire's warmth would be with her through the rest of the night. A deep sleep overcame her and, though she dreamed, she did not remember the dreams upon waking.

Fanndis woke the girl when the suns had begun to break the horizon in the eastern woods. Stigg had already been up for an hour or two and took his breakfast silently in the kitchen. Fanndis smiled, remembering the conversation with her son that morning. He was restless when he came in from the barn and Fanndis wondered at his behavior.

She had asked him earlier, "Whatever is the matter with you?"

"The barn was drafty," he grumbled. "I know we couldn't very well let the girl sleep in there, but I suppose I'll just have to make a fire pit or something for the foreseeable future."

Fanndis proclaimed, "Stuff and nonsense! You and Lord Maslyn will be building an addition onto the cottage for the girl. She'll need a workspace and a place to sleep as well as a fireplace. Work on the project should begin as soon as possible, don't you think? You don't want to spend your entire life in that barn, do you?" Fanndis scolded.

"Hmfph," Stigg muttered.

She shook the girl awake and bid her to wash and dress. Arna did as she was told and enjoyed the feeling of the heavy, knitted clothing that Fanndis had provided. The fabric was a wintry grey color. Fanndis said it would blend in well with the forest when she needed to go out for ingredients or to perform rituals. Everything sounded so mysterious to Arna. She was filled with excitement. When she had woken up, she was pleased to see her fire from the night was still burning brightly. When she asked it to dim, it did. She asked it to blaze once more. It did. Everything about the power she had discovered within herself solicited smiles and increasing excitement. She wondered why she had never commanded the elements in the past.

"Fanndis," she asked. "Why have I never summoned magic before?"

"I suppose it may have been because you did not know how to organize your thoughts properly or because your yreth production was insufficient until recently. There could be thousands of reasons that aren't readily apparent," the old woman replied.

That answer satisfied the girl for the moment. Arna rolled up her sleeping pallet and put it where her master directed. Much of the morning was spent in the kitchen. Fanndis showed Arna how to dry herbs by tying them at the stems and hanging the bundles from the beams that ran across the ceiling. They made poultices, teas, and ointments—for the villagers, Fanndis told her.

"It's very important that a Seidh woman be a top-notch healer. The villagers need to be able to trust that you can help them with your skills."

"Aren't there doctors?" Arna asked, innocently.

"Of course. However, doctors cannot heal certain terminal cases and we can often help where they cannot," Fanndis said.

"How?"

"By making the patients comfortable, or helping them believe there is hope in their healing. Miracles *do* happen, you know. Sometimes when you give somebody hope, a mysterious turn around in their health soon follows. Of course, the medicines we give them help, but a person's faith and hope go much farther than herbs. Besides, hospital medicine is often more expensive than some of the poorer villagers can afford."

They continued this way until the suns reached their zenith. Arna loved the work; from the scents of the herbs to hearing Fanndis say their names. Fanndis explained that she gathered some of them during summer. Some of them came from elsewhere. Fanndis informed her that there was a secret greenhouse in the forest that she had maintained since she was still an apprentice. Arna was intrigued and asked to see it as soon as possible.

"We'll probably need to make a run to it sometime this week. There is a village woman who's about to deliver her first child and there are herbs there that can help ease her labor."

By lunchtime, Arna was ready for a break and was hoping that Bialas would come join them soon. Her hope was rewarded when she looked out the kitchen window and saw Lord Maslyn coming through the clearing. Her heart flipped and she followed Fanndis to the door to greet him.

"Welcome, Lord Maslyn. I trust your lessons went well this morning?" Fanndis politely inquired.

"Oh, yes. Father Kimbli and I had a grand time learning about land treaties and the price of horses twenty years ago." Soryn rolled his eyes dramatically.

"That sounds immensely exciting," Arna chortled.

Stigg had been working all morning in the back of the cottage, clearing snow from around the back kitchen. He came in shortly after the boy's arrival and washed up for lunch. Fanndis and the girl returned to the kitchen to set the table and present a meager lunch of herbs, pickled vegetables, and a soup of salted pork and cabbage.

157

They had let the soup simmer over the fire all morning and the scent filled the entire house with a mouthwatering aroma.

The four sat down at the small table in the kitchen and Stigg grunted as he bowed his head. Fanndis immediately copied her son, followed questioningly by Arna and Soryn. They looked at one another and shrugged. After a blessing, the meal lasted only a half hour or so. When everyone had finished, the women cleared the table while Stigg motioned for Lord Maslyn to follow him to the back clearing of the cottage. Arna winked at the boy and whispered, "See you soon."

Lord Maslyn had no idea what Stigg was taking him to do, but was looking forward to working with his physical strength after a morning of mental activities. Stigg walked towards the woods with an axe and Lord Maslyn assumed he was to follow him. After traipsing through the trees, brambles, and thigh-high snow for several minutes, the boy quickly grew tired of walking. They eventually stopped at a frozen creek bed. Soryn considered asking Stigg what they were doing, but decided to wait and watch. The man began to hack at the ice covering the creek. It took Stigg about five minutes to break through a small section of the frozen water. Soryn could see strong currents flowing underneath the ice. Stigg had a pack on his back that Soryn had not noticed before. The man hauled it off of his shoulder and sat it in the snow by the creek bank.

He retrieved a pair of slickers that went to the waist. Soryn noted they were lined with lamb's wool and would be warm even in the freezing water. Stigg waded into the creek. The water was quite deep—coming up to his upper thighs. He pointed at the pack and Soryn found a pair of rubber work gloves. The boy handed them to Stigg and watched as he slipped them on and then promptly plunged his arms into the freezing water. At first the boy thought they might be doing some primitive form of fishing, but when Stigg picked up a huge stone from the creek, he knew they were not looking for fish.

"Take those back to the cottage and set them near that area I've cleared of snow," Stigg said.

Soryn reached down to pick up the icy rock and shivered at the touch. He cradled it in his arms—it was excruciatingly heavy—and toted it all the way through the woods back to the cottage. When he returned to the edge of the creek, Stigg had already laid out six more of the enormous stones. Soryn knew he would have to work more quickly if he was to keep up with the man.

They carried on in this manner for several hours. Despite the fact that the air felt twenty degrees below freezing, Soryn was drenched in sweat. He eventually worked out a rhythm that helped him to stay caught up with Stigg's work in the creek. Several times, Fanndis' son had to break up newly-forming ice around his legs. Occasionally, he stepped out and dried off before going back in. It was a painstaking process and Soryn's entire body ached by the time Stigg took off the slickers and gloves.

They walked back to the cottage in silence, each carrying the last of the stones in their arms. They deposited them by the cottage and Soryn tried to guess their purpose in hauling a hundred rocks from the creek. There was a shoveled out area of snow and debris next to the left side of the back kitchen wall. Stigg retrieved a strange tool with a large metal roller at the end and set it in the freshly uncovered purple dirt. He rolled it all over the area and Soryn realized it was packing the frozen dirt to make the surface level.

Soryn could hide his curiosity no more. "Stigg, what exactly are we making?"

"Arna will be living here from now on and she'll need a permanent place to sleep and work," he replied.

Lord Maslyn felt a surge of pride roll through him when he knew he was building Arna a place to stay. He helped Stigg for the rest of the evening. They placed a layer of rocks all around the perimeter of the room and put smaller stones under the empty places where the larger ones were set against the back kitchen wall. The suns had not yet set, though they were close to doing so. Soryn wondered if they would be tearing down part of the back kitchen wall or if Arna would have her own entrance. He would find out soon enough.

When the work was over, Stigg simply took the cloth he kept in his trousers' back pocket and wiped his forehead. Without saying anything, he walked into the kitchen and did not come back. Soryn took that as his cue that the day was at an end. He exhaled heavily and rubbed his arms through his coat to help alleviate their increasing soreness.

He entered the cottage and slumped into a chair by the kitchen table. Fanndis and Arna were both there and giggled at the sight of him. Arna brought over a warm compress they had been keeping by the fire. She promptly shut the kitchen door and told her friend to remove his coat. He did, though it caused ribbons of pain to shoot through his arms and shoulders. Groaning, he finally completed the task, and Arna placed the compress on his shoulder blades through his shirt. Soryn sighed as the heat helped melt away some of the soreness.

"You'll need to ask Jori to take you to the hot spring in the bottom level of the castle tonight." Fanndis ordered.

"We have a hot spring in the castle?" Lord Maslyn asked in surprise.

"Yes. Where do you think all that hot water comes from that you enjoyed when Jori brought it for you to wash with?" she retorted.

"I thought they had to boil it."

"Thankfully, there is a bountiful spring flowing under the castle. Long ago, they discovered it when warm water came up through cracks in the stones in the castle dungeon. They immediately tore up the floor and a huge spring was uncovered. It's kept secret from the villagers. There are other springs in the area. Most villagers use the public spring near the mountains," Fanndis explained.

Stigg returned to the room minutes later carrying a lantern. The boy knew it was time to go. Arna helped him put on his coat over the compress and Soryn followed Stigg out the door. They walked in

160

silence through the forest until they reached the tree line. From there, Soryn walked alone through the snow—aching every step of the way—to the bottom tower door. When he was halfway there, he heard a familiar voice.

My, my…what have they done to you in those woods? Ulla's velvety voice was a welcome distraction.

"Good evening, Ulla. Pardon me while I feel like dying after hauling rocks for four hours," Soryn replied, groaning intermittently.

Hauling rocks, is it? That Fanndis is a slave-driver if ever I saw one.

"Not Fanndis; her son, Stigg. That man is a workaholic. He may be the death of me unless I can bulk up some muscle."

Ahhh. What project requires so many rocks?

"We're building a room for Arna off the side of the kitchen, since she'll be living there once we get it completed—which, at Stigg's pace, could be by tomorrow night." Soryn hoped they would not work that quickly on it. He was sure he would faint at the exertion.

Well, you certainly won't be in prime work condition the way you're carrying on.

"I'd like to see you haul rocks for hours on end. You'd be complaining, too," Soryn replied, indignantly.

I'm sure you're right. Why don't you have Jori take you to that hot spring that they keep in the dungeon?

"That's exactly what I'm going to do," Soryn said as he made it to the tower door. He truly thought he might die as he slowly climbed up the stone steps to his room. It did not occur to him to ask how Ulla knew about the spring.

Come now, little Maslyn…show me what you've got. I know you can climb those stairs more quickly than that! Ulla's words sounded like ridicule to Soryn, who wanted to say a few choice words to the pig.

Instead of generating creative mental insults, Soryn just continued on, trudging up the stairs. When he made it to the tower room, he promptly collapsed on his bed. He knew that in order to get Jori, he would have to pull the cord near the doorway to the castle passage. That meant he had to get up again. He almost did not know if it was worth it, but the promise of the warmth of the hot springs was too tantalizing to ignore. Minutes later, he finally pulled the chain—twice to be sure Jori would hear it if he was in his room or if he was in any other important part of the castle. After that, he went back to his bed, collapsed once more, and waited for his manservant to arrive.

Jori came after about five minutes. Soryn was nearly asleep on the bed, though the pain was enough to keep him from falling completely unconscious.

"Is there something I can do for you, sir?" Jori asked, amused by the display.

"Jori, is there a hot spring in the castle basement? Fanndis' son had me toting rocks most of the day. If I don't get some warm water for this, I think I might be dead by morning…" Soryn thought his dramatic flair was sure to work on the manservant.

Jori merely chuckled and nodded.

Lord Maslyn carried himself in as dignified a manner as he could while they passed servants going about their nightly routine. Many of them bowed, excited to see the master of the house finally released from the tower room. Others continued their business and ignored him. Soryn did not care at the moment. All he cared about was making it to the water below.

It took almost twenty minutes to navigate the enormous castle passages and stairways down to the dungeon. Though no one had been imprisoned recently, the entire area felt confining and desolate. Jori continued to lead his young master through a long hallway with cells on either side—all of them empty. The manservant opened a heavy wooden door and moist heat filled the dungeon passage. Jori handed Lord Maslyn a towel and change of clothing.

"I'll return for you in an hour, sir. Do be careful in the spring," Jori announced and left, shutting the heavy wooden door behind him.

Soryn looked anxiously around, assuring himself that he was truly alone. The windowless stone room was enormous. Torches were set about in each of the four walls, reflecting yellow light off of the grey stones. The spring bubbled up through the floor. Soryn saw that it had been contained in a stone pool cut in the center of the room. The water was murky, but he saw that a fissure at the bottom of the pool allowed the warm water to flow in and drains on each side allowed it to flow out so that the level remained the same. He also saw that there was a shelf-like precipice in the pool where a person could sit.

Sighing in contentment, he stepped into the steaming water. It was so warm, it hurt at first—his body was still freezing from the outside air and the drafty castle. He slowly immersed his legs; kneeling first, then sitting. A groan escaped as he settled into the wonderfully hot water. The tension in his muscles began to release and though he was still sore, he felt much more relaxed after a few minutes.

It was strange for him to think that just days before, he had been locked in the same tower he had lived in for so many years and that, now, he was completely free to move about anywhere he wished. Soryn had enjoyed his lessons with Father Kimbli that morning, though the subject matter bored him. He also enjoyed the work with Stigg, even if his body screamed at him for having participated in it. Perhaps he would become strong more quickly this way. He was glad he did not have to be completely cut off from his friends, but could also pursue his mayoral duties.

He settled down into the water and let the warmth of the spring flood his senses. Rivulets of heat washed over him and he wanted nothing more than to remain in the pool as long as possible. Suddenly, he felt inspired to give thanks to whoever had watched over him during his life. He wanted to thank those people who were helping him now. Bowing his head, he said a silent prayer to anyone who might be listening. Though he could not see the stars in order to count his blessings like his mother taught him, he counted them by the stones lining the walls.

* * *

Fanndis hummed quietly by the fire while Arna stirred the cauldron that hung over it. Their dinner smelled delicious. Herbs, salted pork, and cabbage mingled together in the broth, swirling as she rotated the wooden spoon. Stigg could smell it from the back room where he worked on making netting for a bed he was building for Arna. All was quiet in the cottage, save for the gentle tune the older woman hummed. When the soup was finally finished, the three of them sat down to a nice warm meal.

Chapter Ten

In which the children face unforeseen perils…

Ulla sat in the study, brooding. He felt upset about being left out of all the excitement. He knew that he could leave the study if he wished, but he was not sure if he wanted to, yet. Geri and Freki had already visited him and he had had enough animal company for one day. The little Maslyn would be down at the spring and Ulla's mental telepathy would not reach him there. He was bored. He wanted excitement, intrigue…he wanted to be human again.

Hopping down from his perch, Ulla went to the hole in the stone wall underneath the table with the miniature Adden. Sucking in his ample waist, the pig squeezed through the small hole and out into the empty space in the bottom of the tower. There was a particular nasty scent that dirtied the air—Ulla guessed it was from the refuse of rats or even his feline lackeys.

Piles of the mess were everywhere and Ulla used his nose as a guide to carefully pick his way between them. By the time he reached the precarious stair that led to the grate between the tower and the castle passage, he was revolted with the stench and thought he would retch. Using his snout, he lifted the loose grate and slipped into the duct that ran underneath the castle passage between the tower and the main edifice. Thankfully, the majority of the tunnel was clean and the darkness masked any unsettling arachnids. Ulla climbed down the stair at the end of the tunnel into the ducts below the castle's main floor. Such small spaces had allowed him great mobility when his human body had been stolen from him. He knew if he had walked around among the humans, they might have put him in the barn with the other pigs or he might have become someone's pet, or worse…someone's dinner. He shivered at the undignified thought. He knew that, if he ever *did* get his body back, he would never eat pork again.

He skirted his way through the ducts, hearing footsteps above him. His memory had faded in some areas of the castle layout and he had to retrace his steps several times until he successfully climbed out through the grate in the dungeon with the hot spring. Ulla was startled by a great commotion in the pool. It was Soryn, splashing madly in the water. At first, the pig chuckled because he thought the boy was trying to swim. Then he heard gurgling sounds and grew alarmed. He raced to the edge of the pool and looked in. Soryn floundered around in the water because he could *not* swim and was unable to keep himself above the surface.

Soryn! Calm down! Still your body's movements or you'll just drown yourself! Ulla tried to force his mental voice enough that the boy's thoughts of panic would be interrupted.

"Ack! Ulla—!" The boy's words were overtaken when he fell again under the water.

Try your best to move your arms and legs to tread the water! It will keep you afloat!

Soryn panicked. He had no idea what he had been thinking when he moved off of the ledge to try his hand at swimming. The water had a strong whirlpool current and he had been dragged under several times. Being unable to swim, he panicked. The boy tried to do as Ulla said and moved his arms and legs in downward motions, trying to keep his head above water. When his head started to clear, he used his limbs to push through the strong current over to the side of the pool.

That's it. Try and move to the ledge. Move your legs and arms together in the same motion. That's it. Good.

Soryn climbed out of the current and onto the ledge, totally exhausted and frightened. He had been so afraid when the water pulled him under. It would have been horrible to die just after gaining freedom. Breaths came in and out as if his very life would extinguish if he did not take in as much air as he could.

Rest now. You're out of danger. What in the world were you thinking, going down into the pool? Did Jori not warn you about the current in the bottom?

"No…he…didn't…say anything…about it," Soryn panted.

The fool. People have drowned down here before. You can't move off the ledge…even if you are an advanced swimmer. You're very lucky, Lord Maslyn. It looks like I showed up just in time.

"I'll…say …How did…you…get here…anyway?" Soryn asked, still trying to catch his breath.

There are ducts that run underneath the castle, even as far as the tower. I know them very well. I just choose to spend most of my time in the study.

"How do you know so much about swimming? I didn't think pigs swam," Soryn inquired, having regained his voice.

That answer is simple. I haven't always been a pig.

Soryn felt as though someone had smashed him over the head with a club. "You haven't?!"

No. I was human once. You remember I told you I was a prisoner of sorts, as well?

"Well, yes…"

My body was transformed into this hideous shape many years ago. I've spent so much time in the study to see if I could find something out about how to get my body back. After all this time, I've had no success. I was hoping that you and I could work out a fair exchange. I did help you get out of the tower. I was wondering if you would help me find out how to get my body back.

Ulla had not expected to be so truthful with Soryn, but since he had almost lost the child only moments earlier, he determined that it was best not to delay any further. A strange look came over the boy's face. The pig was not so sure he liked what he was seeing.

"That's why you wanted me to learn magic. That's why you wanted me to find Fanndis, isn't it?" Soryn was perturbed by this idea.

I confess it played a part— however, before you decide to hate me, I did know that you and that girl were interested in the Seidh. I just thought I'd make everybody happy with one go.

Soryn imagined that, if a pig could smile, Ulla would be doing so to gain his favor once more. The boy had to admit that Ulla's suggestions had led to his freedom, as well as his friendship with Arna.

"I suppose your little game worked out well for everyone," he allowed.

See? I'm not entirely selfish.

"Entirely?" Soryn raised an eyebrow.

I am a little selfish. Aren't we all?

"I suppose…" Soryn felt he was being swindled by the animal in some way, but he was far too fond of the creature to abandon him now. "I'll help you find a way to get your body back—if I can. It may be impossible, you know."

Yes, I know I may remain in this disgusting form forever, but it's worth a try.

The two of them sat listening to the spring's bubbling. Soryn worked up the courage to stick his toes into the water for a few moments, then his calves. Pretty soon, he was sitting on the shelf in the water again—careful about holding onto the side of the pool with his arms so he was not drawn into the currents.

I'll be going now. That manservant is on his way to get you. I'll see you some other time.

Before Soryn could reply, the pig had dashed back under the grate in the wall and was gone. The boy was thankful the pig had shown up in just the nick of time to save him from drowning. The water had just seemed so warm and inviting. However, his hand had slipped off the ledge of the seat and he was sucked into the fierce current. He had panicked, swallowing water and thrashing about. Ulla had come right at the moment he was about to give up. Again, he thanked whoever was watching over him.

Jori opened the large heavy door and summoned the boy. Soryn got out of the pool and dried off, dressing quickly. He followed Jori back up the stairs to the main castle level and into the great hall where he shared a late meal with Father Kimbli. The two of them discussed the events of the day and how Soryn had nearly drowned in the hot spring (Lord Maslyn conveniently left out the part about Ulla saving him). Father Kimbli gave Soryn some tips for swimming and keeping one's head above the surface.

By the time dinner was over, Lord Maslyn's eyelids were drifting closed and Jori promptly led him back to the tower room. Soryn saw that a roaring fire awaited him. Sadness settled over him when he saw it. Arna wasn't the one who made it. He missed her. The bed had been turned down with fresh sheets and blankets. Jori left him with promises that he would return in the morning to fetch him for breakfast.

Soryn's aching body was less sore than before, though he knew he would be still be stiff in the morning. He dressed for bed and crawled under the heavy blankets. The red lanterns cast a pale, comforting glow about the room, mingling with the light from the fire. He watched the hearth for a while, listening to the crackling twigs and whistling logs. Outside his window, he heard the wind howling and the Night Bells ringing in the darkness. He thought he heard the cry of a wolf somewhere in the direction of the woods, but he brushed it off as his imagination. Without noticing it, the young Maslyn of New Kristiansand fell asleep and dreamed of a childhood spent in the shadows of his older, twin brothers.

* * *

The next day brought sunshine and frigid winds. It was Suns' Day, which meant he had the day off from tutoring, so Soryn went to Fanndis' cottage after breakfast. He and Stigg worked for hours on the addition to the cottage that would become Arna's room. Before they worked more on the structure, they had to create a putty-like mortar that Soryn abhorred. It smelled like vomit and the boy was not so sure it was mortar at all. He was of the opinion that it came from some unfortunate animal. Soryn mentioned his suspicions to Stigg. The man scowled at this suggestion. They slapped the mortar over their first layer of stones and put the next layer down. They continued with another layer of mortar, another layer of rocks…for *hours*.

When they ran out of stones, they went back to the creek, broke open the ice, and carried more back to the cottage clearing. Fanndis approved of their progress. She saw it from her brief treks to the barn for straw or to visit with Eira. Arna was thrilled that she would soon have her own space in which to sleep and work. In two days, Arna had learned to summon fire in more creative ways. She had also learned to summon water, and make the most useful health poultices and salves. Fanndis was an excellent teacher and Arna already knew the names of the herbs they used and where they grew. She could not have been more excited about her apprenticeship. She and Fanndis got along much like grandmother and grandchild. It was an exciting time—made even more so by Soryn's presence, though she really only saw him at mealtimes.

Stigg seemed shy around her, though she wasn't sure why. Arna's attempts to make conversation had proved fruitless and he usually grunted or mumbled unintelligible replies to her questions. Still, he helped her with any heavy lifting when he was inside and he made sure to set out warm blankets for her by the fire before he carried his own to the barn to sleep. She felt a sisterly affection building for Stigg. It made her glad, considering she was an only child and her parents had passed away some time ago.

By the time the suns set, Lord Maslyn was far worse than the day before, as far as aches and pains went. The little room was only about four stone levels high. They had begun to leave a space for the door, which helped the boy picture the end result. Stigg finally went into the cottage for dinner and Soryn sighed. Exhaustion slithered underneath his skin. He thought he would have at least built up a few small muscles the day before, but he slumped into the house like a rickety old man and the women put warm compresses on his shoulders again.

Lord Maslyn returned to the castle later on and asked to go down to the spring again. Jori obeyed his master's request and took the boy down to the warm water below. Ulla met him there after the manservant had gone and the two of them talked about the goings on at the cottage and so forth. By the time Lord Maslyn had gone up to the great hall and had a second dinner (his appetite had grown exponentially), he was nearly falling asleep in his chair. Father Kimbli chuckled at the boy's behavior and asked Jori to take him off to bed.

Another roaring fire met him when he returned to his room. He fell into the covers without even undressing. The manservant simply covered Lord Maslyn with the numerous blankets and went about the rest of his nightly duties. That night, Soryn dreamed of Arna and how she might look in the summertime. He saw her short hair blown by the wind and they laughed over some shared joke his mind was too tired to remember. They watched the suns set together and held hands, enjoying the warmth the summer suns exuded.

* * *

The sound of the forest birds drifted in through the cottage windows. Though they were shuttered against the cold, Arna could still hear the birds' song. Fanndis' wind chime also fluttered with the wind and the soft, lyrical tones of the bells made the girl want to fall back asleep. Still, she was very excited about the day ahead. The night before, the old snow woman had assured Arna that they would make a trip to the secret greenhouse deep in the woods. Arna washed, dressed, and rolled her sleep pallet. After years of living as a servant, she still woke before everyone else—even Fanndis who awoke at dawn.

All was dark, save the glow from the fire. Arna had summoned it the night before. It burned a pleasant amber color. She was reminded of how her closed eyelids lit up with the sunshine in summer. Being the only one awake in the house, Arna tidied up her sleeping pallet and set about making breakfast for Fanndis and Stigg. Birds sang outside the cottage windows and she smiled as she went about her work. For a moment, she felt the same fascination that Soryn had for the fifa birds. It was remarkable that they could survive in Niflheim's incredibly cold climate. Arna created a fire in the kitchen hearth and asked it to burn hot and strong all day. She knew, without looking or checking, that it would do as she had commanded. She made oatmeal in the cauldron over the fire and added some honey to it. When Arna had asked about the honey, Fanndis told her that Stigg kept a few bees in the shed attached to the back of the greenhouse and harvested the honey before the heavy snows returned at the end of summer.

Sometime later, the old woman walked into the kitchen and greeted the girl through stifled yawns. Stigg entered from the back kitchen doorway and the three of them sat down to a nice quiet breakfast. He muttered a nigh unintelligible "thank you" before he went out to work on the chores. After the dishes were cleared from the morning meal, Fanndis dressed for trekking through deep snow.

"You'll need to bundle up well, Arna. The greenhouse is a ways away and we'll need to pack lunch. Bring a large basket, some shears, and twine, if you please."

Arna did as she was told and by the time the suns had barely peeked over the northern mountains, the two of them set off.

"Will we be back in time to see Lord Maslyn?" Arna asked.

"Not in time to see him for very long, I'm afraid. It will take an hour or so to get to the greenhouse and then we have a lot of work to do when we arrive. We will need to visit the greenhouse each week at the same time. The plants get ornery if they don't have structure and consistency," Fanndis replied.

"Plants?" Arna raised an eyebrow.

Fanndis' face showed surprise, "Of course. Plants are finicky creatures. High maintenance."

Arna laughed.

They walked for a long time, avoiding snow drifts and renegade roots from the giant trees they passed. Arna spotted many creatures in the forest: a fox, a hare, even an enormous winter deer. It was three times as tall as Arna and she marveled at its white coat. It stared at the two travelers and sniffed. When it moved on to other haunts, the old woman and the girl continued carefully.

"Fanndis, what sort of plants do you grow in the greenhouse?" Arna inquired.

"Many of the plants in *this* greenhouse are unlike any you will find in the village. Most of these are ancient specimens from the time of Ancient Earth. The seeds have been passed on generation to generation in my family and kept very safe. I think I was the first person to dare plant them. It took me a long time to figure out how to care for them properly."

Arna was delighted with the prospect of seeing plants that had once grown on the humans' old home world. Colonization of other planets began nearly a thousand years ago and people had lived on Niflheim a little over nine hundred of those years. It was mind-blowing to think of vegetation even older than that, crossing countless light-years of space to grow on a new planet. Just when Arna's feet had begun to ache, she saw a glass-walled building. The glass was translucent, but not entirely see-through. She thought she could already make out some of the greenery within.

"We're here," Fanndis remarked.

The old woman went to the door and pressed her hand against it. Arna came to realize that the door had been sealed with magic to prevent intruders. When the apprentice examined the walls, she saw that they were very thin, though sturdy enough to allow the material to absorb sunlight. The door swung open and Fanndis walked inside. Arna followed. What Arna saw took her breath away. An entire scene of green filled her eyes. There were plants on almost every

173

available surface. Herbs grew in pots on the floor, trees grew in the back of the building that had huge, curtain-like leaves—Fanndis called them "palms". Other plants were small and lived in long rectangular beds. One of them was called, "clover". Flowers in varying colors were dispersed here and there and Arna's heart gave a delighted leap at such beauty. She let her nostrils fill with the clean, vibrant scent of life. The air was moist and very warm. Fanndis shed her outer layer of clothing. Arna did the same.

"How is it so warm in here, Fanndis?"

"Look up," she said.

Above their heads, at the top of the arched ceiling, five floating, miniature suns hung down. They were like the small Adden in Ulla's study. The humidity came from sprinklers running down the ridge of the roof. The spray became a mist as it descended over the greenhouse inhabitants. As she was studying the ceiling, Arna was startled by a wolf's howl. It sounded dangerously close to the building. Fanndis saw the girl's alarm and smiled.

"That's just a friend of mine. He lives near here with his mate and cubs. Don't worry. He won't bother us," Fanndis assured her.

"You mean you talk with him?"

"Of course. It took a while for me to gain his trust, but he's a gentle creature at heart. He fiercely loves his mate and pups and is very protective of them. When I befriended him and helped with a thorn in his back leg, he promised to protect the greenhouse. He's too far away for me to really hear what he's saying in that howl, but I am sure it is kindly meant."

Living in a castle most of her life, Arna had not had too much experience conversing with animals. Before she lived in the Maslyn's house, she had lived with her mother and father—both of whom were allergic to most house pets. Ulla was the first animal she had talked to. She wondered what a wolf's personality would be like. Eira did not come into the cottage much, but Stigg had already told Arna that the cat did not talk to humans anyway.

The wolf's howl was joined by another. Soon, they promptly ceased.

"Ah, must have been trying to call his mate to him. I suppose it worked," Fanndis said casually.

She took Arna around and named every single plant in the greenhouse. In the end, there were only about one hundred seventy eight varieties or so (Fanndis put great emphasis on the *only*) and Arna knew it would take several weeks to remember them all. She gingerly touched every one and tried to feel the texture of the leaves against the pads of her fingers. Living on a planet where such greenery only blossomed for a month or so during the summer, it was like a miracle. She wanted very much to bring Bialas to this place. She wondered what he would think when he saw the lively plants in such a cold forest. Fanndis brought Arna out of her reverie and began to instruct her on the rudimentary skills a person needed to work with plants: trimming, weeding, and fertilizing. Arna picked up the work very quickly, but a thought came to her and she asked Fanndis, "Why don't we use the Seidh to grow the plants and tend them?"

"Because it is good to get one's hands in the earth and feel the life there. When someone gets too dependent on magic, it can tarnish their love and appreciation for growing things and good hard work," the old woman smiled. "It can also lead to yresses—a sickness caused by using too much of the Seidh. Nasty stuff."

They continued their work in silence, listening to the wind beat against the sides of the greenhouse and hearing the wolf's howl. When it was time for lunch, they sat on the packed dirt floor and Fanndis told Arna stories about her youth. Arna enjoyed her teacher's stories and was a little sad when it was time to work again. For several more hours, they made their rounds to each plant in the greenhouse—giving each one attention and care. They cleaned their utensils and then locked up the secret building.

It was almost evening when they walked back into the cottage clearing. Arna was met with a sight that nearly took her breath away.

She noticed the addition to the kitchen side of the cottage had grown considerably in her absence. Instead of four levels, there were now ten or more. A space for a door and three windows were evident. Stigg and Soryn had also started building the fireplace and chimney. She was so excited, her heart nearly burst. Though she had had a warm place to sleep in the castle, she had to share it with four other serving girls. It would be wonderful to have a private place.

She ran up to Bialas and wrapped her arms around him in a firm hug. She gave Stigg one as well. Fanndis' son half-smiled before clearing his throat and promptly getting back to work. Arna did not see the fiery blush that flooded Stigg's cheeks once his back was turned. After brief comments on the progress, Arna followed Fanndis inside and helped her start dinner. Meanwhile, outside, Soryn was sure his cheeks were the same color as the red lanterns in his tower room. He had never expected her to do that. The fact that she had done the same to Stigg flooded his chest with jealousy. Stigg kept his face away in his own embarrassment. They continued to build.

Soryn was no longer bothered by the vomit-scented mortar and he was glad of it, because he was the one responsible for putting it on the stones between each layer and in all the cracks. By the time Fanndis called them in for dinner, they had gotten twelve layers of stone completed. The room was now up to Soryn's middle. He hoped they would be done by the end of the next week. The work was *killing* him. He kept waiting for muscles to show up, but so far none had. It was certain that he would need them if Stigg intended to work him like this for the foreseeable future.

He was stiff as an old man in Niflheim's darkest winter by the time they went inside to eat. Again, the warm compresses were placed on his shoulders. Again, he nearly fell asleep before it was time for him to go. Soryn groaned as he left for the castle, but assured them all he would return the next day. Arna stood at the door of the cottage and watched him leave with Stigg into the woods. The night had turned cloudy and she expected a huge snowstorm. An

176

ominous feeling grew in her chest. Something about the storm ahead would be different than their usual snows. Arna did not know how she knew this, but she knew it was true. Brushing these thoughts aside, she shut the door of the cottage and started the fire for the night. It was not quite time for bed and she was antsy for some physical activity.

More than anything, she wanted to get outdoors and go for a walk before the bad weather settled in. It would be good to be alone for a little while, to explore, and think. She slipped on her thick fur-lined boots and cloak and went out through the front door. Fanndis was still in the kitchen. After skirting around the cottage, she made certain that her teacher was not hanging around the back kitchen door. Carefully trudging through the snow, she walked into the woods in the direction they had gone to the greenhouse. She spared a glance at her soon-to-be room and smiled—knowing that Bialas and Stigg had worked so hard on it for her. It would be wonderful to have a private space of her own. The path they had taken during the morning was littered with their footprints. Again, she looked up at the clouds. Swirling and black, she felt sure they meant trouble. She would have to be swift.

When she made it to the greenhouse, she tried to open the door but something stopped her. A wolf sat, mere feet from her, in front of a giant rock formation. She had not seen it at first, because it was white and blended with the snow so well. Its yellow-amber eyes burned a hole through Arna's boldness and she felt sweat beading on her forehead, panic rising in her throat to form a scream. The wolf did not growl. It simply cocked its head and peered at her quizzically. It reminded her of the way Ulla tilted his head when he talked. "That's odd," she thought. It did not seem like a very animalistic gesture. Without a single sound, the wolf moved from its seated position and circled her. She stood very still, frightened that if she moved, the creature would attack. She hoped it was the "good" wolf that guarded the greenhouse for Fanndis.

Speaking to the animal never occurred to her. Instead, when the wolf finally made a rumbling in its throat, she ran—unfortunately in a direction away from the cottage path. She sprang towards the rock face behind the greenhouse and climbed. The wolf growled and barked at her. Tears of fear and frustration ran down her cheeks as she tried to grab a hold of the slick rock ledges. When she made it up halfway, she heard a terrible, piercing howl and lost her hold on the ledge.

It was only when her body slammed into the hard-packed snow that she realized something was terribly wrong. Intense, clawing pain throbbed through her left leg. Dizziness overtook her. The wolf was quiet. Arna tried to look for him, turning her head. A blazing stab of pain snaked across the back of her skull. Somewhere in the depths of her mind, a thought kept screaming, "Get help!", but she was far too dizzy and weak to heed its advice. Arna groaned, knowing she was in real trouble. Not knowing what to else to do, she looked up at the sky and waited for the snow.

She did not have to wait long. Soon after, white flakes drifted towards her in a beautiful lazy dance. Smiling, her eyelids began to drift closed. Alarm ignited in her chest and quickly raced through her. "I shouldn't go to sleep…" she thought. Just before her eyelids shut completely, she noticed a bright light above her. It came from behind her body.

"Is it morning…?" she asked the falling snow.

Chapter Eleven

In which there is much discussion…

Stigg was terrified when he discovered Arna had disappeared from the cottage. He looked all around the barn and house before he noticed her tracks leading towards the greenhouse. His alarm grew when he saw the portentous sky overhead. A terrible storm was coming. It surprised him that he was so overwhelmed by the thought of danger befalling her. This girl was upsetting the delicate balance he had carved out for his life. Stigg was a solitary, careful man—not prone to change or social interaction. Arna was causing him to feel differently about his methodical existence. She was good for him. Knowing he had no time for such distracting thoughts, he pushed them away. He followed her tracks before the storm hit. About half-way to the greenhouse, snow started to fall in great heavy sheets. Wolves howled in the distance and Stigg quickened his pace. The lantern he carried swung like a great pendulum as he lumbered through the deep snow. The howling grew louder. Then, up ahead, Stigg saw the white wolf running towards him.

"What's happened?!" Stigg demanded.

The girl's hurt. I was guarding the greenhouse and she saw me. I did not mean to frighten her. She climbed up the rock face. When I tried to stop her, she couldn't hear my words. She lost her footing and fell. I think she's broken her leg, the wolf told Stigg as he ran in Arna's direction.

"Did she hurt anything else?" Stigg asked, laboring through the thickening snowstorm.

I'm not sure. As soon as I saw her fall, I ran to get one of you, the wolf answered.

Man and animal ran as fast as they could through the oncoming storm to get to Arna. Since the wolf's speed was far superior to

179

Stigg's, he made it back far earlier than the man. He lay down next to the girl, who had passed out, and attempted to warm her body with his. The light from Stigg's lantern revealed her still form long before he reached her. When he made it to her, he knelt next to her body. It was already covered in a thin blanket of snow, though the side closest to the wolf was beginning to melt. Stigg's heart pounded as he checked for Arna's pulse. It was there, faint. The wolf had said her leg may have been broken. He pushed her skirts up, exposing her stocking-covered legs. He examined each one and saw that the bone of her left thigh was threatening to break through the skin and tights. It would be very painful to splint, but it needed to be done before they could move her. It was a blessing she was unconscious. He gingerly examined her head but could see no gash or wound. There was a deep hole in the snow where her skull had made contact, however, and he imagined she would have a sore neck for the next few days.

"I'm going to splint the leg before any more damage can be done", Stigg told the wolf.

The white creature nodded and settled over her body so that she would be still if she awoke during the process. The wolf inclined his head. When Stigg had a good grip on the leg, he exhaled and jerked the bone back into place. Arna did not stir, which troubled him. He tore strips from his jacket and grabbed several pieces of wood that had fallen from snowy trees. Tying them around the leg, he secured the splint. Stigg picked her up immediately after—careful to cradle her head in his arms. The wolf carried the lantern in its jaws as they got her back to the cottage as quickly as possible. Already, the storm had made it almost too difficult to travel.

Stigg noticed the way Arna smelled of lavender and jasmine— the varieties his mother hung in their kitchen. His fear almost paralyzed him. Though he had not known her for very long, he felt responsible for her protection. He cursed himself for failing to notice her absence sooner. Clenching his teeth, Stigg pressed on through the blinding snow. Fanndis was frantic when Stigg carried Arna's limp body through the open kitchen door.

"Lay her on the table," Fanndis barked as she wadded up a spare towel to cushion the girl's head.

Stigg showed his mother Arna's broken leg and his setting. Fanndis nodded; Stigg had done an expert job of it. Fanndis tore strips of linen from her medicine kit. With Stigg helping, and the wolf watching from the doorway, she removed Arna's skirts and tights. Then, Fanndis thoroughly cleaned the wound and the entire leg with warm cloths and lavender oil. She rubbed a foul smelling salve over the wound that would stop internal bleeding and speed the healing of the bruised skin over the break. Using several layers of linen, they bound it from Arna's knee to the top of her hip near the thigh. Then, they wrapped the entire leg so that it would keep still. They set the wrapped leg on a stack of pillows that Stigg fetched from the den.

Next, Fanndis examined Arna's head. She felt as gently as she could around the back of the girl's skull and felt an enormous bump—Arna probably had a severe concussion. She knew it was bad that the girl had fallen asleep and Fanndis promptly slapped Arna across the cheek. That didn't work. Fanndis resorted to the Seidh and put both hands on either side of Arna's face. She willed herself to enter her pupil's mind and aroused her consciousness. Arna's eyes fluttered open and grew wide as she screamed in her pain. Stigg bristled at the sound, his body tensing.

"Arna, your leg is broken and the pain will be intense for a few moments. We're getting something for the pain now. How is your head?" Fanndis spoke slowly and loudly so the girl's eyes focused only on her.

"My….head…" Arna mumbled, dazed.

"Does it hurt?" Fanndis prompted.

"I'm…dizzy…" Arna said, trying to stay focused on Fanndis, who currently had two heads.

"A concussion; I'm sure of it," Fanndis said to Stigg and the wolf. "We're going to give you something for the pain. It will make you sleepy," the old woman continued as she nudged Arna and carefully guided her back down to the pillow.

While Stigg watched over the girl, Fanndis went about the kitchen gathering herbs: hops, lavender, and devil's claw to mix a powerful painkiller. She took the kettle from the fire hook and immediately poured it into the powdered herbs. It made a strong tea for Arna to drink. After three or four minutes, the old woman supported her apprentice's head and helped her sip the tea until Arna had drunk all of it. While the girl started to doze off, Fanndis quietly asked Stigg to ready the bed in the back of the cottage. While her son did as he was asked, Fanndis requested that the wolf watch Arna while she went into the room with Stigg to make a sun spire to keep the girl warm through the night.

Since Fanndis had not fashioned a spire big enough to support the sun she needed to make, she had to make do with a broom propped between two chairs. Fanndis summoned as much energy as she could and moved her hands in spherical motions, as if she held a great orb between them. Within seconds, a bright, hot, brilliant sun sphere spun between her hands. She set it to float above the broom handle and anchored the sun she had made to her make-shift spire with a hovering spell. When the room had heated through and there were enough blankets on the bed, they brought Arna in and set her on top of the covers. The sun spire's warmth would keep her comfortable enough and the leg needed to remain uncovered. Though the sun spire warmed the room, it did not glow very brightly. Fanndis asked it to burn a dim orange so that it would not wake the girl.

Stigg watched over her throughout the night, with Fanndis checking in on her every hour or so to make certain that the leg was not infected. Arna had been very lucky that the wolf had been guarding the greenhouse. It was unfortunate, however, that he had been the unintentional cause of her injuries. Yet, if he had not been there, they might never have found the girl. As soon as they had her down in the bed to sleep, the snow storm began to beat and whip the cottage with savage winds and sheets of ice. The air howled viciously and Fanndis gave credit to Stigg's thatching that the roof did not cave in. Stigg knew he would have to go on the roof in the morning and shovel the snow off the thatching so it would not buckle and break under the thick blanket.

The night passed slowly for Fanndis and her son. By morning, they were both exhausted, but Arna was not stabilized yet. The storm had calmed to a gentle snow shower by dawn. Stigg finally ordered his mother to bed, though she fought him every step of the way to the sleeping pallet by the hearth. Within minutes, she had dozed off. Stigg returned to the bedroom and sat in the chair by the bed. Arna breathed normally; no sign of fever, and her heartbeat was strong. He knew he should sleep, but instead, he took her small hand in his hands and prayed that she would get better. All was quiet well into the afternoon.

* * *

Soryn woke suddenly in the night when he heard the frightening storm beating against his tower window. Thunder crashed and the wind roared. It sounded like the hurricanes he had read about in the books from Ancient Earth. He knew better; it was one of Niflheim's ferocious blizzards. Though he tried, going back to sleep proved futile.

Can't sleep? Ulla asked quietly.

"No," Soryn admitted.

Want to come for a visit?

"If it's all the same to you, Ulla, I'm pretty tired. Even though I can't sleep, I think I'll stay in bed."

Wish I could sleep in a bed...I suppose it would be rather odd trying to sleep in a bed as a pig.

"I suppose it would," Soryn agreed, yawning.

Nighty night.

"Goodnight."

Eventually, near dawn, Soryn did go to sleep again. Too soon after that, Jori came for him and took him down for his breakfast and morning lessons. The manservant informed Soryn that he would not be able to travel anywhere outside the castle that day because the snowstorm had dumped over seven feet of additional snow during the night. Soryn was disappointed that he would not be able to see Arna or to work on her room, but he thought it would be a good opportunity to explore the castle. He followed Jori into the great hall and ate with Father Kimbli like he always did. Then, they had tutoring. The boy was learning about the New Kristiansand government and how it operated. After his lessons, Soryn had lunch in his room and made his plans to explore the castle once he was done.

He wanted to explore the rooms branching off of the passage that led to the great hall. Also, he wanted to learn more about the portraits hanging between the doors to those rooms. Perhaps he would loiter about the upper floor where the guards' barracks were. The most intriguing rooms to him, however, were those of his brothers. His parents' rooms should probably have been the most interesting, but he remembered them well. Olan and Fenris' rooms were another matter. When he was younger, Soryn had rarely spent time with his twin brothers. They were six years older than him, so they were always off studying or consumed in personal matters.

Soryn pushed his lunch tray away and went down the passage to the main body of the castle. The first room he explored was filled with dusty old furniture in random positions throughout the room—a storage place, he guessed. The next room had chests lining every inch of the walls. In the center of the room, there was just enough of an aisle to walk around and access all of the chests. Soryn opened several of them and discovered bed linens, quilts, blankets, napkins, table cloths, towels, and other fabrics. He figured that it made sense to store excess items in forgotten corners of the castle; forgotten places like his tower.

The next few rooms were just as uninteresting. They were filled with old silver or brass fixtures and textiles that had gone out of fashion. Soryn grew increasingly drawn to his brothers' rooms. His older siblings were identical twins, who had looked exactly like their mother. They had her silvery-white hair, red-brown eyes, and the pale skin of the northern people that dwelt in the polar mountains. A shiver passed over him as he recalled their faces. Both brothers had seemed odd to him...almost otherworldly. Soryn could not remember Fenris smiling a single time. Olan was always off in the woods studying nature or pursuing some new hobby. Soryn's parents had treated the three of them with love and respect, but he remembered that Fenris spent most of his time getting into trouble. Their mother often watched Fenris with wary, concerned eyes.

Soryn frowned. Walking more quickly, he headed towards his family's quarters. As he went on his way, he passed the portraits. It made sense to him that the rooms beside them might be filled with something worthwhile or extraordinary, but those rooms were strangely devoid of contents. Feeling discouraged, he went down to the main corridor of the castle and passed the great hall. When he saw no one there, he visited the office that he and Father Kimbli used for lessons. The old man sat at the small desk, reading over a document with his spectacles balanced precariously on the end of his long nose.

"Hello, Father," Soryn greeted.

"Good day, Lord Maslyn." Father Kimbli looked up and smiled.

"Can you show me the rooms my brothers used to live in? I'm exploring the castle today and I would like to look around in my family's quarters, if that's alright."

"Follow me." Kimbli extended his hand and rose from his chair.

They went up a staircase that branched off the main passage, taking them up to the second level of the castle. Father Kimbli pointed out the room where Soryn's mother and father had lived, then the two rooms his brothers used. The boy had never really thought about his own old room and could not even remember what he had kept there. It would be interesting to explore that place as well. Father Kimbli bowed his head and left Lord Maslyn to himself.

Soryn first entered his old room. The four poster bed he used to sleep in was on the left side. Wooden shelves lined the right wall, housing toys for infants and young children. Dust clung to every surface—he suspected the servants avoided those rooms because of the superstitions surrounding the night of the fire or some other such nonsense. He found his old room entirely dull and went next to explore his parents'.

A giant bed rested in the center of the room with polished mahogany posts, head and foot boards. The coverlet was fine blue velvet. Desks sat on the left side of the room and painted portraits of the entire family covered each one. Soryn took one of the framed pictures and put it in his coat pocket. He would look at it later.

Since his curiosity about his brothers' rooms was so strong, he left his parents', deciding he would go back to it at a later point and examine it more closely. The room closest to his parents' had belonged to Fenris. The door creaked as he pushed it open. Cobwebs stretched out from the door to the threshold as he nudged it wider. All was pitch black inside. Two moth-eaten drapes covered the window on the back wall. A peculiar scent offended him as he stepped inside. Soryn imagined rats or other vermin might have taken up residence in the abandoned space. He wondered why the odor was not in his old room or his parents'.

Light from the open door did little to illuminate the place. It appeared as though everything in the room was painted grey with shadow. A chaotic, disheveled mess covered the floors. Lord Maslyn almost stepped on what looked to be a rusty blade. When he picked it up, he saw that there was fur or some other fibrous material stuck to dark matter on the knife. The blade fell from his hands and clattered to the floor. His heart raced. Memories of his childhood flooded back to him—images of Fenris, skinning a deer in the woods

186

or bringing rabbits home to dissect in his room. Soryn had watched from the door when one unfortunate creature had been the object of his brother's fascination with living things. When the animal had squealed, Soryn had run away to get his mother.

She had comforted him and promised to talk with Fenris about his behavior. Soryn's eldest brother never brought another animal back to his room—at least when Soryn was around. Lord Maslyn knew that did not mean Fenris never brought them back at other times. Fenris had been a vicious hunter—often letting his prey struggle for hours before he finally ended their lives. Olan never hunted. Olan preferred to sit in the woods and draw the animals or observe their activities. Soryn used to follow him, too.

Now, standing in Fenris' old room, Soryn felt a strange feeling growing in his heart. The boy looked over to the table in front of the bed and saw the skeletal remains of some creature that had suffered one of his brother's cold necropsies. The entire room exuded a sinister aura. Soryn left. When he opened Olan's door, the room looked much brighter than Fenris'. Olan never kept drapes over his window, Soryn remembered. The window glass was dirty with grime and it was difficult to see through. Considering the snow storm raging outside, there would have been nothing to see, anyway. This room was arranged much like Fenris'.

Books were strewn out on the bed and on every other available space. Most were open to specific pages with notes scattered about. Lord Maslyn was instantly reminded of Ulla's study. It had the same look and feel. There was no sun spire, however. Soryn looked at one of the open books. He was shocked to see it was about the Seidh. A particular sentence caught his eye:

"Animal transmutation is far more difficult than object transmutation."

Soryn immediately thought of Ulla and how he claimed to have been human once. The boy wondered what had happened to Ulla.

How had he been transformed into a pig? Next to the open book, Soryn saw an open journal—written in Olan's curly script. Excitement coursed through him…he was about to read something his own brother had written! Though it did not bring Olan back, it made him feel closer somehow. One entry read:

I wonder what it would be like to walk about in an animal's skin. I know if I transmuted myself, it would be my own skin, but I would be changed; other. I have always pondered the animals in the barn. Whenever I visit, they seem so at peace with themselves. The cows are content to sit in their stalls, chewing their cud and standing for hours. The horses are content to swat flies with their tails and stomp their feet at regular intervals. The pigs—ah the pigs—are by far the most intelligent of creatures. There is a cunning cleverness behind their dark eyes that speaks of knowledge. When I spoke with some of them, they carried on perfectly rational conversations. One pig in particular, Ulla, is a wise old soul. He's a large, pink Harkjoran pig. He often speaks of the theoretical notions behind animal communication with humans and the implications of it. I find him fascinating. If ever I were to change myself into the form of a pig, I would seek him out immediately and spend hours talking with him.

Soryn's heartbeat went from quiet, even strokes to rattling whips. Chills rose on his arms. *Ulla…pigs…the desire to become one.* "What if Ulla is really my brother? What if Ulla is Olan?" these thoughts raced through Soryn's mind. Soryn knew that "Ulla" was not the same pig that Olan had written about in his notes, but what if his brother Olan had transformed himself into a pig the night of the fire? What if that was the only way he could escape? What if Olan had taken the name "Ulla" because he had so admired the wisdom of that particular pig in the barn? Soryn grabbed the journal and fled the room. He took the journal to his tower and immediately accessed the secret door to the study.

Coming for a visit? Ulla chimed.

"I've got to show you something and ask you some questions."

Goody.

Soryn made sure to keep his mind only on Arna, Fanndis, and Stigg so that Ulla would not be able to read his real thoughts just yet. When Soryn reached the study, Ulla sat on the chair next to the table. Soryn smacked the journal down on the cluttered surface and asked, "Did you write this?"

Ulla glanced down at the journal and answered with another question:

Why do you want to know?

"I want to know if you are my brother! I want to know if you have been alive all these years and haven't told me! I want to know what happened the night of the fire!" Soryn yelled.

Soryn, calm down. These are big questions. Important questions. You won't get the answers you seek if you scream at me like that. I had my reasons for neglecting to contact you.

"So, you are my brother," Soryn stated.

Yes.

Soryn looked away from Ulla and tried to wrap his mind around that news. This meant his brother was alive. Perhaps Fenris was alive also. Perhaps his parents…

"Are my parents alive? Are they somewhere safe?" Soryn whispered.

No, Soryn. Our parents died in the fire that night. Nothing will change that. I couldn't save them. It was too late…

"Why didn't you tell me this from the beginning? Why couldn't you tell me you were Olan from the start? I would have done everything within my power to free you from your animal form in an instant. Why didn't you trust me?" Soryn asked, heartbroken that his brother had not told him about his predicament.

It's complicated. I didn't tell you right away, because I knew you would be upset that I hadn't spoken to you in six years. I knew you would be angry with me. I haven't spoken to you, because I've been ashamed, Soryn. I failed our family. I saw what our brother was doing to us—tearing us apart—and when I tried to stop his madness, it backfired and caused the death of our parents.

"How so?" Soryn demanded.

This is quite a long tale. You might need to sit down.

Ulla hopped from the chair to the table and Soryn took his seat.

How much do you remember about Fenris and his...personality?

"I remember he liked to hunt—a little too much. He used to bring animals back to his room and examine them. When they were dead, he would dissect them."

He didn't dissect them, Soryn, he vivisected them.

"What does that mean?"

He dissected them while they were still alive. I believe that's why you ran to tattle to our mother about his behavior once, is it not? You might not have realized what he was doing, but you had sense enough to be bothered by it.

Soryn tried to block the memories that surfaced because of Ulla's words.

Take your time, Soryn. I understand that this is difficult.

Soryn nodded. "Thank you, Olan."

You can still call me "Ulla" if it is more comfortable for you. I know that I look and feel quite different to you than the brother you knew as "Olan".

"Alright. Did you rename yourself after that pig you met in the barn?" Soryn said.

Yes. Ulla was a great friend of mine. It broke my heart when he passed on.

Soryn tried to maintain his composure...hoping Ulla would continue with his story. Sensing the boy's thoughts, the pig went on with his tale.

Right, well, you saw in the journal that I was very interested in animal transmutation? Long before the night of the fire, I had thought about trying to transform our brother Fenris into an animal.

190

I thought he might not hurt them so much if he knew what it felt like to be in their skin. I found every book I could on the subject and studied it deeply. Before I could attempt it, however, something happened.

"What happened?"

Our mother went to her room to prepare for bed. Father had not come up to our wing of the castle yet. I heard terrified screams down the hallway and ran to her room. Her hands covered her face. Fenris had laid a dead rabbit on her pillow with its brain exposed. I could see that the brain had two small pins sticking out at particular places—the Wernicke and Broca's areas—the speech and language centers of the brain. I'll admit that I was fascinated. Next to the pillow on a scrap of paper was written, "Like what you see?"

"Couldn't he have just put the pins there to fasten it to the pillow?" Soryn pointed out.

Fenris and I shared a...connection. I can't explain it, but it was always as though we could read each others' minds. We knew each other well. I knew he had placed those pens in those spots for a reason.

"I see," Soryn said—a little envious of their deep connection.

Naturally, our poor mother fainted. She had not studied biology in university, but I had studied it with Father Kimbli and I knew that our brother had found something extraordinary about animals' brains. Their language center was exceptionally well developed on the planet of Niflheim and it was clear he wanted to find out why. Sure, many scientists had already studied this—with little success— but Fenris wanted to find groundbreaking discoveries. He had always been obsessed with the inner workings of the body— the brain specifically. Still, to leave that animal on our mother's pillow, in a desperate plea for attention, was vile to say the least.

I told Father about the incident. He was the one who found Fenris out in the woods checking his traps. Our brother was dragged back to the castle and locked in the dungeon to "think" about what he had done. Of course no harm came to him—the guard brought him food and he was well tended. I visited him, but he did not say much to me. I could not understand why he hadn't just told mother about his theories. He had put the rabbit there just to frighten her, I was sure. The message had been for me. When I asked him about his reasoning, he simply cocked his head and smiled. He said, "Didn't she find it interesting?" It was as though he had just put a bundle of summer flowers on her bed.

I left, frustrated. Later, Father went back down to the dungeon to check on Fenris and talk to him about what had happened. When he got to the cell, our brother was gone. The guard had been knocked out and had a nasty bruise on his forehead. A rock lay nearby. They eventually discovered that the Fenris had escaped down a passage accessible by a loose stone tile on the floor. Fenris was extremely good at figuring out secrets and puzzles. He probably knew every secret passageway in this castle.

"How did the fire happen?" Soryn asked.

Well, Fenris did not surface again until a particularly cold winter night about a month later. Our mother had been worried sick about him and prayed night and day for his return. We were all having a grand dinner in the great hall that night. Officials from the town council were present and father was celebrating a treaty he had made with New Herning's council. The other town was high in the mountains and needed permission to pass their exports through New Kristiansand. Father needed to be able to allow his exports to pass through their mountains. It was a celebrated and monumental agreement.

Well into dinner, the hall doors burst open. Fenris walked in covered in blood, holding one of his skinning knives. The entire room fell silent. The guards' hands were on their swords, but they were all looking at Father trying to discern what to do. Fenris had tribal markings on his face—the kind of those who live in the Eastern caves. In his eyes there was a strange pride. In my mind, I began to recite incantations for transmuting human beings into animals. I had already decided if Fenris posed a threat to our family or himself, I would change him into an animal. That way, the guards would catch him more easily.

Fenris walked calmly across the hall to the end of the table where our parents sat. He raised his knife. I immediately used the Seidh to send my brother into the body of an animal. Unfortunately…it worked.

"Unfortunately?" Soryn asked.

He changed into a wolf, but he was disoriented. His animal body was huge in comparison with his human one. He thrashed about wildly and everyone in the hall panicked. Most fled the room at once. Fenris flailed and raged against his new form and knocked down several hanging oil basins from the hooks on the walls. The fire spread so quickly… I could do nothing to stop it.

Snippets of memory fell into place in Soryn's mind. Images of a white wolf causing chaos…the fire…

I had not learned that when a human transmutes another human, a price must be paid. My price was that I, too, was turned into an animal. A pig. In his rage, Fenris burst through the eastern glass window and ran to the woods. I could vaguely see that a group of guards had run off to catch him but I knew it would be a fruitless endeavor. Being turned into such a small animal, I was able to navigate through the commotion and make my way into the tower and the secret study.

I did not know our parents had died until the next day. They say the fire consumed them so completely that they did not even find their bones.

Soryn did not know what to say. The news that his brother was a pig…that his own brothers were inadvertently responsible for his parents' death…it was too much. They were both quiet for a long time. Finally, Soryn stood up and started for the passage.

"I think I'll go up to my room for a while," he said, emptiness seeping through his words.

He left the study and managed to climb back up to the hearth without paying much attention to his steps. Once in his room, he sat down at the long table. A tear escaped, followed by many more. Before Soryn knew it, he was sobbing into his shirt sleeves. He thought he wanted to know the truth about the past. But now that he knew…he wished he didn't. Memories flooded back to him—the terrible fire, Father Kimbli grabbing him and hauling him to the back of the room away from all the commotion. The sight of the wolf breaking the glass window…It had been the most frightening night of his life. It was no wonder the memories had remained buried so long.

Soryn did not eat dinner that night—not even when Father Kimbli offered to bring it himself. He stared at the fire. Some time when he had been talking with Kimbli, one of the servants had made one. He just watched it burn, letting the orange light lull his eyes into a numbed stupor. A furious wind blew outside his windows. Lord Maslyn wondered if the snow storm would last forever. Ulla said nothing more throughout the night and Soryn was glad of it. He closed his eyes and fell asleep with his head on the table. His dreaming mind listened to the sounds of the wind crying and the Night Bells ringing.

Chapter Twelve

In which a new discovery is made…

Arna grumbled at her broken leg and eyed the white wolf with a sour expression.

"It's your fault," she muttered. "You could have just spoken to me. Then I wouldn't have thought you were trying to eat me."

I did try to talk to you. You weren't listening.

"Well," Arna sighed. "Looks like I'm stuck in bed all day. Probably tomorrow and the rest of the week, too. It's a good thing Fanndis has four million books for me to read or I would go insane being cooped up in here," Arna whined.

You wouldn't want to go outside right now. The whole world is buried under twelve feet of snow.

"How did you get in, then?"

The window. My mate and pups had to dig their way out of our den this morning in order to find food. Stigg is up on the roof shoveling off the thatch. Fanndis is in the kitchen. Everyone is busy, but you and I. Is there anything I can do for you?

"You could tell me your name," Arna suggested.

You may call me Ulf.

"Ulf?" she remarked.

Yes. Ulf. Shall I fetch you something? Though you were not listening when I tried to warn you of how slippery the rocks were, I do feel responsible for frightening you. I will do whatever I can to help with your healing.

"I think I am fine for now. I must say, you are a very pretty thing. I've never seen a wolf up close before." Arna studied his abundant white fur and large paws. "How many pups do you have?"

Seven. They are quite a handful, but my mate is an excellent mother.

195

"May I meet them one day?" Arna asked.

Perhaps. They live very near the greenhouse. Maybe the next time you come, I can arrange something.

"That would be nice." Arna smiled.

She gazed at the giant sun spire that Fanndis had created for her. It was warm and beautiful. Arna wondered if she could make one if she tried. An attempt would be made once she could get up and move about. Ulf's movement caught her attention. He slinked quietly out of the room. Once he was gone, she reclined on her ample pillows and closed her eyes.

The back of her skull pounded from the concussion she had sustained hitting the snow bank. The lump on her head was huge. She hoped it would go down soon so that she could sleep comfortably. Whenever she touched it, a wave of nausea crashed over her stomach. Her leg looked like a swollen, snow-covered log. Fanndis had changed the linens once Arna had woken up earlier that afternoon. The white fabric contrasted with the grey homespun quilt over the bed. Arna missed Lord Maslyn. She missed being in the kitchen or at the barn with Fanndis and learning the Seidh. She missed mobility. Appreciation for the ability to walk would never be lost on her again.

Ulf returned about an hour later. Arna sat reading from a text on herbal cures. She looked up when his claws tapped against the wooden floor. In his mouth was a giant ball of fur. At first, the girl thought Ulf might have been carrying his tail in his mouth, but then she realized he was carrying one of his pups. He sat it down on the bed and Arna felt her entire body disintegrate into mush.

"Oh, my goodness!" she squealed as she reached down to pick up the little wolf pup. He yawned, looking bored. He tolerated her petting.

His name is Derik. He's our youngest. He was whining when I went home to visit, so I thought he might like to meet you. He's too young to talk with humans.

"You are so precious! I wish you could stay with me!" Arna beamed, hugging him close to her neck where his soft fur could touch her skin. He licked her cheek and she squealed again.

Stigg watched from the threshold and smiled. Arna was such a vibrant person. The work on the thatching had taken all morning and he was enjoying a much needed break. Wanting to give the girl some space and time to enjoy the wolf pup, he went outside to shovel snow away from the cottage walls. The scene from the previous night played through his mind. He was so glad Ulf had come to him. If not, Arna might have been buried under the snow and never found until summer's thaw.

In the kitchen, Fanndis prepared soup for dinner. The ladle made calming circular motions in the cauldron as she hummed to herself. Though Arna's broken leg and concussion had scared her to death, Fanndis was quite recovered and cheerful after a nearly sleepless night. When the soup was finished, she brought a bowl to Arna in the back room of the cottage.

"Thank you," Arna said gratefully.

"You're welcome. Who's this little fellow?" Fanndis asked, rubbing the tiny wolf pup behind the ears.

His name is Derik, Ulf answered.

"Well, you're a handsome little thing aren't you? Yes you are!" Fanndis could not help herself. She gushed over the tiny wolfling as well.

You'll both spoil him if you're not careful, Ulf chided, though he gave a growling wolf chuckle at the women's behavior.

Arna passed Derik to Fanndis' excited embrace and ate her soup. Its soothing heat filled her chest with warmth and she smiled. Her leg ached, but thanks to a cleverly made poultice, it was mostly numb. Fanndis, Ulf, and Derik eventually left the room, though the girl was glad she got to see the precious baby animal yawn one more time (eliciting a chorus of squeals from the females in the room). She grew tired and slept again. The suns had not even set.

197

Fanndis and Stigg both checked on her during the night. She was out of danger, though, and the older two slept most of the night themselves. In the morning, Stigg began work on a crutch for her, with some help from Fanndis. By the end of the day, they had helped her out of bed and Arna was able to hobble around the room a bit. Unfortunately, due to the enormous amount of snow that had been dumped during the blizzard, Lord Maslyn was still unable to visit that day. After Arna fell asleep that night, Fanndis and Stigg slept the whole night through.

* * *

Lord Maslyn could not stand any more time away from his friends, so he carefully walked on top of the neck-high snow with his snow shoes until he came to the cottage. Stigg had obviously been busy uncovering the cottage foundations, so Soryn climbed down until he could knock on the front cottage door. Fanndis hugged him around the neck when she invited him in. Warmth from inside the cottage was overpowering compared to the frigid air outside. He was almost entirely frozen from the waist down and sat by the fire for a long while, letting his stiff limbs thaw out.

"Where's Arna today?" he asked when he did not see her.

"She's in the back room. I think you'll want to see how she's doing. She had an accident the other night," Fanndis replied.

"An accident? Is she alright!?" Lord Maslyn shrieked.

"She's fine. Just go see her," Fanndis laughed.

Soryn trailed into the back bedroom, blankets wrapped about him. Arna was napping. On top of her covers was an enormous leg cast. Soryn gasped. Because she was sleeping, he peeped his head back into the main cottage room and whispered, "How did it happen?"

"She was startled by our wolf friend that guards our greenhouse in the woods. When she thought he was a threat, she tried to climb the icy rock face and fell and broke her leg. She also suffered a concussion. She's doing much better now," the old snow woman told him.

"I'm glad she's alright," Soryn sighed in relief. He wondered if he could sit with her. "Can I stay with her today? I know I should help Stigg, but she's my friend and I want to be there when she wakes up."

"I think that would be lovely. I'll have a word with Stigg." Fanndis smiled—knowing all too well that the two children cared deeply for one another.

Soryn wrapped up in several more blankets and brought a chair from the other room. He sat it closely to the floating sun spire so he would be warm while he waited for Arna to awaken. Naturally, his gaze rested on his friend. She looked so beautiful lying on the bed. Her broken leg lay wrapped up in countless strips of linen and looked about three times its size. Soryn frowned. It was unfair that she had gotten hurt just when she was beginning her life as a Seidh apprentice.

He moved his chair close enough to put his hand over hers. Arna's skin was soft and cold. He blushed and started to pull away. Soryn was startled when she shifted her arm and curled her hand around his. Looking up at her face, he was sure that she was still sleeping. Embarrassment flooded his chest when she slyly opened her left eye to look at him. Arna smiled.

"Hello, Bialas," she said, yawning.

"Hello, Arna," he replied, gently removing his hand.

"Oh…" she said, surprised.

Soryn timidly reached out and put his hand back around hers.

"I'm sorry about your leg," Soryn muttered.

"Oh, it's alright. It was my fault, running from Ulf. He's the white wolf that guards the greenhouse. He was growling and I got frightened. He was just trying to speak to me, though. I'm not sure why I couldn't hear him at the time. Ever since I fell, I've been able to hear him just fine. Is he still here?" Arna craned her neck, trying to see over Soryn's head.

"I didn't see him. Is he nice? I mean, aren't wolves supposed to eat people?" Soryn asked, uncomfortable.

"Oh, no. Fanndis said that wolves never attack humans," Arna assured him.

"He seems kind," Lord Maslyn said, trying to be polite, but still wary of the creature—especially after finding out that Ulla was his brother. What if the wolf was Fenris?

"Well, his pup Derik is really my favorite. I think I may talk Ulf into letting Derik stay with me once he gets older. Not really sure if he would agree, though," Arna giggled.

"Arna…I need to tell you something. I hope I'm not interrupting, but…you see…I just really need to talk to someone about this." Lord Maslyn felt he could not delay his tale.

"Of course, Bialas. You can talk to me about anything."

"It's about Ulla," he said, fidgeting with his hands.

"Ulla?"

"He's my brother, Arna. He's my brother, Olan." Soryn told her.

"Your brother? But how? I mean…how is that possible, Bialas?" Arna was astonished at Lord Maslyn's confession.

"I don't know. He said that it happened when he turned my other brother, Fenris, into a *wolf.*"

"I remember hearing about that as a child. I was a kitchen maid at the time. I heard the older girls talking about it for days. I didn't want to say anything to you until you found out more on your own. I didn't know if I should…"

"It's alright," Soryn sighed. "Anyway, everyone was so distracted by the wolf's disastrous thrashing that no one noticed a small, black pig running out of the room, terrified for its life."

"Did he tell you this?" Though Arna believed Soryn thought he was telling her the truth, she still did not trust Ulla.

"I figured it out when I visited my brothers' old rooms and found Olan's journal. He spoke of a pig he admired in the barn named, 'Ulla' and how much he hoped he would be able to try animal transmutation one day."

"You asked him about it and he confirmed it, right?" she asked.

"Right."

Arna was troubled by this news. Though she was extraordinarily happy that Soryn might have at least one family member alive, it still bothered her that Ulla was always so sneaky. He never did anything overly suspicious, but Ulla's whole demeanor felt devious to her. She hoped that she would not offend Bialas if she said something about the validity of Ulla's claim.

"Do you think he's really telling the truth?" she whispered.

"I wouldn't have believed him if he came out and told me—he knew that. He said so himself. Because I found the journal, because of what I read, Arna, I truly feel that he *is* my brother."

"He wants us to learn how to turn him human, doesn't he?" Arna had suddenly put all the pieces together: Ulla's apparent support in getting Lord Maslyn out of the tower, encouraging them to find Fanndis, leading Soryn to believe he was his brother...It all made sense. If he were really Olan, he would have known about Fanndis because he would have seen her in the castle—perhaps even learned about the Seidh from her. It was clear, however, that he was not adept enough at magic to perform it without turning himself into an animal along with Fenris. It was also clear he did not have enough skill to get himself out of his predicament.

"He admitted that, yes," Soryn confessed.

"Do you want to help him?" Arna asked pointedly.

"Of course I do, Arna! What kind of a question is that?"

"What if he's lying, Bialas? I would never want to accuse him of that without cause, but you have to admit that he's been somewhat cryptic the entire time we've known him."

Soryn didn't want to acknowledge her words, but he knew them to be wise. Somewhere in his mind, the suspicion was there. What if Ulla was not who he said he was? If Ulla was Olan, like he claimed, then there would be no harm in investigating to be sure.

Arna?

The girl nearly jumped out of her skin when Ulf's voice came into her head.

"Yes, Ulf?" Arna said, looking around Lord Maslyn to see if the wolf was in the doorway. He was not. "Where are you, Ulf?"

I'm outside with Stigg. Can you send Soryn out? Stigg needs help with something.

"Sure, but why don't you just ask him yourself?" Arna suggested.

Ulf did not reply. Soryn was confused at her dialogue with the absent animal. "What's going on?" Soryn asked.

"Stigg apparently needs some help with something and can't be bothered to come and tell you. Ulf relayed the message. You better go on and see if you can help him. That man will work himself to death one of these days." Arna shook her head.

"I'll be back, later. Please get some rest, Arna." Soryn smiled. As he headed for the door, he mulled over her words.

"Bialas, please don't misunderstand what I said about Ulla. I'm very happy that you may've found your brother. I just want you to be careful, that's all. He hasn't exactly been very straightforward with you, you know."

With that Arna waved him out of the room and tried to go back to sleep. However, her mind was decidedly active. It was running through every encounter that she had had with the pig.

Ulla always made her feel uncomfortable. Not like Ulf. The white wolf was somewhat aloof, but very kind and a loving father, from what it looked like. She trusted Ulf. She did *not* trust Ulla— even if he *was* Lord Maslyn's long lost older brother. It seemed overly convenient that, when the pig wanted to become human, he just so happened to be Lord Maslyn's brother. Then again, he could be telling the truth. Maybe. She could not be sure. Perhaps Fanndis would have some insight into the whole thing. Her teacher did not seem overly fond of Ulla either, which might cause some unnecessary bias. Still, Arna would ask her.

The herbs that Fanndis kept putting under Arna's pillow made her sleepy again. She closed her eyes for what felt like a couple of seconds and she was out again. A dream of snow and the northern mountains drifted into her mind. Though she had never been to the place her dream depicted, she felt sure she was seeing a real place. A woman dressed in heavy furs of various pelts hiked ahead of her on a narrow mountain trail. The way was rocky and steep, but the woman led her to the strongest footpaths and often extended her hand to her to help Arna keep her footing.

A goat bleated somewhere higher up the track. The sound startled Arna and when she slipped, the woman caught her hand. Her face was shrouded in shadow beneath a dark cowl. She was old, that much was clear from her hunched stature and that raspy voice that said many times, "Keep to the path." After a while, they entered a cave lit up by a blazing interior fire.

The cave was sparsely furnished, but large. Her guide went about putting away the heavy traveling cloak. Arna watched her curiously. The girl sat when the old woman sat. A goat rested by the fire. When Arna extended her hand to pet the beast, the woman swiftly swatted her hand away.

"Do not touch," the stern voice barked.

Arna mumbled an apology. The woman grew quiet and began to sway. She brought her hands up over her head before bringing them down suddenly and stretching them out towards the goat. What looked like tendrils of smoke curled out from the old woman's hands and wrapped the goat's body in a smoky cocoon. Before Arna's eyes, the goat's body changed into that of a human man. He was very pale and looked ill. He stared at Arna with the saddest eyes she had ever seen. Before she could say anything to comfort him, the woman withdrew her hands and the man became a beast once more.

"This man cannot be human or he will die," she said, as if she were explaining the weather.

"Why?" Arna asked.

"He is sick. The disease spreads less quickly in the goat's body. He will live longer this way. I have done this to help him. However, he misses his human body. He begs me to return him to his human form permanently. I change him back once each day just to remind him how much pain his human body is in. Though his animal body is sick also, it does not feel as much pain as when he is in his own. It is a kindness that I do not change him back."

Arna said nothing and looked on the goat with pity. She wondered what had made him so ill. Why did he not simply get medicine for what ailed him?

"He cannot get medicine because there is none to give him. He has cancer. Even on Ancient Earth, they were unable to cure that particular evil. He is beyond hope. He will die very soon. I keep him here so that he may die in peace," the old woman explained.

The goat exhaled heavily and then struggled up on its four legs. He sniffed the air and walked out of the cave mouth onto the mountain path.

"Will he be alright out there?" Arna asked, concerned.

"He'll be alright. He'll come back when he's hungry. Why have you come to visit me?" the old woman asked.

"I'm dreaming. I've been thinking a lot about human transmutation." Arna was a very adept lucid dreamer. No matter how real her dreams felt, she always knew they were not.

"Oh you know you're dreaming, do you?" the old woman raised her eyebrows.

"Yes."

"What if I told you that you are *not* dreaming?"

"I'd say that you're just my subconscious mind trying to convince me otherwise," Arna said, not at all intimidated by the woman's suggestion.

"What would convince you?" she asked.

"I could tell you that. But, you—being a figment of my imagination—will simply confirm what I say in order to make me believe that I'm not dreaming," Arna countered.

"That makes a lot of sense." The old woman nodded.

"I suppose if you predict the future I might believe that this wasn't a dream," Arna suggested.

"When you wake up, Soryn will be sitting by your bedside," the old woman stated.

"That's likely to be true since he is visiting the cottage. You'll have to do better than that," Arna quipped.

"He'll profess his love for you in three and a half years' time, on a night when all of the moons are full. You'll be in the mountains. You'll also be asked a question soon after. You will say 'yes'." The old woman's voice was gravely serious, though her words were of love.

"What?" Arna felt a strange chill creep up her neck.

"If this happens, and it will, you must come see me soon after. There won't be much time."

"What is all this? This is just a dream!" Arna grew angry.

"Is it just a dream?" the old woman asked, staring at the mouth of the cave whimsically.

"Yes!"

"Open your eyes," the old woman ordered.

But they were already open when the girl tried.

* * *

"Arna?!" Soryn yelled, trying to get Arna to snap out of whatever trance she was in.

Vague sounds registered in Arna's head. First, she was staring at the old woman. Then her confusion grew when the cave, the fire, and the mysterious woman faded. Arna found she was staring at the sun spire, sweat soaking her body. She blinked until the whole room came into focus, then looked over at Bialas. He looked petrified.

"W-What happened?" she asked. Whatever she had been doing, it was not dreaming.

205

"You were just lying there with your eyes completely open and you stopped breathing! I thought you had died! What happened?!" Soryn demanded.

"I don't know…" Arna rubbed her eyes and forehead. She had a headache.

"What's going on!?" Fanndis boomed from the doorway.

"Arna was unconscious with her eyes open and she stopped breathing!" Soryn's heartbeat rattled his chest and his breathing was erratic. He had been terrified that something very wrong had happened to his friend.

"What's this?" Fanndis looked at Arna.

"I fell asleep after Lord Maslyn went outside to help Stigg. I was having a strange dream," Arna began.

"That was no dream. Who was speaking to you?" Fanndis interrupted.

"What?" Arna asked, confused again.

"Who was speaking to you in your vision? Was it a woman? A man? An animal? I need details if we're to solve this riddle. We need to know who summoned you," Fanndis said, folding her arms.

"It was a woman—an old woman. She was dressed in wolf pelts and we were hiking in the mountains until we reached her cave. Inside, there was a goat. She changed him into a human before my eyes, but then turned him back. She said that he was sick and that she kept him in animal form as a mercy. She said that he would not die as quickly in an animal body." Arna did not know who this woman was, but by the look in her teacher's eyes she knew that this ordeal was very significant.

"Did you see her face?" Fanndis asked, very serious.

"No. It was shrouded in a cowl and it was too dark to see under it."

"That's because the old bat hid it from you purposefully. She probably wanted me to know that she was testing you."

"Who is it, Fanndis?" Arna asked, suddenly starting to believe that she been in the other woman's actual presence. How was that possible?

"Her name is Valkyrie and she's an old Seidh woman of the north. I, myself, trained with her many years ago. She's a few years older than me. At the time my training began, she had already mastered magical powers that many do not even attempt until they are far advanced in their practice. Valkyrie's quite a force to be reckoned with. If she's taken an interest in you, we need to keep close watch on your dreams."

"How did she find out about me in the first place!?" Arna was exasperated at the idea of some strange woman monitoring her mind when she was unconscious and vulnerable.

"It's hard to say. She may have been passing through the village and heard about you or she might have sent her spies here to keep watch on *me* and might have learned about you by accident," Fanndis admitted, her lips drawn tight.

"You mean she spies on you?" Arna felt a little afraid of this Valkyrie woman.

"She likes to…how shall I put it?" Fanndis tapped her cheek, thinking. "She likes to collect information about her former apprentices in case she needs to entice one of them to aid her in her wild experiments. Some of my friends, who also studied under her, just say she's morbidly curious and a busybody. I think there's more to it, personally."

"Great. Now, not only do we have Bialas' brother Ulla to worry about, but we have some meddling intruder entering my mind!" Arna snapped her head away from Fanndis and Soryn. She was quite put out.

Stigg had come in by that time. He was unsure of what everyone was discussing, but he could tell it was a distressing topic. Stigg's mother tapped her foot frantically on the floor and Soryn paced about the room biting his lip.

"What about Ulla?" Fanndis' foot stopped and she grew very still.

Arna, realizing what she had blurted out, covered her mouth and looked apologetically at Bialas. He caught her gaze and frowned. Soryn knew there was no taking it back now. He might as well go ahead and tell Fanndis about what Ulla had told him. Perhaps she would help, perhaps not, but he certainly trusted everyone in the room not to tell anyone.

"Ulla is my brother Olan. He didn't tell me. I found out on my own when I read through some of Olan's old journals. When I approached Ulla about it, he admitted it was the truth." Soryn stared at the floor, afraid to meet Fanndis' gaze.

"How did you come to this conclusion?" Fanndis asked, still calm and quiet.

"After the snowstorm the other night, I couldn't come visit you, so I went to the old family quarters of the castle. I found Olan's journals next to a book about animal transmutation. The entry was definitely in Olan's handwriting and it mentioned how much he liked a pig in the castle's barn named 'Ulla'. It also mentioned how much he wanted to be able to transform into an animal. He was fascinated with animal transmutation—just as my other brother, Fenris, was fascinated with the biology behind animal communications with humans."

"And you asked Ulla about this?" Fanndis asked.

"Yes. I confronted him and probably backed him into a corner, but he told me the truth. He had already told me that he was a human trapped in a pig's body. I never suspected it was Olan until I found the journal entry," Soryn said.

"You're sure of this, Soryn?" Stigg asked from the back corner of the room.

It startled the others in the room when Stigg spoke. He rarely contributed to conversations unless it was strictly necessary. Soryn nodded at the man.

"Yes. I'm sure he's my brother."

"Well…this certainly makes things more complicated, doesn't it?" Fanndis remarked.

"He helped us get out. He told us to find you, Fanndis. I think it was because he thought we might learn how to turn him human again," Arna suggested.

"That may be true, but I think we should help him no matter how selfish his motives were," Soryn said, on the defensive.

"I meant no offense, Bialas, but there is the possibility that Ulla was using us all along. He may not be your brother at all. I just don't like the way he went about it. He's too sneaky," Arna admitted.

"Ulla is *not* Olan, Lord Maslyn," Stigg declared from the doorway of the room.

"How do you know? I would know more than anyone!" Soryn protested.

"Stigg is right, Lord Maslyn. I don't believe he's Olan, either. It doesn't add up. We need to investigate further," Fanndis agreed with her son.

"How can you know this?" Soryn said, tears stinging his eyes.

He had been so lonely and Ulla helped him find friendship and freedom—they were all forgetting this. So what if he was going to use them just to become human again? He had lived for six years as an animal. His sensibilities were bound to be skewed.

"Soryn, think about it. What do you remember about Olan's temperament? I can tell you that the animal I met in my old study was nothing like the Olan that I remember and trained all those years ago," Fanndis said.

In Lord Maslyn's mind, images of Fenris beating Olan up in the woods flashed by. Olan would never cry, though he was a timid and sensitive boy. He would just grab Soryn's hand and walk away, leaving Fenris laughing. Other images entered Soryn's head: Olan befriending birds in the woods and sitting with patience while he drew their delicate feathers; Olan speaking to the cats or rats he kept as pets. Ulla did seem very different from the brother he remembered. Soryn's mother had always called Olan an "old, gentle soul". Ulla did not seem like Fenris either—too reserved and not nearly malicious enough. However, he did feel strangely familiar to Soryn.

"Perhaps you're right," Soryn conceded, though he did not want to believe it. He finally thought he had found his brother. Now, perhaps he had not. Sitting down on the bed, he put his head in his hands. He felt Arna's small hand rest on his shoulder.

"We'll sort this out, Bialas. Don't worry. Perhaps he *is* your brother, but just changed or something. It may take a lot out of a person's personality to be transferred into a different body." Arna attempted to comfort him.

Ulla is lying to the boy, Ulf spoke only to Stigg's mind.

"Obviously," Stigg scowled under his breath, only loud enough for Ulf to hear.

We need to know more about this pig. I'll investigate and see what I can find out. Eira and I will talk to all the animals we have connections with in the castle, Ulf said.

"Let me know what you uncover."

Will do. With that, Ulf was gone and Stigg heard Eira meow outside the cottage. He could certainly count on those two to find out the truth. Stigg gave his mother a meaningful glance and she could tell that the wolf had left the cottage and had gone in search of knowledge about this situation.

"Arna, you need to get some rest after your encounter with Valkyrie. Soryn, come with me," Fanndis commanded.

Before the girl could protest, Lord Maslyn and Fanndis had left the room and she was alone with Stigg. He looked troubled and pensive.

"What's the matter, Stigg?" Arna asked.

"I don't like the pig. I don't care for anyone who makes people deliberately uncomfortable. I know for certain, however, that he is *not* Lord Maslyn's brother Olan."

Arna was also troubled by the conversation. She wanted to get to the bottom of it all. If the pig truly was Lord Maslyn's brother, she wanted to help turn him human again once she was strong enough. If it was not, she wanted to find out who it really was and fast. Confounding Fanndis' sleeping draughts, Arna fell asleep again. Her rest was, thankfully, free of that Valkyrie woman's meddling.

Stigg watched from the doorway, deep in thought concerning the events over the last week. He knew much about the Maslyn family and its past but that girl in the bed…he knew nothing of her. Though she was some years his junior and far too young for him, she was enchanting and wholly unique. In some ways, Stigg was reminded of Fanndis—with her devil-may-care attitude and her sense of humor—but there was something else there that made Arna entirely herself. He just couldn't place what it was. She was certainly diverting and that was a welcome change from the boring life of the son of a powerful Seidh woman. In all of Stigg's twenty three years, he finally felt that something extremely interesting had taken root in his dusty heart.

Since Fanndis was busy with Soryn, and Ulf and Eira had gone to gather information, Stigg felt he should sit with Arna awhile. That protective feeling he had experienced the night she had fallen from the rock face had not waned. He did not want her to be alone so soon after Valkyrie had invaded her mind. Because it still nagged him, he labeled the feelings he was having towards her as brotherly affection. When he was a boy, his mother had birthed another child—a baby girl—but she grew very ill during the summer and soon died. Stigg had been eight years old; old enough to be devastated by the incident, but young enough to recover. He supposed he was thinking of Arna as some shade of the little sister he lost long ago.

The warmth of the sun spire soothed his tired body. Angry winds whipped against the stones of the cottage and the sound was like the rocking of a boat. Soon, Stigg fell asleep in the chair. When Fanndis found him later, she smiled and walked softly into the room. Fanndis looked from Stigg to Arna. The girl had been such a comforting presence in the house. Fanndis wanted to protect her. In

211

order to do that, she had to know why Valkyrie was so interested in the girl.

She walked up to Stigg and gently shook his shoulder until he woke up and stretched.

"Sorry I fell asleep. I didn't want to leave her alone," he muttered, still groggy.

"It's alright, son," Fanndis whispered. "It's good to see you at rest."

"Where's Soryn?" he asked.

"He's outside shoveling out around Arna's room so that you two will be able to resume work soon," Fanndis informed him.

"Ah," Stigg yawned.

"Stigg, I want you to find out more about Ulla. I know that Ulf and Eira will help you. I must take care of another matter and I might be gone a night or two. Please watch over Arna and Soryn. Don't let them out of your sight for long. Send Kimbli a message and ask him to come here for Soryn's lessons for the next two days. I don't want the boy anywhere near that pig until we know exactly who he is. Kimbli must be apprised of the entire situation—he's the only one in that town we can fully trust."

"I understand. Are you going to go visit that woman?" Stigg was concerned for his mother traveling alone through the mountains.

"Yes. Unfortunately, I must face Valkyrie once more. I suppose I was overdue for a visit, anyway. I'm getting too old for these sorts of escapades," she grumbled.

"Mother…you're only fifty-nine years old." Stigg pursed his lips.

"Yes, but Soryn and Arna call me the 'old snow woman' so perhaps I *should* trudge around like some ancient crone," Fanndis smiled, trying to get her son to cheer up.

"Nonsense," Stigg said, smirking.

"Well, I need to leave before it gets dark. I'll take your horse and leave Liv here, if that is alright with you. Ivan is a much stronger animal and I know he can travel longer distances without growing tired," she said.

"That's fine. Mother, please be safe. It's dangerous up there on the mountain," Stigg said gravely.

"Ah well, it can't be helped."

Fanndis left. Stigg massaged his temples with his fingers. He was tired. He hoped he would be able to keep up with all the indoor and outdoor work along with caring for Arna as she healed.

"This will be interesting," he mumbled to himself.

He left Arna to sleep and went to the barn. Waving at Soryn, who was working hard to rid Arna's building of snow from the storm, Stigg crossed the waist high snow to the stables. In the barn, Stigg put his fingers to his lips and gave a shrill whistle. From the rafters of the barn, his hawk friend, Vrik, ascended to light upon his extended arm.

"Vrik, I need you to deliver a message to Father Kimbli," Stigg told him.

What sort of message?

"Tell him that we need him to travel to the cottage to give Soryn his lessons for the next two mornings. Let him know that my mother has urgent business in the mountains and I need Soryn's help tending to Arna, who has a broken leg."

It will be done, Vrik promised and flew away into the darkening sky.

Stigg went back and helped Soryn with the shoveling.

"Where did Fanndis go?" Lord Maslyn asked, breathing heavily.

"To see Valkyrie. It's about a day's ride up into the mountains. She may not return for two to three days. Father Kimbli will come to give you your schooling in the mornings at the cottage until she returns. I need help tending to the chores and checking on Arna. You don't mind, do you?" Stigg had never spoken so many words to the boy, but he was beginning to feel more comfortable with Soryn.

"That sounds great! It's so cold in my tower room, anyway. I'd love to sleep on the floor by the fire tonight."

"Well, I'm getting very tired of sleeping in the frozen barn. I'll sleep in the den, also, and that way, if Arna should need something in the night, one of us will be able to reach her quickly."

"Do you think she'll be awake again before nightfall?" Soryn wondered aloud.

"Probably not. The sleeping draughts my mother has been giving her are very strong. She needs her rest. Her leg will take a while to heal. Tomorrow, she will need to get up out of bed and walk around with her crutch for a while—just to get moving," Stigg informed Soryn.

"What if she needs to go to the bathroom?" Lord Maslyn's eyes widened.

"She has a chamber pot. I'd rather not get into her personal business. If she has an urgent issue, I'm sure she'll let us know." Stigg laughed on the inside at the boy's awkward practicality.

"Ah," was all Lord Maslyn said, turning an impossible shade of red.

When the two of them finished clearing out the snow, there was still about an hour of daylight left. They looked at each other and immediately, began working on the room. Now that Arna was injured, it occurred to each one that it would be a nice surprise for her to have a finished room when she was up and moving around by herself again. By the time it was dark, they had put another two layers on the room. Stigg estimated they would be finished in about four days if they could avoid any more blizzards. That did not include furniture for the inside, however. Stigg had almost finished building her bed, but she would still need a desk, chair, and shelf for books.

When they reentered the cottage, Arna was still sleeping and breathing softly. Soryn thought she looked very peaceful and angelic. A hint of smile curled on her lips and there was a tender beauty about her. He wished he could wake her up so that they could talk and laugh together. After several, minutes, however, he knew he should let her sleep. Returning to the main room, he helped Stigg lay out their sleeping pallets for the night.

Before settling down for sleep, Stigg smoked his pipe and started reading from a book entitled, *Aartiksen: Philosophy in the Niflheim Woods*. Soryn felt that would be a bit too dense for him, so he browsed the bookshelf on the wall next to the fire place. There, he saw many books on philosophy—Stigg's he assumed—and some on topics like hunting in the Obanian mountains. He chose one on the natural life in the woods and opened it to see an image of a wolf-pack. It was not a photograph like they had on Ancient Earth, but it was a very detailed drawing.

The two of them, man and boy, sat reading silently just as comfortably as if they had lived their whole lives in the same house. When it was time for sleep, without a word, they settled down. It was utterly peaceful and tranquil. Somewhere off in the woods, Ulf's mate howled for him to return to her. Soryn wondered when the white wolf would go home to his family and when Eira would be back at the cottage. He yawned and supposed he would find out in the morning.

He thought it strange that he felt no sort of suspicions about Ulf. Though he was a white wolf, he was wholly unlike Fenris, whom Soryn remembered to be cruel and sadistic. Ulf was a leader; a *father*. Soryn never suspected him at all. After all, on a planet covered in snow, there were most likely thousands of white wolves. It was a relief knowing Ulf wasn't Fenris. Ulla was enough to worry about.

Chapter Thirteen

In which a mountain is climbed…

Fanndis felt entirely too arthritic to be climbing mountains. Yet, there she was, leading Ivan up a very steep, but steady path towards the peak of Mount Aibek. It had been many years since she had completed her training in the caves of this same region. Then, Valkyrie had been a much younger woman and far less intrusive into other peoples' business. Fanndis wondered what had made her so curious of late. Her old master had often intruded into Fanndis' own dreams and visions years before, when Stigg was a child and she was actively assisting the Maslyn family.

Her displeasure, at the time, with Valkyrie's actions proved to the older woman that Fanndis was not interested in being spied upon. Even so, Fanndis knew her former teacher would never leave off spying on her completely. Ivan snorted and shook his ample mane. Fanndis, drifting back to the present, patted him gently on the side of his neck.

You're doing just fine, Ivan.

He snorted again. Ivan, in common with Eira, preferred not to speak with humans mentally. Also like Eira, he was a reliable and devoted friend, though he would not say anything to the people he knew. Fanndis found animal communication mores very interesting. Some animals relished contact with the human world. There were even animals who had published books (using trusted human translators and scribes) about animal preferences in human communication and population to population communication. Other animals had even written novels. It was something Stigg found fascinating. Fanndis and her son often talked late into the night over such things—trying to tempt Eira to speech, but failing every time. The cat simply meowed or ignored them altogether.

A harsh gust brought her mind to the path once more. The wind bit into her clothes down to her aging skin. She felt thinner than she had when she last came up the mountain. Perhaps her age had made her more susceptible to frostbite. Fanndis truly hoped not, because she still had several hours of travel before she could make camp. The jagged peak loomed high above her. She scowled at her former master for choosing to live so high up some God-forsaken mountain.

Fanndis meditated as she rode the remaining hours away until she came to a familiar cave—one she used to stay in when she traveled down the mountain for supplies to fill Valkyrie's pantries and storage caverns. Ivan trotted into the cave mouth. It was very large and he sat down after Fanndis dismounted. Within minutes, the great animal had fallen asleep and, again, Fanndis patted him on the neck. Ivan would most likely find that sort of gesture patronizing, but she did it anyway.

After settling into the cave, Fanndis made a fire near the mouth so that the smoke would not smother them. The howling wind would never die down, so she just took out her wool travel blanket and settled in for a long, windy, frigid night. Ivan's long coat would keep him warm, she knew, but she put another blanket over him just in case he started to feel the cold. Still too early for sleep, Fanndis calmed her mind enough to reach out for Valkyrie. She inhaled deeply, exhaled slowly. Yreth welled up within. Soon, her mind went utterly still and filled with only one thought: Valkyrie. Images of the mountain's summit entered her dark head. She smelled the wind, heard its cry. Her mind's eye noticed the fire burning at another cave mouth—Valkyrie's cave. Somewhere within her vision, the mournful bleat of a goat rang out.

"Valkyrie," she tested.

At once, Fanndis felt another person's presence enter her mind, but she was well-trained—almost as well as Valkyrie—so Fanndis did not let Valkyrie take control as the older woman had with Arna.

"I see you've improved at this, Fanndis," Valkyrie observed, her spectral image sharpening in Fanndis' vision.

218

"A little," Fanndis admitted.

"How is our girl doing?" Valkyrie inquired.

"I assume you're talking about Arna when you say, 'our girl'?" Fanndis' dry skepticism dripped from her reply.

"Of course. I heard that she had a broken leg. Poor little dear. I wonder how that happened?" Valkyrie pondered aloud.

"It's none of your concern unless you plan on stealing my apprentice," Fanndis spat, coming to the point.

"Oh, I wouldn't think of it. Besides, I have too much to deal with, what with taking care of Annar and everything. He's quite temperamental as a goat, but the cancer will only spread faster in his human body. I've tried to tell him I'm doing him a kindness," Valkyrie told her.

Fanndis ignored Valkyrie's remark about Annar and said, "If you don't want to be her master, then what *do* you want with her? It's not like you to meddle with someone's mind and then leave them alone as if nothing ever happened."

"I just wanted to see who you were spending your time with these days. I see little Lord Maslyn has finally escaped his fairytale tower," Valkyrie remarked.

"Yes. He's working with Stigg, learning to build and take care of the land. A lord should understand the toil of his people." Fanndis stretched her neck muscles, trying to sit comfortably through her vision.

"Ah, feeling philosophical are we, Fanndis? Has that son of yours been entertaining you with his reading?"

Fanndis overlooked the older woman's barb and spent some energy trying to see what the area surrounding her old master looked like. There was a fire. Valkyrie sat cross-legged, and the goat, Annar, was by the stone hearth, wheezing. The cave glittered with trinkets given by mountain folk. Herbs hung from every available space on the ceiling.

"I see you like my home."

"It's lovely. Let's get to the point. What do you really want with Arna?" Fanndis said, almost to the point of rudeness.

"My, aren't we feisty this evening?" exclaimed the other woman.

"Valkyrie!" Fanndis prompted in as commanding a tone as she could muster.

"Oh, alright. I sense a strange energy in that girl. I feel that she will be very powerful—perhaps more than you and me. I felt her presence all the way at the top of my mountain without trying. I wanted to find out more about her. Is that a crime?" Valkyrie scowled.

"No. I know what you mean. As soon as Lord Maslyn introduced me to her, I felt a strong depth of the Seidh already within her. Perhaps it is just because she is so strong willed or perhaps it is truly because she has a great store of powerful yreth within her. I am not sure yet. Her training has been interrupted because of her broken leg. She also suffered a concussion and has been sleeping a lot," Fanndis said, feeling a little more comfortable with Valkyrie now that she knew the older woman would not steal the girl away.

Both women were silent for some time. Soon it became apparent that neither had anything to say further. Fanndis spoke up, "I'll see you in the morning, Valkyrie. I'm rather tired." A large yawn escaped her mouth before she could stop herself.

"Pleasant dreams," the old woman said.

"We'll see," Fanndis remarked.

Both women let go of their mental focus. Fanndis' body slumped where she sat. Despite the tired, draining sensation crawling through her, she was relieved. She had been afraid that her old master would have wanted Arna as an apprentice. Because Valkyrie was extraordinarily powerful, she could have taken her. Fanndis could have lost the girl. It would have been shattering. Already, maternal affection had taken root within her for the child. It would have destroyed Stigg as well. The relief Fanndis felt only grew as she prepared for bed.

Ivan snorted and looked up.

"All is well, Ivan. Go on back to sleep now."

He snorted again and lowered his head.

Fanndis fell into a dreamless sleep and when she awoke the next morning, it was not yet dawn. Ivan stood up because his legs were getting stiff resting underneath him. He whinnied a "good morning" and Fanndis grunted in response. Her bones were screaming at her from sleeping near the top of a frozen mountain. The pressure in the air was abominable. Still, she managed to lift herself off of the rocky floor and wrap up enough to set off on the path towards Valkyrie's cave.

Snow fell in violent spurts at that altitude and the way was icy. Ivan inched forward, one step at a time, until they came to a terrace. There, the path was level for a few feet. That's when Fanndis spotted Valkyrie's cave above their heads.

Fanndis scowled. It was the most asinine place to live that she had ever visited. She could not fathom why some old woman would want to subject herself to thin air, frozen ice all around, and torrential winds. Ivan snorted, directing her attention to the skinny, steep, zigzagged path leading up to the cave mouth. It was not passable for the horse. Fanndis knew she was going to have to hike up herself.

"Wretched woman; living in a place like this!" Fanndis grumbled. The slick rocks were treacherous to say the least. She could not imagine how her former master traveled back and forth from the mountain villages to the cave. It was near suicide just to *get* from the terrace up the twenty or so feet to the opening. Ivan nudged her with his head, helping her up.

"It's easy for you to say, 'go on up'. I'm the one that has to do it!" In spite of her protests, Fanndis plucked up her courage and climbed. Beforehand, she tightened up the laces on her boots and pulled her heavy coat tightly about her. She hiked in much the same way she imagined a hundred year old man would walk down to the market. It took *forever* to scale the path. By the time she was at the mouth of Valkyrie's cave, she was exhausted, cold, frustrated, and cranky.

"Woman!" Fanndis barked.

"Good morning, Fanndis," Valkyrie chimed. Her voice sounded distant.

"Get your old carcass out here at *once* and give me some tea and a blanket!" Fanndis demanded, panting.

"Wait just one minute, youngling. I'm still the master here," the older woman's voice rang out from a nearer distance.

Fanndis walked in and slumped next to Annar who was sulking by the fire. She petted him gently on the belly and he looked up, mournful despair clear in his eyes.

Hello, Fanndis, Annar whispered.

"Hello, Annar. I am so sorry to hear how ill you are. Is there anything I can do?" Fanndis asked him.

It hurt to take in his changed appearance. He had been so strong and handsome once. The body of the goat hid the human form that had grown old and weak. Fanndis wished there was something she could do to help. However, she knew that Valkyrie was wise to keep him an animal. The transmutation would have slowed the illness, confusing the bacterial and viral cells.

It seems I'm destined to die an animal, he groaned.

"Oh, Annar, it isn't all bad. You get all the food you want, you get to sleep by the fire. Sounds heavenly to me!" Fanndis knew that he would not agree with her assessment, but she hoped she could bring some cheer to his grim mood.

"Here is your blanket, *Madame*, and hot tea. Can I get anything else for you?" Valkyrie's sarcasm leeched all the good will from her offer.

"That will be all, thank you." Fanndis swiped the mug of tea from the older woman's bird-like fingers and snatched the blanket as well.

Alright, you two. I don't want to hear any of your bickering. I'm tired and all I want is some peace and quiet, Annar ordered.

Considering how much each woman respected the man, they obeyed him. Valkyrie jerked her head in the direction of a deeper cavern. Fanndis patted Annar on his belly again and followed after. Darkness hung over the women as they maneuvered the uneven cavern floor.

"He doesn't have much time left," Valkyrie confided.

"I can tell. Poor man. I wish the Seidh had been able to be of help in cancer research but, it's just one of those things that even magic can't touch. It's a grand shame."

"Yes, it is," Valkyrie agreed.

Fanndis followed her former master into the old training room which was a wide chamber full of stalagmites and stalactites. Bits of furniture littered the floor. Among the pieces was a desk. Fanndis remembered many long nights spent sitting there, writing her notes and observations. Dried herbs decorated the ceiling, mirroring the mats spread about the floor. The blankets were still piled in the far corner. Near them were the three sun spires Valkyrie had made to keep them warm while they worked. A giant bucket sat in the middle of the room, serving to catch snow that fell from the asymmetrical hole in the roof. It was full, of course. Nostalgia soaked right through her irritation with Valkyrie. Fanndis' expression softened.

"Brings back memories, eh?" Valkyrie sighed.

"Yes, many. Not *all* of them bad." Fanndis smiled, her narrowed eyes lighting up with challenge.

"I can send you straight back down that mountain with nothing, you know," Valkyrie teased.

"Bah. You don't scare me." Fanndis waved her off.

Valkyrie walked towards the desk and ruffled a few papers that sat on the top. The younger woman walked around and took in the familiar sights, touching objects here and there that sparked arbitrary memories. It even smelled the same: like dried sage and juniper.

"I wanted to show you something," Valkyrie informed her, her brows furrowed in thought.

"What is it?"

223

"It's something I found when I went down to the woods a few days ago," she said.

Fanndis was confused when Valkyrie began to dress for riding and going out into the cold.

"Are we going somewhere?" Fanndis asked.

"Well I certainly couldn't move it, now could I?"

"Why not?"

"You'll see," Valkyrie promised.

"Very well." Fanndis resigned herself to an unwelcome adventure.

The older woman went back to the main chamber of the cave and whistled while meandering into another chamber off to the side. That one, she used as her barn because there were several holes coming through the rock ceiling and it allowed light and ventilation for the few animals she kept there. One such animal was a magnificent, black longhaired horse. His name was, Nar, Fanndis remembered. Valkyrie had named him after Annar whom she had always loved in secret.

"I suppose Ivan is down below?" Valkyrie asked, knowing the answer already.

"I wasn't going to be so cruel as to require him to hike up your front 'steps'," Fanndis spat.

"Stuff and nonsense. He would have been fine. Watch how my Nar navigates the path perfectly."

"Mmhm." Fanndis rolled her eyes and followed the old woman out of the cave mouth and down the slippery incline.

She had to admit that Nar moved gracefully as he stepped behind Valkyrie. He was an impressive horse—about two hands taller than Ivan and far broader. It was amazing he had the grace necessary to go up and down Valkyrie's formidable path.

"Put your eyeballs back in your head and congratulate my friend, here," Valkyrie said, head held high.

"You were magnificent, Nar. Truly," Fanndis encouraged.

I don't prefer your patronizing tones, Nar snorted.

"You would get along with Ivan," she chuckled.

When Fanndis and Ivan were ready, the older woman led them down an unfamiliar groove in the mountain and into the woods. It took quite some time and she knew that she would be staying with Valkyrie and Annar that night. She was glad she had told Stigg to plan for her delayed return. About an hour passed. Valkyrie took Fanndis to a particular rock formation deep in the woods towards the west.

As they rode closer to their destination, a strange, slithering dread crept into Fanndis' heart. She could not explain what it was like—it was *almost* like the presence of death, but subtler. It was a harrowing, terrifying presence that made chills rise on her neck.

"What is this place, Valkyrie?" whispered Fanndis.

"You feel it don't you? That presence like death, but different? You'll see why when we go inside."

They dismounted. Valkyrie knew that the animals would not want to see what the women were about to see. She gestured for Fanndis to follow her. They had not moved very far into the cave before Fanndis' eyes were drawn to the thing Valkyrie had wanted to show her. Bits of leaf detritus and bones of small animals were scattered about the floor. But it was what rested in the back of the cavern that commanded her attention. Lying on a bed of twigs, leaves, and fur was the body of man. The naked flesh looked grey in the limited light and the face appeared to be sleeping, but Fanndis knew he was not sleeping. He was not dead either. Silvery white hair coiled around the man's shoulders and limbs like a net. The closed eyes were rimmed with dark lashes and brows and Fanndis knew if he opened them, they would contain haunting red-brown irises. She knew at once that it was the body of one of the Maslyn twins.

"How can this be? He's not dead...he's not asleep...I don't understand..." Fanndis' mind was stretched taut with the effort of untangling the mystery before her. "It's Olan's body," she stated, dumbfounded.

It did not make sense. She had guessed that Olan was alive and well in some animal form since the night of the fire. The transformation had happened right before her in the great hall. Never had she forgiven herself for teaching Olan magic before he was ready for the consequences. It was her fault the former Maslyn and his wife was dead. Guilt swelled within as she stood blinking at the man before her. She had been so sure about how it all had turned out. Yet, the image of Olan's cold, lifeless—but not dead—body gave her pause.

"What does this mean?" she asked Valkyrie.

"It means that when Olan performed his magic all those years ago, he did not transmute Fenris' body into that of an animal. Instead, he *switched* Fenris' body with an animal's and also his own. Their human bodies were instantly comatose and in the place where the summoned animals had been originally. He was not ready for that sort of magic, Fanndis. There is always a price to pay when spells do not go as planned," Valkyrie explained, looking at her old apprentice with a furrowed, accusatory brow.

"I did not teach him *this*—I swear it! He asked me about animal and human transmutation, but I told him he was too young for it. I suppose he went off and learned about it on his own. His curiosity was far too strong for his own good. Oh dear, look at him." Fanndis reached out to touch the pale skin.

It was stone cold. She pressed two fingers to his neck to feel for a pulse and could just barely make one out. It was extremely weak and pitifully slow. How long it had been lazily pumping like that? For six years, she supposed.

"We need to find Fenris' body. I would feel better knowing where both of them are, should Soryn and Arna get any ideas to change them back. If Olan's is way out here, Fenris' could be anywhere. Olan's spell wasn't transmutation. It was transference—a different sort of magic altogether. Dark magic. I doubt he had any idea what he had done until it was far too late," Valkyrie commented.

"What do you think happened to the animals' spirits when their bodies were taken by Olan and Fenris?" Fanndis asked—far out of the realm of her magical knowledge. It was obvious an animal's soul was not living in the cold, naked body on the floor of the cave.

"They're dead. If not, they may have remained within their own bodies with Olan and Fenris' spirits and fused their souls with the twins'. Who knows? This kind of magic is forbidden—stuff that Olan will pay dearly for should he ever regain his own body. I am sure he never meant to perform such work, but he did and he will pay the price." Valkyrie sighed, saddened by her own words.

"We should leave him here. He's safe this far from the villages and so deep in the forest. I'll send Stigg to check on the body every now and then until we can figure this mess out with that dratted pig in Soryn's tower," Fanndis said, recognizing she had let their problem with Ulla slip.

"Pig?" Valkyrie was intrigued.

"Yes," Fanndis pursed her lips. "Soryn is convinced that the pig living in the basement of his tower is his brother Olan."

"Really?" Valkyrie's mouth hung open in surprise.

"It's not. It can't be. Ulla's demeanor and personality are wholly different from Olan's. However, what I don't know is whether or not he is Fenris. If he is, we are in a world of trouble should he ever regain his human body. I sensed a terrible sorrow and fury within that animal. I knew it was really a human at once. I just need to find out which human it is," Fanndis sighed.

"Let me check into it," Valkyrie pleaded.

"You want to help us now?" Fanndis asked, still not trusting that Valkyrie had totally pure intentions.

"Don't make me out to be a harpy, Fanndis. You know very well that I have always been fond of Olan—especially when you brought him to visit me that summer. Though I don't know the new Lord Maslyn, I have been a strong supporter of his family and I want to see him succeed."

"We all do. He is a very dear child—highly motivated to succeed and enjoying his newfound freedom in honorable ways," Fanndis said, her fondness for Soryn shining through every word.

"Is he much like the others?" Valkyrie asked.

"You mean the twins?" Fanndis clarified.

"Yes."

"Not at all. He's much more like his father—stoic, reserved, *very proper*." Fanndis chuckled at the last remark.

"The twins were completely different from either parent. It is a shame they did not inherit their mother's gentleness and grace. She was a woman of great poise and intellect," Valkyrie mused.

"Olan would have grown into a fine Seidh man if he merely had the chance, but it was ripped away all in one night by his own unfortunate hand." Fanndis grew pensive.

"We can change them back you know. It wouldn't be hard for either of us," Valkyrie suggested.

"Well, we certainly can't do anything until we know where Fenris' body is. His may be somewhere near Soryn or Olan's body, and then we definitely can't change them back yet. I want to know more about who he is in the *animal* world before we do that. If Fenris is Ulla, I don't trust him. Ulla is devious and sneaky and I don't like the feelings I get when I'm around him." Fanndis shuddered, just thinking about her encounter with the pig.

"Well, I'll put my sources on it as well," Valkyrie said. "Don't worry. We'll get this all sorted out. Perhaps after six long years, these boys—well...I suppose they're men now, aren't they?—will be able to return to their bodies."

"Yes, hopefully so," Fanndis agreed.

The two women covered Olan's frozen body with leaves and other materials from the cave. They left for Valkyrie's home. On the way, both women were gloomy in their thoughts and did not speak much. When they returned to the cave, they were met with a terribly sad sight. Annar lay by the fire, utterly still. His body had returned to his human form and his eyes were fixed on the light coming from the cave mouth.

Valkyrie cursed inwardly at the silent tears that slipped down her cheeks.

"Wretched old man. Had to go and die on me," Valkyrie muttered through her quiet sobs.

Fanndis stared at Annar's waif-like body and felt her own heart implode within her chest. He had been a good friend to her when she was still an apprentice. Valkyrie knelt before him on the floor, rocking slowly back and forth. Fanndis knew Valkyrie had never faced her feelings for Annar. Fanndis bowed her head and let the tears fall peacefully while she prayed for his departed soul.

Valkyrie could not control her reaction to Annar's death. She had never told the man that she loved him. Not once. In all the years they had lived together as friends and companions, she had never said it. They had come close several times to declaring their love, but in all her sixty-eight years she had never been so ashamed of failing to do something right. She collapsed over his thin, wan body and pressed her hands to his chest and face.

Fanndis rested a hand gently upon her master's back and prayed for her—also willing some power into her friend to help calm her so that she would not give in to despair. Whatever feelings Valkyrie had held in her heart for Annar, her former apprentice knew they were powerful. It pained Fanndis that she never saw her two friends' love fulfilled.

The night grew dark. Wind blew harsh and violent against the dreary cave. The fire burned on despite the gale outside and the darkness in their hearts. Sometime before dawn, Valkyrie finally slept against Annar's still form. Fanndis sung ancient tunes under her breath that she remembered from her youth. She fell asleep just as the first light from the suns peaked over the mountain. Valkyrie startled awake and covered Fanndis with a blanket before going to the back of the cave. When she made it to the training room, Valkyrie tore her clothes and fell in the middle of the cavern floor. In her hands were sheers, like one would use for sheep. Without much emotion, Valkyrie began cutting off her hair—short to her scalp like Arna's. She knew it had been Annar's favorite thing about her appearance and now that he was gone, she could not bear to feel it brushing against her body.

When she had finished, she took the hair back to the main cavern, braided it, and laid it gently across Annar's chest, folding his hands over it. Then, she left and traveled far up the mountain. There, she sat and stared at the suns rising. Emptiness took root in her heart like she had never experienced before. It was as though nothing else would ever fill it again. And yet, she felt a gentle tugging on her spirit—as though there were someone there trying to get her attention. When she looked, there was no one around, yet she still felt it strongly.

"My heart is broken," she muttered to whoever or whatever it was.

All of a sudden, she felt a warm presence beside her on the rocks. A white wolf had perched himself next to her. He said nothing. The great animal simply gazed at the rising suns and the effect they had on the white clouds stretching over the horizon. Valkyrie had never seen a wolf so close. He was breathtaking. His fur swirled with the wind and his yellow eyes lit up with borrowed sunlight. Valkyrie's despair somehow shifted to some foreign place in her mind. All she could think about was the wolf's beauty and his serene glare.

At some point during the suns rising, the wolf turned his head and his golden eyes bore into her. Valkyrie stared back. Though no words were spoken, somehow, she was comforted by his presence. Soon after, he stood on his four paws and slinked away into the darker parts of the mountain not yet touched by the suns' light. She stared at the space he left behind and felt like she had just been destroyed and rebuilt into a wholly new creature. The pain of Annar's death had not lessened, though now she knew it would; in time. Someday. An unexplainable peace settled in her heart and she knew that she had just had an encounter with something strange and fierce and wonderful. Despite the sadness that still swarmed in her chest, she looked up at the rising suns and laughed in the wind and felt the pure flakes of snow dance across her face.

Chapter Fourteen

In which the summer comes…

Fanndis returned to the cottage several days later to see Arna's exterior room nearly complete. She supposed that the only way Stigg knew to while away the time was to work to the bone on some project. Arna had been reading a great deal and learning various bits of magic from Fanndis' books. It was clear there had been much productivity while she had been away. Father Kimbli was in the kitchen, reading his Bible with his spectacles pushed way down on the end of his nose. She chided him for neglecting his duties as steward.

"It's Suns' Day, Fanndis. Even stewards don't work on Suns' Days," he laughed warmly.

"Is it truly? I lost track of the days," she sighed.

Dropping off her riding clothes, Fanndis told everyone that she would be at the hot spring that lay about a mile north of the cottage. The others continued their work while she was away. Father Kimbli stayed and admired the building being done on the room for Arna. The girl herself was in the bedroom, napping.

While at the springs, Fanndis thought long and hard about the situation with Ulla. Finding Olan's body in the cave had been a shock and she was hopeful, for the first time, that the situation with the twins might be resolved soon. Heat rose in ghostly swirls of steam and the woman was distracted by them. For a short time, she bathed and let the water splash around her without thinking about much. Sometime later, she hauled herself up on the bank and dried off. Because the springs were so secluded, she had no fear of being watched. Standing up, she dressed at her leisure before heading back to her cottage.

By the time Fanndis returned, the men were in the kitchen in the middle of some heated debate about philosophy. Smiling, she skirted passed them without interrupting and went to check on Arna. The girl slept on the bed and Fanndis, making sure not to disturb the girl, unwrapped the linens around her thigh. The entire section above the knee was terribly swollen and bruised. It was not a pretty sight and Fanndis hoped her healing abilities would make it so Arna's thigh would be beautiful and supple once more by the time the break healed.

Fanndis brought poultices and linens from the kitchen. She set about cleaning the skin around the break and rewrapping it tightly. Thankfully, Arna was an obedient patient and had not insisted on getting up and moving about a lot. Her break should heal within eight weeks. The girl would be able to walk about on crutches much sooner than that. Fanndis was about to finish her work when Stigg knocked on the door and walked inside.

"How is she?" Stigg asked.

"I believe she'll be just fine. The area's bruised and swollen, but you did a good job setting the leg. It will heal properly in a couple months," Fanndis replied.

Stigg nodded and made to shut the door, but Fanndis interrupted him.

"Yes?" he inquired.

"You're a kind soul, Stigg. I'm glad my son is so compassionate." Fanndis inclined her head and went back to work.

Color rose in Stigg's cheeks and he shut the door, heading back to the kitchen. Father Kimbli leaned back in his chair, resting his eyes from his reading. Soryn had his face buried in one of the books Stigg had let him borrow, turning pages back and forth looking for answers to unspoken questions. A half smile came to the man's lips as he watched the boy and the old man acting so at ease. Stigg, himself, was troubled so he went to the barn to feed the horses—and to get his mind off of what was perturbing him.

Ivan looked tired after the journey into the mountains. Stigg forked some dried greenhouse hay into the horse's trough then patted him on the neck. The horse snorted and chomped at the food with obvious greed. An owl hooted in the rafters. Despite his own unrest, Stigg was struck by the peacefulness of the night. He wished that peace would descend upon himself. It was as though all of their lives were about to change—even more than they already had in the last few weeks. A portentous nagging kept twining itself about his mind. He was worried. The business with the pig and with Arna's accident weighed on his mind and he frowned.

Ivan whinnied, gobbling his hay. Stigg shook his head, banishing his thoughts. Patting the horse again, the man turned and sat at the base of the stall door and leaned his head against the wood. Ever since he was a young man, the barn had been his place for privacy and solace. The pure spirits of the animals and the familiar smells allowed him to rest even if his mind was in turmoil. He closed his eyes, just for a moment, but was soon drifting off to sleep. Frigid night air whirled about them, but the warmth from the bodies of the horses, the cow, and their chickens helped to take the edge off.

Sometime later, Father Kimbli found Stigg asleep in the barn. The old man called for Soryn to help him walk Stigg back to the hearth fire and his bedroll. The three of them staggered their way back into the house where Stigg and Soryn went to sleep. The old priest chuckled at the two of them. They looked exhausted. Fanndis walked into the room and found Kimbli smiling at them.

"I think it's high time I left for home," the old priest said.

"It's getting late," Fanndis observed.

"Did you find anything out when you went to see that woman?" Father Kimbli asked.

"She showed me something unbelievable in the woods near the west," Fanndis admitted.

"What?"

"We found Olan's body. His *human* body, still alive but in some sort of comatose state."

235

"How is that possible?" Father Kimbli whispered.

"I don't know. Apparently, Olan performed transference instead of transmutation. It's a giant mess to be sure," she muttered, rubbing her temples.

"Hmm." Father Kimbli rubbed his chin, not really knowing what to say.

"Well, sleep well, old friend. It's a cold night out there." Fanndis turned to get his coat for him.

"Oh, I will. I'll be glad when I'm back in my room at the church and buried under my mound of covers. These old bones are getting rather snappish about the cold nowadays," he chuckled.

Fanndis watched him ride away and endured all of the thoughts and emotions that flooded her once he was gone. She wanted to get to the bottom of the quagmire they were in and she wanted to do it quickly. All of the doors and windows were fastened before she went into the bedroom and lay down on a pallet next to the bed. Arna rattled out strange little puffing snores which helped lull the older woman to sleep. Fanndis dreamed about Annar, Valkyrie, and the days of her youth.

* * *

Months passed and Arna's leg made a full recovery. When she was up and about walking again, Stigg and Soryn introduced her to her new room. In the end, it had taken about a month to finish because of another snow storm that delayed them. She loved it. Inside there was a bed, a worktable, a small fireplace, and a shelf for books. The space was very simple, but it was all her own and she was ecstatic to have it. The three of them moved all her few possessions into it immediately. That night, she was able to sleep in her own bed.

Soryn came to the cottage every spare minute. Things had grown quiet back at the tower. He found it strange that Ulla had not spoken to him at all for the last several weeks. Often, he tried to talk

236

to the pig and even visited the study, but Ulla was not there. Lord Maslyn had no idea where the pig had gone and grew uneasy that nobody knew of his whereabouts. Soryn, of course, reported everything to Fanndis, Stigg, Arna, and Kimbli. They had heard nothing from Ulf or Eira about who Ulla was in reality or the pig's intentions. They had been unable to find any information.

Because they were at a standstill with that situation, Stigg kept teaching Lord Maslyn how to cut firewood, build rooms, work with animals, carpentry, forest knowledge, and signs for the changing seasons. Soryn was happy in his work and was thrilled with the muscles he had developed under Stigg's tutelage. Every now and then, Soryn would catch a glimpse of his growing biceps and smile to himself. Stigg laughed every time—a strangely natural sound coming from such a silent person.

Stigg told him that soon, summer would come. Because Niflheim was buried in snow most of the year, there was no spring or fall—just winter and a brief summer that lasted about three months. One month, the snow thawed a bit. The next month, one could see some green leaves, flowers, and hints of purple earth. The last month, the heavy snows began and everything was buried fully in white once more. Even in the "warmest" period of summer, snow still dominated.

Soryn asked, "How do you know that summer is coming?"

"Because there are buds on the trees under the snow and because the wind has changed. In summer, the winds are much stronger and warmer, because our world is closer to the suns."

"Oh," Soryn replied.

The boy was in awe of Stigg. He had never really been around a grown man before—well, other than Jori or Kimbli. Stigg was soon to turn twenty-four. The man was young, strong, and active. Still, the fact that Stigg rarely said four words to Soryn in an entire day made it difficult to feel connected to him. Sometimes, the boy thought he could see a smile gracing the man's lips at some good piece of work that Soryn had produced, but he was never sure. Stigg was more a brother figure to him than a father figure, but Soryn knew in his heart that Stigg could never replace the relationships he wished he could have with Olan and Fenris. Soryn expected he would never see his brothers again at this rate, and had no idea what had happened to Ulla—who *claimed* to be Olan.

Fanndis whiled away the days teaching Arna everything she knew about herbal lore and where to find plants in the greenhouse and in the wild. Because vegetation on Niflheim had adapted to such frigid conditions, there *were* still some plants that grew even in the dead of winter. Arna loved the work with the herbs and the medicinal preparations. She had started going into the village and helping those who needed poultices and salves. She was becoming a favorite face among the women in New Kristiansand. Fanndis also continued to teach Arna how to harness her magic and to alter the elements and produce them.

Days, weeks, and months passed as they all grew in knowledge and friendship. It was no secret to anyone—Father Kimbli included—that Soryn and Arna were developing a relationship that was more than platonic. Soryn turned thirteen sometime before the summer and began the process of becoming a legal adult. On Niflheim, boys were seen as men around the age of fifteen due to the responsibilities given to them at that age—a profession, sometimes their own piece of land—in rare times, a wife. Girls were considered women at fourteen or so—not only because they were sexually maturing by that time, but also because they were given a great share of responsibility at that age. It took everyone pitching in to help with the hard life on an ice planet.

Both Soryn and Arna grew secretly excited about their looming manhood and womanhood. Fanndis and Stigg often chuckled to themselves hearing the two of them talking in adult-like tones when they thought no one was listening. Fanndis remembered her own days of maidenhood and her excitement at turning fourteen and being viewed as a woman in the village.

Kimbli continued to tutor Soryn about the responsibilities and tasks that fell to the Maslyn of New Kristiansand. The boy developed an interest for such things and an aptitude for his lessons. Before the summer came, he went with Kimbli on outings in the village to help with disputes and treaties and such. Arna was very proud when he told her about his daily exploits and he listened with rapt attention when she told him about hers.

Stigg continued to check on Olan's body in the cave near the northern mountains. Nothing changed. Ulf kept an eye on it for them when Stigg couldn't make it himself. The man worked harder each day than the day before. Stigg's feelings for Arna grew into more than brotherly affection, but he buried them as often as he could, knowing she would never love him in return. She was far too besotted with Soryn. Stigg respected that. She was almost eleven years his junior anyway. He supposed he was just lonely for female companionship. He had been a man, now, for nine years. He felt it was high time he had a wife—especially when he was bombarded with young, adolescent romance at every turn.

The trees grew heavy buds beneath the snow on their branches. The winds changed. By that time, no one had heard anything from Ulla for several months. It was unnerving that he had just disappeared into thin air—especially when they had gotten so curious about his true identity. Everyone was shocked when the first day of summer came and Ulla contacted them suddenly out of nowhere with a strange sort of message.

I found it! My body! It's there in the cave!

A dark chill settled over everyone in the cottage. Fanndis set down her knitting. Arna paused with the kneading she performed on a ball of bread dough. Soryn looked up from the book he read. Stigg put aside his ax. Each one heard the pig's voice. Ulla was nearby. Even the summer sunshine and winter thaw could not assuage their feeling that something was terribly amiss.

* * *

239

The fact that they could all hear Ulla was troubling enough, but his words frightened them the most. Soryn and Arna did not know what Ulla was claiming other than he had found his own human body. Fanndis and Stigg knew that he was claiming to be Olan. Both looked at each other with frowns on their faces. They either had to believe that what he said was true or a terrible lie.

Fanndis spoke, "Ulla, where is this cave?"

In the woods, near the northern mountains. I've found my body! You must come and help me!

Two things went through Fanndis' mind. First, if Ulla was telling the truth and was in fact Olan, then Soryn could potentially have one of his brothers back tonight. Second, if Ulla was *not* Olan and was someone else, he would have to have some sort of plan if he was meeting with all of them at the place where Olan's body was hidden. It was a gamble, but they had to go out and find that pig—if only to imprison him until they could make him tell them the whole truth.

Fanndis tried to remain calm and think through what she thought they should do. She ordered Stigg to saddle the horses (they had acquired Soryn's own horse, Sable, and a small mare for Arna to ride in the months past). She gathered coats and riding clothes for each of them. Arna gathered water skins for the journey and Soryn sat in the chair by the hearth, silent. He was in too much shock to think about preparing for anything. He just wanted to know what was going on. When everyone else was ready, they stopped and looked to him.

"Soryn?" Fanndis prompted.

Arna reached out and put a hand on his shoulder.

"Are you alright?" she asked.

He looked up with utter confusion in his eyes. Arna held his hand and helped him stand. He followed them all out into the melting snow and mounted his horse. They rode off into the woods towards the north. Stigg rode at the head of the group. Beside them,

240

Ulf ran—blindingly fast—circling to make sure they were all safe. Ulf's mate joined them further into the forest.

Hurry! It's here! Ulla repeated about halfway into the trip to the cave.

"How do you know where you're going?" Soryn finally demanded.

"Talk later, Soryn," Fanndis ordered over the sounds of hooves and jingling harnesses.

Soryn glowered and sulked the rest of the way—wanting so badly to know what was going on and feeling left out that no one would tell him. Arna kept looking over at him, trying to comfort him with kind, concerned looks. It took about an hour to reach the cave near the western base of the mountain. Everyone dismounted in front of the cavern mouth. Ulf and his mate, a black-furred wolf, stayed a fair distance away in the tree line. Soryn wondered if they were wary of Ulla, too. A strange, eerie aura hovered about the area and Soryn shivered.

"Where are we?" he murmured.

"Come inside, Soryn. I hope everything will become clear to us when we enter," Fanndis said.

He looked at Arna, unconvinced. Stigg went first and Fanndis followed. Arna grabbed Soryn's hand and they, too entered the dark mouth. Ulla sat on his hind legs beside a pile of leaves and twigs.

Good evening, all. I did not expect you to get here so soon, Ulla said, cocking his head.

"Why have you brought us here, Ulla?" Fanndis asked, her voice carefully controlled.

I've found my body. Didn't I tell you? I'm your brother, Soryn, and here is the proof. Ulla tugged with his teeth at the twigs, leaves, and other detritus covering an oddly shaped mound.

Soryn's eyes grew wide with surprise and fear when he saw the naked body of a man. Silver-white hair flowed over deathly pale skin. It tangled in great knots over the limbs and muscled torso. Lord

Maslyn stepped closer, amazed at the sight before him. It *did* look like one of his brothers—just grown up.

"Olan?" Soryn muttered, quietly. He knew it was not Fenris' body. Olan had a mole below the left eye that Fenris did not. It was the only thing about the twins that enabled others to tell them apart. Though the body had clearly aged and the white hair had grown down to the man's thighs, Soryn knew it was really Olan.

"Ulla, if you are telling the truth, you have nothing to fear, but you must realize we cannot turn you back into your human self until we know a little bit more about you," Fanndis warned.

Why would I bring you to a body that is not my own and ask you to turn me human? You would know the instant the spell was performed whether or not it was true.

"You have a point, but I will perform no such magic today—not until I have had a nice long chat with you, pig," the woman declared, as firm as stone.

Very well. Soryn...I hope we will be reunited in human form very soon.

Soryn said nothing—he was too shocked by what he saw on the cavern floor. His very own brother...now a man. Ulla trailed after Fanndis outside the cave. Arna and Stigg eventually exited as well. The youngest Maslyn lingered. He reached out and touched Olan's cold skin. It was uncanny how the body before him felt so alien and yet so familiar. Arna called for him. Soryn snapped out of his focus and turned around. She gestured for him to come out. Stigg had mounted his horse. Fanndis and Arna were mounting theirs. Soryn ascended to his own saddle in a daze. They left Olan's body where it was—knowing it would be protected by Ulf and his mate. Ulla spent the trip in silence, trotting alongside the horses.

When they returned to the clearing around the cottage, they confined Ulla to the kitchen—Fanndis performed barrier incantations to ensure he would not leave. She wanted the pig in one place until she could get the answers she sought. Soryn just watched Ulla, trying to imagine the pig's personality in Olan's body—were they really one and the same? Arna stayed in her room researching human and animal transmutation and transference without Fanndis' permission. She wanted to know what was going to happen to Ulla and the body in the cave. Stigg remained in the front parlor, calling Lord Maslyn to join him.

Fanndis slammed the kitchen doors shut and put a warding spell all around the room against eavesdroppers. She wanted to know exactly what was going on before she performed any magic either way. In the other room, Soryn and Stigg smoked their pipes and waited for Fanndis to get her answers. By the time the Night Bells rang from the distant village church, Fanndis opened the door, but sealed the pig inside.

"Soryn, you must not talk to Ulla tonight. I've put a stop to your communication with one another through a warding spell around the door. I'm sorry to do this to you, but I must run an errand. I'll be back and in the morning. I swear I will tell you everything I know— and it is quite a vast amount of catching up that will need to be done. I'm sorry." With that, Fanndis left the cottage without another word and sped off into the night with Ivan.

Within an hour, the cottage settled down for the night and Soryn knew he would not be getting any sleep. He knew the barrier spell around the cottage would only work on Ulla, so he got up and climbed out the shuttered window without a sound. Looking around to ensure no one saw, he knocked on Arna's window. She opened it after the first knock—wide-eyed and anxious.

"We've got to get him out of here. I don't know what's going on, but I've got to switch him back. I don't care if he is my brother or not, but I've got to know, Arna. I've just got to," he pleaded.

Arna could not stand to see her friend in such distress. She simply nodded, and grabbed the spell book she had been reading. She knew enough about Fanndis' barrier spells to weaken it enough to remove the pig from the cottage. Soryn opened the back kitchen door and tiptoed across the floor, grabbing Ulla from his perch on the wooden table. When they got him out, he simply said,

Thank you.

In silence, they went to the barn and saddled one horse. Sable was a huge gelding, strong enough to hold two children and a pig. In silence, they rode to the greenhouse. Because Ulf was watching the cave, she knew she would be able to retrieve what the book said was needed in order to perform a reversal transformation. It only took her several minutes to gather the necessary herbs and then they were off again, riding in the darkness.

Don't head back to the cave, Ulla demanded.

"Why not?" Soryn and Arna queried in unison.

You don't think they'd leave my body there now that I know where it is, do you? They are suspicious of me. They don't really believe me. I know you two *do. I can take you where I think they will have taken it,* Ulla said.

"Where?" Arna asked.

Start riding to the east and I'll show you the way.

With Ulla giving them directions, they traveled to a desolate, barren grove of trees in the eastern woods. There was a large burrow at the base of a giant fir tree that he steered them towards. Summer winds brought in a gentle, freezing rain while they rode. It was a welcome change from the snow. Soryn and Arna were not suspicious about the lack of tracks. If Fanndis had come that way earlier, the rain would have washed away any signs in the snow.

Down in the burrow, they saw the body—just as Ulla predicted.

"How did you know she would move it here?" Soryn asked, a nagging suspicion in the back of his mind.

Remember I can read thoughts? Apparently, your Lady Fanndis forgot that I possessed that power. She let her thoughts slip to this location in her mind. I knew instantly the spot she meant, having visited the same place when I was outside the castle for an errand and a snowstorm started. I used to hide here.

"Oh," Soryn said, convinced.

Arna set about making the casting circle and tracing out the symbols in the proper order. She called forth a small fire and set it in the center of the circle. She asked Ulla to get into the middle of the fire—assuring him it would not hurt.

"Are you sure, Arna? Are you sure you can do this?" Soryn asked, a sudden terror overtaking him at what they were about to do. He believed in her, but he wanted no mistakes and he was even more convinced that Ulla was his brother then than ever.

"I can do this, Soryn. I know I possess the power and other than that, it's mostly following directions. It will be alright," she promised, laying a hand on his shoulder.

Arna then gazed at Ulla, held the open book in her lap and closed her eyes. For several minutes, she breathed in and out— slowing her fluttering heart. Then, she chanted the focus words in the book that would help her visualize the end result in her mind. She knew that she wanted to have the original spell reversed and each spirit returned to its home body.

When the time came, Arna's brow was bathed in sweat and her eyes were clenched as tight as possible while she fought to keep her concentration. She knew that the process would have started because her mind would not let the image that she had conjured disappear. Never opening her eyes, she focused all her energy on the change.

Soryn grew very uneasy when a reddish glow surrounded Ulla in the fire and the naked body on the pile of leaves. Something within gave him pause and made him feel that they were tampering with darker magic. However, he saw Arna's deep concentration and the sweat that ran down her temples. He saw Ulla's eyes grow dim and dark and a new, brighter light settle over the human body. It only took a minute for the light to seep down into flesh and bone.

Soryn could not look away from his brother's body. He did not see when Arna fainted. He only watched and waited for there to be some sign of life in his brother. Slowly, the red light faded entirely and a hum he had not noticed before stopped. All was quiet save for the rain pounding on the snow outside. Darkness filled the burrow.

"Hello, Soryn," a voice said—a voice that Soryn could not recognize as Olan's because of its deepening with age.

"Olan?" Soryn tried out the name now that Ulla had returned to his former self.

"It's quite nice to use my own voice again, little brother, thank you," the voice crooned.

Still, Soryn could not see Olan in the poor light and for some strange reason, this frightened him. A dark foreboding overcame him and a fear he could not explain gripped his heart.

"Olan?"

"I knew I could count on you. You were never like the others— mother, father, our brother...you understood the world in a more sensible way. I knew I could trust you," the voice said—Ulla's voice.

Soryn backed away. He thought he might make it to the entrance, but then he remembered Arna. Despite the sense of danger he felt, he had to make sure it was truly Olan that stood before him. By some stroke of luck, the clouds above the ground cleared and some of the moons' light slipped into the opening of the burrow. What Soryn saw filled him with misery.

There before him stood not Olan, but Fenris. Olan and Fenris were identical except the small mole near Olan's left eye. He knew as soon as the blue light fell on the man's face that he and Arna had made a terrible mistake. Just as Ulla exuded an aura of disquiet and confusion, Fenris exuded an amplified aura of utter malevolence. Soryn could not explain it, but it was there all the same—as though his brother were evil.

"Fenris," he stated.

"Soryn," Fenris returned, smiling wickedly.

Gone was the impotent Ulla. Gone was the illusion that all was becoming right in Soryn's world. With the return of his brother, it was as if all his childhood fears had flooded back into him. Fenris had been creepy as a child and was proving to be absolutely terrifying as an adult. Soryn did not know what to do. He could not flee without leaving Arna and he could not grab her in time to get away from Fenris. But then...he was only thinking of Fenris attacking him. "Why would I think that?" Soryn thought to himself. Terrifying or not, it was still his brother before him. Fenris had just tricked Soryn into thinking he was a different brother.

"Why did you trick me?" Soryn demanded, his voice as steady as he could make it.

"Trick you?" Fenris said, cocking his head in the same fashion Ulla did.

"You told me you were Olan!" Soryn screamed—hoping it would wake Arna, but it did not.

"Ah, that's where you are wrong. I told you that I was your brother, but I never said I was Olan. You assumed I was him, so I let you believe it. When I talked to you all in the cottage, I told the truth—I had found my body and that it was in a cave. Look around you—doesn't this look cavernous?" Fenris' diabolical smile set Soryn's nerves even more on edge.

"How did you find Olan's body?" Soryn demanded.

"Well, that was easy. Because this location is far nearer the cottage, I was still able to read minds and I could see the place Stigg was picturing in his. My sources told me that your little group had found a body in the woods and I could only assume it was Olan's if I had already found mine here. So, I traveled quickly—more quickly than you all—to the cavern to the north and I waited. I was lucky that you were all so far behind me or else I might not have made it in time.

"I waited by Olan's body—marveling at the fact that while he and I were in animal form, our human bodies had grown into men. When you all arrived, I thought it could go two ways. Fanndis would finally believe my deception and reverse the original spell right away. I wouldn't have been able to take Olan's body, but Olan was not but a few feet outside the cave. He would have reclaimed his own body."

"What?" Soryn felt confused.

"The white wolf—that mangy thing—is our brother Olan," he informed Soryn.

"Ulf is Olan?" Soryn was fitting all the pieces together.

"I knew he had taken up with that female wolf and started a pack—I kept tabs very closely on Olan, even if he entirely ignored me. The animal kingdom is a small world, Soryn—it was quite rude of him to shut me out like that. However, since Fanndis did not turn me back on the spot, I knew you and Arna would be fools enough to do it yourselves. You two are entirely too adventurous, you know. I expect Fanndis won't be too pleased with you when she sees what you've done."

Soryn felt as though he had died and was merely observing the whole scene as a ghost. He was too surprised and full of fear to be anything but detached and helpless.

"Fenris, Arna is hurt. We need to take her back to the cottage." Soryn shifted towards her unconscious body.

"You won't be taking her anywhere. I have some business to attend to concerning your little witch, here." Fenris' voice was full of shadows.

"Leave her be, Fenris," Lord Maslyn said from some hidden reservoir of courage in his soul.

Before Fenris could reach her, Soryn sprang forward— attempting to grab her and carry her out of the burrow. Fenris knocked him back and out of the way. Soryn's head flew backwards and slammed into the packed dirt of the burrow walls. The last thing he saw was Fenris stooping over Arna's helpless form before all went dark.

Chapter Fifteen

In which the cottage is seized by despair and hope…

Birds chirped nearby. Soryn was bathed in warmth. This confused him since he last remembered being in a dank, dark burrow under the earth. He listened—the reality of what happened not yet registering in his mind. A crackling sound—a fire— and the scrape of something metal struggling against another hard surface caught his attention. A soft sleeping pallet lay underneath him. Opening his eyes, he was astonished to find he was back in the cottage. Looking up, he saw Fanndis standing over the hearth stirring a small cauldron of soup.

"I see you're awake." Her voice was low, angry.

"Fanndis?" Soryn mumbled, still not understanding how he had gotten back there.

When he rose up, a sharp, stabbing pain rippled throughout his head and neck.

"Don't move. You've hurt your head. I expect it's that idiot Fenris that's to blame for that—though you're certainly to blame, too!" Her mood was clearly volatile.

Suddenly, the memories of the previous night rushed back to Soryn and he shot up, ignoring the blasting pain throughout his body and cried, "Arna!"

"Calm down. She's here with us. Though, you'll not be talking with her today." A despairing look settled upon the old woman's face and she appeared to have aged in the night.

Soryn felt an icy weight drop in his stomach. "What's happened, Fanndis?"

"See for yourself." She jerked her head towards the cottage's front door.

Soryn followed her gaze and nearly jumped out of his skin. A man sat in a chair, wrapped in a patchwork blanket. At first, Soryn thought it was Fenris, but then he saw the mole beneath the left eye: Olan. He was shivering and had streams of tears flowing down his cheeks.

"Olan?" Soryn whispered.

Olan stared off into empty air and did not appear to have heard Soryn's questioning utterance. Fanndis exhaled.

"In all my years…I would never have expected something like this. Never!" Fanndis sighed, clanking the ladle onto the soup catcher on the hearth.

She stomped off into the back room. Her heavy footfalls made Soryn shudder. He stared at Olan. His brother sat there, eyes wide and gazing into space as if his entire world had been ripped from him. When Soryn thought about it honestly, he supposed it had—if Olan truly had been the white wolf they had all come to know. Ulf had a mate, a family of cubs; another life. Soryn and Arna had destroyed that. It had been unintentional, of course, but they had destroyed it, nonetheless. Lord Maslyn grimaced at the bile that rose in his throat. He raced to the window, opened the shutters and retched into the snow.

Soryn looked over towards Arna's room, but the shutters were closed. The sound of harnesses caught his attention and he looked up to see Stigg bringing Ivan around to the barn. When Stigg saw Soryn, he just looked away—as though it were too painful to look upon the boy. Soryn retched again. After he pulled his head back into the room, he closed the shutters. Fanndis beckoned him into the kitchen. Olan remained in his chair, eyes still staring and empty. In the kitchen, Fanndis sat at the table and gestured for Lord Maslyn to take a seat.

"We need to have a conversation, Soryn," Fanndis quipped.

"Yes, ma'am," he said, trying to hold himself together.

"Soryn, what you and Arna did was reckless to say the least—but let me finish. I understand that what you did was done out of love and the desire to return your brother back to his original form. However, once I talked with Ulla in the kitchen, I knew he was Fenris. I knew, because Olan told me. Ulf had come back with us to the cottage and Ulf told me never to trust Ulla. He explained that the pig was really Fenris and the white wolf, himself, was Olan. Because I have known Ulf for many years and I trust him, I believed him at once. I had not kept a guard on my mind and Ulla found out I knew the truth. Because of that, I had to run to Valkyrie to see what could be done to keep you all safe.

"Unfortunately, before I could get there, I had a terrible feeling of foreboding. I turned around and came home. When I returned, I could see that you and Arna had run off, taking matters into your own hands. I remembered a binding spell Valkyrie had told me about long ago that could make Ulla dormant until we knew what to do with him, but I needed his physical presence in order to perform it. By the time I had located you in the burrow, it was too late. If I had arrived minutes later, Arna might have been…" she stopped herself and looked towards the kitchen fire with tears in her eyes.

"Might have been…what?" Soryn asked in a dead, monotone voice.

"Fenris tried to rape her, Soryn. I trust you understand what that means." A small tear tumbled down Fanndis' aged cheek.

"Oh, God," Soryn burst into tears.

"He didn't succeed. When I got there, he had torn off most of her clothing but, thankfully, Stigg is a lot stronger than him. We were able to get him away from her and take her out of there before he could do her any harm." More tears rolled down Fanndis' face.

"But why would Fenris *do* that!?" Soryn asked, tears stinging his eyes.

"I suspect that waking up as a man was quite a confusing experience. His body and hormones are entirely new. As well, your brother has always had a knack for making impulsive, bad decisions."

"What have I done?" Soryn asked, broken and defeated under the weight of all that had transpired.

"Soryn, there's more. Arna is in a coma. We can't wake her up and I've tried everything. Reversal magic is very powerful and has dark consequences. She had no idea of this, I understand, but she was not ready for a spell of that magnitude. It is a wonder she's alive at all. If it were just yresses, she would be fine in a few weeks, but this drained every last drop of energy from her body and I have no idea when she'll wake up." Fanndis wiped her forehead and sat with her hands clasped as though she were praying.

When Soryn heard her muttered words, he prayed, too, for forgiveness and for help for Arna. He didn't know to whom he was praying, but he did it anyway—hoping some gracious deity would have pity on such a miserable creature as him. He wished they had never tried to reverse the original spell...he wished he could take it back.

"What about Olan?" he mumbled.

"He is still in shock. He hasn't said a word since it happened. Fenris broke free from Stigg and ran off into the woods. Stigg wasn't able to find him," Fanndis remarked.

Soryn sat and cried, his head in his hands.

Fanndis got up and left him there at the table. When she walked through the cottage's main room to go check on Arna, Olan was in the exact same position—eyes open, body still. His face looked vacant, his mouth slightly ajar. He had the blanket clutched about him like a life line and she imagined it was his only tangible connection to reality. Fanndis opened the door to the cottage bedroom and sighed. Arna rested there, eyes closed. Anyone would have thought she was sleeping. Not for the first time, Fanndis wondered if Arna had traded spirits with an animal, that it might be her punishment for reversing an animal transference spell. That would be the best case scenario. If Arna was inside an animal body somewhere in the woods, she might be able to make her way back to the cottage somehow.

The old woman prayed that would be the case. If Arna was in fact in some magical coma and not in an animal body…Fanndis would cross that bridge once they had given it some more time and thought. She sat on the bed and placed her hand on the girl's chest, giving her Seidh power one more try to see if it would wake the girl up. It did not. Feeling defeated, she called out to Valkyrie with her mental powers.

Fanndis? Valkyrie was startled to hear from her apprentice after the turmoil of the night.

Valkyrie, something terrible has happened.

I'm on my way, Valkyrie replied, not waiting for Fanndis to say more.

Fanndis was thankful she was not going to have to explain everything just yet. It gave her more time to regroup and to make sense of it herself. She was so angry at Arna and Soryn for not waiting, but at the same time, she understood why they didn't. It was out of love and the desire to make right something that had gone wrong long ago. She knew they were just trying to do what they thought was right. It pained her that it had backfired so badly for them both. Though Soryn seemed physically unaffected, she knew that his heart was devastated by the results of Arna's spell.

Stigg opened the door to the bedroom. His stern face was stained from weeping. He came over to the bed and knelt down next to it. Taking Arna's near lifeless hand into both of his, he cradled it to his face and let his tears fall. Over the last few months, he had grown to love her far more than he imagined he could. Stigg was so furious with Soryn that he could not even look at the boy. Gazing at Arna's lovely, still face he kissed her hand. He felt ashamed that he had not been there to protect her. Then and there he vowed that if she ever regained consciousness, he would ask her to marry him when she was old enough. He knew she loved Soryn, but perhaps that would change if only she would wake up…Stigg wanted to spend his life protecting her.

In the main room, Soryn sat next to Olan in complete silence. He had nothing he could say to his brother that could fix what had happened. Then, he had a spark of an idea. He knew that he was already deep into the mire that he had created, but he had an inkling of an idea how to fix it. Getting up, Lord Maslyn clothed himself for riding. The wind was chill, but not frozen, when he stepped outside. The snow had begun to melt around the back yard and the rain had stopped. In the barn, his horse whinnied nervously—knowing something was amiss in the house.

What's happened, sire? Sable asked.

"Terrible things, Sable. We must go look for a friend," Soryn replied.

After saddling the horse and mounting up, he led the great animal off into the woods in the direction of the greenhouse. He knew Ulf's den had been around there somewhere, because that was where Arna had gotten hurt back in the winter when Ulf had come to warn everyone. The woods were dark, the moons low on the horizon. It was nearly dawn when he reached the greenhouse. Continuing past it, he searched around the granite outcroppings for caverns. When he did not see any obvious openings, he decided to try asking where the wolf den was.

"If you can hear me, Ulf's mate, I have grave news for you! Please come out and talk to me!" Soryn truly hoped Olan's mate would speak with him.

What is it, human? A growling voice entered his mind.

"Ulf is my brother Olan—my human brother," Soryn said, feeling the truth would be the best approach for a dangerous animal.

I know this. What does that matter? He is a wolf—my mate, she replied.

"That's just it…my friend Arna and I performed some magic to return Olan to his human form. We thought that Olan was the black pig and we had no idea that Olan was actually Ulf. I am so sorry." Soryn knew he was jumbling his words, but he stopped to give her time to process this tale.

254

Show me, Ulf's mate commanded.

Soryn peered around, hoping the wolf would not startle him, but when she came out from the top of the rock face, he was astonished by her beauty. She was smaller than Ulf had been, but had ebony black fur that ruffled in the summer wind. She dashed from rock to rock until she was on level ground with Soryn and his horse.

Are they at the cottage? she asked.

"Yes."

I care not if he is a man. I know we cannot be as we were if he is in that form, but he is still the father of my pups and the spirit that I love, she said, more to herself than to Soryn.

He hoped what she said would somehow make everything okay once she saw Olan. He wished that the power of her love for Ulf could change Olan back—now that Soryn saw the terrible thing he and Arna had done. She led the way back to the cottage, running through the wind like a shadow to get there. He found that Sable had trouble keeping up with her. When he saw the light from the cottage shutters through the trees, Soryn dismounted and led his horse the rest of the way through the melting snow to the barn.

Olan's mate went on into the house and Soryn let her go. When he entered some minutes later, what he saw touched him to the core. Olan's mate sat before the human body of his brother, brushing her expansive cheek against his smaller human one. Soryn saw the tears rolling down Olan's face and that his expression had changed to one of utter grief. Olan broke down and sobbed. His cries of sadness and frustration brought Fanndis and Stigg into the room to see what was going on.

Fanndis put a hand to her mouth, stifling a small gasp. She realized it was just Nora, Ulf's mate, and relaxed. Olan brought his arms around Nora's body and cried harder. Soryn guessed they were talking to one another mentally. He *hoped* they were still able to communicate. Everyone felt they should leave the room to give them privacy. No one could imagine the suffering they were facing. Fanndis wished it were as simple as changing him back into a wolf—but since the wolf's spirit most likely died when Olan performed the original spell, there was no spirit to reenter the body. It was already decaying behind the cottage.

By the time the suns rose, Valkyrie arrived. Nar had ridden as fast as his hooves would carry him. Nora had gone back to the wolf den to retrieve their seven pups. Most were old enough to walk behind her except Derik. Fanndis had promised Nora that she could live in the barn if they swore not to eat the horses. Nora quickly agreed. Valkyrie was shocked to see a family of wolves inside the barn when she stabled Nar with the other animals. The matron wolf eyed her with a wary curiosity. Valkyrie frowned and ambled towards the house. She wanted to know exactly what had happened.

When she walked into the kitchen and through to the den, all was quiet, though everyone was wide awake and sitting around the fire. She noted that Arna was absent from the gathering. Also noticed was Olan—the youngest of the Maslyn twins—who sat in a chair covered in blankets. His face was gaunt, nearly hollow, and his eyes were sunken into purple-skinned sockets. He looked terrible.

"What has happened here?" she demanded.

"Valkyrie," Fanndis muttered.

Valkyrie observed that Stigg, Fanndis, Olan, and Soryn were in great need of sleep, though no one would get any if they continued brooding by the hearth. Using a small bit of magic, she put them all under a sleeping spell that would last until noon or so. Within minutes, everyone in the room, except for Valkyrie, fell into a deep sleep. Valkyrie went into the bedroom—she presumed that Arna was in there.

When Fanndis had contacted her, Valkyrie had guessed snippets of what had happened. Soryn and Arna had performed reversal magic and now Arna was in a coma because of it. Valkyrie had some experience in this area and knew that the girl was in no danger, but she had no idea when Arna would wake. It could be hours, days, weeks, years…it was hard to tell with magic of that sort. Dark magic. If she had been in the body of an animal, it was likely that she would have found her way to the cottage by now, but there really was no way to be sure. The best thing to do would be to watch and wait.

Valkyrie tried every spell she knew of to wake the girl, but her efforts proved fruitless. She even tried the same reversal spell Arna had done. Nothing worked. Heartsick, the old woman went back through the front room and into the kitchen. She knew the people in the middle room would be hungry when they awoke from their enchanted sleep. Taking some of the hanging herbs from the ceiling and vegetables from the root cellar below the kitchen floor, Valkyrie made a stew in the cauldron. She prepared the spices and herbs in the broth in such a way that it would bring comfort to all in the house. Valkyrie, herself, was in need of comfort after Annar's death, though months had passed since. Her hair had grown a bit since she had chopped it off in her grief.

Many thoughts coursed through Valkyrie's head in the silence of the morning. Summer birds sang bright songs outside the kitchen windows, but she felt none of their cheer. Still, a strange comfort settled in her old bones. She liked the cottage and the warmth it provided. She enjoyed the company of others. A thought came to her, "You could stay here, Valkyrie." She knew that Fanndis would most likely need help with all the extra mouths that had accumulated around the cottage and she could be of help with Olan—helping him get back on track with his Seidh training if he still wanted it.

By midday, the others began to wake. Olan was the first and Valkyrie made sure he saw her before any of the others woke up. She drew him into the kitchen for a talk.

"Hello, Olan," she whispered.

"Valkyrie?" he croaked—not used to his human voice.

"I'm surprised you remember me. You were just a boy when you came to see me last."

"What are you doing here?" he asked, his voice sounded far away, disinterested.

257

"I came to help in any way that I can," Valkyrie replied, smiling.

Olan said nothing. He had no idea how she could help. He felt like dying. He had been responsible for his parents' deaths. At the time, he had been disoriented. Olan had not expected to turn into an animal when he turned Fenris into one. It was all a mistake and yet, he had been the one to knock over the oil lamps and he had been the one who had killed them by causing the fire. It was his fault. Weariness claimed him and he sat. As a wolf, he had found peace about his past actions. Nora and his pups helped. Now…he had no idea how he would face each day. Olan had never wanted to be human again…to feel human emotions. It was suffocating.

"Valkyrie…" he pleaded before breaking down into sobs again.

Because of his crying, the others meandered into the kitchen. No one could say anything. Everyone felt it was their own fault for what had transpired. Valkyrie did not know what to say to any of them. "Let's have lunch. I made soup," she announced, floundering for words.

Olan had trouble with the soup. Living for six years as a wolf had created a pallet that was more drawn to raw meat than cooked plants. Because he could not bring himself to eat, but knew that raw meat would possibly make his human body ill, he decided to go out to the barn and visit his family. He pushed his chair away from the table, clumsily, and walked stiffly out the back kitchen door. Everyone observed how strange he moved on his human legs. In the barn, Olan saw Nora swat at Derik who had jumped onto her head. When she growled, he leapt off with glee. Olan wanted to cry. That was his family and yet, he felt so far away from them.

Ulf, you are still my mate and their father. You know this, Nora encouraged. *We'll sort this out.*

He nodded and went to sit by her and the pups. Derik immediately crawled into his lap and snuggled against his stomach—like he did when Olan had been a wolf. Apparently Olan's youngest had not noticed his father's change in appearance.

It's your spirit that matters—not the outer shell, Nora reminded him.

"Thank you for encouraging me, Nora. I don't know what to do. I want to be a wolf again. I want to return to the forest. I want to run with my four feet. But I don't see how that can happen until I can transmute my actual human body into that of a wolf. I can't use transferring magic again…the price is too high…" Olan was tempted to cry again, but what was done was done and he was tired of running away from what had happened.

He had to deal with it now. At least Nora had relocated to Fanndis' barn for the time being. That way, he could still be with his family while he tried to figure out what came next. Olan had no real feeling towards Soryn. He loved him, of course, but he didn't remember knowing him that well as a boy. Being brothers did not make them automatically familiar with one another. Memories of being children together were muddled and faded. His thoughts about being human before being a wolf were dark and grim. He hated being a human now. It reminded him of the Seidh and of his brother's evil. It reminded him of becoming a wolf and killing his parents. And yet…when he had become a wolf, his life had become simpler; his needs more basic.

When he had mated with Nora, his world had grown quieter, more peaceful and clear. He had finally forgiven himself for accidentally killing his parents, but when Arna and Soryn had flung him back into his human body, it was like a curse. His dratted hair had grown to his knees and Fanndis had braided it for him. Cutting it was unthinkable for some reason. It was the only pelt he had as a naked human. He missed his fur and his wolf senses. He loathed his human body. It meant he and Nora could not be together. It meant he could not wrestle with his cubs when they grew up—they would no doubt tear him to pieces.

Nora leaned her head against him, drawing him out of his thoughts. Olan felt the warmth from her fur and her pulse racing through her body. She was so strong and wild to him. Knowing his mind would only focus on his bitterness at being a human while he was with his family, he apologized to Nora and went back to talk to Valkyrie. Fanndis was extremely powerful with the Seidh, but he knew that Valkyrie was even stronger. Perhaps she could help him in ways she was not considering. He knew there had to be a way to return him to his wolf body or to make one.

"Valkyrie," he called when he entered the kitchen.

"Yes?" she said, looking up from stirring the soup.

"Turn me back. My body is right outside. Make me like I was. I can't stand this," he said, trying to hold onto his willpower.

"Olan…"

"Can't you do it? There is no spirit to return to that body if not my own," he pointed out.

"It's already decaying. It's a dead body now," Valkyrie explained, though she was pondering the idea.

"Then put me back and then heal the parts that have been decaying. I can't be human anymore, Valkyrie. I just can't." It took all his strength not to cry again.

She looked on him with pity and then said, "Show me the body."

Valkyrie was uncomfortable with the idea of using what was essentially necromantic magic, but she felt there was no harm in this—it *had* been his body for six years and the animal spirit had not returned to it. It was not as though she were about to try resurrecting a dead person. Olan was alive and well—just not in the body he was used to living in. Valkyrie followed Olan out into the back area of the cottage and into the woods a ways. There in the melting snow was Ulf's lifeless wolf body. The white fur looked stiff and bunched up. She hoped that what she was about to try would work for him.

Olan leaned down and touched it—it felt strange to touch his own body when he was in his human form. He longed so much to be a wolf again.

"Please, Valkyrie," Olan pleaded, wishing with all his heart that it would work.

260

Valkyrie felt uncomfortable that she had not told Fanndis what she was up to. However, the younger woman had gone to sleep and Valkyrie did not want to wake her after the drama of the previous nights. Summoning her strength and feeling the yreth growing, Valkyrie focused her energy on the wolf body. She breathed deeply of the chill late afternoon air and stretched out her arms—one toward the wolf form and one toward the human body in which Olan's spirit currently resided.

Because transferring magic was just transferring one thing from one place to another, it was more or less spiritual telekinesis. It was only dark when one was transferring one living thing into another living thing's body. When the object body was empty, it was acceptable. It required no ingredients. That was only for transmutation, reversals, and other sorts of physical distortion and spiritual transference. She imagined the result she wanted in her mind—Olan inside his wolf form, the form he had lived in for so long and in which he had grown to adulthood.

Olan stood very still—hoping her magic would take effect soon. As he looked up at the rising moons, he felt his viewpoint grow hazy and distorted. Now, he was looking up at the sky from a lower point and the image looked far sharper than his human eyes could perceive. He felt the sounds of the coming night within him instead of just with his ears. He could smell everything—the kitchen fire and the soup boiling over it, Arna's smell had changed now that her spirit was elsewhere. All of this he knew just from scent.

It had worked. He sprang off of the ground on his four wolf feet. A victorious howl carried into the summer wind and Ulf leapt up to hug Valkyrie who was stooped over the human body on the ground. She laughed, wearily, and patted his furry back.

"I'm glad for you, Olan. Truly. But know this…there will never be a time for you to return to human form. Your human body will now slowly die. I made the transplantation permanent. No one will be able to take your form away from you again. But the price is that your human body will die."

I understand. You can burn it if you like or bury it. I have no more need of my human flesh. I've been reunited with my true form and with my family—including Soryn. It is good to know him as I truly am.

She smiled and extended her hand in the direction of the barn. Ulf ran off, excited and eager to brush his pelt against Nora's and to play with his pups. He was free. As a wolf, he was free to run and roam the mountains. Free to feel true forgiveness for what he had done in the past. It was over. Entering the barn, he saw that Nora was preparing to hunt. When she saw him, her heart gave an extra beat and she bounded towards him, brushing her entire body against his. Next, she pinned him on the floor of the barn. The horses chuckled in their unique voices as they looked on.

Oh, love... Was all she could say. If wolves cried, Nora would have then. Ulf gave a playful growl and licked her nose. The pups bounded across the barn floor and covered their parents with little nips and howls.

"I'm happy for you, Olan," Fanndis said from the doorway to the barn.

Fanndis.

"Please live happily and forgive yourself for what is past. We will deal with what has happened. Go. Live with your family. We'll make sure you know what is going on at all times," she said, teary eyed.

Thank you, master. I am in my true form—the form I was born to be in. Being human felt so constricting and cold...

"You're welcome to stay in the barn as long as you like, but if you wouldn't mind...it would be wonderful if you could remain our greenhouse protector?"

It would be an honor, my lady, Ulf said, as he bowed his head low.

Fanndis patted him on the head and marveled that he did seem more himself as Ulf. She expected Soryn would be very sad, but it was something that had to be done. Now they had to worry about

262

waking Arna and tracking down Fenris. Not knowing where he was made her extremely nervous. When she walked out, she saw out of the corner of her eye the wolf couple settle into the hunt. They sped out of the barn like shadows—the pups were watched by Eira who swatted at them with her claws when they got too uppity.

Back in the cottage, Fanndis found Soryn in the bedroom sitting next to Arna. He whimpered, thinking no one could hear his crying. Tiptoeing, so she did not alarm him, she put a hand on his back and said, "It's going to be alright, Soryn."

"It's all my fault," he said. "I should never have gotten out of that tower. None of this would have happened."

"You can't go through life and think 'if only I'd never' all the time. We cannot know what would have happened if you *had* stayed in the tower. We only know what *did* happen. You can't change it. The only way to make it better is to work hard and live one day at a time." Fanndis encouraged.

"If there's nothing you or Valkyrie can do to wake her, what am *I* supposed to do?"

"Talk to her. Work diligently to be the best Maslyn you can be so that when she wakes up—and it is *when*—she'll be very proud of you," Fanndis told him.

"Alright." He was not convinced, but he just needed Fanndis to leave for a little while. He wanted to be alone with Arna.

Fanndis figured he wanted to have some time to himself and she went back into the main room. It was late. Stigg was already smoking his pipe and reading—almost as if the events of the previous night had not occurred at all. When she looked at the title of the book, however, she knew the incident was fresh on Stigg's mind; eating away at it.

"*Tracking through Ice and Snow* seems a bit dense for light night reading," Stigg's mother commented.

"I want to be ready. He may have gone into the mountains and I *will* find him. I'll make him pay for what he tried to do to her." Stigg turned a page, a determined scowl set deep in his face.

"Stigg..." Fanndis whispered, knowing it was no use when her son set his mind to something.

"He tried to rape her! Just think if he had succeeded! If she had gotten pregnant, it could have *killed* her she's so young! I just...I..." He was overcome with his anger. Sitting up, he threw the book from him.

"Stigg, *you* stopped him. You *saved* her," his mother pointed out.

"Tch—*saved* her. She's in a coma! We don't even know if she'll wake up!"

"You love her."

Stigg looked at the fire. The flames danced in his tortured eyes. "Yes," he admitted.

"She's a whole lot younger than you, Stigg." Fanndis pointed out.

"I can't help it. She's almost a woman. I would certainly never approach her until she was. I know she doesn't love me and that she won't marry me one day, but I have to try; as soon as she's a woman," Stigg said.

"She'll marry Soryn, you know." Fanndis didn't want to hurt her son, but it was the truth. She and Valkyrie had already seen glimpses of it with their foresight.

"I don't care. I'll be surprised if I ever love another woman. She's the one for me or I'll have no one."

"Stigg, you may not feel that way someday."

Instead of replying, Stigg picked up the book from the floor and continued to read. Since Fanndis knew pushing more conversation would be useless, she walked back to the kitchen and sat down at the table with Valkyrie, who was sipping hot tea.

"Stigg is full of rage, isn't he?" Valkyrie noted, having overheard their conversation.

"Yes. I'll be surprised if it dissipates anytime soon. He loves that girl, even though he's nearly twice her age. Obstinate boy..." Fanndis rolled her eyes.

The two women sat in silence for a while. Soryn stayed in the back room with Arna. Stigg fumed over his book. Depression hung like a heavy vapor over the cottage. Everything had gone wrong. Fanndis was glad that Valkyrie had been able to give Ulf what he wanted, at least. Fanndis knew she did not have that kind of strength, though she was an advanced practitioner of the Seidh. It took extreme power to do that sort of spell; power she did not have.

"Cheer up, old girl. We'll make it through this." Valkyrie winked at her—suddenly the optimist.

Fanndis had seen a change in the woman—other than the short cropped hair.

"What's happened to you, Valkyrie?" Fanndis asked, curious.

"Something happened up on the mountain after Annar died," she began. "I was so overcome with my grief and regret and I just wanted it all to go away. Someone came to me—a wolf. We merely sat in silence and watched the suns rise together. I've never experienced anything like it. I felt an unexplainable hope, despite my sadness. Since then, I've felt comforted. I know I can go on. It's what Annar would want. Annar wanted to be human so badly, yet I forced him to remain a goat to prolong his life. All I was really doing was prolonging his suffering. When I saw Olan's pain, I couldn't fail to help him. That's why I changed Olan back. It was the right thing to do."

Fanndis did not know what to say. Valkyrie had always been such a sarcastic, blunt person. To see this new calm and compassionate figure was a wonderful change.

"I'm glad for us both, Valkyrie," Fanndis said, touching the older woman's hand and patting it gently. "I'm glad to have my teacher back and to have a friend in all this."

"I suppose we're in for a long summer of waiting." Valkyrie pondered aloud, exhaling and holding the tea mug between her wrinkled hands.

"I suppose. Perhaps we'll know something before winter about Arna—surely it won't take that long to find out where she's gone…"

Valkyrie did not reply. Instead, the two of them sat for the rest of the night in silence, talking occasionally and praying for guidance. It was a chill summer night and the wind battered the stone cottage. Eventually, Stigg fell asleep in his chair with his pipe in his hand, his book against his chest. Soryn fell asleep holding Arna's hand, his head on her shoulder. All were restful in the house and conquered by a brief, fleeting peace in spite of the sorrow; each one weary, waiting for what was to come.

THREE YEARS LATER

Chapter Sixteen

In which a boy has become a man…

Late in the month of Heyannir, 907 PAE (Post Ancient Earth)

Summer soon would end and the winter snows loomed on everyone's minds. Lord Maslyn drummed his stylus on his desk while he waited for the insufferable merchant in his office to agree to stop cheating his customers. The man was a pox on everyone else's businesses since he sold cheap goods for exorbitant prices. Each week, Soryn had some wronged villager in his office complaining about the miser. Finally, Lord Maslyn could stand it no longer and just wanted everyone to shut up about the situation. That is why he had called Knut into his office that morning. The fool's shady business practices would end immediately.

"Lord Maslyn, sir, let me tell you why it is that I run my business in the manner that I do—" Knut began, but Soryn cut him off.

"I'm not interested, Knut. I've heard from nearly every villager and merchant in town. You're a cheat and your goods are in such poor condition that they endanger the lives of the people who use them! You're a ship materials seller, for heaven's sake! What could happen if one of your mooring lines snapped and ended up killing someone because it could not perform its proper function? No, Knut. I'm not interested in your defense. Either sell your goods at a reasonable price or find a new supplier that will provide you with quality materials. End of story. If I find out you haven't done as I've asked, I'll have your merchant's license revoked, *permanently*. You'll never do business in New Kristiansand again."

"Yes, sir," Knut grumbled under his breath, sweating from the pressure of the Maslyn's glare.

"Now, be off with you and start fixing what you've broken. You have a lot of angry patrons to appease," Soryn demanded, flicking both hands in the direction of the door.

Knut mumbled his way to the door and slammed it shut when he left. Soryn groaned and rubbed his forehead. Father Kimbli was ill and had not been able to assist Soryn in his mayoral duties for almost a month. Though Soryn, being a man now, was quite used to running the village alone, it was nice to have Kimbli around so he could take a break every now and then. He wanted to go help Stigg, Fanndis, and Valkyrie with their cottage repairs before the winter snows came in full. He wanted to sit with Arna and talk to her.

He endured three other meetings until it was time for him to move on to his other daily duties. Jori waited in the tower to assist Lord Maslyn with his afternoon paperwork. After his meetings, Soryn had to review all the treaties and licensing requests, and other flotsam and jetsam that had to be signed and documented. It was tedious work and Soryn always grew cranky by the end of it. The only thing that gave him pleasure was saddling Sable and galloping into the woods to visit the cottage.

That day, as the suns were sinking low on the horizon, Soryn decided to walk to the cottage to let his head clear. All the guards waved at him on his way out and even told him some jokes—they were about his age, after all. Soryn was surprised at how many people were comfortable with him as their village leader. He was only sixteen—but since boys became men at fifteen, he had been a legal adult for over a year. It was nice to be treated with respect and support, though he was still very young. Stigg still treated him like a boy and had grown so disagreeable to work with over the last three years that Soryn was just about to explode from frustration.

Fanndis always tried to assure Soryn that Stigg was just sad and irritated with himself that he still had not found Fenris. Soryn didn't care. He never wanted to see Fenris ever again and he silently wished about twenty times a day that Stigg *would not* ever find him. Perhaps that was why the older man always grunted when Soryn asked a question or when he did not perform his chores well. Stigg was a proud person. Perhaps he knew that Soryn did not approve of his tracking activities.

Ulf had become a great friend and confidant. It was hard for Soryn to view him as his brother when he looked like a wolf, but he and Ulf had developed a deep camaraderie and it was nice for him to have someone to talk to that did not always want something from him or have something critical to say about his actions. Ulf and his pack—for his pups were all grown now and several other wolf families had joined them in their den—guarded the greenhouse well. Whenever unsuspecting travelers tried to investigate the unusual structure in the forest, the pack could be counted upon to frighten the poor people off.

When Soryn broke through the tree line and into the clearing where the cottage rested, he saw Valkyrie and Fanndis out in the front yard tying bundles of thatch. The roof had gotten old and everyone had agreed it was time to replace it before the winter snows. It was backbreaking work and Soryn and Stigg got the worst of it, having to lay thatching on the roof across the rafters. Still, working with his hands was always preferable to working with the mind and Soryn relished physical activities. It helped get his thoughts off of Arna who was still in a coma, resting in her room. He never stopped thinking about her. In all his spare time, Soryn researched methods for locating wandering spirits or medical dictionaries for waking coma patients. He had found nothing in the last three years; neither had Fanndis, Valkyrie, or Stigg.

"Hi-oh, Lord Maslyn!" Valkyrie waved—she had become such an annoying, perky human being of late. It was unnatural to be so happy all the time, in Soryn's opinion.

"Hello, Soryn," Fanndis said, smiling.

"Hello," he muttered.

"Bad day?" she asked.

"Annoying, frustrating, soul-killing…," he sighed. "Yes, a bad day."

"Cheer up! A whole roof worth of thatching waits for you! Just the thing to get your mind off your frustrations!" Valkyrie beamed, trying to rub his unhappiness in his face (or so Soryn thought).

"Valkyrie…could you tone it down *just* a bit?" Soryn narrowed his eyes.

"Well, excuse me if I'm not as glum as the rest of you lot all the time. I think it would do you some good to cheer up."

"Hnn," was all Soryn uttered in reply.

Stigg motioned for Lord Maslyn to come on up to the roof and Soryn waved back. First, he went into the cottage and dropped his coat by the hearth. Then, he walked through the kitchen and out the back to see Arna, who had been sleeping in her new room for the majority of the last three years. He opened her door and saw that Stigg had opened her windows, made a small fire, and put flowers out on her desk.

He knew it was Stigg who had done these things because he always picked wildflowers, whereas Fanndis or Valkyrie often chose more cultivated varieties from the greenhouse. Soryn knew Stigg cared deeply about her, though the older man never spoke of it. Soryn looked over at Arna, lying there in the bed. Her blondish, brown hair had grown very long over the years and it curled slightly here and there. Her skin was pale like fresh winter snow. His heart gave an uncomfortable lurch. Every time he looked at her it was the same: a sea of regret.

His fingers brushed over her hair and smoothed it away from her face. He hoped that his touch would somehow bring her back, but each time he drew his hand away disappointed.

"Soryn!" Stigg barked from above.

"Coming," he mumbled too soft for Stigg to hear.

He left the door open for Arna, more habit than anything. At least the fresh air would do her a bit of good. The temperature had already started dropping to the customarily frigid winter norms. Soryn shivered a bit as he climbed the ladder propped against the slope of the roof.

Sweat trickled down Stigg's bare back and he carried two bundles of thatch under his left arm as he tiptoed down the ridgepole of the roof. Soryn followed behind and helped the man without any instruction. Though he and Stigg did not talk much, they worked together in a seamless cadence. Perhaps it was more due to familiarity of work patterns than communication of any kind. They worked until time for dinner when the women called them in. They had almost finished half the re-thatching by that time. If it was a clear night, the light from Niflheim's three moons would allow them to get it all done.

Talk at dinner was less lively than usual. Everyone could tell Soryn was in a sour mood. Ulf and Nora had dropped by earlier to deliver several rabbits for the stew. Even the addition of meat (a rare presence at the table, even in summer) did not brighten the evening. By the time the meal was over, Valkyrie and Fanndis had decided to find some way to bring a smile to Lord Maslyn's face. While the men went back up on the roof, the two women took a stroll to the greenhouse.

"I wonder if he'll ever snap out of it." Fanndis sighed.

"Snap out of what?" Valkyrie inquired.

"This stupor he has about his life. It's like when Arna went into the coma, he did as well. He's just been so detached for so long. He rarely speaks unless it is to grumble about something. He's more like Stigg than he knows. Stigg has changed much of late as well," Fanndis explained.

"She may still wake up, you know," Valkyrie said pointedly.

"Yes, but…" Fanndis hesitated.

"But what?" Valkyrie prompted.

"I just don't want either of them to get their hopes up. She could be like that for quite some time. Years more perhaps. Maybe forever," Fanndis admitted.

"Mm."

The greenhouse was always a welcome diversion. It was full of life and green beauty. They spent time pruning overgrown areas and more time picking ripened fruits and vegetables. Their baskets were full when they walked back. On their way through the moonlight, they spotted Ulf and some wolves in his pack. Both women waved and they were surprised when Ulf turned towards them and ran.

"What's the matter, Olan?" Fanndis asked.

We think we may have found something, Ulf told her.

"Like what?" Valkyrie asked, her heart racing.

Something that could be related to Arna.

"Where?!" Fanndis shouted.

Towards the base of the mountain. Do you have time to follow me? Ulf inquired.

Fanndis and Valkyrie glanced at one another and nodded. The wolves trotted at a pace the humans could follow. Though the night was well upon them, the three moons gave plenty of light to pick their way through the forest. The base of the mountain was very distinct and almost a straight climb up. Both women were thankful the wolf had said *towards* the base of the mountain and not *in* the mountains.

It was not long before they each saw what Ulf had been talking about. A hot spring bubbled up near the bottom of a cliff face. There in the water was a strange illusion—or so Fanndis thought at first. It appeared to be a young boy but on closer inspection, Valkyrie noticed the figure was far too womanly and the hair was simply cropped short.

"My God..." Fanndis started.

There in the water was Arna, naked and bathing in the spring. Her body had a soft glow all around it and Fanndis thought she could clearly see through it to the rock face. It was as though they were staring at a ghost. Ulf and the wolves crouched low and stepped soundlessly through the underbrush.

"Arna," Fanndis whispered.

"It's her spirit," Valkyrie confirmed.

Fanndis skirted down the path to the spring and saw Arna's spirit reach into the water, bring its arms up, and smooth the air

274

down its skin as though it were washing. She wondered if the spirit really thought it was getting wet at all.

"Arna?" Fanndis tried again.

The apparition turned her head. A confused expression haunted the girl's face. She looked just like Arna did three years ago.

Fanndis? Arna's spirit mouthed the words, but the sound was in Fanndis' head.

"It's me, Arna. Where have you been?" Fanndis asked, as calmly as possible.

Been? I'm here, she replied in dreamy tones.

"Yes I can see that you're here, but…you've been in a coma for three years!"

Has it been that long? The spirit looked up at the moons above.

"Yes it has. Soryn has been worried sick about you," Valkyrie spoke up.

My…and here I was…all this time…

"You've been in the hot spring for three years?" Fanndis asked, disbelief clear in her voice.

No…I've been here in this form, wandering…not knowing where I was. I was lost, Fanndis. I couldn't find my way back. I saw the other side of the world…the southern mountains…the oceans…the great frozen rivers…I didn't realize I had come so close to home…It is strange…being…unfettered. The spirit looked down at the water and continued to "wash".

"Unfettered?" Valkyrie prompted.

When I performed the spell, I felt my own spirit slip away, so I forced my spirit to fly and I lost track of time and space. It has felt like centuries and, at other times, only hours…it is strange…I am free to go where I wish…though I have begun to get homesick…

"For your own body?" Valkyrie inquired.

No…for Soryn…

"Come home with us, Arna," Fanndis coaxed, motioning for Arna to follow them with her hands.

Home?

"To the cottage. Soryn is there. He longs to see you," Valkyrie joined in the plea.

Home. Yes…I will come…

Fanndis and Valkyrie kept their backs to the forest and faced Arna's spirit. They beckoned to her with their hands. Eventually, Arna's spirit walked onto the shore of the hot spring and followed the two women. Valkyrie doubled around the apparition and walked behind her so that Fanndis could look where she was going. Fanndis turned around and walked ahead. They kept Arna's shade between them.

Neither had experienced an incorporeal form before. It was strange seeing the girl in this way. Her lithe figure looked entirely carefree as she gazed about at the stars and trees. Each older woman wondered how the girl had changed in three years of "unfettered" wandering. It took longer to get back to the cottage, but the women had to take care not to rush the spirit—for she was bemused by many things in the woods: a frosted leaf here, an ice-capped bud there. They had to guide her back to the present often, reminding her that Soryn waited for her.

When they did reach the cottage, a heavy cloud of smoke billowed out of the chimney. The men had finished with the thatching. Fanndis and Valkyrie gave one another a look. It would be best to reunite Arna's spirit with her body first, before Soryn or Stigg saw her. Valkyrie opened the door to Arna's room and marveled as the spirit lifted her hands and attempted to touch the stones that made up her extension of the house. She even went so far as to rest her head against the stones.

Soryn made this place…

"And Stigg," Fanndis added.

Stigg…Soryn…

Valkyrie cleared her throat, prompting Fanndis to usher the spirit girl inside the room. Arna's shade tiptoed towards her physical body and ran her hands up the covers. When the spirit's hands brushed Arna's face, sparks of light popped upwards and Arna's spirit faded as her fleshly body reclaimed it. Fanndis and her companion held their breath—not daring to release it until they knew Arna had returned to herself. Arna's human body seemed to change in color; it looked brighter, fuller somehow. Within moments, they saw the chest lift and fall rhythmically as though she had merely been sleeping and not in a coma. Fanndis reached out a hand to Arna's skin and it felt miraculously warm and *fully alive*.

"Oh, Valkyrie…she's come back." Fanndis felt tears pool at the corners of her eyes and she knelt on the side of the bed weeping.

Valkyrie patted her friend's back and laid her other hand on Arna's shoulder. Arna's eyes fluttered a bit, opening. She looked around her little room and at the old women gawking at her.

"Fanndis?" she asked, her voice hoarse and dry from years of silence.

"Arna! You've come back to us…" Fanndis could not even begin to stop the flow of her tears. It was as though her long lost daughter had returned.

"Come back? Have I been somewhere?" Arna inquired, looking about at her surroundings with puzzlement.

"You've been in a coma for three years, Arna," Valkyrie informed the young woman.

"Three years? How can that be? I remember the spell…I remember…What happened? Did it work?!" Arna queried, trying to sit up and coughing at the effort it took to speak and to move.

"Don't rush yourself. You haven't been out of this bed in a *long* time, girl. You mustn't overdo it," Fanndis chided with a smile.

"Yes, it worked," Valkyrie began. "But we had to quickly undo what was done for Olan."

"Olan was Ulla after all?" Arna asked.

"No. Ulla was Fenris and he tried to do you great harm. If Stigg hadn't made it in time…We weren't quite sure what would have become of you," Fanndis answered.

"What about Olan?"

"Olan was Ulf—your wolf friend. We were all surprised as well, but he could not stand being human in the end. Valkyrie paid him a great kindness in returning him to his wolf form. We burned his human body shortly after. He wanted nothing to do with his humanity after all the painful memories it brought back. Besides, he had his family to think of. All his pups are grown now. Derik still visits often and asks about you," Fanndis continued.

"What happened to Fenris?" Arna asked, anger bubbling up inside her.

"We haven't seen him since. He escaped the same night of the spell and Stigg has been searching for him high and low to no avail. It's as though he simply vanished," Valkyrie supplied.

"I messed everything up didn't I?" Arna felt miserable.

"No, dear one. You were trying to make right something that just didn't really need to be fixed. Your heart was in the right place, your motivations pure. It is Soryn who has truly suffered since. He and Ulf were able to become friends and brothers again, now that he knows Ulf is Olan, but he blames himself for what happened to you," Valkyrie explained.

"Idiot. It was *my* decision to perform the spell," Arna scowled.

"Yes, but it was Soryn who asked you to do it. He longed so much for his lost family. He has never been the same since the night of the spell. All the hope has been driven out of him. It's like he didn't even wish to go on living in the world if you were not in it with him. He has visited you and talked with you every day since it happened. I expect your return will cause him great reason to celebrate and live again," Fanndis hoped.

"He's here?" she whispered.

"Yes. Would you like to see him?" Fanndis inquired.

"Yes, please," the girl nodded.

Fanndis and Valkyrie grunted with the effort of carrying Arna's weak body into the main cottage. Though the girl tried to get up on her own, it proved to be a useless endeavor—they imagined her muscles had atrophied from being unused for so long. It would take a while for the girl to regain her strength. When Fanndis nodded, Valkyrie used her free hand to open the door from the kitchen to the main room. Stigg and Soryn sat reading and smoking their twin pipes.

"Ahem," Fanndis cleared her throat.

Soryn saw her first. He shot up, knocking over his chair in his surprise. Stigg, too, stood and gaped at Arna's conscious state.

"Arna...my God..." Stigg whispered.

"Yes, we must praise heaven for this miracle!" Valkyrie exclaimed.

Both men walked towards her and marveled at her beaming cheeks and bright eyes. Arna soaked it all in—admiring each of them and studying their aged faces. Soryn was a man now and he had a strong look about him that had replaced the childish features of his younger days. Stigg looked much the same but with a few more lines on his weathered face.

"Hello," Arna finally said.

The men let out the breath they had been holding in and laughed as they reached for the girl. She was swallowed by their embraces and giggled at the attention.

"Don't break me," she laughed.

Soryn's heart was full and warm for the first time in ages. It was like the first time he and Arna had gone down the passage in the tower together and shared in the sun spire's warmth. He had not realized how dead he had felt until she had come back to life. He needed to touch her to make sure she was real.

"Soryn," Arna said, looking up at him with vibrant eyes. "I have missed you."

Soryn reached out his hand and stroked the long hair away from her face. Her skin was warm and full of health. A tear rolled down his cheek.

"Arna," he said, bringing her hand up to his own face, weeping.

Stigg was crying, too. His arm rested around the girl's shoulders. As he gazed at her, he poured all the love he could into his eyes—hoping she knew how much she meant to him. Joy filled every corner of his being that she was awake and healthy.

"Stigg, I hope you've been getting along fine without me?" she teased.

"Just fine now that you're *back*," Stigg admitted.

Valkyrie and Fanndis found their arms were giving away on them and the old women appealed to Soryn to take their young charge. He obliged, a huge smile spreading over his lips, and held her between his two strong arms. Arna marveled at his muscles.

"*These* are new," she giggled, touching his biceps.

"Stigg's been working me to death while you've been away." Soryn blushed at her mention of his physical strength. He had changed quite a bit while she had been in the coma.

"Stigg, didn't I tell you not to work too hard?" Arna smiled at him.

Stigg blushed and shrugged. His heart was overjoyed that she was alive and happy, but it broke a little to hear her praising Soryn in such a loving manner. He knew that she loved the boy, and he wanted to be happy for the two of them, but he brushed those thoughts from his mind and concentrated on cheering up. Despite all he felt, he knew that Arna would not want him to be sad.

Soryn carried Arna to the chair by the hearth and held her as he sat down. He figured the fire's warmth would do her good. Stigg sat after he set his chair back on four legs. The women collapsed in the other vacant seats, laughing at their exhaustion after carrying Arna's small body into the house.

"How did this happen?" Stigg looked up at his mother.

"Well, Ulf and some members of his pack came to find us, because something strange was in the woods near the base of the mountain. We followed them to the hot spring and Arna's spirit was there, in the water. It was the first incorporeal spirit I had seen," admitted Valkyrie. "But we knew it was Arna, because, though we could see through her, it looked just like she did years ago before the coma. We were able to talk to her spirit and get it to come back with us."

"You saw her *spirit*?" Soryn remarked, surprised.

"Yes," Fanndis shivered. "It was quite an odd experience."

"I don't remember any of that," Arna confessed, a frown on her delicate face.

"I suppose that a person's spirit is somehow connected to the subconscious," offered Fanndis.

"It's a shame. I would have loved to remember all the wonderful things I might have seen and witnessed," Arna sighed.

The joyous group talked and laughed well into the night. Though Arna had gone into her coma a child and awoken a woman, it felt as though nothing had changed between any of them, as though three years had passed with the blink of an eye. When night came, Soryn carried Arna to her room and made up the fire (she was far too weak for magic) and tucked her in. As he turned to go, she reached out for him and tugged his sleeve.

"Don't go just yet," she pleaded, her wide eyes mirroring the moonlight pouring from the open shutters.

Soryn's heart leapt and he felt the uncomfortable flutter of anxiety in his stomach. He loved her so much and yet he did not know how to express that to her.

"Alright." Soryn turned back toward her.

He sat on the edge of her bed and she made sure her legs were pressed up against him. Arna was so cold, she felt she might never be warm again. Soryn's body was almost hot.

"It's strange to see you all grown up, Bialas."

"It's strange to be called 'Bialas'," he said, inclining his head towards hers. "You're the only one who calls me that, you know."

"I like it. It's like a special name only I know." She smiled.

"Arna…I cannot begin to tell you how sorry I am." Soryn could not hold back his guilt any longer. Though he was overjoyed at her waking, he was overcome by his part in what had happened three years earlier.

"Don't…"

"You don't understand! I put you in that bed for three years. It's my fault you were in a coma. You'll never get those years back, Arna. Ever. All because of me," he groaned, putting his head in his hands.

Though it was a struggle, Arna propped herself up on her arms. She laid a weak hand on his back.

"We were fooled, Bialas. Ulla was a liar and he's responsible for this, if anyone is. You were just trying to help your brother. As it turned out, you were right. Ulla *was* your brother, just not the one you supposed. I bear no ill will for what we did. It was as much my decision as it was yours. Please don't blame yourself," she begged.

"You speak as though you didn't lose three entire years of your life, Arna."

"But it wasn't as though I really noticed. For me, it's as though I just woke up from a very long dream. I remember everything like it just happened. You can fill me in on the rest." She wanted desperately to encourage him and get him to be the hopeful Soryn she remembered.

"There's not much to fill me in on. I'm the Maslyn. I work in the village until late afternoon each day and then I spend my evenings here, helping them out, visiting with you. Not much to tell. Father Kimbli is ill at the moment, but recovering. He asks after you often." Lord Maslyn shrugged.

"Hopefully my return will add some excitement to life," she teased.

"Well, Stigg *did* say about five words to me today, which is a new record."

Arna punched him in the arm for that comment, but then recoiled in pain when she realized that she was nowhere near strong enough for such displays yet.

"It *is* mind-boggling to have all this hair tumbling down everywhere," Arna confessed. "That is definitely new for me. I've had my hair short most of my life. I think I kind of like it—"Arna stopped when Soryn suddenly ran one of his hands through her hip-length locks.

"It's beautiful," he corrected.

"Thank you," she said, color rising to her cheeks.

Before he could think better of his impulse, Soryn leaned forward and kissed Arna full on the lips. Though startled at first, Arna melted into the embrace and brought her arms up around his neck. It seemed entirely right that they should be kissing. She *did* love him after all and she knew he loved her back. Being inexperienced at kissing, Soryn had no idea what to do after he had acted so rashly. He broke away, his face aflame, heart beating madly.

"That was a nice surprise." Arna smiled with his taste on her lips.

"I'm *so* sorry. I have no idea what got into me, I-I…" Soryn was mortified at what he had done, but despite his embarrassment, he found he wanted to do it again.

Since he could not summon the words for how he felt, he hoped that a kiss would do the job. He thought he should do it again. Just so she knew what he felt for her. He looked over and she was smiling with her intoxicating prettiness and her smell—he only noticed it right at that moment. It brought memories to his mind of their escapades before her coma. She had always smelled of jasmine and lavender. Her scent comforted him, he realized, and having it back filled some hole in his heart.

"Bialas," she prompted.

His heart was overwhelmed with love. Soryn was a man, old enough to marry, but he did not want to ask her just because they were both grown now. He did not want to ask her just because he was afraid of what might happen now that she was awake. Still, there was some underlying desperation within him. They had missed so much time—time they could have spent together over the last three years.

"I love you," he said, gazing into her eyes.

Tears rimmed Arna's eyes. She had loved him from the very beginning—even as a child. She knew she would never love another man. It was as though she had been reborn into a woman overnight. Three years had made her an adult while she slept. Her heart and spirit told her to move, to pursue the one she loved.

"I've always loved you, Bialas. It began when I was first assigned to your service in the tower. I've always known it would be this way between us," Arna confessed.

He leaned forward, heart feeling as though it would explode, and nearly touched his lips to hers but first whispered, "May I kiss you again, Arna?"

Though it took considerable effort, the girl brought his face to hers and kissed him with as much passion as she could. Soryn made sure he was not crushing her and wrapped his arms about her frail body. They kissed and held each other for a long time, content to be together. When they pulled away, both were filled with a complete peace.

"When you are well, I want to take you somewhere," Soryn said, stroking her arm.

"Where?" she replied.

"Somewhere in the mountains. It's a special place."

They said nothing more, simply touched hands and entwined their fingers. Soryn stayed with her until she fell asleep with a comely grin on her face. Only then did he leave her. He made sure her shutters were sealed to ward off the chill of the night air. Then, he turned towards the barn and his horse. He expected everyone else to be in bed already, so he was surprised to see Stigg sitting in the barn, leaning his back against one of the stalls.

Stigg had his knees pulled up and his forearms propped over them. He appeared more relaxed than Soryn had ever seen him. That man rested for no one. Lord Maslyn smelled alcohol—*strong* alcohol—and surmised that Fanndis' son had been drinking for quite some time.

"Stigg?" Soryn attempted.

He heard the sloshing of liquid in a glass bottle that Stigg picked up, uncorked, and then drained.

"Are you alright?" Lord Maslyn prodded.

"This is happy drinking…" Stigg slurred.

"Happy drinking?"

"Couldn't be happier that the young lady's alive and well. Couldn't be happier…" he said, every other word nearly unintelligible.

"Stigg, give me the bottle." Soryn had *never* seen Stigg drink any alcohol over the last four years. It was unnerving. He wondered what in the world had caused him to get drunk.

"Want some?" Stigg offered.

Soryn took the empty bottle.

Lord Maslyn sat next to Stigg and saw extreme sadness in the man's eyes, despite his declaration that he had been "happy drinking".

"Stigg, please tell me what's wrong. I know we don't exactly get on that well, but I am your friend." Soryn was worried. He wondered if he should go and fetch Fanndis or Valkyrie.

"I love her…" Stigg said, clear as a bell.

Soryn knew he meant Arna without asking. A lead weight settled into his heart. Arna loved him, not Stigg. Soryn ached for the man. He honestly had not guessed that Fanndis' stoic son had fallen for Arna so deeply, though now that he saw the depth of Stigg's emotion, he suspected the man had loved her this much for a long time. Even before the coma.

"Stigg…"

"But I'm happy for you and…for her…" Stigg said, concentrating on his words.

Stigg's beard had grown unkempt over the last few days because of all the work with the roof thatching and his hair was disheveled. He looked like he had not crawled out of the village pub for days—just like a man despairing in his barn over a woman. Stigg must have been drinking for quite some time to be this inebriated.

285

"Stigg, come on, I'll help you to the cottage." Soryn stood up and extended his hand down to the man, but Stigg just patted the noble's hands away.

"I want to stay here a while," Stigg declared, looking at nothing in particular, but certainly not at Soryn.

"Alright," Soryn relented.

As Lord Maslyn turned to leave, he saw out of his peripheral vision a solitary tear roll down Stigg's cheek. Fanndis' son closed his eyes and leaned his head back against the wood of the stall. More tears followed the previous one and Soryn felt a swelling of pity in his chest. He knew he needed to leave. Since Soryn did not see any other bottles, he figured no harm would come to Stigg if he went in and told Fanndis what had happened. Thankfully, both women were up and sitting by the fire when he entered from the back kitchen door.

"Soryn, we thought you'd gone," Valkyrie said.

"No, Arna and I talked a while and then I went to the barn to saddle up my horse. When I got there, I found Stigg with *this*." He extended the depleted vodka bottle towards Fanndis. The woman eyed it with a moderate degree of skepticism.

"But Stigg doesn't drink," Fanndis said, perplexed as she took it from Soryn.

"Well, he must have forgotten that he doesn't drink. He's about to pass out, I think. He's sitting in front of Ivan's stall," Soryn informed them.

The two women sat still, not really knowing what to say. Their silence was interrupted by a strange sound. It was coming from outside, from the direction of the barn. Fanndis and Valkyrie strained their ears to listen and could make out words.

"He's drunk! And *singing*!" Valkyrie exclaimed, putting a hand to her chest.

"Oh dear…" Fanndis sighed. "I'll go get him. Wait here. I may need your help, Soryn."

"Alright."

286

"Be careful, Fanndis," Valkyrie cautioned.

"He's my own son. He won't hurt me."

"Have you ever seen him drunk before?" Valkyrie interjected.

"Well, no, but I saw his father quite intoxicated many a time and he was never violent. I'm sure Stigg means no one any harm. I know what caused this." Fanndis rolled her eyes, heading out the back door.

Soryn tried changing the subject, "Valkyrie, who is Stigg's father?"

"Oh, him? He was a fisherman down in the village. One winter, he was very ill and Fanndis tended to him. I suppose they grew to be good friends, although nothing more came of their relationship, except for Stigg and the daughter that passed on in her infancy. Fanndis remembers him fondly, but the fisherman died at sea some years ago. Stigg never speaks of him, as far as I can piece together. I think he may have died while she was carrying Stigg's little sister. She doesn't talk about him that much," Valkyrie replied, looking away.

Soryn rubbed a hand through his hair, scratching his scalp with the pads of his fingers. Being so happy and yet so sad and confused at the same time was taking a toll on the young man. He slouched in the chair nearest the hearth and exhaled.

"What's wrong, lad?" Valkyrie inquired.

"Honestly, no offense, Valkyrie, but I don't want to talk about things right now. I just need a minute to process everything," he admitted, hoping she would not be angry.

"I understand. I think I already have an idea of what's going on. I'm not as unobservant as all that." Valkyrie went back to the knitting that Soryn had not noticed before.

They heard some rather destructive sounding noises from the direction of the back door. Soryn stood up to help Fanndis. A loud crash prompted him to hurry. Soryn opened the door. Stigg collapsed through the threshold onto the floor, snoring. Fanndis panted and heaved her hands on her hips. Stigg's mother shook her head as she looked at one of her favorite clay pitchers in several pieces all over the floor.

"I may skin him alive when he wakes up," she spat.

Fanndis sat down at the table and sighed, putting her head in her hands. "Soryn, I've *never* seen him like this," she confessed.

Soryn felt responsible, like it was his fault that Stigg had fallen in love with Arna. Knowing it was nonsense, he sat down next to Fanndis and wrapped his arm around her.

"He's in love with Arna," he stated the obvious.

"I know. He told me some time ago, but I thought it would fade. I suppose I don't know my own son very well," she smirked.

"He's never been drunk before? *Ever*?" Soryn raised an eyebrow looking at the unconscious man on the floor. "He seemed an expert tonight."

"He delved into the pub with me when he was about your age. I bought him a drink, but Stigg promptly spat it out on the ground raving about its terrible taste," she chuckled. "I guess he got over it once he started tonight, though. We'll have to hide all of my medicinal vodka, just in case."

"I'm sorry, Fanndis. Somehow, I feel like this is my fault," Soryn mumbled.

"What, that my son's a fool for falling in love with someone half his age? Soryn, that's just idiocy and you know it. Stigg knew better and I told him so, myself."

"You did?"

"Of course. Arna looks at him like a big brother figure. She would never love him like that. He knew it to begin with," Fanndis glowered.

"Love has a mind of its own it seems," Soryn said, feeling the flutter of happiness he had felt earlier when he and Arna had declared their love.

"That it does," agreed Fanndis, thinking back on her brief romance with Stigg's father and her old flame for Governor Frey.

Shaking her head, Fanndis bumped Soryn in an attempt to lighten the mood.

"Do you think he'll be alright, Fanndis, truly?" Soryn was not so sure.

"Help me get him into bed and I'm sure he'll wake up feeling just fine in the morning. Well, all except for a devil of a headache."

Chapter Seventeen

In which an old enemy returns to the woods…

Stigg awoke with a searing throb in his head and a stomach that twisted itself in cruel knots.

"Oh, God," he groaned, knowing the previous night's drunkenness had left him the worse for wear.

He looked up and saw his mother sitting next to the bed, her legs crossed and a wooden bucket held out towards him. An eyebrow lifted on her aging face.

"Hello, Mother," he muttered, gratefully accepting the bucket and regurgitating the contents of his stomach into the crude receptacle.

"You gave us all quite a stir last night, Stigg. Anything you'd like to talk about? A latent penchant for binge drinking perhaps?" Though her tone sounded light, Stigg could tell she was deadly serious.

"No, nothing like that…I just…well," he ran a hand over his head and mussed his already unkempt hair into a matrix of tangles. "I don't know what made me do it, to tell you the truth."

"That's an impotent excuse if ever I've heard one. Tell me the truth. Tell me how you really feel about Arna and Soryn, Stigg. For once in your life, give me a sermon, if that's what you feel like doing," his mother pleaded. "I'm here to help you."

"You can't help me," he whispered—attempting to keep the noise level down for his sore head.

"You're right. I can't if you don't tell me how," she countered.

"I'm a fool. I love a girl who's far too young for me, who's in love with a fine young noble. She *does* not and *will not* ever love me back." The words flowed out before he could think better of them. Strangely enough, it made him feel better.

291

"I tried to warn you, Stigg. I know you're lonely, but I *did* try to warn you, son," Fanndis admonished.

"You did," Stigg sighed, waving her off. "I didn't listen."

"You've always been headstrong—I have no *idea* where you got that abominable trait," she smirked.

"Mmhm." Stigg laughed.

He instantly regretted it, for it stirred up the already terrible ache in his head.

Stigg leaned back down on the pillows, a cold hand to his brow. The room felt chill. He peered at the empty, blackened hearth. The fire must have burned out in the night. Fanndis marveled at her son—long since grown and so sad, despite his hard work. She pitied him. He had never been social and had only met one woman in his life, other than Fanndis and her friends: Arna. It was bound to happen, she realized. Fanndis always knew he would love the first woman he laid eyes on and that he would love her with all of his heart, forever. She wished she could have been wrong about that.

"Do you want me to make you breakfast before you start to work?" she asked.

"No, that's alright. I'm going to take the day off," he declared, pulling the covers over his head.

Fanndis thought her mind had gone bad. Stigg had not voluntarily taken a day off from work in his entire life. He was the hardest working human being she had ever laid eyes on—and that was taking Stigg's own father into consideration. After her shock subsided, she stood up and patted him on the head like she used to when he was young.

"Well, you rest. If you get hungry, just let me know, alright?" She stepped out of the room.

He nodded before falling asleep again, his hand on his aching head and his heart still full of holes. Fanndis shook her head and shrugged. She looked to Valkyrie who was sitting by the hearth darning some of their winter stockings.

"How is he?" Valkyrie lifted her brows.

"Well, he's as lovesick as it gets, even though he clearly knows better, by the looks of it. I suppose I didn't really make it any better," Fanndis confided, striding through the main room into the kitchen.

Valkyrie set aside her sewing basket and walked behind her old apprentice. Soryn was still at work and Arna was asleep—Valkyrie had checked earlier. The house was quiet. Without Stigg's usual business about the cottage (inside and out), things felt unnaturally still. Both women set about preparing poultices and salves for the villagers and performing small bits of magic in order to tidy up the house. Valkyrie kindly put the broken pitcher back together using a small spell. Fanndis smiled in thanks.

By noon, Ulf dropped by the cottage and inquired after the events of the previous night with the apparition they saw in the woods. The women invited him in and he sat on his hind legs, flicking his tail every now and again as he listened to the recounting of the story.

Well, I'm glad that Arna is back to normal. It was terrible that she got caught up in my family's misfortunes. I felt bad for the child, Ulf remarked.

"She's not a child anymore. She may have gone to sleep as one, but she woke up a woman," Valkyrie pointed out.

So it would seem. Any sign of Fenris? It looks like he's the only one not accounted for after that night. My pack and I have seen neither hide nor hair of him over the years.

"Stigg goes out on his tracking missions to the west and east every now and then, but I suspect Fenris sailed south long ago, unless he's a great fool. He would know we're after him," Fanndis replied.

That would make sense, but my brother is an arrogant creature. He may not be through toying with all of us yet. I pray you are right and I am wrong.

Fanndis nodded her agreement. "I would be happy if we never heard from him again, but I know Stigg will never be satisfied until he can see Fenris behind bars or worse."

The conversation ended with Ulf's promise to send Derik to visit Arna later. The women went back to work. Arna awoke a little after the wolf left and the two older women helped her lean on them as she took the smallest of steps from her room to the kitchen. Pillows were brought from the main room and they made a cushioned seat out of one of the wooden kitchen chairs so she could sit and talk with them. Her color was still good, though they knew the girl was exhausted. It would take a while for her to regain her full health and strength.

"Is it very strange waking up and finding three years have passed?" Valkyrie asked, curious.

Arna's bell-like laughter lit up the kitchen. "I suppose," she grabbed a long tendril of hair and gazed towards her chest. "These are new," she blushed.

The women laughed. They made small talk and settled into a comfortable conversational rhythm about all that had passed over the last few years. Arna was most curious about Soryn's role as the town's Maslyn.

"Oh, he's done wonders for the village—don't let him fool you. He grumbles about work every night he visits, but Kimbli tells us that the local economy has improved substantially and the people have better access to the resources they need. He's really accomplished a lot to have only been publically working with the community by himself for a year," Fanndis informed her.

"How is Kimbli? Soryn said he was ill."

"He had a bout of pneumonia, but one of us visits him every day and brings him medicine and herbal teas. He's almost well now. I'm sure he'll want to see you." Fanndis smiled.

"I'd love to see him. It will be nice when I can walk properly again," Arna said, her voice sounding gloomy for the first time since she regained consciousness.

"Cheer up. You're a living miracle. It is unusual for the Seidh to be so forgiving. Typically, when people meddle with magic they're not ready for, they suffer much harsher consequences. You're most fortunate, you know," Valkyrie pointed out.

Arna blushed, knowing she was mostly to blame for what had happened. It all felt as though it were just yesterday. It was strange to know that no one had seen Fenris in three years and that Olan had chosen to live as a wolf and that Soryn was a man now. It was stranger to know that she had lost three years of time. She had not even dreamed when she had been in the coma. It felt odd. *She* felt odd. Though she had been a precocious adolescent, Arna felt too young to be sixteen and a grown woman.

"Where's Stigg? Shouldn't he be out working himself into a stupor about now?" Arna inquired.

"He claims he's taking the day off. I think yesterday wore him out," Fanndis said, leaving out the fact that Stigg loved Arna and had drunken himself to the point of passing out the night before.

"Is he sick?" Arna gasped.

"He *did* throw up this morning," Valkyrie muttered.

Fanndis shot her a poisonous look.

"It's true he's not feeling well," Fanndis admitted, all the while wanting to slap Valkyrie later.

"Can I see him? I could cheer him up, maybe," Arna offered.

"No." Fanndis knew that would be a disastrous idea. "I think he's asleep. Best to leave him be, I think. We wouldn't want you to catch whatever virus he's gotten—especially after you just woke up and all."

Arna nodded.

For the rest of the day, the women talked, laughed, and worked. They gave Arna some tasks that would help her build up the strength in her hands and fingers. She tried her hand at sewing and kneading bread dough. Arna could do nothing for longer than a few minutes at a time, but she was able to accomplish a lot before Soryn came in through the door later that night. He was not alone. Behind him hobbled Father Kimbli. Stigg remained in the back bedroom.

"Bialas! Father Kimbli! It's so wonderful to see you both!" Arna greeted.

"Hello, Arna," Father Kimbli bowed his head. "It's so good to see you awake and healthy."

"I could say the same for you. Valkyrie and Fanndis told me you were sick," Arna retorted.

"Ah, well, thanks to these two ladies, I'm doing much better now. Right as rain." He smiled, patting Soryn's helping hand away. Kimbli groaned, bending down to sit. "Hope you don't mind if I sit, Fanndis?"

"Not at all. May I get you anything?"

"No, I'm fine, thank you," Kimbli assured her.

Soryn thought about sitting, but he wanted to check on Stigg first to make sure there was no ill will between them. He slipped out of the kitchen without attracting too much attention. The women's minds were on Kimbli and they asked after every aspect of his health. Walking through the main room, Soryn saw that the door to the back bedroom was shut and that no light escaped from underneath the door. He cracked it and stepped quietly inside.

Stigg lay on his side. Covers were strewn all about the bed. Perhaps Stigg had kicked them off in the night. Soryn looked about the room for a blanket or something to lay over him. Though Soryn felt distinctly odd and motherly noticing something like that, he picked up a quilt that was draped over the back of a chair. Opening it up, he spread it over Stigg's body and turned to leave.

"Mother?" Stigg murmured.

"No, it's me. Soryn."

"Oh."

"Sorry if I woke you up," Soryn apologized, turning back to the door.

"Can we talk, Soryn?" Stigg asked.

Soryn had never heard Stigg ask him to talk about anything. He felt an icy foreboding creep into his chest.

"Alright," he said, pulling the chair nearer the bed.

"I'm sorry for what you saw last night. I wasn't myself," Stigg admitted.

"It's alright." Soryn felt increasingly awkward. Stigg was not someone who shared feelings.

"I know what a fool I am for loving someone who doesn't love me back. I just wanted you to know that I am happy for you and Arna. I would never do anything to jeopardize what you two have." Stigg pulled the quilt tighter over himself, shivering. His head was still battling the hangover.

"Stigg…" Soryn did not know how to respond.

"Thanks for the blanket."

"You're welcome." Soryn guessed that their conversation was at an end.

Standing up, Lord Maslyn stretched and walked to the hearth to build a quick fire before he left—hoping it would banish some of the chill from the room. Just as Soryn was about to cross the threshold into the other room, Stigg spoke up, serious and alert.

"Take care of her Soryn. If you don't, I'll be there. I won't let any harm come to her; emotional or otherwise."

"I understand." Soryn shut the door and left Stigg in the darkness of the bedroom.

* * *

The company in the kitchen roared in laughter as Soryn walked through the door, a slight frown on his face. Valkyrie noticed, though she said nothing. Arna looked up at Lord Maslyn and smiled.

"Come sit, Soryn." Arna patted the seat next to her.

He acquiesced and sat without saying anything. Soryn felt guilty for being so pensive, but he was worried about Stigg and worried about the entire situation with their apparent rivalry for Arna's love.

A half smile came to his lips, for her sake, and he looked at her with as much happiness as he could manage. He *was* happy that they were together, but he had come to care much more for Stigg than he had previously thought. It was as though he was betraying a brother. Soryn supposed Stigg was far more of a brother to him than Olan or Fenris had ever been.

"Father Kimbli was telling me how much you've done to improve the economy in the village," Arna encouraged.

Soryn shot Kimbli an irritated glance. The priest lifted his hands in surrender.

"Soryn, you're far too modest about your accomplishments," the old man admonished.

Lord Maslyn rolled his eyes.

Everyone laughed at that.

"You've changed, Bialas. You're very business-like, now," Arna observed with some amusement.

"He's become a very shrewd leader, indeed. Governor Frey has had to back down at Soryn's desk many a time. The boy is just as great as his father before him. Perhaps greater," Kimbli beamed.

Soryn cleared his throat, a slight blush rising to his cheeks. He desperately wanted the conversation to turn away from himself.

"Is Stigg up yet?" Valkyrie asked, sensing the young man's discomfort.

"No, he's still feeling ill, I think."

"Odd," Father Kimbli opined.

"He must have caught something rather nasty," Fanndis blurted out. It was not *entirely* untrue, she assessed.

"Hopefully he'll return to good health soon," the priest said, concerned.

An awkward silence followed. They were rescued from it when Derik scratched at the door, whining to get in. Valkyrie let the now-grown wolf into the kitchen. Fanndis felt it was a good thing Ulf's wolves were such clean creatures. Otherwise, she would have bristled at the presence of so many animals in her kitchen throughout each week. Derik had aged into a large, intimidating beast. He had the dark fur of Nora and some patches of white like his father Ulf. Wholly magnificent to gaze upon, Arna gasped—not realizing it was the same pup she had held and cooed over so long ago.

Hello, Arna, Derik greeted.

"Hello there," Arna said, still failing to make the connection with the past.

You don't remember me, do you? He chuckled.

"Well, no, not really," she admitted.

It's me, Derik. Ulf's pup.

"Derik! You've grown up!" Arna exclaimed.

Yeah, I suppose. Still not as tall as my old man, though. I've got a ways to go before I'm as formidable as he is, Derik mused.

"I think you're entirely as formidable as your father," Valkyrie encouraged, knowing the adolescent wolf was fishing for complements.

You're very kind, Valkyrie.

"I know." Valkyrie's mouth spread into a sly grin.

"Are you here to visit or is there some business you need to attend to?" Fanndis remarked.

Originally, just a friendly visit was intended, but my father brings news—not so good I think, Derik admitted.

"Is anything wrong?" Valkyrie asked.

Well, we're not entirely sure. There have been very strange things going on in the woods lately, not the least of which is Arna's apparition in the springs.

Soryn was disturbed. The rough hair covering Derik's spine stood up and he seemed on edge. The wolf kept picking up his front two paws and placing them back on the ground, over and over—as though he were doing the wolf version of human pacing.

"What's wrong, Derik?" Soryn demanded.

It's just that we've noticed someone has been trying to get into the greenhouse. We can smell him, but he's smart, whoever he is, and we've been unable to catch him in the act. He knows when we change the guard and seems to try and tamper with the greenhouse when we're not watching—though it's only for a few minutes at a time. As far as we can tell, he has been unsuccessful in his attempts to get in.

"Fenris?" Soryn lifted an eyebrow.

Perhaps, though Ulf thinks not. He says the man's scent is nothing like Fenris'.

"Who would be trying to get into our greenhouse?" Valkyrie wondered aloud.

"Perhaps a villager in need of a specific herb?" Kimbli offered.

"Why would they not just ask? We have no reason to refuse help to anyone in the village," Fanndis retorted.

"Perhaps they are too ashamed or poor to compensate you," Soryn suggested.

"That's never kept us from helping those that need it," Valkyrie countered.

Hmmm. Derik was still pacing in his odd wolf-like way.

"I'll go check it out, since Stigg's still feeling sick," Soryn offered, heading towards the main room to retrieve one of the rifles they kept in the chest.

"Wait! What if they're dangerous?!" Arna protested.

"Stigg has trained me well in tracking and moving silently through the forest, Arna. I'll be just fine," Lord Maslyn assured her, feeling a little abashed that she did not have more faith in his abilities. Then again, she most likely found it hard to believe that he was a grown man now.

"He'll be alright," Fanndis promised.

"Be careful, Soryn," Valkyrie cautioned.

"I'm coming with you."

Everyone in the kitchen turned to look towards the main room. Stigg stood in the doorway, his skin as pale as the moons, dark shadows beneath his eyes. His clothing looked as though it had been hastily thrown on. In his hand was the second rifle. Soryn lifted an eyebrow. Stigg nodded towards him.

300

"Stigg, are you sure you're in any condition to be traipsing around the woods?" Fanndis pursed her lips and crossed her arms.

"I'm fine. Let's go Soryn," Stigg said with finality. He avoided Arna's gaze as he stormed out of the back door into the snowy yard beyond.

Soryn shrugged. "I'll look after him, Fanndis. Don't worry."

"I would appreciate it. He's not himself today." Stigg's mother sighed.

With that, Lord Maslyn smiled at Arna, squeezed her hand, and then followed Stigg into the woods. The nights were growing frigid with promises of oncoming winter snows. They were only a few days off at the most. The summer had flown by, just like all other summers on Niflheim. Soryn mourned the loss of the warmer weather, but he was glad the snow would be coming. It was far easier to track in the snows. Stigg, he knew, hated summer and would be glad as well.

Stigg was well ahead of him, but Soryn followed his path with ease. The younger man knew that Stigg had not even tried to conceal his tracks. Lord Maslyn suspected that this suspicious business would have something to do with Fenris in the end. Stigg had gotten rather worked up about that prospect. So had Soryn. Up ahead, Stigg gave one of their signals—an owl's call—and Soryn crouched until he caught up with the man.

"See anything?" Soryn whispered only loud enough for Stigg to hear.

"I'm not sure. Take a look," Stigg replied, his voice low.

Soryn peered up ahead through the briars they were hidden behind. They were still a ways from the greenhouse, but both men could see the angled roof and the rock face behind it. For several moments, Soryn saw nothing, but then, he understood what Stigg had mentioned. On the greenhouse roof, there was a glinting light that seemed to be going in and out like it was a signal of some sort. He peered harder. He had better eyes than Stigg and he kept staring until they hurt. *There.*

"A piece of the roof is loose. It's flapping in the wind and the light we're seeing is coming from one of the anchored sun spires inside, I would imagine," Soryn said.

"Well, we better go investigate and make sure it's not the work of that prowler."

"Mm." Soryn followed as Stigg made his way to the greenhouse without a sound.

Ulf sat on a higher embankment above the roof and stared at the loose panel in puzzlement, his tail undulating behind him.

Hello, gentlemen, Ulf greeted.

"Do you know what's going on?" Stigg asked.

No. I've been watching all day and the roof panel came loose on its own with the wind. It wasn't the work of whoever has been trying our patience—unless they loosened the panel during our watch change in the hopes it would come loose later. This entire situation is baffling for my pack and me—especially considering we are master hunters.

"You stay here. We'll skirt around back and see what we can," Stigg said.

No need. I've got several of my best already staking out each side of the greenhouse and the corners from strategic positions in the woods, Ulf informed them.

"So we wait?" Soryn arched an eyebrow.

We wait. He's tried every night for the last few nights, so if history can tell us anything, he'll try again, Ulf replied.

Stigg and Soryn coiled around the perimeter of the greenhouse and settled near another of Ulf's pack members so that they could see the front door of the building. They all sat, waiting for nearly two hours, but nobody wanted to leave in case they missed something crucially important. Soryn thought, several times, that he heard some telltale sign of human movement through the woods, but each time it was a rabbit or a squirrel. He figured he was getting anxious waiting for someone who could be connected to his traitorous brother.

Finally, there was movement in the trees. The wolves crouched low, ready to spring. Through a break in the tree line came a cloaked figure—walking with purpose towards the greenhouse. Soryn and Stigg allowed the wolves to move into action and watched as five or six of them pounced on the stranger, pinning him to the forest floor. Only then did Stigg and Soryn move from their position to inspect the man lying before them.

It wasn't Fenris. It was an older man from the village that Soryn had seen once or twice in the market. He was shivering and looked scared out of his wits.

"What are you doing here?" Stigg growled.

"I-I-I...*please* don't hurt me! I was just doing what he told me to do!" the man stuttered, shielding his face with his forearms from the wolves that surrounded him.

"What *who* told you to do?" Stigg asked, already knowing the answer.

"He never told me his name. H-He told me to come and tamper with the greenhouse for a couple of nights. He told me where it would be and showed me how to get here without being noticed, that's it, I swear! He told me he'd hurt my family if I didn't do it! Please! Please don't let the wolves eat me! I never wanted to hurt anybody!"

Soryn's spine froze when he realized that the old man before them was just a decoy. He sprang before Stigg could question the wretched diversion further. Soryn felt like a fool for being taken in by such a trick. He prayed and hoped that he would make it back to the cottage in time. Stigg followed behind Soryn, leaving the man shuddering and sobbing in the snow. Ulf's wolves would look after him. Stigg's heart beat frantically in his chest; he knew what awaited them at the cottage. Fenris had fooled them and was most likely at the house wreaking havoc. Neither Stigg nor Soryn wanted to think of what the traitor's intentions were.

Chests heaving and legs cramping, Stigg and Soryn came within view of the cottage. All looked just as it should. The windows were bright with firelight and smoke puffed out of the chimneys. Yet, both men felt ice settle into the pits of their stomachs as they took in the sight, knowing that nothing good awaited them inside.

"Let's go," Soryn announced.

He took the rifle in one hand and kicked open the door.

Chapter Eighteen

In which Lord Maslyn becomes a man of action…

The kitchen was vacant. That was not so unusual, Soryn allowed. It was nearing bedtime after all. He hoped the women were safely tucked in their beds, but something told him this would not be the case. Stigg stormed into the main room and scowled. Both men looked at each other when they saw that it, too, was empty. Not a sound could be heard—no creaking of the bed in the back bedroom, no laughter or conversation. It was unearthly quiet. No one was in the cottage at all. There was no sign of struggle or attack. Everything was in its place and tidy.

Stigg scowled and violently ran his hands through his hair. "Check everything—look for any sign of what could have happened. I'll check the barn."

Soryn nodded, feeling the dread smother him. Something was very wrong. In the interest of remaining calm, he searched everywhere for a note, a clue, *something* to help them know what had happened. The kitchen and main room were no help. However, in the back bedroom discreetly settled on the chair underneath the window was a scrawled note that read:

We've gone after them. He's headed for the mountains.

"Stigg!" Soryn shouted, taking the paper with him as he ran to the barn.

Stigg was still inspecting the stalls in case someone had hidden there. He looked up when Soryn came in.

"What did you find?"

"We have to go, now! They're up in the mountains. We may still be able to catch their trail," Soryn panted as he began undoing saddle ties from the hooks on the barn wall.

"Soryn."

"Hurry up! We have to catch them!" Soryn yelled, frightened beyond thought.

"It's going to be alright. We can handle this. *You* can handle this. Arna will be alright," Stigg promised, his eyes sincere.

Putting a hand on Soryn's shoulder, Stigg nodded his support. Soryn nodded in return and continued to loosen the saddle from the wall. Stigg sprang into action, saddling Ivan within minutes. Soryn had Sable saddled in comparable time. Apparently, Fenris did not care if they followed him—if it was in fact Fenris they were pursuing. They rode as quickly as the horses would tolerate. The path snaked around the front of the cottage and into the woods— approaching the mountains from the east. Stigg sneered at the petty attempt to throw them off the trail.

Though Stigg was not a religious man, he prayed the entire way that his promise to Soryn would ring true. Adrenaline pumped through his veins when he thought about what *could* happen when they made it to the mountains. He pushed the thoughts away and focused only on the trail ahead of him and following as fast as he could. There was no way to tell how much of a head start Fenris had. Occasionally, he looked back at Soryn to see how the young man was doing.

Soryn sat, grim-faced in the saddle. A murderous tint shrouded Lord Maslyn's eyes. More than that, he was afraid. More afraid than he had ever been in his life. All he could think about was Arna, taken by a fiend into the mountains for some unknown purpose. He worried for the women who had become like grandmothers to him. He worried that he and Stigg would be able to do nothing to save them. They made it to the base of the mountain and saw the path the others had taken. There was no way for them to tell how far behind they were, because of the snowy trees that guarded the way. A few minutes up, they met Valkyrie. She was badly hurt and groaning on the ground. Soryn dismounted and went to the old woman. She panted and clutched her leg.

"Well, some heroine I turned out to be," she said between labored breaths.

"What happened, Valkyrie?" Soryn demanded.

Stigg knelt next to them and took a look at Valkyrie's leg. The shin bone had come clean through the skin. He made a splint from some sticks around and a strip of cloth that he tore from his shirt. She said nothing to Stigg, but focused all her attention on Soryn.

"He came. Fenris. Just after you and Stigg left for the greenhouse. He came in through the kitchen door, just like he belonged there with us. We didn't know what to do. He had no weapon that we could see and he was smiling kindly. No one could say anything. We realized then that Fenris had somehow silenced us with powerful magic. When we tried to move, we found we could not. Fanndis and I were planted where we stood as though we were statues. He'd done that, too. He picked Arna up and left without a word. We could hear Arna screaming and crying for help, but we were unable to move.

"Finally, Fanndis and I were able to break the spell he'd put us under—powerful spell it was—and we clambered out into the yard and saw that he'd taken Nar and fled into the woods, towards the mountains. Fanndis wrote the note while I saddled Liv and we followed after."

"How did you hurt your leg," Stigg asked, trying as best as he could to stabilize the area where it was broken.

"I fell and told Fanndis to go on without me," she said.

"Go, Soryn. If I don't set her leg, this could be very bad. I'll catch up," Stigg said eyeing the path up to the peak.

Soryn did not need to hear anything else. He sped up the slope as quickly as he could, urging Sable along with quiet yips and squeezes of his thighs. The trail was becoming more difficult to follow and it became clear some ways up that Fenris and Fanndis had gone off the path towards the north instead of continuing towards the west.

"Just what are you up to, Fenris?" Soryn whispered to himself.

He fought the dread that threatened to paralyze him. He could not afford to brood about his brother's intentions. Breathing in and out, Soryn fought for calm. He just followed the path, listening to the wind rustling the leaves of the trees and the clipping gallop of Sable's hooves in the night.

Soon, he found what he sought. Up ahead on a small terrace branching off of the mountain sat Fenris, Fanndis, and Arna around a fire that rested in a hastily thrown together hearth. Fanndis sat ramrod straight—unnaturally so—and Arna leaned against Fenris with her eyes closed and her body slumped as though she were unconscious. Soryn led his horse into the clearing and dismounted, tying the reigns to a nearby tree.

"Hello, Soryn," Fenris said.

"Fenris," was all Soryn could manage.

"Sit. You're among friends here," Fenris extended his hand to the ground in front of him.

Soryn never took his eyes off of the traitor as he lowered himself to the ground and sat on his knees, poised—like Stigg had taught him—for action should there be a need for it. Fenris sat across the fire from him, looking as though he had not changed a day in three years. His brother had left his hair long instead of cutting it in a more manageable fashion. His red-brown eyes, the eyes of their mother, peered out at Soryn like sinister orbs. Fenris had tainted those eyes; they were the eyes of a monster now. A crooked smile arranged itself on Fenris' face. Soryn found he wanted to smash it in. Sadness welled within him that his brother had deteriorated to such a crazed state. How did that happen?

"It is strange to see my little brother all grown up, Soryn. Tell me, how does it feel to find yourself a man and in a new body?" Fenris' velvety voice filled the silence much like Ulla's used to fill Soryn's mind.

"Why did you take Arna? What could you possibly want with her?" Soryn ignored Fenris' question.

"My, how rude you are, ignoring your older brother's inquiries. Well, given that I am the *polite* one, I'll answer you. Nothing. I care nothing for this girl. I just wanted to see you, that's all. I enjoyed our little game in the woods, didn't you? I knew you and that oaf would figure it out sooner or later and come running." Fenris smiled, curling his long-nailed hands through Arna's hair.

Hatred seethed through every fiber of Soryn's body. Still, he figured it was more prudent to bide his time and wait instead of acting rashly. Fenris had apparently lost his telepathic powers that he had while in Ulla's body. Just as that thought passed, Soryn was startled to hear a voice in his mind.

Soryn?

It was Fanndis. Soryn felt his tension release a little.

Soryn, can you hear me? she continued.

Yes. Fanndis what is happening?

No time. Listen. He thinks I am still under his spell and that I cannot move, but I've long since broken it. Wait until I give you my signal and then go for your rifle. I'll stun him long enough to keep him from thwarting your attempt. Then, we'll have him. I'll take care of Arna.

Alright. Soryn was nervous, but knowing that Fanndis was not defeated bolstered the young man's courage.

"You seem deep in thought, little Maslyn. What are you thinking about?" Fenris mused aloud, still stroking Arna's long hair as though he was her lover.

"I'm just wondering how my eldest brother became such a waste. You had talent and ambition, but now you're just…evil," Soryn said, trying to keep his brother occupied while Fanndis readied herself.

"Oh, I'm not evil, Soryn. I'm just tired of being the cast-off child. The one everyone views as a beast. I had grand ideas, little brother. I could really have been something great had I only the right encouragement, but Olan stole all that away from me when he turned me into an *animal*. All of my future was stripped away."

"We made you human again, you fool! You could have gone after your 'future'," Soryn spat, disgusted with the man in front of him.

"Ah, yes, little Soryn came to save me, and for what? To learn that I was too old for training and for school? Too old to pursue my goals? The world is not forgiving to someone they consider dried up and useless," Fenris sneered.

"I'm sorry to disappoint you. I was doing what I thought was best." Soryn threw up his hands.

"As always, just like our parents, your best failed to meet my standards, Soryn." Fenris' acid words seared the air.

Soryn knew it was meant to sting him, but it did not. He didn't care. Any feeling for Fenris had long since died in him.

Now Soryn! Fanndis cried.

For an instant, Fenris cocked his head just like Ulla used to and for a split second, Soryn mourned their lost fraternity. Banishing his despair, he sprang into action as Fanndis stood up with her hands outstretched. Soryn did not see when Fanndis created an orb of concentrated wind and shot it directly at Fenris. Soryn's brother was blown backwards—almost to the edge of the terrace. Fanndis grabbed Arna before he could get up. She dragged the girl back towards the path down the mountain. By then, Soryn had grabbed the rifle and had his boot thrust into Fenris' stomach, the gun pointed at the face he hated.

"Lie still," Soryn ordered.

"Well, well, well…someone *has* become a man while I've been away. Did the great Stigg teach you all of that? I know that Olan wouldn't be man enough to teach you such violence. Good for you, Soryn. Truly I'm touched by your display of masculinity," Fenris chuckled, that crooked smile still in place.

Soryn breathed evenly. Stigg had trained him well and he did not waver for an instant. He hated looking at Fenris' hair spread over the rocks like a net and his red eyes almost glowing in the firelight. He looked so much like their mother and Soryn gritted his teeth at the sight of him. It was sickening. He did not want anyone so heinous to share any likeness to his dear mother. Their mother had been all things good and kind in the world. Fenris stared up at him, hands held aloft in apparent surrender, but Soryn was no fool.

A moment passed by and Soryn heard Arna's soft gasp of alarm when Fanndis succeeded in waking her up. Soryn could not afford to turn and look at her. He knew if he let his guard down for a minute, Fenris would take advantage of it. Indeed, even with Soryn holding firm, Fenris thought he saw an opportunity and tried to get up. Soryn promptly shot him in the thigh. The shot reverberated off of the rocks and everyone's ears rang with the deafening sound. It took them all a minute or so to realize that Fenris was screaming in pain.

"Don't move." Soryn narrowed his eyes.

Sweat broke out on Fenris' face. Blood spewed from his injured leg. Still, he smiled through gritted teeth. Soryn shifted his foot. He was growing uncomfortable. Why was Fenris still smiling? His older brother's hand moved to a pendant around his neck that Lord Maslyn had failed to notice. Fenris' other hand extended towards Soryn and suddenly, he found he was being blasted backwards into the fire. He cursed under his breath and patted at the flames that threatened to burn away his clothing. Looking up, he saw Fenris leaning over him holding a knife that had been concealed in ragged clothing.

Fenris stomped on Soryn's chest, breaking several ribs. Soryn sputtered for breath as his older brother brought the knife down in a graceful arch. A gasp rang out when it collided with flesh and bone. Soryn coughed and looked down to see the knife sticking out of his right side. Fenris' face held only a bored amusement at his actions. Dark hollows surrounded his fiery eyes.

"That wasn't nice to shoot me, little brother. But you see? My power is such that I have already closed the wound you gave me in my leg. But your wound…that will take real medicine and I'm afraid you'll bleed out before help can get to you." All Fenris' white teeth were on display as his malicious sneer distorted his face.

Fenris wrenched the knife out and walked towards the women, leaving Soryn heaving for breath and losing his life's blood. Fanndis covered Arna with her arms and whispered to the girl not to be afraid. Fanndis began to weave a barrier around them that even Fenris, with his stolen power, would not be able to break so easily. Just as Fenris almost made contact with Fanndis' barrier, he was tackled to the ground. An intense battle for the knife ensued. At first, Fanndis imagined it was Soryn, fighting on despite his injuries, but then, she saw it was Stigg.

Stigg grunted with the effort of controlling his opponent and once or twice, Fenris snapped at the man like he was still an animal. Stigg made sure to keep Fenris' hands extended so that the knife could not harm him.

"Get his pendant! Stigg! That pendant is giving him power! Get it!" Fanndis shouted.

Stigg and Fenris both looked down at the necklace. Fenris fought back with a ferocity that Stigg had never seen before in anyone. Stigg used every ounce of effort he had and inched his way to the pendant. Grabbing it securely in his hands, he tried to shove Fenris' face away into the snow, but Fenris used his body to roll back and threw Stigg off of him. Springing up with surprising agility, Fenris rose from the ground, knife still in hand looking for his attacker.

But Fanndis and Arna had hands to their mouths. Soryn had a stunned expression on his face. Stigg had fallen off the side of the terrace. Fenris sauntered towards the edge to confirm that the man had met his demise below. To his pleasure, Fenris saw Stigg's body crumpled on a rocky precipice. Blood stained the cliff and Stigg's abdomen. A smile of satisfaction crossed Fenris' face and he turned around, intending to finish Soryn off and the women as well.

Fanndis looked up above her, intending to beseech the heavens for help when a flash of white and black caught her eye. Up on another rock outcropping stood Ulf, Nora, Derik, and several others of their pack. She said nothing and tried to look afraid, though she was afraid no longer. Fenris neared their barrier and went to touch the pendant on his neck. He paled when he felt only the fabric of his tunic. Stigg had torn it off when he was thrown over the cliff. Fenris cursed himself and thought about retrieving it, but he did not have time to plan his next move. Ulf sprang from above and clamped down on Fenris' shoulder with his iron jaws.

Fenris shrieked. Ulf shook his brother's body—now limp—from side to side in savage movements. Fenris was thrown against the mountainside and hit his head on the rocks. His body went still and Ulf crouched over him in case he came to. The pack surrounded Fenris on all sides. Sighing, Fanndis released her barrier. Arna was in shock and still unable to walk on her own. The older woman reached down and helped her up.

Near the edge, Soryn had hoisted himself up, clutching his side where Fenris had stabbed him. His breathing came out heavy and erratic, but he refused to faint until he could check to see if Stigg was okay.

"Do you have Fenris?" Soryn asked Ulf.

He's not going anywhere, Brother, Ulf replied, inclining his head.

"Is Arna alright?" Soryn asked Fanndis.

"I've got her. Go." Fanndis' fear took hold of her. She did not know what she would do if her son had died on the rocks below.

Soryn peered over the edge and saw that Stigg had fallen twelve feet or so to the next precipice. He lay on his back, but Soryn could see that his eyes were open and he was breathing, though it was laborious. There was a lot of blood. Soryn worked up all the strength he had left and began to climb down, one hand clamped to his side in an attempt to staunch his own blood loss. He felt the hot liquid oozing down his torso and leg, but he didn't care. All he could think about was Stigg and he prayed that his friend was alright.

When he made it to the ledge, he hurried over to him. Stigg coughed and a small red stream ran down the sides of his chin onto his chest. Soryn saw that Stigg's back had been gashed by a rock when he fell and it had punctured something. Fear coiled in Soryn's chest and he knew that Stigg was badly hurt—the kind of hurt one does not recover from.

"Stigg?" Soryn attempted.

"S-Soryn?" Stigg muttered, but then coughed up more blood and sank onto the rocks, closing his eyes. His breathing gurgled and caught in his throat.

"We're going to get you fixed up in no time, you'll see," Soryn promised, tears pooling at the corner of his eyes.

"Y-You're a terrible liar, Soryn," Stigg laughed, despite the wracking cough that followed.

"I'm not lying."

"Did we get h-him? I-Is Arna alright?" Stigg shuddered, his eyes beginning to lose focus.

"Yes. He won't be able to hurt her again," Soryn assured him.

Stigg smiled and seemed to relax into the rocks. Soryn tore strips from his shirt and crumpled them against Stigg's back—the source of the blood. He knew it was futile, but he had to try.

"Stop," Stigg whispered.

"I'm not going to just let you die, Stigg. You should know I'm too stubborn for that. You are, too, for that matter," Soryn panted, losing focus from his own blood loss.

"You're hurt," Stigg pointed out, struggling to raise his hand to indicate Soryn's side.

"I'll be fine. It's you I'm worried about."

The world seemed to stop for a moment. The wind went still and the snow fell in silent, lazy flurries. Soryn kept pressure on Stigg's wound and looked up at the moons above. They were all full tonight and it gave him some strange sense of comfort. Above on the other precipice, he heard several of Ulf's pack howling. The stars twinkled

314

and the entire scene made Soryn think of the Night Bells that would be ringing right about that time. A thought came to him.

"Arna!" Soryn shouted.

"Soryn?" Arna and Fanndis peered over the rock ledge above.

"Can the Seidh help Stigg?" Soryn felt hot, desperate tears tumble down his cheeks.

Above on the precipice, Arna's heart filled with a strange, overpowering sensation. Something about Soryn's question pierced her mind with urgency. She searched her brain for an answer. Then it dawned on her...*In three and a half years' time, Soryn will profess his love, then, in the mountains he will ask you a question when the moons are full. You must say 'yes'...then you must come to me...there won't be much time...*

"Oh, God," Arna breathed.

"What is it?" Fanndis asked.

"We have to get Valkyrie. Now!" Arna shouted.

"But, Arna, the Seidh can't heal a wound like this," Fanndis insisted, her cheeks stained with weeping.

"We have to get Valkyrie!" Arna turned around and stumbled as she tried to walk. Cursing her useless body, she screamed for Derik.

The young wolf perked up his ears and looked towards her.

What is it, Arna?

"Run! Get Valkyrie! She's down below somewhere on the mountain! Go!"

Without reply, Derik sped off down the path like the devil was at his heels.

"Help is coming, Soryn. Make Stigg hold on! Someone is coming that can help him!" Arna yelled.

But below, Soryn slumped over Stigg's body, unconscious. Stigg's head turned to the side, his eyes closed.

* * *

Valkyrie leaned over the edge, situating her splinted, broken leg so that she could extend her head far enough to see all of Stigg's body. She frowned. Fanndis eyed her, bewildered. Fanndis had no idea how her former master would be able to heal such terrible wounds. Arna had every ounce of faith in Valkyrie's abilities. After all, the old woman had warned her of this incident years ago, had she not? When Valkyrie started to swing her body over the edge to climb down, both younger women protested.

"What are you *doing?* You've got a broken leg, Valkyrie!" Fanndis spat, exasperated.

"I'll be fine. I've got two strong arms and a whole other leg. You just watch me." Valkyrie stuck her chin out defiantly, nodding towards Fanndis. "I'll be alright. Right now, it is very important that I reach Stigg."

Fanndis only nodded, still worried to death about her son. Arna put a weak hand on the woman's shoulder. Fanndis put her own hand over the girl's and sighed.

"If anyone can do it, she can," Fanndis admitted.

Despite their protests, Valkyrie ascended the rock wall with three limbs. It was an incredible sight to see such an old woman navigating scarce hand and footholds like she was a spry child. Fanndis wondered just what her former mentor did to keep herself in such spectacular shape. Fanndis wondered about a lot of things to keep her mind off of her son's portentous death.

Once she was firmly situated on the rocky terrace, Valkyrie stretched her broken leg out and sat. Then, she scooted her body closer to Stigg's and Soryn's. Both men had fainted, though both were breathing. This was an encouraging sign, at least. Casting her gaze to either side of the bodies, she searched.

"What are you looking for!?" Fanndis shouted.

"That pendant that Fenris had. I've seen it before. I'll need it," Valkyrie replied, searching Stigg's clothing in case it slipped inside.

Valkyrie smiled when she spotted it clutched in Stigg's left hand—a hand that lay precariously close to the edge of the rocky shelf. Using all of her waning strength, she leaned over Stigg's body and retrieved the round pewter pendant. Its weight was shocking for so small a thing, but Valkyrie remembered that its wealth was not in its weight but in its *power*. Her own master, a Seidh woman of great renown, had worn a similar trinket around her neck all of her life. Valkyrie wondered how Fenris had obtained something so impressive.

Fanndis, Arna, and Derik leaned over the ledge above and stared in amazement as Valkyrie placed the pendant on Stigg's gash. It began to glow a dull amethyst color. Valkyrie waited, praying and hoping that the pendant would work. Fanndis gasped when Stigg's color returned and he jerked up, gasping. He was shocked to see Soryn, fainted, across his chest. He looked over at the older woman in confusion.

"You're out of danger." Valkyrie patted Stigg's leg.

Stigg looked at the blood pumping, more slowly, from Soryn's side and watched in amazement as Valkyrie extended the pendant towards the open flesh. Stigg's eyes grew wide when he saw the glowing light and Soryn's skin begin to close, the flow of blood to cease. Soryn came to, coughed, and tried to right himself, disoriented. Both men turned to see Valkyrie smiling, looking off towards the sky.

"Just what is that thing, Valkyrie?" Stigg asked, his voice weak.

"This is an Amplifier—a magical trinket used to strengthen Seidh powers. My own master used to use one in her work. This is an especially powerful talisman. I have no idea where Fenris would have discovered such a thing. He must have had his own latent magic buried deep inside himself even to use this device. Still, he perverted its intended purpose. He used it for evil. I have used it to heal the two of you—not all the way, you understand. Just enough to get you home where we can patch you up. Perhaps it will heal my leg so that I can climb back *up*." Valkyrie chuckled even as she placed the pendant on her broken shin and watched with satisfaction as the bone reconnected with itself and the pain eased. Her skin closed, though an angry red swath of skin still spread over the area.

"It's amazing the amount of damage that wretched man was able to cause just from his misplaced rage," Valkyrie grunted, her brows furrowed.

"Mm," Soryn and Stigg muttered in unison.

They looked at each other and laughed deliriously before descending into coughing fits.

"Be careful, you fools," Valkyrie warned. "The pendant has helped you along your way to healing, but you won't be fully healed for a while yet."

Up above, Fanndis and Arna held one another and cried despite their grins. Fanndis nodded her head in deference to her master and Valkyrie inclined hers in return. Near the mountainside, the wolves fidgeted and Ulf ordered most of them to leave. Nora and Derik stayed to help see to the removal of Fenris from their mountain. The man was still unconscious, but no one made to heal his head wound with the pendant—Valkyrie refused. He had far too much malice in his heart. It would have to heal the old-fashioned way.

Epilogue

In which this tale comes to a close and another story begins…

It took several hours to get everyone up the rock face, down the path, and back to the cottage. Fanndis rode into the village to wake Father Kimbli, telling him they had a favor to ask of him. Valkyrie, now able to hobble around on her healing leg, tended to those who were worse off. Arna, who had been strengthened by the power of the pendant as well, provided encouragement and aid to Valkyrie. Stigg had his shirt off, sneering at the pillow of white linen wrapped around his torso and the salve that smelled like death plastered to his wounds. He wrinkled his nose at the stink and tried to read his book in peace despite the constant distraction.

Soryn, too, had linen strapped to his knife wound. The same foul scented salve nestled within the gash that was quickly healing itself. He sat by Stigg, a new and strong camaraderie between them, and read from another book. Both men begrudged the fact that they could not smoke their pipes, but Valkyrie persisted that smoking was counterproductive when one's body was trying to right itself. Each one had scowled at that. Arna laughed at how alike the men had become since she had been in her coma. For some reason, she found that the older, more mature Soryn was even more attractive and appealing, though she missed his boyish optimism and hope. Perhaps he would gain it back now that Fenris had been dealt with and she was awake.

Fenris sat dazed in the corner with Ulf, Nora, and Derik lying about him on the ground. They had taken it upon themselves to act as watchers in case Fenris chose to do something foolish. The head wound he received from the rocks on the mountain had been bandaged, as well as his shoulder where Ulf had bitten him. Though Valkyrie despised the man in their midst, she could not let him be

319

neglected when it came to care. She was a healer, after all, just as Fanndis was. Fenris did not even struggle at the rope bindings that had been tied a little too tightly. No one made a move to loosen them.

Once Valkyrie had a chance to sit down around the fire, the door to the cottage flew open to reveal Fanndis and Father Kimbli, both shivering at the increasingly cold wind outside.

"I do believe winter may be upon us," Fanndis exclaimed, through chattering teeth.

"Shall we put the kettle on?" Valkyrie offered.

"Please do," Fanndis replied.

Father Kimbli hung his coat and stared at the assorted casualties of the night's battle. He frowned at the wrapped middles of Soryn and Stigg, the crutch Valkyrie used to get around, and the person responsible for it all hunched over in the corner. The frown deepened when he saw no penitence in Fenris' lethargic face. Though he was an old man now, Kimbli straightened himself up and walked over to the corner. The old priest crouched in front of the man who had once been a boy under his care. Memories of Fenris' troubled childhood and violent adolescence jumbled in Kimbli's mind.

"I want you to know something, Fenris," Kimbli began.

"What? You intend to throw me to the wolves?" Fenris' words came from a weak and slurring mouth. He chuckled at his private joke.

"I intend to see you fully repent for the chaos and shame you have wrought in this family and I intend to see you smile again, with kindness and gentleness in your heart; not this evil, vengeful sneer you have now," Kimbli told him.

"We'll see, old man. You tried it once. We know how successful *that* rehabilitation attempt was," Fenris cackled, trying to focus his gaze on the face before him.

Kimbli straightened up and asked Valkyrie for some of the tea she had just brought in on a tray. The old priest brought the cup to Fenris' lips and let the man drink, though the eldest son of the dead

Maslyn did so with bitterness and resentment in his heart. He contemplated spitting it out at the man, but Fenris knew he was beaten and that he was at their mercy. His head felt as though it would crack in half and he was nearly dead from exhaustion. The pendant had drained him of his energy even before his head had been smashed on the mountainside. Fenris was no fool, contrary to what everyone around him believed.

"You will come with me to the church," Kimbli declared. "You wolves may visit us whenever you like and, Fenris, I hope you know that if you try anything malevolent again, they'll be there to remind you of the scars you will always bear from your brother's fangs," Kimbli said.

Fenris merely smirked and glared at his captor. "Like I said, we will see."

Kimbli sighed and sat down in a chair by the fire, gratefully accepting another cup of tea from Fanndis' hands. The old priest felt entirely too old to have a willful, deceitful, beast of a man as his ward, but he knew that everyone else in the room had experienced a little too much of Fenris over the years. If anyone could deal with him, it was God. Kimbli smiled, knowing that in the end, things would turn around for Fenris, if only he would have ears to hear and eyes to see. The warmth of the tea settled into the old man's bones and set a small blaze burning there. It was nice to feel a fire for some greater purpose every now and then. He knew that Fenris would be his last test, his last challenge on this world. Kimbli hoped he would rise to meet it and that he would be successful.

A hush descended over the cottage as the suns rose. When everyone was sure Fenris was unconscious and would not escape his bonds, the rest of them drifted to sleep; all but Soryn and Arna. The pair of them hobbled out to the front of the cottage and watched the suns light up the world. The sky brightened with fiery reds and oranges that promised a gorgeous last day of summer. Somehow, they both knew the heavy snows would come that night and all would be shrouded in white and mystery once more. They held hands, sitting on the bench that Fanndis sometimes used for rest while she worked. Arna leaned her head on Soryn's shoulder and he rested his head on her hair.

The entire scene was almost surreal. Peace and comfort spilled over them. It was over. Soryn knew it was time to ask his question. It may have been premature, it may have been reckless, but he knew it was *right*. Without breaking their closeness, Soryn braced himself and whispered, "Arna?"

"Mmm?" she muttered dreamily.

"I need to ask you something; something important," Soryn confessed, trying to maintain his calm.

"Alright," Arna replied, a grin hiding in the corners of her mouth.

"I want you to understand that it's not because of what happened last night and it's not because you've been in a coma and it's not—" Soryn stopped when he felt Arna's small finger pressed against his lips.

"What is it, Bialas?" she prompted.

"Will you spend your days with me like this? Will you marry me?" Soryn asked, his heart a thunderous pounding in the cage of his chest.

"Of course," she promised, as though it had already been decided long ago.

Soryn sighed and wrapped her tightly in his arms, laying a gentle, chaste kiss on the top of her head. Smiling, he inhaled her scent and was comforted by the odors of lavender and jasmine. Inside, he knew the house was sleeping, but he felt like he had woken up from a long and perilous dream. The suns' rising felt wholly new to him, like it was the first dawn he had ever truly seen. Arna looked up when they heard the distant ringing from the church. Morning Bells held a new hope for Soryn. He had always associated the dark events of his life with the ringing of the Night Bells and with troubled sleep. Now, he knew that he and Arna would greet the day together, listening for the quiet, placid sounds of the chimes that rang in the day.

When he realized Arna had fallen asleep, Soryn did not move. He stayed there listening to birds in the trees and watching the suns rise ever higher in the sky. Sometime mid-morning, his arm fell asleep, but he didn't move it. Instead, he leaned into his future wife and smiled, resting in her presence and in the peace that blossomed in his heart. The clouds came later and sounds in the cottage prompted him that he should probably move and wake Arna. But he did not. He sat a while longer and fell asleep as the first silent snowflakes ushered in the white of winter. He dreamed of snow falling about them under a spotted field of twinkling stars, and of the Night Bells ringing.

Thank you for reading *Night Bells*! If you enjoyed the story and would like to read more tales from Niflheim, consider giving it a review on Amazon, Barnes and Noble, or Goodreads.

About the Author...

    L.M. Sherwin has been writing since she was too young to hold a pen. Her first stories were dictated to her mother who wrote them down to preserve for posterity. As time went by, Sherwin moved on to write amusing short stories. In middle school, she wanted to tackle her first epic novel. Things kept getting more involved and, though she still has all the notes from this novel, Sherwin put it aside to pursue other story ideas. In college, she started work on a manuscript she intended to finish. After marrying her high school and college sweetheart, her husband encouraged her to pursue her life-long dreams of becoming an author. She started writing an hour a day. After a year, she had written four manuscripts—three novels and one novella. The first manuscript became *Night Bells*, the first Tale from Niflheim. The second tale from Niflheim, *Silent Shades,* was published in late 2012. She plans on publishing another Tale from Niflheim in early 2013.

Other Books by L.M. Sherwin
TALES FROM NIFLHEIM
Night Bells
Silent Shades

Find L.M. Sherwin
Website: http://lmsherwin.com/
Twitter: http://twitter.com/LM_Sherwin
Facebook: http://www.facebook.com/L.M.SherwinBooks
Goodreads:
http://www.goodreads.com/author/show/6505775.L_M_Sherwin

The Tale Continues...

Silent Shades

Book Two in the Tales from Niflheim series, a subset of The Primoris System Novels

By L.M. Sherwin

Frigg is a hired killer—a mercenary who belongs to a group of elite assassins ruled by a fierce commander. After completing a contract that leaves her close to death, Frigg is rescued by a surgeon and taken to his cabin to recover. When she is well enough, Frigg escapes and returns to her life as an assassin. Frigg receives a new contract from her commander and travels to New Kristiansand to murder Lord Maslyn, the mayor of the city. Upon arriving, she discovers more about her mark than she ever anticipated. Can Frigg put aside her personal feelings in order to complete her contract, or will she abandon her vocation to protect the person she was sent to kill?